ALSO BY LJ SHEN

DAMAGED GOODS

L.J. SHEN

Bloom books

Published by Bloom Books, an imprint of Sourcebooks
P.O. Box 4410, Naperville, Illinois 60567-4410
(630) 961-3900
sourcebooks.com

Cataloging-in-Publication data is on file with the Library of Congress.

Printed and bound in the United States of America.
WOZ 10 9 8 7 6 5 4 3 2 1

This book is dedicated to my beloved husband, who vetoed the name Lev for all three—count them, THREE—of our sons. You, sir, are a big meanie.

"Someday, somewhere—anywhere, unfailingly, you'll find yourself, and that, and only that, can be the happiest or bitterest hour of your life."
                                        —Pablo Neruda

"Ever has it been that love knows not its own depth until the hours of separation."
                                        —Kahlil Gibran

TRIGGER WARNINGS

This book contains subjects and issues some may find offensive. For a full list of trigger warnings, please visit this site:

Cutting
Drug abuse
Prescription drug addiction
Loss of parents
Mentions of death and suicide

PLAYLIST

"Rehab"—Amy Winehouse

"Falling Apart"—Michael Schulte

"The Show Must Go On"—Queen

"It Ends Tonight"—The All-American Rejects

"Be Alright"—Dean Lewis

"Him & I"—G-Eazy and Halsey

"Boys of Summer"—The Ataris

"Die For You"—The Weeknd & Ariana Grande

"ceilings"—Lizzy McAlpine

"people pleaser"—Cat Burns

"Freak Me"—Silk

"Goodbyes"—Post Malone feat. Young Thug.

PROLOGUE
LEV

AGE FOURTEEN

I'm standing over my mother's grave, wondering why the fuck my eyes are dry.

I couldn't look at the coffin back inside the church. Knight said she looked pretty. Calm. At peace. But also…nothing like herself.

I squeezed my eyes shut the entire way through, the way I did when I was really little and went on spooky rides at theme parks. Now I'm freaking out because maybe I made a mistake, because it was the last time I could look at her face not through a picture.

That's the thing about losing someone—there are so many losses along the way that make up a big loss.

No more cuddles in bed on rainy days.

No more heart-shaped fruit in my lunch box.

No more singing lullabies to me when I'm sick, with me pretending I'm embarrassed and annoyed by it when actually Mom singing lullabies is the best thing to happen to this universe since sliced bread.

Bailey is hugging me so close, my bones are about to dissipate to dust. She's about four inches taller than me now, which is stupid and embarrassing and just my luck. My face is hidden deep inside her hair, and I pretend to cry because it seems rude and screwed up if I don't. But the truth is, I'm not sad or gloomy or any of those things. I'm fucking *pissed*. Angry. Enraged.

Mom's gone.

What if she's cold? What if she's claustrophobic? What if she is struggling to breathe? What if she's scared? Reasonably, I know she isn't. She's dead. But logic isn't my friend right now. Not even an acquaintance. Hell, I doubt I could spell the word in my current state. I feel like Bailey is physically keeping me together. Like if she loosens her arms around me, I'll collapse into thousands of little marbles, scatter and disappear into the nooks and crannies of the cemetery.

Everyone files back to their cars. Dad claps a shaking hand over my shoulder and steers me away from the grave. Bails reluctantly releases me. I clutch the tips of her fingers. She's gravity. She's oxygen. In this moment in time, she's everything.

Sensing my unspoken need for her, Bailey turns to my dad. "May I please catch a ride with you, Uncle Dean?"

Thank you, Jesus.

"Yeah, Bails, sure," Dad says distractedly, laser-focused on Knight's back. My brother is going through his own stuff right now and my dad is trying to ensure he doesn't lose another member of our family. Usually, I'm cool with being the low-maintenance, "background" kid. Not today, though. I just lost my mom at fourteen. I want the world to stop, but it disrespectfully keeps on spinning and functioning like my life wasn't just destroyed.

Before we hop into the car, I clutch Bailey's fingers and pull her to me. "If I told you I want to run away from here, somewhere really far, like…I dunno, Kansas far, what would you say?"

Her big blue eyes hold mine like my eyeballs are about to fall off. "We ride at dawn, bitch."

"Really?" I ask.

She nods once. "Try me, Lev. You're my best friend. I'll never let you down."

It's weird, but the possibility of Bailey and me running away from all this is the one thing holding my ass together right now. She might be everyone's good girl, but to me, she's a bad addiction.

The drive is silent. I'm a page torn out of a book. Out of place and floating aimlessly. All I have is the memory of once belonging. Then, we're in front of my house. Everyone trickles inside in their black frocks. They look like ghouls. Home without Mom isn't a home. It's a pile of bricks and expensive furniture.

Invisible ivy roots me to the ground. Bailey is the only one who notices. She loiters behind with me, and suddenly, I really hate that I'm putting all my dreams and hopes on her. Because she could be gone tomorrow too. Bus accident. Freak heart attack at fifteen. A kidnap-and-murder plot. The options are endless, and I have really shitty luck with people.

"Kansas?" She grabs my fingers, playing them like they're keys on a piano.

I shake my head, too choked up to produce actual words.

"We don't have to go inside." Her hands slide up to grab my arms and keep me standing. How did she know I'm close to falling? "We can hang out at mine. I'll make fondue. We can watch *South Park*." Her blues gleam like sapphires.

Fresh irritation floods me. Bailey is being *soooo* understanding, even though she doesn't understand jack shit. She *does* have a mom. A healthy one. And a dad. And a sister who isn't an addict. Her life is perfect, while mine is a pile of calamities.

She's a blossoming flower, and I'm dirt, but that's okay because the thing about flowers is they're buried in dirt, so I know exactly how to cut her off.

Shaking her off, I swivel and stomp my way out of our cul-de-sac. She races after me, calling my name. Her Mary Janes clap the ground urgently.

"Lev, please! Did I say something wrong?"

To be fair to her, she stood no chance at saying anything *right*.

But screw being fair. I'm hurting, and she is baggage. Just another person to love and to lose.

I pick up my pace, running now. I don't know where I'm going, but I'm eager to get there. The sky—completely blue just seconds ago—cracks like an egg. Thunder rolls, gray washes over it, and rain starts pouring in thick sheets. It's summer in SoCal and shouldn't rain. The universe is angry, but I'm angrier.

Whenever Bailey manages to catch the sleeve of my shirt, I speed up, but even after thirty minutes of running in the rain, soaked to the bone, she doesn't quit. Somehow, we find ourselves in the woods on the outskirts of town. The thick, tall branches and blankets of leaves intertwine together like laced fingers above us, creating a makeshift umbrella. I can sort of see my surroundings now, and it's pretty and it's calm and far enough away from that stupid cemetery. I stop running when I realize I'm not gonna escape the new reality: Mom's dead.

I finally understand the term *heartbreak*. Because that thing in my chest? Split open clean in two.

I turn around, my lungs scorching. Bailey is pale and sodden, her black dress clinging to her body. Her lips are blue and her skin is so pale, I see a map of purple and red veins under her flesh.

"Go home," I growl. But I don't want her to go home. I want her to never leave.

She steps closer, tilting her chin up defiantly. "I'm not leaving you."

"Fuck off, Bailey!" I fold in half, screaming. I feel like she kicked me in the stomach.

She'll leave. She'll let you down. Don't fall for this, Lev.

"I'm so sorry." Her eyes are full of tears, and she flexes her fingers, itching to grab me.

Hug me.

Go away.

Fuckfuckfuck.

My mouth opens again and more bullshit spews out. "Don't be

sorry for me. Be sorry for yourself. You're the loser who hangs out with an eighth grader instead of people your own age."

"I wish it didn't happen." She ignores my insults, trying to grab my fingers again and play them like a piano, like she does every time I'm upset.

Laughing, I rasp, "I wish *you* didn't happen."

"I wish it were me who was dead." Her face is covered with tears and pain and mud, and I can't do this anymore. I don't care how much I'm hurting, I can't ruin the only good thing about my life right now. She gives me something to fight for when every cell of my body wants to give up.

"Now you're just talking outta your ass." I spit phlegm between us.

She shakes her head, quivering fingers darting to her hair, massaging her scalp. I believe her. And it kills me that even though I feel like someone slashed me open and my guts are pouring out, I still wouldn't want Bailey to be in Mom's place.

"I'm not. I'm serious. I would die before willingly watch you suffer."

There's a beat of silence. Then I open my mouth and the most feral, scary, loud cry I've ever heard tears out of it. It echoes in the sky and bounces off the trees. A flock of ravens takes flight from the treetops.

And then I go to the only place I need to be right now—I go *mad*.

Anger pierces through my skin. I rip through a thick curtain of cobweb, grab a young tree like it's a neck, and crack it in half with my own two hands. Blood gushes from the creases of my palms, and a fingernail snaps clean out of my skin. It falls into the wet mud under my feet. I can't even feel the pain.

Bailey is screaming, but I can't hear her. I punch into oak trees, kick dirt, pull flowers from their beds, holding them like decapitated heads and tossing them into the river in a white, blind, hot rage. I destroy nests and uproot a whole-ass bench, throwing it into the river. I'm annihilating anything and everything in my path. It's me against nature, and once—just this once—it seems like I'm winning.

At some point, I notice through the mist of rain that I'm not the only one wreaking havoc. Bailey is on a bender too. Ripping flowers, peeling chipped tree trunks, screaming into the wind. Her face is muddy, her hair crazy, and I don't think I've ever seen her like this—wild and free and rabid.

I think it's the first time either of us has done anything less than perfect. Seeing her destroying instead of mending for once in her life does something to me. She punches a tree, and I realize that she is bleeding, and that realization, that she is hurting, finally snaps me out of my trance. I pause. Look around. Breathe. *Really* breathe, feeling the oxygen filling my lungs and the carbon dioxide leaving them. The wind ceases to weep. The rain stops. Bailey stops too.

Time moves, but we don't. We stand there like two trees, the soft ripples of the river nearby the only sound penetrating the silence. For a moment, we're the only two creatures existing in this world. The sole survivors of my mental apocalypse. Then I hear it. The chirp of birds. Bailey and I both look up at the same branch, where two doves are huddled together, slightly damp from the rain. One of them cleans the other with its beak. The other is tweeting.

I swear it's looking at us while it chirps. Am I losing my mind? Why the fuck not? This seems on par with the rest of my crappy week.

"Look, Levy." Bailey points at the birds, her eyes flaring. "Know what they are?"

"Rats with wings." I scowl, not in the mood for a wildlife lesson. Bailey is full of useless facts about animals. And every other subject under the sun, really.

"Turtle doves," she corrects. "They're notoriously loyal. Symbolizing friendship and everlasting love."

"Parasitic disease hubs." I wipe the blood on my fists against my wet black suit, spitting on the ground.

"When they puff their chests out, their wings look exactly like a heart pressed together. Don't you get it? A heart. *Lev.*"

I blink steadily. "Are you high?" I really can't afford having another addict to worry about. Like, Knight is already doing my head in.

"Can't you see?" She grabs both my hands, pulling me to the tree where the doves sit. "This is hope in tragedy. A message from above!"

"A message from my mom?" I repeat slowly so she can hear the full dumbassery of the sentence, though I'm desperate to believe her. And if there's anyone who can convince me to believe supernatural shit, it's Bailey. She's crazy smart.

Bailey nods, her eyes shining like lighthouses in the pitch-black. "The sudden rain? The rainbow? The doves? Rosie is telling you something."

"That global warming is about to go batshit on our asses?"

Bailey shakes her head vehemently. "That you're not alone. That you will always have people who love you." Now she does take my fingers and plays with them.

"What kind of people?" I grunt.

"People like me," she whispers, tightening her hold.

"Yeah, but eventually you'll leave." A grim smile slits my face. "I've seen this movie before." Knight is going through the same thing with Luna, and they were best friends too. "You'll go to college, and I—"

"Even then, I'll be at your beck and call." She tugs and pulls, her voice begging me to believe her. "Try me, Lev. Pick up that phone and call when I'm in the middle of the semester. I'll drop everything and come. No questions asked."

I ignore her. "You'll find a boyfri—"

"Romance is fleeting. Friendship is constant. I will always choose a good friend over a great boyfriend." She shakes her head. "You're my soul mate."

It is not the time to tell her I'm in love with her. It is not the time to tell her *I* want to be that hypothetical boyfriend. That she is becoming an ethereal weapon of self-destruction for me. That when I jack off, it's to her image. That when she laughs, my chest feels funny. When she cries, I want to suck in her pain with a kiss and suffer on her behalf.

My knees sink into the muddy ground. Bailey descends with me, our fingers still knotted together. My head drops to her shoulder. And I finally feel them. The tears. They're coming hot and fast, running down my cheeks like they have somewhere important to go. Bailey swallows me in her arms, stroking my head, my back, my arms. Her lips are in my hair, whispering all the things I want to hear.

That it will be okay. That happiness will find me. That rainbows appear after thunderstorms because the universe is a balancing act of good and bad.

I cry and I cry and I cry until I'm all dried up. Heartbreak gives way to exhaustion. I can barely open my eyes, they feel so puffy. But still, I don't lift my head up. I want a few more minutes buried in my best friend.

"Can we stay like this?" My lips move against her shoulder blade.

"Forever," she confirms, pressing her lips to the edge of my ear. "I have nowhere to go. Other than Kansas, maybe."

She's attempting a joke. Checking the temperature to see if I'm ready to stop being a jackass.

My face is still in the crook of her neck. I'm too chickenshit to look up. "How's the sky looking, Dove?"

Bailey stiffens at the sound of her new nickname. For a second I'm worried she'll laugh at me. Say it's a cliché. Worry I'm calling her a feathered rat. Then she relaxes against me.

Her voice floats like a bird's song: "Blue and clear as day, Levy."

CHAPTER ONE
BAILEY

AGE NINETEEN

"Duuuuuuude. Can you believe Lauren sprained her ankle porking a tourist? I would *die*." Katia, my roommate, runs a contour stick under her cheekbone, all the way down the tip of her jaw. She glides her tongue along her upper teeth to get rid of lipstick residue, her eyes glittering as she studies herself in the mirror.

Our Juilliard dorm room is smaller than my walk-in closet back home and haphazardly furnished. Two bunk beds. One rickety desk. An immeasurable amount of Broadway posters, throw pillows, and inspirational quotes scissored into hearts. Daria says trying to make this place look livable is like putting lipstick on a pig: *"Only you got yourself a dozen pigs and one stick of cheapo lipstick."*

But Daria is also a high school counselor, not a world-renowned ballerina. She never made it to the Big J, so it's probably the jealousy falling out of her mouth.

"Hello? Earth to Bailey? Should we send a search party to find your brain?" Katia dumps the contour stick on the desk, picking up a brush to blend in the makeup. "Bitch finished her career because of a Tinder date! It's more pathetic than Kylie, who gained a bunch of weight and lost her spot at the Bolshoi."

"Dude, Kylie has *lupus*." I rear my head back. Holy mean girl.

"So does Selena, and she's still hot shit." She rolls her hazel eyes. "There are always excuses, aren't there? If you wanna be successful in our industry, you gotta hustle."

"You know I like Lauren. And that story hasn't really been confirmed by reliable sources." I refuse to engage in shit-talking, even if it's my peers' favorite blood sport.

"Not confirmed?" Katia shrieks. "Bitch has a cast and a one-way ticket back to Bumfuck, Oklahoma. What more do you need, an in-depth article in *The Atlantic*?"

I hug a throw pillow to my chest on our bunk bed, eager to change the subject. "Okay, but can we talk about how I *love* this eye shadow on you?"

"You know throwing shade is my passion." Katia twists her head and winks, a shock of platinum-blond hair slinging over her shoulder. She straightens her posture and tosses the brush inside her makeup bag. She's wearing my sequined Gucci minidress. A hand-me-down from Daria.

Katia is on a scholarship here. She migrated to the U.S. from Latvia with her mom eight years ago and got into Juilliard on a full ride. We got paired in the freshman dorm room and now live on a steady diet of ramen, pizza rolls, and motivation, much to her chagrin. She tried to stage an intervention when I canceled the organic, gluten-free food subscription my parents placed on my behalf when I moved in here. But I made a conscious decision to cut myself off from their bank account when I turned eighteen. So far, I've been doing pretty well.

Thing is, the more you swim in money, the drier your creativity pool is. Art comes from a place of depravation. In art, privilege is a disadvantage. Art is about bleeding. Dying onstage. Telling your story through a medium—be it paint on canvas, clay, dance, or song. What's *my* life story? A couple bad manicures and an unfortunate braces phase?

I read a quote somewhere by an author named Amy Chua: "Do

you know what a foreign accent is? It's a sign of bravery." I can't stop thinking about this. About how neatly and insipidly I've always fit into the world around me. With my Valley-girl twang and pastel cardigans and cushy trust fund.

Until now. Until Juilliard.

"*Ohmygosh*, Bails, stop being such a party pooper. I like Lauren too. Even though she's a bitchbag for hooking up with Jade's ex." Katia's voice daggers through my fog-filled brain. I'm in excruciating pain. I have three stress fractures, one in each of my tibias and one in my spine, and they're all throbbing, demanding to be acknowledged.

"He gave her a ride upstate." I scrunch my nose. "This is all specula—"

"It's just a shame because it was her last year," Katia cuts me off. "She signed a Broadway contract, you know. *Hamilton*. Ensemble member. Now she has to go back to Oklahoma—"

"Montana," I correct, choking on the pain.

"To like…work at her dad's pig-racing ranch—"

"Her family doesn't farm."

"Whatever, Bails. You're literally the worst person to talk shit with. Haven't you heard? Nice women don't end up in history books." Katia downs the remainder of her pregame beer, slam-dunking the can in the trash.

"That's not true," I murmur, knowing I'm being an annoying brainiac prude and still not able to stop myself. "What about Eleanor Roosevelt? And Harriet Tubman, Ma—"

"La la la la la." Katia pretends to block her ears, strutting to the door. "This is college. I'm here to have fun, not learn something new." She puts her hand on the door handle, stopping to glance behind her shoulder. "Sure you don't wanna come to Luis's party? The textbooks aren't going anywhere."

"I know. And I'm still positive." I drop my phone on the throw pillow I'm clutching and gesture toward my ankle. It is currently the size of a tennis ball. "I should probably stay off my feet."

Katia winces. "Did you at least kill it in the audition?"

More like the audition killed me. Hence why you need to get out of here so I can drown in painkillers, low-stakes reality Netflix competitions, and self-pity.

"Yup," I pop the *P*. "You have fun for both of us, okay?"

"Scout's honor." She raises two fingers.

"Text me if you feel unsafe," I say, as I always do whenever she goes out. That's me. Bailey Followhill. Designated driver. Straight-edged, straight-A mathlete. Charity enthusiast. Voted Most Likely to Become the First Female President. Mommy and Daddy's pride and joy.

Always there to pick up the slack my older, shinier sister leaves behind. That's just who I am. Little Miss Goody Two-Shoes.

"See you in the a.m., babe." Katia finger tickles the air.

She leaves me in a cloud of hairspray fumes and despair. I swing my gaze to the ceiling. The room smears behind a coat of my unshed tears. The pain in my legs and spine is so acute, I have to bite my inner cheek until blood fills my mouth. I know what to do. I've been doing it for weeks. Okay, *months*. It's a temporary solution, but it works wonders and makes the pain go away.

Inhaling sharply, I fling myself off the bunk bed and skulk my way to my padlocked diary. The one Mom gave me the day I moved into the dorms.

"Document everything, Bailey. Every tear. Every smile. Every fail, every win. And remember—diamonds are made under pressure. Shine always, my lovebug."

I unlock the diary with the key, which I keep buried under a potted plant—yes, I keep plants here to ensure Katia and I get good, clean oxygen. Inside, there are no pages. No words. No ink. I guess it's a good metaphor for my existence. The way I gutted the glittery, pink-leathered journal my third week at Juilliard and placed a five-and-a-half-by-eight-and-a-half-inch box containing my pills there instead. I don't have a prescription drug problem—mainly because my doctor hasn't been prescribing me drugs for months now. So I found other ways to get them.

Dr. Haddock had wanted me to get a cast on my right ankle and go on a four-week bedrest followed by physiotherapy. *"I can't prescribe you more Vicodin, Bailey. May I remind you we're in the midst of an oxy epidemic?"*

I pleaded and begged, argued and bargained, then dished out anecdotal facts to support my quest for painkillers. He ended up prescribing me some Motrin 800 to pull me through my audition today. An audition that was supposed to redeem my failing grade at ballet and dance composition. I gave it my all. Every ounce of energy. Stretched every ligament and muscle to its limit. But it wasn't enough.

I wasn't enough.

"I can tell you want this badly, Miss Followhill." One of the senior choreographers tapped her pen over her clipboard rhythmically, her mouth downturned in dissatisfaction. *"But passion without skill is like fuel without a vehicle. You need to work on your Alexander Technique. To relearn how to work your basic movements. You need to revise your plié and tendu. Go back to the roots."*

Slamming my eyes shut, I shake my head, making her words dissipate. Half the time I don't even know if I want to be a ballerina or if it's the only thing I've ever meant to be. My destiny was written for me from the moment I was born, and I went along with it. Mom saw a potential, scouters agreed, letters of invitation from ballet institutions began pouring in when I was around eleven, and that was it. I was on the fast-track to becoming a ballerina.

I reach for the box and pat its insides. There's only one Motrin left. Not a benzo to pick up my mood or a Vicodin to take the edge off.

"What the luck?" I hiss. Katia must've stolen a bunch. She somehow got her hand on my key. I *know* I had a couple Xannies lying around. No way did I consume all of them in less than a week.

I grab the pill and swallow it without water, then pick up my so-called diary and hurl it against the window with a yelp. It slams against the glass and collapses on the floor. The empty cardboard dislocates, placed face down on the old carpet, like a prima ballerina in dying swan position. The professors' voices twirled in my head a few minutes after they thought I left the room. Instead, I was still kneeling behind the curtain, holding my ankle and trying not to sob through the pain.

"Not flexible enough."

"Not enough energy."

"Isn't she Melody Followhill's daughter? Figures. I remember her mother. Wasn't the brightest star in the sky. If you ask me, she was lucky to break that leg. Got a cushy marriage out of it. Followhill Jr. is better but still no Anna Pavlova."

That was after I managed to convince them to let me retake the test, go onstage again so I could pass the semester. There's no way I, Bailey Followhill, brainiac extraordinaire, am going to fail my freshman year of college.

I grab my phone, scroll down my contacts, my thumb hovering over one name. *Payden Rhys.* The chisel-jawed ballerino from Indiana who got a lead role in *La Sylphide* without even breaking a sweat. He makes his pocket money selling Vicodin, Xanax, and other party favors. Shadier than a cowboy hat and a man I despise with all my heart, but somehow I find myself increasingly spending more and more time with.

There are only a couple months left before the semester ends, and my grades outside the dance studio are flawless. I can't go home early. Can't show the world that my best isn't *the* best. Besides, I just need to retake this test, get a good grade, then I'll have the entire winter break to allow my injuries to heal and ditch my very recent, *very* manageable drug habit. I text Payden.

Bailey: Wanna party?

He knows exactly what I mean by that.

Payden: How hard?

Translation: How many do you need?

Bailey: Spring break hard.

As many as you got.

Payden: Be there in five.

I plaster my back against the door and slide to the floor, nestling my head between my knees, sobbing noiselessly. I hate that my body is not keeping up with my ambition, with my drive, with my academic grades. And I hate that it gives someone like Payden power over me.

Sometimes I want to unfurl like the satin ribbons of my pointe shoes. To spin rapidly, the layers of my self-consciousness and anxiety uncurling, loosening, until I am left bare. I secretly resent my older sister, Daria. It's easy to be her because the expectations placed upon her are slim to none. She embraces her imperfections. Wears them proudly like battle scars. She showed her husband, her friends, our parents, the worst sides of her, and impossibly—*implausibly*—that only made them love her harder.

That's not an option for me. I'm Bailey Followhill, the perfect little ballerina. No mountain is too high, no test is too difficult.

Got a problem? Ask Bailey. She knows everything.

Well, spoiler alert: I have no idea what I'm doing right now.

Three minutes later, there's a knock on the door and Payden is standing in my room, a mischievous spark in his brown eyes. He greets me by helping me up to my feet and slapping my ass, leaving a punishing sting. There's a casual maliciousness to him that always sets me on edge.

"Damn, Bails. I love a good thigh gap, but this is too much, even for me." And he is a body-negative prick who prides himself on making people feel bad about themselves. Word around is he landed in hot water with his professors last year for telling his dancing partner she was too heavy for him to ballroom lift. She was less than a hundred pounds *and* he used the F-bomb.

"You look like a mess." He pulls up his pant leg and tugs a Ziploc bag from his holey sock. Inside it are smaller individual bags with pills. "You been crying?"

"No. Just the stupid injuries bugging me," I lie, pulling my sleeves over my fists and rubbing at my nose. I want him to leave. I hate him. But he's the only person who ever sold me benzo that passed my chemical tests and carries genuine Vicodin.

"Those fine legs giving you trouble again, Followhill?" He flicks a small bag full of Vicodin with his thumb and forefinger, a cigarette clenched between his lips. "Well, the offer to wrap them 'round my neck still stands. I'll be your best painkiller."

"Been there, done that," I mutter, trying to suppress the lackluster memory of us together. "You're no Vicodin, Pay. Barely half an Advil."

"*Oof.*" He laughs. "If I gave half a fuck what some spoiled little princess from Todos Santos thinks, I'd take offense."

"You were the one who wanted in my pants," I remind him.

"Can you blame me? Fucking a virgin had always been on my bucket list."

I glare at the Vicodin dispassionately, wondering if it'll do the trick. I took two Motrin before my audition today and still messed up the choreography. My tibias feel like they're about to snap.

"Got anything stronger?" I honestly don't recognize myself in this conversation. I graduated from high school without even trying *pot*. Lev once had to pick me up from a party because I thought I got too high on the fumes when *other* people were smoking it.

"Than V?" Payden pauses, a look of confusion painting his face. "Sure. I've got oxy if you wan—"

"Yeah, I'll try oxy."

His features darken. "I was gonna say 'if you want to kill yourself.'

I don't sell oxy to students, and I'm definitely not gonna sell it to *your* lightweight ass."

"You're exaggerating." I pull my hair into a tight bun, my scalp screaming with pain.

"Nuh-uh. You're fast approaching tweaker zone, and those assholes tend to die and get their dealers into all kinds of trouble." He runs a hand through his sandy hair. "Look, I know you're good for the money, but you ain't worth the risk." His eyes lick me from head to toe appreciatively. "Sure you don't want a repeat of our night of passion, for old time's sake?"

I'm too polite to tell him his lovemaking skills match those of a dead hedgehog. "Positive. Give me ten of the Vicodin and go on your merry way."

"*Ten?* Bailey…"

"Payden." I arch my eyebrows pointedly, stretching my palm open in front of him. When he remains a pillar of salt, I seize my wallet from a drawer and pull out a wad of cash, fanning it like a magician doing card tricks.

He swallows. "Dude, this is no longer recreational. You're getting a dependency."

"Dependency? Don't be ridiculous. I know WebMD like the palm of my hand. I just need to finish this semester. I can handle it."

He says nothing.

"Since when do you care about me?"

"I don't," he says dispassionately. "I care about *me*. My ass is too talented, young, and hot to end up in jail. You know what they do to people like me there?" He frames his face with his fingers.

Avoid them, because you're a horribly annoying human?

"I'll be fine, Pay."

Ultimately, his survival instinct trumps his pesky conscience and he sighs, taking the money. He shoves the bag of pills to my chest, raising his finger in warning. "Shit, dude. You're my steadiest client on campus. Didn't see that one coming."

Didn't see me coming, either. Seriously, why did I ever think sleeping with him was a good idea?

"Thanks so much. Enjoy your night." I jerk my chin to the door. Which is literally less than a step away from him. "See ya around."

He shakes his head. "You're one messed-up chick, Followhill. I'm glad we never got together seriously."

Feeling's mutual.

I push him out of my room, though he takes his time looking around, loitering, hoping I'll change my mind about a hookup. "Done anything to your room? It looks different…"

"Payden!" I chide. "Get out before I tase you."

After the door shuts, I hop on my bunk bed with the bag of Vicodin pinched between my fingers and take a slow, steadying breath. I could take one and wait for it to kick in, facing more pain and anxiety…*or* I could take two and get knocked right to sleep. I'll be able to wake up tomorrow ready to conquer the world. Kill it onstage. Get perfect grades. Payden is wrong. I'm not an addict. I'm just trying to save my career like every other dancer out here. And…*maybe* forget about how cold, isolating, and unfriendly New York is.

Sliding two pills into my open palm, I knock them back with some water. After twenty minutes of pacing and pretzeling from the pain, I take a third one. Finally, it kicks in. I let my body sink down onto my bed. Only it feels like I'm soaked into the mattress. My head drowning in the pillow.

I'm falling…

Plunging…

Plummeting to a place deep and dark where light can't break through.

A place where dreams go to die.

————

I wake up groggy and shivering.

It's not supposed to be this cold in here. The heater is on full blast, and I'm wearing Daria's oversized Valentino sweater. Last time I felt this cold was when I got mugged this November and the prick forced me to strip down to my underwear so he could steal Daria's Vivienne Westwood ivory silk dress. An incident I conveniently forgot to tell my parents about so they wouldn't freak out. I check my Apple Watch. It's only been twenty minutes since I fell asleep, yet I'm struggling to keep my eyes open. My breathing is labored, and my arms feel like they're nailed to the bed. Good news is I can't feel the pain in my legs. Bad news is I can't feel my legs, like, *at all*.

I've been to enough D.A.R.E. classes to recognize the signs of an overdose. A violent shudder tears through my flesh. I throw a heavy hand down on the carpet, where my phone is charging. My balance is so off, I twist out of the bed, falling to the floor. I can't move. I can't stand up. *Holy crap, what do I do?*

Somehow, my fingers curl around my phone. I yank it off the charger and aim the screen at my face, shaking, sweating, panicking. A lifetime passes before it unlocks. I think about calling Katia, then realize I can't afford to waste my one call on someone untrustworthy. Instead, I punch the first name I call when I'm in trouble. Or that I *would* call if I ever got into trouble. Doesn't matter that things have been weird between us. Doesn't matter that I yanked his heart out of his chest, put it in a blender, and set the speed on x4. Doesn't matter that he pretty much hates me.

Doesn't matter that all that's left of us are bittersweet memories and two ragged bracelets. Or even that his absence is the most present thing in my life, and something tells me that if we were still us—*really* us—I never would've gotten hooked on Xanax and Vicodin.

While I wait for him to answer, the world shrinks in front of my eyes. Like a photo being devoured by fire, the edges blurring inwards.

"Bailey?"

He sounds flippant, disinterested; he has good reasons to be. #Bailev is dead. I killed it with my own hands. His background noise is sultry music, laughter, and beer bottles clinking together. He's at a party.

"Lev…" My tongue is a half-dead thing in my mouth. I can't believe I'm saying these words. "I've overdosed."

"What the…?" A door shuts in the background, and the noise fades. He went somewhere quiet so he could hear me. My throat is all clogged. *Shitshitshit.* "Repeat that?" he demands. "Like, right the fuck now."

"I overdosed! Drugs. I…I think I'm about to die."

Even though up until this second Lev has had absolutely no knowledge of my ever consuming anything stronger than Infants' Tylenol, he catches on quickly.

"What did you take?" His voice turns soft, raspy.

No judgment. No anger. I can't believe we grew apart. Can't believe I *tore* us apart. I can't believe this is the last time I might be speaking to him. *Ever.*

"Vicodin, supposedly. But it feels…different. Wrong." My breathing shallows; my body is shutting down. "I need you to call an ambulance." I try to swallow. Fail. "And send someone in the residence hall to my room with Narcan. In case…you know…"

Who says being a nerd doesn't pay off? I listened carefully during those D.A.R.E. classes.

"Actually, I don't fucking know, but that's a conversation for later." The sound of him frantically rummaging through something fills my heart with stupid, unwarranted hope. "Wait on the line… *shit! Fuck!* Where is it?" he growls. "I'm using Tha—someone else's phone to make the calls. Count to ten for me."

Normal Bailey would do it backward, in Latin, just to show off. *Current* Bailey isn't even trying. Current Bailey is also dumb enough to wonder who is Tha—? A girl? A girl*friend?* Is he hooking up with people now? Now's not the time to be jealous. My oxygen levels are way down. Everything is going darker by the second.

"Lev, I'm scared."

"Don't be," he barks, but he sounds more scared than *I* am.

I gulp, and he can sense my panic because he asks, "When have we ever let anything bad happen to each other?"

"Some things are bigger than us."

"*Nothing* is bigger than Bailev," his voice is resolute. "Repeat it."

"Nothing is bigger than Bailev," I say weakly.

"Atta girl. No lies detected."

My eyes flutter shut. I'm too tired. Too heavy. Too numb. In the background, I hear Lev talking to a 9-1-1 dispatcher, then to the Office of Housing and Residence Life. He is calm, in control, and bossy as hell.

Lev is the epitome of a heartthrob. Broad-shouldered, pillowy-lipped, with drowsy sex eyes and a body that makes Adonis look like a dude with a dad bod. But that's not why I'm in love with him. I'm in love with him because he's the boy who drags me every first rain of winter to dance among the raindrops, barefoot, since he saw me doing that once when I was six. Because he kisses my forehead when I'm sad and watches cheesy Netflix rom-coms with me when I'm PMSing but also has a side of him that races sports cars and bungee-jumps from cliffs.

He is hardness and softness. Air and water. He is my everything and yet nothing to me at all these days. And I'm ripped to shreds even thinking about it right now.

"I...Lev, I'm..." I croak.

"You're getting through this is what you are. Help's on the way. Now, remind me what year did they allow women to start dancing ballet?"

1681. He is trying to distract me, and I appreciate it, but my mouth is too heavy to answer.

"Dove?" His voice is a lullaby, wrapping around me like a wooly blanket. "You there?"

My eyelids droop, darkness engulfing me. Death is cold and quiet and beautiful, and it's so close, I can feel its breath on my skin. The first thought that pops into my head is how selfish I am for putting him through this, hearing me die, after everything he's been through.

"Answer me, Bailey!" I hear the smash of glass breaking, followed by a string of curses. A startled voice *what-the-fuck*s him in the background. It's male, and I don't know why I'm so relieved, seeing as I'm about to *die*, but at least Lev has a friend there to take care of him.

I hear Lev tromp out of the party, shrugging off pleas to play donut on a string. "Just wait," he keeps chanting in my ear desperately. "They should be there any second, Dove. You hold on tight for me, okay?"

"Lev…" I choke. "Come? Here? To Newyeeeek?" I slur.

"Yeah," he says without missing a beat. "I'm on my way. You just keep waiting, all right?"

Foam coats the back of my throat, the tears making it impossible for me to see. I clutch my bracelet. A black tattered string with a silver turtle dove. Lev has a matching one he never takes off.

No wonder your name means heart in Hebrew, I want to tell him. *You captured mine between your teeth and swallowed it whole.*

"How's the sky looking, Dove?" I hear his car door slamming shut.

The last words I'm able to produce before I log off are "Cloudy… with a chance of rain."

CHAPTER TWO
BAILEY

THREE DAYS LATER

My cheek is pressed against the cool window of Dad's Range Rover. I watch as the Californian spring bursts forth in greens, yellows, and blues. The flight from JFK to Lindbergh Field was so quiet, the three of us could've easily passed as strangers. The few words that were exchanged were emptier than my stomach.

Mom: Would you like some lunch, hon?

Me: No, thank you.

Mom: You haven't eaten properly in days.

Me: I'm not hungry.

Dad: Sure about that, Bails? Mom bought you sushi from the airport. We know you hate airplane food.

Me: It's not the food, it's the environment. The humidity and pressure in the cabin at thirty thousand feet changes our sense of taste and smell.

Dad: Roger that, Einstein.

Me: Pasterski.

Dad: What?

Me: "Roger that, Pasterski." After Sabrina Gonzalez Pasterski. A genius female physicist. How do you expect us to break the walls of patriarchy if every notable figure in cultural reference is a man?

Dad: Oh. Kay. At least you're back to sounding like Old Bailey.

Mom: How's the pain now, Bailey?
Me: Better, thank you.

I don't think the pain from the fractures and back injury is actually better. It's just numbed by everything else that went down these past three days. Since my call to Lev, a few things happened. Someone busted down my dorm door and shoved Narcan up my nostril. I came to, then started vomiting *everywhere*—floor, walls, carpets, you name it. They hoisted me onto a gurney and took me to Mount Sinai Hospital. The student hall was crammed wall-to-wall with curious bystanders. They hooked me to machines. Stabbed my veins with needles. Ran a ton of tests. Pumped my stomach clean. Mom and Dad got there in the middle of the night, ghostlike in texture. The first few hours, I pretended to sleep just so I wouldn't have to face them. Mortification didn't begin to cover it. OD'ing is the kind of messed-up even Daria didn't bring to their doorstep. A drug problem is something that happens to other people's children. Children who don't grow up in one-and-a-half-acre Spanish colonials with two swimming pools, a timeshare in the Hamptons, and monthly shopping sessions in Geneva.

By the time the morning rolled in, I reluctantly opened my eyes.

When they bombarded me with questions, I lied. I could count on one hand the number of times I'd lied in my entire life—honesty is a no-brainer when you never do anything you're ashamed of. But, I realized, this was no longer the case. Now I did have a secret—I craved downers and painkillers all the time. Depended on them to push through my daily anxiety and injuries. Thus, my affair with dishonesty began. In truth, *affair* was an understatement.

Bailey Followhill and Dishonesty are now in a steady, all-consuming relationship.

I told my parents it was a one-off. The first time I bought painkillers.

"I thought I was buying heavy duty Motrin, not Vicodin laced with fentanyl!" I explained earnestly, trying to look as scandalized as they were. "You know I'd never do something stupid, Mom."

She gave me a *you're better than that* look. But honestly, right now? I'm not so sure that I am.

Now here we are, three days later. Back in my hometown of Todos Santos. My second semester was cut short, and Mom told me the board was going to reevaluate my enrollment and give us an answer by the end of the academic year. See if I'm good to retake my physical test.

A million thoughts hysterically run inside my head, arms flailing, bumping into one another. What if they don't take me back? What about my failed grade? And all the classes I'll be missing? How am I supposed to face the people who have seen me ushered out on a gurney, trails of my ramen and stomach acid dripping down my chin? Does Daria know? Does Uncle Dean? And what about Knight? Vicious, Millie, and Vaughn?

One thing is for sure—*Katia* knows and turned out to be a fair-weather friend, judging by the messages she left on my phone.

> Katia: I can't believe you did this in our ROOM.
> Katia: You vomited all over my clothes, FYI. Like, I need to borrow leggings from Petra to go to the laundromat.
> Katia: You could've gotten both of us into so much trouble, wtf.
> Katia: Honestly I feel SO slighted.
> Katia: Is someone coming to water your plants? I have too much on my plate right now.

My head is spinning. I want to throw up, but there's nothing inside my stomach but water and anxiety. And that anxiety? It feels like a mythical creature that devours my inner organs hungrily. Slithering, growing, taking up more space.

The Range Rover glides into downtown, past the hilly golf courses and palm trees dancing in the wind. The surf shops, cafés, and pastel-colored storefronts scream familiarity and comfort. The thin cord where the ocean kisses the sky glitters with promise.

Ruthless motivation stabs at my chest. No. This can't be the end. This break is going to help me get *my* big break. I will practice harder and go back to Juilliard better than ever. It's far from over. In fact, it's only the beginning. I'm not gonna let Mom down. *Or* myself. I've been wanting to be a ballerina since I learned how to walk, and a little setback isn't going to kill my career.

"Bails, baby, want an orange?" Dad asks, peering at me from the rearview mirror. Jaime Followhill is the best dad in the world. He is also Captain Random, which I normally adore. It's fun to be offered fruit out of nowhere or wake up to your dad jumping on your bed, announcing, "Legoland today. Last to make it to the shoe rack is the placeholder in the lines for the rides!"

"I'm good, thanks." I seize a lock of blond hair from behind my ear and run my fingers through it, looking for fuzzy, damaged hairs to pluck. I don't deal with imperfections well.

"So I *did* find something interesting." Mom is going for chirpy but sounds off-key and panic-stricken. "A wellness center just outside Carlsbad. *Gorgeous* setting. All luxurious suites. Looks just like the Amangiri. Michelin-starred chefs, massages, yoga, energy-healing. Honestly, I would check in myself if I could take the time off!"

She wants me to go to *rehab*? Is *she* high?

"You can't be serious, Mom." I press my lips together, keeping my temper at bay. I never lose my cool. Never yell, never talk back, never rebel. My parents and I don't have arguments. We have mild disagreements. "That so-called 'overdose' was a one-off." I air quote the word.

Rehab is for addicts, not for people who meddle with painkillers and Xanax during super stressful, short times. Not to mention, Juilliard isn't going to sit around and wait for me while I namaste with desperate housewives who went too hard on their drinking habit.

"You ended up in the ER with your stomach pumped," Mom retorts.

"Yeah. And they pumped *nothing*." I fold my arms. "I took one pill." *Three, but that's practically semantics.* "I'm not a druggie."

"Don't mock substance abuse victims, Bails. Druggie isn't a term we use in this house." Dad's voice has a jagged edge. "Sure you don't want an orange? They're sweeter than sin."

"Your daughter has been doing enough sinning for one decade, judging by the last three days," Mom mumbles, swiveling her body to me. "Look, I don't know how you ended up with fentanyl in your system, but—"

"You don't believe that I thought it was Motrin?" I don't know why I'm genuinely offended, considering I've been popping pillies like I'm a Post Malone song. "The guy who gave it to me said they were a European brand." That's my third lie in a row. I need to write them all down somewhere to keep my version straight.

"You still haven't told us who it was." Mom's eyes narrow on mine in the rearview mirror. "He could get someone killed, you know."

"I don't know his name!" Fourth lie. Wow, I'm on a Molly-less roll here.

In one of her texts, Katia said Payden skipped town and went to dance on a cruise ship after what happened to me. He probably knew his wrongdoings were about to catch up with him and decided to bail. As long as he doesn't hurt anyone anymore, it's none of my business.

"All I'm saying is—" Mom starts.

"This is the first time I've ever let you down. Like, *ever*. My first oopsie—"

"Okay." Mom slaps her thigh, looking ready to explode. "Let's not pretend me picking up my nineteen-year-old daughter from a hospital across the country is an oopsie. It's a *travesty*. We're not trivializing what happened this week, missy."

"Did you limber up before stretching that far? It was a mix-up! I thought it was Motrin." I throw my hands up in the air. "It's not like I'm gonna go score heroin on the streets when we get home."

"Why not?" Mom bites back, and this *is* different. Mom never bites back. She coos. She fawns. She giggles happily whenever I breathe in her direction for Pete's sake. She makes me feel so cherished, it gives me more drive and fuel to stay perfect. "You did it in New York. And please, don't embarrass yourself with the Motrin excuse. I don't recognize my daughter in this action. Getting drugs off the streets. Getting drugs at *all*."

"I wasn't going to make it a habit." What am I saying? I'm blowing my own Motrin cover. "I just needed something to ease the pain for my practical exam."

"Is this about your fractures?" There's an edge of panic in Mom's voice. "Are you struggling to perform?"

"No!" I lick my lips, piling up the lies like dirt over a coffin. I can't tell her I'm broken. That it was me against ballet, and ballet won. "My performance is fine." My throat bobs. "Great."

"Honestly, that you didn't get a leading role in the recital is obscene. I'm tempted to give them a piece of my mind about this. No way do they have a more talented ballerina—"

"*Mel*," Dad clears his throat. "Off topic."

And herein lies my problem. The pressure is so suffocating, I feel like I'm crushed under the rubble of expectations, broken dreams, and hopes. Mom forgets herself when we talk about ballet. There's no room for failure—only for success. And I want to be everything Daria wasn't—the best ballerina to come out of Juilliard.

In the back seat, I'm slowly peeling a dry scab off my knee like it's apple skin. In a long, curly line of scar tissue. Pink, raw flesh pops beneath it, and I know I'll be left with a scar from this car ride home.

"I got a bagful of these oranges," Dad tells no one in particular, eager to change the subject. "From Florida. They don't last as long as the California ones, but they're sweeter."

"Well." Mom rummages through her purse, popping a Tylenol

into her mouth. "If you don't have a drug problem, I don't see why going to rehab for eight weeks is such a biggie."

"I'm not going to spend two months in rehab to prove a point to you."

"Then expect some less-than-ideal conditions under my roof while I assess your situation, missy."

"Are you sure you don't want an orange?" Dad singsongs.

"Fuck, Dad, no!" I bang the back of my head against the leather seat in frustration.

Holy cannoli. Did I just drop the F-bomb? I never say fuck. *Fluck, frock, frap*—rarely. Our household has iron-clad rules about profanity. We don't even say God's name in vain. We use Marx instead. The antithesis to God. The father of atheism.

Dad stares at me through the rearview mirror like I slapped him. My knee is bleeding. And I could really use some Vicodin and Xanax right now.

Realizing I veered too far off character, I sigh. "Sorry. I overreacted. But seriously, I'm okay. I get that you're scared, and your feelings are valid, but so is my experience. You're right, Mom. I asked someone for a painkiller, and I thought they were going to give me a hospital-grade pill. It ended up being off the street. Lesson learned. Never again."

I recognize the silence that follows. It's the same one they gave Daria every time they thought she was being difficult and unreasonable. Which was *always.* Homegirl straight up almost ruined her now-husband's twin sister's life. I stood on the sidelines and watched her drama unfold.

But I'm not Daria. I'm responsible, smart, level-headed. I could've gotten into any Ivy League university I wanted.

I decide to take a gamble.

"Look, I'm good with doing the outpatient program until I go back to Juilliard if it puts your mind at ease."

As expected, Mom pulls the "you shouldn't be doing this for us, you should do this for yourself" card.

I'm the first to admit I got carried away with the drugs these past few months, but it's not like I dropped the ball. My grades are still amazing, I do charity work volunteering in a soup kitchen, and never dog-ear my books. Still a civilized human being all in all.

"I'll do the outpatient program," I repeat. "And use the rest of the time to train so I can retake a studio exam."

"You *failed*?" Mom clutches her pearls.

"No!" My pride, like my knee, is bleeding all over the floor. My anxiety is a ball of poison sitting in my throat. "I just…want a better grade, you know?"

"Good news is, you'll have plenty of time to practice because you sure as heck ain't getting out of the house unsupervised," Dad announces in an end-of-story tone.

"You can't hold me hostage!"

"Who's holding you hostage?" Dad drawls. "You're an adult and free to go. Let's go over your options, shall we?" he says conversationally, raising a hand and starting to tick off people with his fingers. "Your sister's? Tougher than military school. Forged in adolescent hell. Also lives in San Francisco, so good luck with the fog. Dean, Baron, Emilia, Trent, and Edie? Will send you straight home after they hear what landed you back in town. Knight, Luna, Vaughn?" He is on his second round of ticking off people with his fingers. "Have young kids and—no offense—not gonna host a substance user under their roof if you paid them. Which brings me to my final point—you can't pay them *or* a hotel because you're flat-out broke."

He's right, and I hate that he's right. My new reality closes in on me like four walls that keep on inching toward one another.

"From now on, you're under our watchful eye. When you leave the house, it's either with me or Mom. Never alone."

"Or Lev," I bargain breathlessly. "Lev too."

I'm not sure why I'm insisting, since Lev is no longer my prince in Bottega Veneta. He never arrived at the hospital, even though he promised he would when we talked on the phone. And even though he texted sporadically these past three days, he's sounded more pissed-off than worried. Has he given up on me? On *us*?

Mom sighs. "That boy loves you way too much."

"Agree to disagree," I mutter, looking out the window.

"Lev ain't dumb and knows what's gonna happen to him if Bailey takes something under his watch," Dad argues. "He can keep an eye on her."

"Fine. And Lev." Mom scrubs her face tiredly. "He *did* save you. Oh, and, Bailey?"

"Yeah?" I bat my lashes innocently. Perfect Bailey resurfaces. Or at least, I'm trying to drag her back to the light, kicking and screaming.

"Stop scratching your knee. You're bleeding all over. That must hurt. Can't you feel it?"

I can't, actually. I'm numb and in excruciating pain all at once, all the time.

"Sorry, Mom." I tuck my hands under my butt to stop myself. "I'll take that orange now, Dad."

He flings it behind his shoulder and watches in the mirror as I peel it methodically, in one go, then sink my teeth into it like it's an apple, rather than break it into slices. A rumble bubbles from his chest. Laughter fills the air-conditioned car.

"Love you, Bails."

"To the moon and back, Captain Random."

CHAPTER THREE
LEV

AGE EIGHTEEN

Miserable Fact #2,398: Roughly 67.1 million people die in the world every year.

"Trash offensive game today, Cap." Austin barrels into the locker room bare-chested, spitting his mouthguard to the floor. I peel off my gear and dump it on the bench. I amble into the showers dead-ass naked, even though the door to the field is wide-open and a bunch of sophomores can probably see me during PE. I shake my head. Austin ain't worth a response. Grim joins me on his hoverboard, also bare-assed.

"You can't ride that inside the locker room, you creepy fuck." I scowl.

"How's a hoverboard creepy?" He pops popcorn-cola gum. His signature scent is smelling like an AMC's sticky floor and first base in the dark. "Please enlighten me."

"Your balls are flapping in the wind like a flag on a cruise ship."

"It's a free country."

"It's not the only thing that's free is the problem."

Grim jumps off the board and kicks it back. It crashes against the wall noisily. "Aye, aye, Captain."

My being the captain of the All Saints High football team is a point of contention between us. Not because he is a better player, a better leader, a better *anything*—he's none of those things. I'm God's gift on and off the field, and that's indisputable. Grim's second best. Everyone knows that. But because I don't give a quarter fuck about the game and he wants to play college football, I'm supposed to bow down, step aside, and give him all the glory. In his warped mind, hunger trumps merit.

I turn the faucet on and shove my head beneath the water, rubbing my face. I haven't heard from Bailey in four days, which is screwed up considering our last phone call. Austin isn't wrong. My head's not in the game. It's not even in the same fucking state. It's in New York.

An *overdose*. What the fuck? The Bailey I know doesn't drink caffeinated beverages after two p.m. I'm also wondering, Why did she call me when we've been practically strangers since the day she left for Juilliard? I've been living the past year in a coma since she left and was fine with it—if you love someone, let them go, right?—but what if you love someone, and the idiot decides to accidentally kill themselves and they reach out to you? What's the protocol on that?

Grim and Austin join me on either side of the showers. Around us are Finn, Mac, Antonio, Ballsy, and the rest of the squad. Ballsy's real name is Todd Ostrovsky, but he has this weird condition that makes his balls gigantic. Like, so big his run times are affected.

I grab curd soap and rub it over my body and my hair, letting the bubbles slither down my abs. "Instead of being butthurt about not being captain, worry about our game with St. John Bosco next week."

"How 'bout I'll do both?" Grim Kwon—a certified smartass, extra tall, extra dark, extra handsome, *extra* fucking period—grabs the bar from my hand and shoves it in his ass, rubbing. "Ever heard of multitasking?"

"Ever heard of *boundaries*?" I hiss out. "That was my soap."

"That was my captainship," he retorts. "You didn't even put your name forward. Coach did."

"Maybe because he didn't think your sorry ass should lead," I tease. Captainship aside, we're good friends. Best friends, actually, now that Bails isn't in the picture.

To say I'm on edge is putting it mildly. I'm off the goddamn cliff, spinning rapidly down a deep, dark abyss.

Grim offers me the soap back, and I remove one of my Versace slippers and hurl it at him in retaliation.

"I'll take that as a no." He shrugs, tossing the soap to Finn, fingering his chin thoughtfully. "There ya go, buddy. I have a spare."

"Thanks, bro." Finn starts scrubbing his body with the soap. Everybody gags and laughs. "What? What's happening?" He eyeballs Grim nervously.

"Nothing, man." Grim pops his gum. "You just smeared my skid marks all over your body. We're bonded for life now. *Soapmates*."

"I see you woke up and chose violence today, Kwon." Finn drops the soap and launches at Grim. They wrestle naked on the wet tiles while the showers spray their bodies. Too bad they aren't hot chicks. Anyway, I root for casualties in this fight.

I see why getting a full ride to a good college is important to Grim. Even though he's loaded, his parents are pretty clear about their expectation that he becomes a lawyer and takes over their family business. Unfortunately for him, he barely has the grades to graduate, let alone get accepted to a good university. So either he sneaks in through football or his name comes off his grandfather's will.

"Break this up before you break his spine, Grim," I order tonelessly. Even though I hate football, I still care about being a good captain. And Finn won't win this fight. Grim is a lineman the size of a tractor.

"Aw, you're not my real dad, Levy."

"That what your mom said? I'll ask for a paternity test."

Everyone laughs. So does Grim.

But because he knows me well, he can hear the edge in my voice. Grim untangles himself from Finn and slips back under the showerhead next to me. Other than being a Bitter Betty about the captain thing—a title I snatched sophomore year—we get along pretty great. We're off to the next topic on our agenda—which parties are worth crashing this weekend—when I overhear Austin telling Ballsy, "Confirmed, man. Saw her beat-up Toyota driving down Spanish River yesterday, her hot momma in the passenger seat."

There's only one person in town with a Toyota Corolla older than the Bible—which is also eggplant purple with a mismatched yellow door—and that's Bailey Followhill. Senior year, she insisted on saving up the money she made working summer camps and bought her own vehicle. She's been financially independent since she was eighteen and probably the only person in our zip code to drive a non-luxury car. Uncle Vicious once threatened to sue Jaime for the eyesore that is his daughter's vehicle parked in our cul-de-sac.

But since Bailey is supposed to be in New York, locked up in some rehab, that can't be her he's talking about. Maybe Mel took the car to the shop?

Ballsy says, "Dude, impossible. She got into Juilliard or some shit."

Austin sucks his teeth. "Nah, bruh. She's back in town. Saw her with my own eyes, getting Froyo from that place near Planet Fitness." *YoToGo*. Bailey's favorite. She always gets the Irish coffee and red velvet cake. Every hair on my body, head to balls, stands on end. Grim notices the shift, glancing at Austin and Ballsy with sudden interest.

"I always thought she was a seven outta ten." Ballsy tugs at his dick roughly, lathering it with soap. "Too Goody Two-Shoes for my taste. But I'd tap that because she is...ya know, legacy. Daria Followhill's sister."

Bullshit. She's a goddamn hundred out of ten, and everyone with a working pair of eyes knows it.

Bailey is a legend in All Saints High. Her grades. Her pedigree.

Her *president of the debate team* status that won us the nationals. She is kind, put-together, smart as a demon, and fuckable to a fault. I don't know one guy who wouldn't want a piece of her. Which coincidently makes me want to butcher half the people in my life into microscopic pieces.

"You sure she's back in town?" Finn wonders. Same.

Austin nods. "OD, man." He turns off the faucet and my mouth is bone fucking dry. He plucks a towel and slaps it between his thighs, wiping back and forth. "My cousin's girl goes to Juilliard. That fall from grace was from a fucking skyscraper, man. She was ushered out of her room on a gurney foaming at the mouth like a rabid dog."

"Shut up."

"It's all over social media."

Ballsy laughs in disbelief. "Bailey Followhill? OD'ing? I have a bridge to sell you in Brooklyn. Who the fuck would buy *that*?"

"Dude, I'll send you a TikTo—"

"That's enough," I roar.

Austin turns to me, a crooked, sadistic grin on his face. "What's the problem, Cap? It's not like I'm trashing a teammate. You can't do shit."

"I can do a whole lot of shit." I step in his direction.

"Yeah? Like what?"

"Fuck around and find out."

A shit-eating grin on his face, Austin drops the towel to the floor, walks over to the bench in front of our lockers, and picks up his phone, sliding his thumb over the screen. "Y'all gotta see Bailey Followhill getting picked up by the EMS—"

The video starts playing, and that's when I lose it. Every ounce of self-control in me dissipates. She's my blind side. My weak spot. She is my Achilles' heel.

I dart toward him faster than an F-22 Raptor and slam his back against the lockers. My nose touches his as I get in his face. We're both naked and dripping water. Not ideal, but I want him to know I am going to make lasagna out of his inner organs if he speaks about her like this ever again. Don't ask me why, but Austin's favorite hobby is pissing me off until I can no longer see straight.

He steps back, chuckling. "My bad." He raises his palms in surrender. "Maybe it's someone who looks *just* like her and attends Juilliard and drives the same car."

"Yeah. Maybe." I pluck his phone from between his fingers, direct it at his ugly face to unlock it, and report the video. "There." I shove the phone into his mouth, deliberately slamming it against his teeth. "All better now, yeah?"

I secure a towel around my waist and pick up my duffel bag, digging for my clothes. Unlike Bailey, I can lie through my teeth any day of the week. I'm not necessarily a good person. I'm just good to the people I love. Morally fluid, and damn proud of that.

"So did she overdose or not?" Finn, who I swear is slower than a sleeping sloth, pokes.

The lie slides out of my mouth effortlessly. "No, fuckface. She got ushered into the ER last week. But she fainted, not overdosed. She is taking some time off because of her sports injuries."

"Sure, man. Sure. Just like I'm taking time off from Margot Robbie because she is too sexually demanding to keep up with." Austin grabs his junk, laughing. That's strike two, and I'm not waiting for the third. He bends over to pick up his shirt from the metal bench. I grab him by the back of the neck and slam him face first against the blue metal lockers so roughly I leave an asshole-shaped dent on the fucking metal.

"Let's try this again," I taunt into his ear. "Shall we?"

"You're handling this whole situation tremendously well," Grim points out dryly from the bench, rolling his socks on. "Twelve out of ten for self-control. Supreme captain material."

Ignoring him, I crash Austin's head against the locker again. He spits out blood. I don't care. I'm past seeing red. This is somewhere between burgundy and black. "Promise me you'll never utter this bullshit again to anyone with ears."

Austin struggles, flailing as he tries to escape my hold, attempting to throw a punch in to save his pride.

"Hey, hey!" Antonio and Finn rush to get between us, trying to deescalate the situation. Grim is the only one not to butt in. He loves tea so much, I'm surprised he didn't bring biscuits. Plus, if I fall, he's next in line to step into my shoes.

"*Dafuq* are you doing, Cole?" Antonio shrieks but doesn't put an effort into pushing me in the opposite direction. He knows Austin overstepped.

Austin gurgles on a mixture of blood and saliva, thrashing against my death grip. "Jesus, Cole. That ego of yours has gotten too big for the rest of you."

"Stop spreading lies about Bailey," I repeat, voice flat, eyes dead.

"Just because you can't handle the truth doesn't change it."

"One thing I can and *will* change is your fucking face if you speak about her ever again."

I grab him by the neck and hurl him to the floor. He falls down with a loud thud, shimmering, fuming eyes directed at me.

Lifting my finger up, I hiss, "This is your last warning. Next time I hear you say her name, I'm feeding Ballsy's nuts to you with a spoon."

"It's a medical condition!" Ballsy kicks my duffel bag angrily as he scurries out the door.

"That doesn't make it any less funny, bro." Finn claps his shoulder, trailing after him.

It's only when Austin, Finn, Mac, Antonio, and Ballsy are gone that Grim opens his smart mouth again. He's slouched against the door with his arms folded, looking smug. "I ran out of Royal Canin."

"Huh?" I shrug into my varsity jacket.

"Your version of Snickers. You know, because you're acting like a little bitch right now."

I swear this is his version of a pep talk.

"Fucker had it coming."

"He goaded you to get a reaction, and you fell right into his trap." Grim pushes off the door, ambling toward me. I know he's about to lay into me, and he has every right to. "Bailey isn't God."

"Never said she was." I hoist my backpack over my shoulder.

"She didn't even tell you she's in town."

"Yeah, well, I'm not her fucking parent, and I don't actually care all that much." I'm glad there isn't a lie detector attached to me or the graph would jump so high, it'd hit the fucking moon.

Grim runs a hand over his overgrown hair, looking like a commercial for an eighty-buck shampoo. "All I'm saying is she's not yours to protect. Every time she's near, you lose yourself."

"And?" I sneer.

"And right now? You have too much to lose."

Fully clothed now, I grab my bag and leave without sparing him a glance.

Cupid botched the job. He only hit one of us.

But that arrow? It pierced through my heart and stabbed at my back.

A few hours later, I walk into the Great Hall. We call it that because All Saints High legit has the best cafeteria space in the whole of SoCal. Probably the West Coast. While it's a public school, it's in the most affluent county in the state. Parents and donors hemorrhage money into it, throwing themed balls and charity events to subsidize whatever their aristo-brat spawns desire. Personally, I think it's the ultimate cop-out. Sending your kid to a public school because you're an upstanding citizen fighting for equality but paying through the nose to make sure said school stays bougie as fuck.

The lunch lady piles a Kobe burger with swiss cheese and coleslaw, and lime and chili-flavored tortilla chips onto my tray. Grim is getting a four-cheese quesadilla with truffle fries and fruit.

A pair of slender arms wrap around me from behind, hugging my waist. A hot, lollipop-scented mouth latches onto the side of my neck. "Hmm. Smells like teen spirit."

"Sweat, spunk, and crushing expectations?" Grim asks blandly, cracking open his can of La Croix as he slides his tray along the conveyor belt of the lunch line.

Thalia nudges her small body between us, grinning from ear to ear. "Opportunity, youth, and ambition!"

I call Thalia my girl-something because she's more than a friend but less than a girlfriend. Someone I'm casually seeing to pass the time. We have this unspoken agreement she can never have my heart.

My dick is a different matter, though.

Thalia pulls at the elastic holding her messy bun together to release her long blond hair.

Grim shoots me a look that says, *I know you see it too, cum-hole.*

And I do. I see it.

Thalia looks kinda like Bailey. Okay, fine. *Exactly* like Bailey, if you look at her from behind. Which happens to be my preferred position when we tumble into bed. Last year, when Bailey was a senior and Thalia a junior, people would mix them up all the time. But that's not why I'm dating Thalia. I'm dating Thalia because she is cute, fun, and doesn't mind verbally sparring with Grim whenever he's being an asshole. Also because she is the only girl who was persistent enough when I turned her down the first hundred times.

"You getting something?" I unfurl my fingers from hers when she tries to hold my hand, my thoughts traveling back to Bailey. *Bailey.* She has no clue I have a girl-something. Things have been weird between us. Now that she's here unexpectedly, she's in for a surprise.

"Hey, by the way, I've been dating Thalia Mulroney for two months. Yup, your hologram with a heartbeat."

"Got my own, thanks." Thalia raises a bag of kale chips and a Diet Coke. I suspect Thalia doesn't have a ton of money for lunch every day and I don't want to offer to pay for her because I don't want to embarrass her, so I slip her favorite kale chips and soda in her locker a few times a week.

"You know, your eating disorder really complements your eyes," Grim says in a fake Valley-girl drawl.

"Why, thank you." Thalia puts a hand to her chest. "But does it go together as well as the chip on your shoulder and in-desperate-need-of-cut hair?"

We all pivot and grab a seat. A sophomore sitting three benches down from us shouts, "My ideal weight is Grim Kwon and whatever his duvet weighs!" Her friend stands up and flashes us her bra. "My ideal weight is three Lev Coles on top of me!"

The entire cafeteria erupts in laughter. Thalia perches her ass in my lap, joining in on the laughter. She turns to Grim, looking slightly annoyed. "I eat a light lunch on Wednesdays. I have back-to-back practice from one till three."

Thalia is on the varsity gymnastics team that won us the district championship and third place state championship last year.

Grim stares at her vacantly. "Shit. You're still here." He yawns. "I muted you out somewhere between chips and shoulders."

She turns to me. "You're gonna let him talk to me like that?"

"Hey, at least he talks to you. Most people, he doesn't even acknowledge."

She laughs and swats my chest. "Asshole. You're so lucky you're hot. And a jock."

I didn't always hate football. In fact, once upon a time, I even sort of liked it. But then the competitiveness, expectations, and *In Lev Cole I Trust* bumper stickers became a thing, and it got out of control. I now do it out of obligation. To my family. To my community. To my never-ending guilt trip.

Thalia grabs my turtle dove bracelet. Or whatever's left of it. "When will you let me get you a new string? The dove's gonna fall off any day now."

I gently pull away. Having her fingers on it feels wrong. "I'll get to it."

"So. Grim. Found a reaper to mate with yet?" Thalia wiggles her brows, turning her attention to him. I chuckle, finishing half my burger in one bite.

"No, why? Do you know another gold-digging, social-climbing, semi-hot gymnast in need of a rich boyfriend?" His eyes mockingly light up. "All I ever wanted was someone to love me for my bank account."

I kick Grim under the table. "Cut it out."

Thalia blushes, throwing a kale chip at him, and he catches it in his hand without looking up from his plate, shoving it into his mouth. "Hmm. I just love the taste of nothing."

Having enough of Grim's bullshit, Thalia turns to me. "Are we still on for today, babes? Early dinner at yours?"

Grim's gaze snaps up from his food, a taunting smile on his face. "Yeah, *babes*, are you still on?"

I'm going to break his pretty nose one day. My misery seems to be his favorite comedy genre.

I run a hand over my buzzed head. "Sorry, T. Bailey's back in town. I gotta see her."

Lay into her, more like it. *If* she's even here. I'm going off Austin's word, which is slightly less trustworthy than that of a Nigerian prince-astronaut stranded in space with a fifteen-million-dollar fortune he wishes to share with complete strangers.

"*Ohmigod*, she is?" Thalia's eyes twinkle with excitement. "Wait, is she okay?"

Alarm bells blast in my head. "Why wouldn't she be?"

"It's just..." Her shoulders hitch up. "I heard some stuff."

"From Austin?" My brows furrow.

Thalia bites down on her lower lip. "No...from Lakshmi."

The video's been doing the rounds already. The whole school probably knows. Good job, Bails. Ruining a nineteen-year flawless reputation on one drug binge.

Thalia smooths my shirt over my pecs. "Will you let me know how she's doing?"

"Why?" I ask. They weren't friends or anything.

"Because she wants to know what she's competing with," Grim coughs into his fist.

"Because I've always liked her." Thalia glares at Grim with a scowl, shaking her head like he's a lost cause.

"Sure," I say, because it seems extra shitty both to bail on her ass and not keep her in the loop. Especially since I blew her off twice this week to work on a vintage car Dad bought.

"No. Let's open this up. Why do you like the girl your fuck buddy is in love with, Thalia?" Grim pops a fry into his mouth, looking between us with a sinister grin. "Is that because she's you but with a personality?"

"Speaking of personalities, you should use all that money to buy yourself a new one," Thalia sasses back.

The barb doesn't land. Grim doesn't get angry. He doesn't get even, either. He normally just gets bored.

"Are you capable of saying something *without* sarcasm?" I grind out at him.

"Hope not. That might invite a real, meaningful conversation." Grim shudders.

"Hey, do you want me to come with you? To see Bailey, I mean?" Thalia puts a hand on my shoulder.

"Yeah, Lev, do you?" Grim blinks expectedly.

Rather than throw a tortilla chip at him, I hurl the entire tray and everything on it. He dodges quickly, and my food ends up splattering over Raul Ortega's back. A varsity wrestler with a taste for shenanigans.

He turns around, death in his eyes.

"Foooooooooooood fight!"

CHAPTER FOUR
LEV

Miserable Fact #2,993: The Turritopsis dohrnii jellyfish is the one and only immortal creature in the world.

I floor it the entire drive home in my Bugatti Chiron Sport. I love a good monster engine, which is why I am obsessed with planes, among other things.

We, the Followhills, Spencers, and Rexroths all live in the same cul-de-sac. It's the size of a golf course, but it's still close enough that we always have our noses in each other's business. Both a blessing and a curse.

I park my car, blocking Dad's Maybach, and torpedo my way to Bailey's doorstep. I don't knock or ring the bell. We're all practically family. Which is a gross-ass idea, considering the things I've been fantasizing about doing to my ex–best friend these past five years.

I punch in the code to their door and throw it open, kicking my Nike Blazers against the wall. Mel's voice greets me from the kitchen. "Lev, honey, you hungry?"

She must have seen me coming through the cameras on her phone app.

"Perpetually." I stop in front of her with my good-boy smile. She turns around and walks over to hug me, holding a spatula. She is making dynamite shrimp and zucchini fries. Bailey's favorite. Rather than acting on my impatience, I spend twenty minutes small-talking her. Bailey probably knows I'm here and it's driving her mad I'm in no rush to see her. *Good.* Only after Mel and I cover every subject under the sun—weather, school, summer plans, college applications—do I finally ask, "Is Bails upstairs?"

"She better be." Mel's friendly smile morphs into a scowl. She looks like she's aged five years in the last four days. "Hey, thanks again for…" She swallows, her fingers fluttering the air to indicate, *you know.* She's *this* close to bursting into tears.

I shrug. "Bailey saved my life every single day for two years straight after I lost Mom."

"She was amazing," Mel agrees. Past tense. *Yikes.* Bails is in the doghouse for real.

"Still is," I say, low enough that Bailey can't hear me from upstairs. "She's just going through the adolescence she never had, I think."

"Maybe," she whispers. "I didn't think you'd grow apart, you know."

But we didn't outgrow each other. Bailey outgrew *me*. She changed, and I stayed the same. Stretched her wings when I wanted to clip them to ensure she never left. It backfired. Big time.

"Don't let me keep you." She steps back, wiping her eyes. "Please tell her food's ready."

I feel bad for Mel. She means well. Everyone always criticizes her parenting skills, but the truth is, it's fucking hard to raise two smart, independent girls. And mothers always get double the blame for everything. Nobody said shit about Dad back when Knight's favorite hobby was blow and alcohol.

I take the curved marble stairway, passing floor-to-ceiling portraits of the entire family. Daria is impishly grinning back, wearing an Oscar de la Renta golden sequin dress. Bailey is in a Navy blue v-neck dress, embroidered with little flowers. Her smile is serene, polite, contained, her eyes two clear pools under a cloudless sky.

They're so different it's comical. Daria is a she-devil who loves her parties and designer clothes. Bailey is an angel with a love for books and charities.

My stomach bottoms out when I step into the second-floor hallway of the Followhills' house. Too many things have happened since I last saw Bailey. I have a new girl-something, and she has a new fucking drug problem apparently.

I follow the trail of warm vanilla and new book scent leading to her room.

I knock on the ajar door, then remind myself she's an addict and doesn't need privacy right now. I barge right in. "Bailey?"

Someone jumps me from behind. Long, muscular legs coil around my back, her arms are circling my shoulders. She giggles in my ear, her breath toasted cinnamon and vanilla. She's fucking everywhere, gorgeous and alive and warm as a perfect August day, and for the first time in my life, I want to break her instead of mending her, because FUCK. THIS. SHIT. She broke my heart, then went and almost killed the girl I love. Who does that to a person?

"Levy!" She plasters her lips to my cheek, oblivious to my mood. Her blond hair rains down on my face, an avalanche of yellow and gold. "Holy shrimp. I haven't seen you in a few months and you're the size of a town house now."

She's acting like Old Us. Our families labeled us #Bailev sometime before we turned six because we were inseparable. People shipped us. Everyone thought we'd become a couple. No dice.

Slanting my gaze sideways, I ask dryly, "Sorry, do I know you?"

"Brainiac. Knows your darkest secrets. Obsessed with lists. Your best friend. Ring a bell?" She nibbles at my ear, and just like that, my entire bloodstream goes straight to my dick and I get light-headed.

Still, I play the part of the jaded asshole. "My best friends are mommy issues and a god complex. Try again."

"Nope." She rubs her smooth cheek along my stubbled one. My dick is seriously a second away from unzipping my ripped Amiri jeans and bursting out to say hi. "Those are your *therapist's* best friends and the reason she owns a vacation house in Cancun."

I don't have a therapist, though I probably should get one, considering the amount of rage I'm bottling up inside these days.

"Get off my back, Bailey."

"Or else?" She grins, and who the *fuck* is this girl?

Feeling like I'm goofing around with one of my fangirls and not my best friend, I reach to tickle her armpits and she falls on her back on the sheepskin carpet, giggling and kicking her legs in the air. She's wearing a pair of white boy shorts and a pink Nirvana hoodie. A Walmart bargain, I bet. Her laughter in my ear and her body writhing beneath mine makes me feel like I've woken up from a long, lethargic sleep. How can people find Bailey and Thalia remotely similar? Thalia is a daisy and Bailey is a rose. Thalia is an open book, what-you-see-is-what-you-get kinda girl. I figured her out long before I laid a finger on her. Bailey is a tightly wrapped gift. Her velvet petals are clasped together firmly, each hiding another layer of her.

Dropping to my knees, I continue tickling her sides, the sensitive spots of her neck, not even cracking the faintest smile. She thrashes and pretends to struggle but really just pulls me deeper in, seeking more contact.

We pretend-fight. Let loose some of that tension that's built up the past year.

Bailey presses her socked feet to my face, laughing breathlessly. I'd love to continue this game, but my boner is about to rip through my boxers and run toward her bathroom for a cold shower. Plus, there are some burning topics on my agenda. I stop abruptly. Our eyes lock. Green on blue. I'm on top of her, my weight pinning her down. She looks a little thinner than last time I saw her, but she's still the most beautiful girl on planet earth. I lower my face until we're an inch from one another. Her hot breath prickles the whiskers on my cheeks.

"*Argh.*" She tries to kick me off, but I'm stronger, bigger, and have a zero-bullshit policy. "You have the eyelashes of a giraffe," she moans. "Boys with long, curly eyelashes should be outlawed."

"Heard they're trying to legislate this in Congress. Visit me in jail?" I lick my lips.

She shakes her head slowly. "Nah. Play your cards right, though, and I'll top up your iPay."

I can't help but laugh, pressing my forehead against hers. "You're a pain in the ass, you know that?"

She nods but doesn't say anything. She's sobered up now, and I can tell she wants to ask why I didn't come to see her in the hospital. But she won't. Because she knows. It's written all over my face—I didn't come because I hate her guts for overdosing and she's not off the goddamn hook.

"I'm sorry," she rasps. "I really, really am."

I swipe a lock of blond hair from her forehead. "You okay, Dove?"

"Yeah," her voice is husky. Hoarse. "Thank you for…you know."

Our mouths are an inch apart. She licks her lips, her gaze lowering to my mouth. A small, longing sigh escapes her. There's a moment where I wonder if she wants me to kiss her. There were a lot of moments in our past where I thought she wanted me to kiss her. And just like in all the others, her wispy ballerina body slips beneath mine, and she's up on her feet in a flash, avoiding me. She marches into her walk-in closet and examines the rows upon rows of summer dresses, arranged by color to create a wall-to-wall rainbow. "What took you so long?"

Hopping to my feet, I grumble, "You rolled into town without a text."

Bailey makes a surprised face. She might be a great dancer, but she has the acting chops of an eye booger. "Really? I thought I texted you back."

"No, you didn't. I can deal with you fucking up, but I won't put up with lying."

She gathers her hair into a long ponytail and drops her gaze to her feet. "Sorry. The last few days have been overwhelming. I was building up the courage to call you. Trying to figure out what I wanted to say."

Ambling toward her, I ask, "And have you?"

She bites down on her lower lip, shaking her head.

"Fine. I'll do the talking, then. Do you have a drug problem?" I rest my elbow on the doorframe, blocking her way out of her walk-in closet.

"Jesus, Lev!" She slaps her thigh with the cardigan she's holding. "Why's everyone so upset the moment I start living a little and trying new things?"

"That wasn't a yes or a no." My voice is a steel blade. Sharp. Cold. Cutting.

"My only drug problem is that everyone keeps talking to me about drugs."

"You overdosed."

"No, I experimented with painkillers. Bought something laced. Got burned. I only did it to keep my injuries' pain at bay. But I'm done with all that."

I want to believe her because the alternative is going to drive me nuts. I also don't want to micromanage her, but if it's tough love she needs, she's cruising for some bruising because I'm gonna make it my job to tail her ass and make sure she's clean.

"Then why was it so hard to figure out what to say?" I eyeball her.

"Because what happened to me was embarrassing."

"Yet in that moment, you called *me*."

"Duh." Peevish look.

"Why?" I press.

She swallows hard. "Because."

"President of the debate team, ladies and gents." I slow clap, sneering down at her.

"Because you were the first number I could find!" She stomps like a child. "It means nothing, okay? Don't read too much into it."

I'm torn between calling her bluff and walking out of here.

Bailey sighs. "Look, I have cabin fever. Can I go for a ride?"

Sure can, Dove. You can go on three. On my cock. These are the kinds of thoughts I really should stop thinking about when I'm next to her.

"You need permission now?" I crack my knuckles, whistling. "How the mighty have fallen."

She purses her lips. "Mom and Dad said I can only leave the house chaperoned by them or you."

I *tsk.* "Well, whaddaya know. What goes around really does come around."

She was the one treating me like a Tamagotchi growing up.

"No one's coming in this scenario between us two. I'm not *that* high." She rips the pink Nirvana hoodie from her body, spheres it in her fist, and throws it at me.

I catch and drape it over my face, head tilted up, sniffing it like a pervert. "Joke's on you. This goes into my spank bank." I tuck the hoodie into my back pocket, because she is that small, and I am that big.

Bailey growls exasperatedly in her pink sports bra, her abs tightening with the movement. She really has changed. Old Bailey doesn't growl, huff, scoff, or any of those things. She smiles politely, fusses, and beams.

I rake my eyes over her upper body until my gaze lands on the tape on her arm, the purple marks of the IV. Then I start noticing the wear and tear on her flesh. Her body is marked—painted purple and black and blue. I've seen plenty of sports injuries in my lifetime. This is different. Worse. Way worse.

The knots in my stomach twist harder and tighter, grow bigger like a rubber band ball, and it feels like they're about to snap through my skin. Even if she doesn't have a drug habit, she's a great candidate for one because living inside her body must be painful. As she slips a blue satin dress on, I say, "Maybe it's a good thing Mel and Jaime are keeping an eye on you. You haven't been taking care of yourself."

Bailey rolls her eyes. Bailey *never* rolls her eyes. "And you know this because…?"

"I have eyes. Look at you. You're battered."

"No, *you're* delusional," she snaps. *Whoa.* Okay. I have no fucking idea who this girl is or what she did to my best friend.

"What happened to you?" I frown. Who the hell am I talking to anyway? "You were this insanely successful girl. The pride of Todos Santos."

"And you think just because I work super hard and it shows that I'm no longer that person?" she spits out. "Well, newsflash—succeeding at an elite school comes with a price. Welcome to life outside our childhood bubble, Cole." She spreads her arms theatrically. "You have to bleed to succeed. When you do sports competitively, injuries happen. Of course, *you* wouldn't know anything about it. I've never seen a quarterback who barely breaks a sweat. What's the worst you've ever endured, a scraped knee?"

Shut the front door. This is a top-tier meltdown. Like, amateurly edited, badly written cable reality TV shit. I'm wondering if she's experiencing some type of withdrawal.

Whoever this girl is, she soldiers ahead, grinning at me tauntingly. "Face it, Lev. Even if I did overtrain, you're the last person to lecture me about it. You're cruising through life too scared to tell Daddy Dearest you *hate* football and want to go to flight school. You're a coward. You just hide it well. When are you gonna tell him, by the way?"

I'm thinking never is a good timeframe.

When I don't answer, she makes a face. "You *are* gonna tell him, right?"

My jaw clenches. "We're not talking about me now."

She tips her head back and laughs humorlessly. "Oh. Wow."

Football is a sore subject for me. I'm good at it, but I hate it. It's like being a porn star with a ten-inch dick who aspires to be a celibate priest. Just because I *can* doesn't mean I *should*. Thing is,

I'm second-generation football royalty at All Saints High. My dad played. My big brother, Knight, played. Last year, my letterman jacket went for seven thousand bucks in an auction. It's hard to throw this kinda love away. Truth is, I'm addicted to the glory. Fucking sue me.

"Sorry, I'm on edge." Bailey rubs her forehead tiredly.

You're on something, all right. "You do seem…scattered," I say gently. Because telling her she is one hundred percent a stranger probably isn't going to get me far. "You need anything?"

She shakes her head. "Just need some fresh air. Wanna grab lunch before we head out?"

"Shrimp and zucchini fries with a side of your fucking bullshit?" I arch an eyebrow. "It's a pass from me."

"I'll behave." She gives me a small, desperate smile. "Please? I just need…"

"An urgent trip to rehab?"

She gives me an exhausted smile, and I think I see the real Bailey through the cracks. "A *break.*"

I groan, running a hand through my buzzed hair. "Fuck. Fine."

We both shuffle downstairs and eat Melody's food. It's good, but Bailey makes the best food in the world, hands down. Mainly because in the months before Mom died, she visited her daily and scribbled down all of her recipes so I would never go without my favorite dishes. She learned how to make my comfort everything— waffles (with a dash of cinnamon and silan), chicken noodle soup (celery, dried onion, yolk), chocolate cake (extra-eggy). All the Rosie Cole staples. She would push Mom's wheelchair into our kitchen and make her watch as she made my favorite food and get pointers.

"One more yolk."

"Generous with the salt."

"A little parsley never killed nobody, Bails."

If watching your best girl-friend race against the clock to ensure she knows how to make your favorite home-cooked meals doesn't make you fall in love with her, then I don't know what does. No wonder I'm trash for this girl. My entire history, my making, is in the palm of her hand.

One time, when Bailey was already at Juilliard and we were no longer technically friends, she sat on the phone with me and we FaceTimed for forty minutes at three in the morning Eastern time while she taught me how to make Mom's waffles just because I felt nostalgic and couldn't fall asleep. She had an important exam the next morning, but that didn't stop her. That was always the problem with Bails and me. We were pretty crappy with setting boundaries with one another.

I look across the table at the girl who spent six months of her life shadowing a dying woman so I can still enjoy Mom's waffles and decide I'm being unreasonable. In the past six months alone, two guys from the team have woken up in the ER after partying too hard, Coach barely saying a word. As long as they perform, they're golden. Bailey has made some poor choices, but I can't deny living up on a sky-high pedestal must get pretty boring, never mind lonely. I should know—she and I are both considered the "perfect" ones.

She's banged up from ballet. And so what if she experimented with drugs a little? Who the fuck am I to judge?

I shift my hand under the table and find hers. Squeeze. She brushes her thumb over my knuckles. A shiver runs down my spine. A silent truce.

After we eat, I drive to YoToGo and get us huge frozen yogurt cups, then we make our way to our secret spot in the woods. Now's probably a good time to tell her about Thalia, but something stops me.

Maybe the fact that there's not much to tell—it's just a steady hookup—or maybe it's that I know if she doesn't care, I'll die a little inside.

Fine, a *lot*.

Bailey finally penetrates the silence and asks, "Are they still there?"

She's referring to the turtle doves we found all those years ago. I nod. "They have a tin of food up on that tree. I top it up every week or so."

Bailey slouches back against the passenger seat, plucking at her lower lip. "Why do you think they never had babies?"

"Maybe they're the same gender. Maybe one of them is infertile. Maybe they're platonic. Maybe they value their independent lifestyle and don't bow to outdated societal norms. Also, kids are fucking expensive, yo."

Bailey laughs, covering her face with her hands. "I forgot how funny you are."

I let loose a little smile but refuse to show her how I glow inside out at her words.

"I think they're both female." She pouts. "The doves."

"That'd be my fault." I scratch the stubble on my chin. "I probably manifested it. You know two chicks is my fantasy."

"Didn't think you'd be so literal."

Now we're both laughing, and the ice might not be broken, but it sure is cracked.

It was freaky, the way we found these doves. The *day* we found these doves. An omen. A message from above. Turtle doves aren't common in North America, which meant they were runaways. Just like we were that day.

We park and hike the way to our corner in the woods. A while back, I stretched a huge piece of canvas across four valley oaks and tied it to each of the trunks, so now Bails and I have a giant-ass hammock raised off the ground to hang out on. About twelve-by-twelve feet. It's always full of leaves and dirt, and it's the only instance when Bailey doesn't mind looking less than completely perfect. When we're out here in nature.

We climb on top of the canvas.

Bailey's tongue twists around her neon-green spoon. "What's new with you?"

I have a steady ride and every time I'm inside her I think about you, which is probably the shittiest thing I've ever done in my life. Dad and Knight are pushing me to play ball in college. And every time I think you might not be okay, I want to stab the faceless, nameless asshole who sold you those drugs.

"Same old shit." I crunch a frozen cherry between my teeth. "How's Juilliard?"

"Amazing." Her eyes are two shiny snow globes. "There's so much talent and inspiration there. The city is full of culture. I go to a different exhibition every weekend and tutor a low-income junior in Harlem twice a week. And the food, Lev!" She gasps. "New York is heaven for foodies."

"Mom told me New York was her favorite city," I say. "Her and Dad started seeing each other there. I think they only moved here because she wanted to be close to Aunt Emilia."

Bailey smiles, and for the first time today, I recognize the girl who taught me how to tie my shoes and rock-skip in the river by our house.

"I always think about it," she murmurs. "Remember the time your mom told us your dad ordered her every rose from every florist on the block?"

"Yeah." My smile is about to split my face in half. Bailey pinks, sinking her white teeth into her bottom lip.

"A couple months ago I went down to that street to see if the florists were still there. Four out of the five are. I bought a few bouquets from each store and sent them to Mom. She put them on Rosie's grave."

"That was you?" My eyebrows jump. "Dad thought she had a side piece. You should've seen the meltdowns."

Bailey laughs wildly. "You're kidding me, right?"

"A little," I laugh.

"Yikes! I thought I told you. My cognitive skills should be peaking at nineteen."

Bailey does nice things because she wants to do them, not

because she wants the recognition. A year ago, I'd have exploded into red heart-shaped confetti at this confession. But she isn't the same girl from a year ago.

"Thanks, Dove. That was a nice touch." I press my fist to her arm.

She bumps her shoulder against mine and steals a spoonful of my Froyo. "Don't be a sap, Levy."

"Do you even know what *sap* means?" I quirk a brow.

"Duh. Systems, applications, and products in data processing. One of my APs was computer science, remember?" She taps her temple.

"Nerd," I whisper-shout.

"Stupid jock." She blows a raspberry.

We both pretend to laugh even though I'd rather take her tongue in my mouth and kiss the shit out of her.

As if on cue, both of our turtle pigeons descend from their nest, making their way to us. Perseus and Andromeda. Bailey chose the names. Something about great, unconditional love and overcoming obstacles together. Joke's on her because these bitches are living rent-free in a nest I literally made for them. Privileged assholes.

Andromeda, without blue in her feathers like Perseus, is also missing a leg, so it's easy to tell them apart. They land on the far corner of the canvas, close to us but not too close to comfort. They know us and are happy to see us.

To Bailey, I say, "I wanna go to New York before college. Visit all the places Mom loved. Her old apartment."

"We should do it together!" She lights up, and it feels so stupid. Making plans with this girl who isn't even my friend anymore and isn't even *herself* anymore. "Go on Tour de LeBlanc." She wiggles her brows, putting on a horrible French accent. "St. Paul's Chapel, Lady Liberty, Battle of Brooklyn...*and here, ladies and gents, the dame Rosie LeBlanc handed Mr. Dean Cole his butt back to him!*"

I laugh in spite of myself. Now she sounds like my best friend again. We were the last of the litter. The invisible kids. No issues.

No drama. Perfect grades. Our SATs are crazy—mine is 1560 and Dove's is a perfect, shiny 1600.

"How'd you find your way to a drug dealer anyway?" I can't seem to give this thing a rest.

At my question, Bailey's face rears back, and her nostrils flare. "Does it really matter?"

"Is that a real question?" I blink slowly. "Bastard's going around selling people laced painkillers. Yeah, I think it matters."

She visibly shrinks. "I didn't catch his name, and it wasn't on school grounds anyway."

"What if he sells to other people? What if—"

"*Ohmymarx*, would you shut up?" she snaps, pulling a joint from her pocket and lighting it up like it's the most natural thing in the world. "I'm not the one with the substance abuse genes here. Stop projecting, Cole."

She's back to being a bitch again. I'm getting whiplash, but I'm starting to see this is the new version of her. Nice and normal one moment, then a goddamn hellion the next. She's exhibiting an addict's behavior.

Plus, she's only a year fucking adultier than me. Not a thirtysomething-year-old with a key to all the hard-knock truths of this universe.

My jaw locks tight. "Your mood swings more than a limp dick in a locker room these days." My eyes drop to the lit tip of the joint. "And since when do you smoke?"

"Since I found a joint in Daria's room—probably Penn's—and decided to mellow down a little. What's your problem?" She twists her face like I stink. "You were the one who offered me my first hit when we were in school."

"That's right." I give her a leveled stare. "Before you were a fucking *junkie*."

There. I said it. It's out in the open, and I ain't taking it back. All you need is to take one look at her to see that she is definitely not the same person.

She shoves her Froyo cup into a trash bag with a huff. "Welp. I'm fed up being interrogated."

"I want you to piss into a cup," I hear myself say.

"Excuse me?" Her eyebrows are about to jump off her forehead and attack me.

"Problem?" I drawl. "I piss into a cup every other month. I can do it in my sleep. And I know a lab that gives back test results within six hours. Prove to me you aren't using. Put my mind at ease."

"Your mind is none of my concern." Her face bricks up. "Maybe *I* should be asking *you* to piss into a cup, family history considered."

"Being a bitch ain't winning you any sobriety points." I shake my head. Old Bailey was never this prickly, this testy. And she'd never smoke a joint. She called cigarettes "cancer sticks" and joints "dumb wands." Which sounded kind of erotic, but whatever.

"Being an overbearing asshole doesn't make you my BFF again, either."

Dove has officially parted ways with her faculties. That's how I know she's a user. There's no way my ex–best friend would ever say something so nasty. She knows my older brother overdosed back when my mom was dying. She was the first person I confided in after Luna told me.

"If you don't have a problem," I grit through clenched teeth, "then how come everything I say makes you jump out of your skin? Why do you look like you have a Victorian wasting disease? Why are your pupils the size of dinner plates?"

"Well, that's because when I was discharged they gave me—"

But I don't let her finish. "You have two options—either you let me help you or I walk away from this clusterfuck and we're back to being strangers. Because watching you destroy yourself is not a possibility. I've watched the person I love more than anything in the world die, and *she* didn't have a choice. *She* didn't do it to herself. I won't let you kill yourself on my watch. Got it?"

"Nice little speech." Bailey hops off the canvas, making

Andromeda flee over her shoulder. She dusts off her knees and looks around, her nose up in the air. "I'm ready to go home now, GI Jackass."

A fucking joint. She straight up pulled out a fucking joint.

My thoughts swirl inside my head. We exchange zero words on our way back. After I drop Bailey off, I go home.

I feel like crap. Bailey is okay like I'm a fighter pilot. Which, unfortunately, I never will be, thanks to Dad and Knight riding my ass about going pro and, you know, avoiding getting myself killed.

It's not like Bailey to pussy out of stuff. Normal her would piss into a goddamn milk jug to prove me wrong. I push the door open and drop my duffel bag at the entrance. Dad is shuffling on the patio. His phone is pinched between his ear and shoulder. His voice is muffled through the glass doors, "Lev's home. I'll call you later, Dix."

He slides the glass doors open and steps inside, a kitchen towel slung over his muscular shoulder. There's a pile of juicy steaks on a plate in his hand. Dad's a silver fox. *And* a hedge fund manager. He could have anyone he wants. But what he wants, apparently, is to friend-zone Knight's biological mother, Dixie, into the next century and live like a monk. He also calls her Dix, which is too close to *dicks*. Now I'm not a big romantic, but I would never call anyone I wanted to bump uglies with Dicks. Or any kind of genitalia, really.

Maybe I don't know shit. Maybe he hung up with her in a hurry because they were having phone sex and are actually screwing on the reg. I hope that's the reason. But he doesn't seem like he is ready to move on. When Mom died, they buried his heart right along with her. There's a huge hole in his chest. And the only thing that seems to somewhat fill it is my football.

"Why so secretive?" I steal a pickle from the salad, popping it into my mouth.

"Why so paranoid?" He drops the steak-filled plate on the dinner table. "Just wanted to greet you. Wasn't Thalia supposed to come for dinner?" Dad walks over to the designer kitchen, where there's a freshly tossed salad and Hawaiian bread rolls waiting at the crystal table, along with San Pellegrino.

I follow him with my eyes as I wash my hands at the sink. "I canceled."

He produces a sound from the back of his throat. "Gee. Didn't see that one coming from a hundred miles away."

"Sarcasm is the lower form of wit, Dad."

"Still wit, though. I take my victories where I can find 'em. How was practice?"

Shit. "Good."

"Yeah?" His eyes linger on the side of my face. "Funny, 'cause I saw Coach Taylor at Whole Foods a couple hours ago and he said you were off. In fact, he said that he's met offensive football signs more capable than you were in practice today."

That damn snitch. He knows Dad from his heyday playing football, so he always overshares with him.

"Bailey's back," I grunt.

"So I heard." He plates each of us a sirloin, salad, and some bread. I've already had food at Mel's, plus the Froyo, but I'm already starving again.

"How's she handling things?" He eyeballs me from across the table when we take a seat. To no one's surprise, the house remained completely untouched after Mom died of cystic fibrosis four years ago. Not one picture was moved. One wall painted. We even kept the old light bulbs until we started experiencing some next-level paranormal shit. Lights flickering, electricity cuts, stuff exploding; Dad isn't in denial about Mom dying. He knows she's dead. He just decided to kill any chance for love or companionship right along with her. A true turtle dove.

I hum into my food in response.

"Got that with words?" He studies me.

"Don't be greedy." My utensils clink on the expensive plate. "Next thing, you'll ask for entire sentences with commas and all that jazz."

He pins me with a look. I'm being difficult. I'm on edge because of Bails, and I just wish he'd tell me what's going on with him and Dixie. If he has someone other than Knight and me…maybe it wouldn't feel like a betrayal to apply to the Air Force Academy before the cutoff date. The clock is ticking. I don't have much time left. It makes me uncomfortable that Dad's entire hopes and dreams are around the idea of me becoming an NFL player.

"She seems tired but fine," I relent.

"Keep an eye on her."

"Plan to."

"Addiction is a tough motherfucker."

"She says she's not an addict." I chew a juicy piece of steak, deep in thought.

"I said that too." He sighs. "And so did Knight."

"Thanks, Dad, for reminding me literally every single person I give a crap about tried to off themselves at some point."

Guess it's my destiny to love people who play Russian roulette with their lives. *Thanks a fucking bunch, Karma. Wrong address by the way.*

I stuff my mouth with a bread roll, chewing slowly.

"Change of subject?" He elevates an eyebrow.

"That's a good idea."

"You got a pamphlet in the mail today. The Air Force Academy." He rolls his eyes like I was asked to join a Satanic cult. My heart picks up speed. He has no clue, does he? That's how little he knows me. "If you ask me, it's outrageous that they still send this propaganda to every high schooler who's about to graduate." He spears some meat with his fork, pointing it at me before taking a bite. "I like my kid alive and in one piece."

It's not all about you, Dad.

The Air Force Academy sent that pamphlet because I filled out an interest form. Now I'll have to dig through the trash to find it. I'm equally terrified and excited. I want to read it. Even if nothing is going to come out of it.

"Everyone wants their kid in one piece. Check your privilege, Dad."

"When you're right, you're right."

There is silence. There never used to be silence. But then I built an advanced flight simulator in the attic, complete with a cockpit, TPR pedals, and curved monitor and spent five hours a day in it max, and he and Knight started getting suspicious. When I began volunteering at the local private airport and got connected to their ATC, they really lost their shit. They knew I was serious about becoming a fighter pilot.

Dad ignores the tension. "Next Friday is gonna be a tough one. St. John Bosco has an excellent track record. You nervous?"

"Last time we played them, their coach lit into their quarterback and had the backup warmed up before we even broke a sweat." I shrug. If Dad took a second to get his head out of his ass, he'd see that I don't find football interesting or enjoyable. Last time I watched the Super Bowl, I was, like, twelve. "You gonna eat that bread roll?" I jerk my chin toward his plate. I don't even know why I'm asking. I lost all appetite.

He shakes his head. "Knock yourself out."

We eat the rest of our meal with Dad dishing out football statistics and giving me pointers for the approaching game. When we're done, I wash the dishes, fish the pamphlet out of the trash can, and go to my room and look over the street at Bailey's window. The lights are turned off. Just like her eyes were today. Still, I push my window up and yell to her, "How's the sky looking tonight, Dove?"

She doesn't answer.

Fuck her.

CHAPTER FIVE
LEV

AGE FOURTEEN

"We should probably head back." The words come out of my mouth finally, after Bailey and I have been in these woods for what feels like centuries.

We buried Mom today. Then ran here and went to war against nature. We're both bleeding and exhausted and confused.

Bailey hoists my arm and drags me back to our cul-de-sac. She is bearing my full weight under her slight shoulders. She grunts in pain every step she takes, but I don't make it easier for her because I'm too busy feeling sorry for myself.

When we get to the cul-de-sac, she heads to her house, not mine. I'm sure people are looking for us. Our phones have been turned off since Dad said he'd kill us if he heard a ringtone during the ceremony.

At her house, Bailey brings me dry clothes from her dad's closet and draws me a warm bath, throwing a bunch of girly bath bombs in there to make the water pink and smell like marshmallow. When I get out, I pad barefoot downstairs and find her in the kitchen. Her clothes are still damp, and her hair looks like a hay bale. A mouthwatering scent of fresh pastry and spiced meat curls from the oven. She made Mom's secret recipe for my hands-down favorite meal. Burek.

It's a pie with meat in it, and it's freaking delicious. I first had it six years ago during a family trip to Turkey. Mom swore she'd learn how to make it and ended up giving it her own twist—hers didn't only have lamb meat but also creamy mushrooms and melted cheese.

Bailey's burek—fresh and hot—is a replica in both appearance and taste. Down to the sesame drizzled on top, glued by egg yolk, and spinach-potato dip next to it. The pastry is crispy as it snaps between my teeth. The different tastes unfold in my mouth. I tip my head back, letting my eyelids drop. "How?" I groan. "It's uncanny."

Bailey grabs a seat across from me, her face and dress still caked in mud. "This one took seven times to get right. The dough has to be super thin."

"Tell me her secret ingredient."

"And lose my edge on you?" She curves an eyebrow, blasé. "Dream on, Cole."

"You should do as I ask. My mom just died." I finish the rest of the thing in one bite and lick my fingers, releasing them with a pop.

"Dude, you can't even turn on the oven. You once microwaved a raw turkey on Thanksgiving."

"Dad should've never given me the task." I grab a bunch of paper towels and dab the residual oil from my face.

"He didn't. He asked you to give it to Rosie!" She is on the verge of laughing but bites it down. I think she thinks I'll get mad if she ever shows she is happy again.

I glance down at my watch, and shit, it's already ten at night. How long have we been gone? Are Jaime and Mel still at our place?

As if reading my mind, Bailey bites her lower lip. "Everyone's probably looking for us."

"I'm not ready to face the world yet," I admit quietly.

"That's not true. You're facing me," she points out.

"You're not the world." I shake my head. "Almost eight billion people on this planet, Bailey Followhill, and you're hands down my fucking favorite."

"I may be your favorite." Bailey slides her hand across the surface, lacing her fingers through mine. "But you're my only. And that scares me, Levy. A lot."

I'm about to ask her what she means by that when her front door flies open, crashing against the wall. Jaime, Mel, Daria, and Penn flood inside in a burst of heated conversation and sniffles.

"Bailey? Lev?" Mel's anxiety sucks the oxygen clean out of the room before she even enters it all the way. "Are you there?"

"In the kitchen, Mom." Bailey hops to her feet, blocking everyone's way from accessing me. In this moment, I can't imagine myself ever letting her fall in love with someone else. I will always want every piece and atom of Bailey Followhill. Every cell and smile. Every goddamn breath she takes belongs to me. It scares me, the things I am capable of doing to keep her. I don't think I have boundary lines. No healthy conscience. If it's her or the entire fate of humanity, I'd still not spare it a moment of thought—fuck the world. I choose her.

"*Oh my Marx*, I'm so going to murder your asses! You scared us half to death!" Daria lunges at her baby sister, shaking her shoulders with her pink-tipped salon nails. "I'm going to kill you, Bails."

"Wow, Dar. Total great choice of words. Very sensitive. You should write speeches for presidents," Bailey grumbles as she politely untangles herself from her sister's clutches.

"I'm just getting heavy Pisces energy in this room right now." Daria frowns, looking between us. "Did something bad happen?"

"Yeah," I say flatly. "My mom died."

"I meant besides that." Daria doesn't even blush; she's that much of a badass bitch. "Was Rosie a Pisces?"

"I think so." Daria's fucking crazy. Do I really want her gene pool for my future children? Fuck, for Bailey, yeah, I guess. "Why?"

Daria raps her pouting lips, nodding, like everything makes sense now. "She's here with us. Pisceans have a hard time letting go."

"Daria." Jaime sighs, then turns to me. "Sorry, Lev, her coping

mechanism is trying to lighten up the mood when things are…"
He trails off.

"Tragic?" I finish for him.

"No, really. Do you know what Richard Ramirez, Osama Bin Laden, Ottis Toole, and John Wayne Gacy all have in common?" Daria parks her waist on the kitchen island.

"Deplorable mass killers?" Bailey winces.

Daria shakes her head. "*All Pisces.*"

"Oh." Bailey nods seriously. "Can't believe science hasn't looked into that. Can they just stop with wasting all their time and money on finding a cure for cancer and get on top of this ASAP?"

And just like that, I feel a rumble bubbling up from my chest. Actual laughter. Bailey makes me laugh on the day I buried my mother. Incredible.

When everyone is done telling us how irresponsible we were for going MIA today, Jaime insists Bailey walks me home. Dad is waiting, and I guess neither of them trusts me not to run away again.

When I see Dad, I apologize and change into my sweatpants. Bailey is still around, busying herself, so I go to the kitchen to grab some water. When I flip the light switch on, it's a total mess. Leftover food people have brought over, and there's a bottle of whiskey with a half-full tumbler sitting on the counter.

Swallowing hard, I make my way to it. I've drunk a few beers here and there, but I've never actually *drank*. Thing is, Knight kind of swears by alcohol, and Dad and his friends use it too, when they need a clear head. Maybe I should try it.

My fingers wrap around the whiskey tumbler of their own accord, and I bring it to my lips.

I hear a voice behind my back: "Don't you dare, Lev Cole." *Bailey.*

I turn around to look at her, not feeling shame or annoyance. Just exhaustion. "I need the pain to go away."

"Not like this." She steps forward. "Not by ruining yourself. I won't let you."

She takes the tumbler and washes it in the sink, then grabs the whiskey by its neck and walks off with it, God knows where, hiding it somewhere I can't find it.

Then we both go upstairs and I feel like a small boy again.

She's still shivering. Still hasn't had a shower. She turns around, about to walk out the door. But I'm too selfish to let her go just yet. I grab the tips of her fingers before she's gone and clutch. Her fingers immediately flutter over mine.

"Stay?" I croak.

Her face softens. "Never thought of leaving, silly."

She sits in my room until I fall asleep. *Literally.* She drags a damn rocking chair from my parents' balcony across the hall and sits and watches me as I succumb to my exhaustion. Not just from today—from years of worrying and taking care of Mom. Of going to bed at night praying and bargaining with God that I would wake up in the morning and she would still be alive.

When I wake up the next morning, Mom's not there, but Bailey is. Her head rests on her shoulder, and her mouth is agape. She's asleep. Guilt stabs at my stomach. Shit. She should've had a shower. Something to eat. Gone to sleep in her own bed. I move in my bed, about to stand and wake her up, but at the sound of my rustling sheets, her eyes snap open. She smiles as soon as our eyes meet.

I fucking love this girl.

"Hey, you." Her voice is pure smoke and gravel. She's so sexy, and she's only fifteen. Fuck me sideways, we're going to have some long puberty years. "Don't bother looking for that whiskey because I hid it well."

I shake my head. "Not gonna try that again. Thanks for stopping me."

"Anytime."

"Do you think it'll ever stop hurting?" I ask.

"No," she says softly. "I'm sorry."

"Okay." What the fuck? She should be saying yes, even if she doesn't mean it. Has she ever met a book/movie/TV show before? Clichés were invented for a reason, goddammit.

"Grief is like a monster. That monster is hungry. It eats whatever's inside you. But one day you wake up…and find out that it's full. That it is satisfied."

"What happens when it's full?"

"It's still a monster, but it's no longer scary."

"Sounds terrible." I scrunch my nose.

She leans back in the rocking chair, mulling it over. "Sounds like life to me. We're bound to get hurt. Life is a journey, and no road worth taking is smooth and bumpless. Life is a borrow, not a gift, Levy. Take advantage as long as you have it."

CHAPTER SIX
BAILEY

"How was it?" Mom peers at me behind her oversized designer shades, clutching the steering wheel. I slip into the passenger seat and buckle up, ducking my head down. The last thing I need is to be seen exiting a *rehab center*.

"Great. Can we go home now?"

"Okay, okay." She slides out of the parking space and into traffic while I glide farther down my seat, desperate to go undetected.

My outpatient meeting in rehab was a lot of things: eye-opening, depressing, horrifying…but it wasn't great. The first portion was a one-on-one meeting with a counselor who asked a ton of invasive questions about my life. I kept explaining to him that I wasn't an addict, not according to the *Merriam-Webster* definition nor the clinical one, but he kept on nodding and jotting down notes. It was the first time someone didn't take me seriously in a decade, and I didn't like how it felt at all.

Then there was the support group. I didn't speak a word there. They called us "survivors." I felt like I was in an episode of *The Last of Us*. Even though I found some people's stories heartbreaking, I couldn't relate to any of them. They were *actual* addicts. One girl miscarried while going on a cocaine bender. Another guy DUI-ed, and his mom, who was in the car, lost an arm in the accident. Then there was the veteran who drank himself into a three-day coma. Me? Drug-free for almost a week and I'm doing just fine.

I mean, my injuries are killing me, and I wouldn't put me in a closed room with my enemies and sharp objects, but other than that—totally great.

"Let's go shopping!" Mom yelps. "And before you say anything, I actually found us some great sales, so you won't have to use my credit card. All affordable stuff, I swear."

I check the time on my watch. Lev should be getting out of school in the next hour or so. He'll probably stop by to check in on me after yesterday's debacle, and I'm in the mood to see him grovel a little for his holier-than-thou attitude toward me. "Thanks, Mom, but I'm kind of tired."

"Tired from what? You were home all day."

What is she, the time police? "From the semester."

"You have been working yourself to the bone…" She worries her lips, a tiny frown denting her forehead.

"Speaking of, did you hear anything from Juilliard?"

I know Mom is trying to shelter me from bad news. From *any* news. But this is my life we're talking about. Or whatever's left of it, anyway.

She hikes her Gucci shades up her pert nose. "No, and anyway, you should be focusing on your recovery."

"From what? Your overprotectiveness?" I try to lighten up my tone, but it is obvious I'm annoyed.

"I'm not being overprotective. I'm being cautious."

"You're going through my text messages," I hit back.

"If you act like a child, you'll be treated as one." Her head twists, and she gives me a disapproving glare. "I'm just trying to keep you safe, okay?"

No. Not okay. The opposite of okay. *She* was the one who made me fall in love with ballet. The stage. The costumes. The dexterity of the human body. She sold me her dream, and I bought it with my last emotional penny without reading the fine print. Mom put me on a pedestal as the talented ballerina, and I've spent every waking moment of my life since then trying to prove to her I was a fine investment.

It was all nice and dandy when I brought in championships, awards of honor, and medals. Now that the expectations are catching up with my body, all of a sudden, I can't be trusted with a phone. That's so hypocritical.

"You were the one who pushed me to choose Juilliard." I fold my arms over my chest. "You literally threw away all other acceptance letters the minute we got in."

And it was a *we*. My journey was hers. I didn't have a choice. She wanted me to fulfill the dream that slipped between her fingers, and I was too broken down to pirouette in another dream's direction. Where Daria fought to discover her true self, I was content being molded by mom.

Even *enjoyed* it. Being the chosen one. The girl who succeeded.

"Well, my priorities changed." She purses her lips.

My anxiety is a tide rolling over my entire body, sweeping me away until my head is about to go under. I'm drowning in my own fear, gasping for air. For relief. For *drugs*. Then words fill the air, and horrifyingly, it seems like they're coming from my mouth.

"Your priorities seem as fickle as your morals. And you slept with a student of yours, so that says a lot."

I slap a hand over my mouth as soon as the words leave it. Mom flinches visibly but doesn't answer. What in the world did I just say to her? I'm horrified and disgusted with myself. But honestly, my anxiety is so bad, I feel like I'm trapped in a stranger's body, and that body is lit on fire. Kind of how I was with Lev yesterday.

When we get home, I go downstairs and close the door. Our basement is a makeshift dance studio and a gym. Mom converted it when she gave Daria and me private ballet lessons. There's a ballet barre along the mirrored wall. I practice here, but my body is in excruciating pain since I'm off the heavy-duty painkillers. I blast classical music that shakes the walls and push myself to the limit, ignoring reason, and logic, and my body.

I check my phone and notice three missed calls from my sister, along with some text messages.

Daria: Hey <3

Daria: Answer :/

Daria: Bitch don't pretend like you have a life outside of school/charity/being creepily, bound-to-implode-one-day perfect.

Daria: Heard you went from goody two-shoes to train-wrecked stilettos in less than one academic year.

Daria: Oh, come on, I'm KIDDING.

Daria: I'M OFFICIALLY WITHHOLDING CUTE SISSI PICS FROM YOU UNTIL YOU ANSWER.

She keeps calling and I keep dodging. I'm not ready for the shift in dynamics where she is the responsible adult and I'm the wayward daughter who has more issues than *Teen Vogue*.

At three thirty, the doorbell chimes. Lev took his time, but I'm glad I didn't text him first. He was wrong to poke into what happened yesterday.

It's only when I fling the front door open that I remember Lev never knocks or rings. He barges and swoops in, like the sports car he uses for racing every weekend.

My heart sinks. Don't people know it's rude to exist and call upon someone when that someone is pathetically in love with *another* someone and waits for them? Common courtesy, people.

At first, I think I'm looking into a mirror. Then I remember I'm wearing plaid PJ pants, a sports bra, and have dark circles around my eyes. A pint-sized blond, extremely muscular and lean in a navy cable knit sweater, white tennis skirt, and matching Air Force 1 sneakers is standing in front of me. She's my vibe and a half—Old

Bailey's style, at least—and seems familiar, but I can't place her in my memory bank.

"Bailey?" She beams, shoving a plate full of oatmeal cookies to my chest. "*Ohmygod*, hi! Thalia. Mulroney!"

Not wanting to seem impolite, I take the plate and smile back. Dang it, why don't I recognize her? I've met her before. "Hey. Thanks so much. Did I…mentor you at dance camp?"

The answer to that question is a resolute no because Thalia's hopeful expression crumbles like one of the cookies she just gave me.

"No. I was a junior when you were a senior at All Saints High. People always mistook us for one another?" She tries to jog my memory, giggling with adorable awkwardness.

The penny drops. "Thalia, of course! I am *so* sorry. Come on in."

I open the door wider. She sashays in, following me to the kitchen. We've never been formally introduced, but we shared grins and eye rolls from time to time when others would tell us how alike we looked. I don't know what she is doing here, but I'm grateful that she's here since my parents put me on house arrest. Actually, I'm not even sure I'm allowed guests, but I'm going to play dumb if my parents give me grief about it.

"Want some iced coffee?" I chirp.

"I'd *kill* for some caffeine right now."

"Triple shot it is, then."

"Aww, Bailey. Still an angel."

Who is currently going through hell, but whatever.

I start making coffee, ignoring the persistent feeling that I'm only pretending to be normal, alive, and an actual person. I don't know what's up with my anxiety, but I feel like I'm acting out a role in a tacky coming-of-age show, not actually experiencing this moment.

Mom is on a Zoom call upstairs—she's on this committee that grants low-income students scholarships to dance schools—and Dad is in Seattle for work. Daria lives in San Francisco with her 49ers-star husband, so I'm lonelier than a saltless french fry.

"So, um, how are things at school these days?" I ask, instead of asking the obvious question—*what are you doing here?*—as I dump heart-shaped ice cubes into Mason jars and flick our Nespresso machine to life. I usually take a lot of pleasure in making people feel right at home and doing nice things for them. But right now, I'm just ticking boxes. Making coffee—check. Making small talk—check.

Thalia props her elbows on the butcher block island, studying her surroundings with puckered, glossed lips. "You know, the usual. Cheerleaders be mean, jocks be stupid, people who aren't peaking in high school be hatin'. How 'bout you? The Big J! I'm so jelly."

I add blue agave and cinnamon to the oat milk and top it with fat-free whipped cream. I know why she's asking. I'm not stupid. People in my former high school found out about my so-called overdose. I heard there's a TikTok going around, but supposedly Daria reported it enough times to bring it down. Guilt spears my heart. I really should call my sister back.

"I'm actually super okay."

"I bet you are!" Thalia claps chirpily. "That's what I told everyone—drugs? Bailey? Nuh-huh. Honestly, people's gossip is out of control these days."

Feeling validated, I nod. "It was just an accident. Like, you're in volleyball, right? You know how it is. I took a painkiller. And…guess there was something in it."

"Gymnastics," she corrects, accepting the drink I made for her. We both suck on pink paper straws. She bats her fake eyelashes. "And gosh, I totally get it. I went through an intense Tylenol phase last year. Tore a ligament and had to push through for the state championship."

I snap my fingers. "There you have it."

"And from looking at you now, I also disagree that you are gaunt. You look totally fine to me." People think I look gaunt? Thalia flips her hair. "Honestly, the toxicity in competitive academia is insane.

I hope when they fall—and they *will* fall, we all do—there'll be dozens of cameras recording the whole thing too."

Smiling tiredly, I say, "I hope not. Just because people suck doesn't mean we have to stoop to their level."

"You're right." Thalia chews her lower lip thoughtfully. "Truth is, I'd love a shot at Juilliard, but there's no way my parents can foot the bill for something like that. They're not…you know, like *yours*."

"The Kovner Fellowship gives you a full ride," I say encouragingly. "I know lots of people who are there solely on merit."

She snorts. "I don't make a compelling enough story. Plus, my grades are trash."

"There's always hope."

"Oh, I have hope. *Hopefully*, I'll marry up." Thalia shimmies her shoulders, and I let out a laugh. Then she turns all serious and leans across the island, a conspiratorial smile decorating her lips. "Look, I know it must suck to be stuck here away from college. If you ever wanna hang out, I'm game."

"Thanks." I grab one of her cookies and nibble on it. I lower my guard, even though I'm not quite sure what is up with this girl. "Everyone around me thinks I have a drug problem."

She fake yawns. "If passing judgment were a sport, this town would have a record number of Olympic athletes."

"Right?" I huff. Gosh, it feels good to finally talk to someone who isn't looking at me like I escaped the cast of *Euphoria*. "My parents are being completely overbearing. Locked all the alcohol and medicine in their bedroom…" I don't add that I actually attempted to get my hands on some of those things during a particularly desperate and sleepless night. "And they don't let me out unchaperoned."

"You're nineteen. You can do whatever you want," Thalia points out. "And you look completely healthy and normal to me."

"Is that why you came here?" I ask. "To check if I'm okay?" Gotta love girls who genuinely want to fix each other's crowns.

She breaks a cookie in half, sliding a piece into her mouth as she shrugs. "When I heard about what happened, it kinda hit me hard. I always looked up to you at school. If you got into trouble, what hope is there for the rest of us?"

"Plenty of hope." I smile sadly. "Even the shiniest apple can be full of worms."

I think about the person I had sex with. About the drugs. About the way I've been treating my family and Lev since I got back. I keep trying to do better but feel so raw. All pink flesh and exposed nerves.

"Plus..." Thalia drops her gaze to her lap. "You're super important to someone who is super important to me. I want you healthy and thriving."

"Oh?" This grabs my attention. I straighten my back. "And who's that?"

"Lev Cole."

I bend down like she kicked me in the stomach.

She might as well have cut me open with a butcher knife and poured alcohol all over my inner organs. I don't even know why I'm so upset by what she said, but I am.

Did I expect Lev not to have any friends? Sit at home after school and pine for me? I mean, that's *kinda* what I did at Juilliard, but Lev and I are different breeds. He is a replica of his brother and father. Effortlessly gifted, crazy athletic, hotter than the ninth circle of hell, and honestly way out of my league. He can light up Vegas with half a smirk. Girls stuff their panties and love letters into his locker. He was voted Most Fuckable Jock on All Saints High's anonymous gossip blog. He has honest to Marx fans. What did I think? That he'd ignore the fairer sex for infinity and beyond?

But did she have to look like me?

"Lev. Of course. Yeah." My coffee goes down the wrong pipe and I start coughing. "I'm so glad you're friends. He's a good guy to have on your side."

"Preach it, girl. And All Saints High's boys are usually gross."

"Extra," I agree with a sigh. "A lethal combination of too much money and hair product." Why am I talking shit? Why am I being awful? Who even am I anymore?

"Oh, and I'm not Lev's *friend*." Thalia bunny-ears the last word.

"Is he your tutor?" I ask hopefully.

She shakes her head. "Boyfriend."

That alcohol she was pouring into my insides? Yeah. Turns out it's battery acid.

"Ohhh, Lev's your boyfriend!" My voice is so high-pitched, I'm pretty sure they heard me on Mars. "Wow. That's… Wow. So…" *Terrible. Depressing. Soul-shattering.* "Amazing!" I accidentally fling the plate of cookies to the floor with an unintentional wild hand gesture.

A little voice inside me snarls, *You're the one who left him. Even though you promised you wouldn't.*

"Oops! Clumsy you. Let me get that." Thalia glides from her stool like an erotic mythical creature. She drops to her knees—a position I'm sure my ex-BFF is familiar with—and starts collecting the cookies. I join her on the floor.

She clears her throat. "Sorry. I didn't mean to, like, spring this on you. I just—"

"Don't apologize!" A shriek that's supposed to be a laugh tumbles out of my mouth. I totally forgot how to human in light of this news. What are even words? My vocal cords are their own entity and I've lost all control of them. "I'm not mad. Just a little surprised he hasn't mentioned you."

"Oh, he hasn't?" She sounds like she's about to cry, and now I feel like a bitch. We both pour cookie crumbs back onto the plate. Our heads bump together. Our hair is the exact same shade of yellow. I'm going to throw up.

Thalia says, "I'm guessing he wanted to tell you in person. Which is why I'm, like, *majorly* mortified right now."

"Never be mortified to tell the truth."

"I don't want to cause any problems."

"Trust me, you're not. Lev and I aren't even that tight."

"Oh, you aren't?" She sounds way too perky hearing that. "How come?"

Well, I broke his heart and ghosted him, breaking every promise I made to him because my feelings for him overwhelmed me.

"You know, nothing special. Life happens, right?" I snicker.

There are five million thoughts running through my head. Now I'm thinking about how Thalia and I look the same and how creepy that is, and *ugh, ugh, ugh,* it's like Lev had sex with me, but I didn't get to have sex with *him*. So unfair.

Wait, do they for sure have sex together?

Of course they do, Bails. They're seniors. And hot. And with pulses.

This is almost as painful as watching Vaughn, my childhood friend, taking a stab at mingling.

I can't let Thalia see how hurt I am. Not because I'm too prideful, but because it's not this poor girl's fault I have unresolved, deep-rooted issues with my ex–best friend. I cannot believe he didn't say anything yesterday.

I reach to hug her while we're both on our knees. I pat her back awkwardly. "I am *so* happy for you two."

"Yay. Thanks. He's just so perfect, you know?"

Trust me, I know.

After it is clear I'm not going to release my hold on her anytime soon (what is wrong with me?), she gently breaks apart from the hug and rinses the plate in the sink. I watch from the sidelines, like it's her home, not mine. She licks her lips, drying the plate with a towel and slipping it into a dish rack. "I really do want to become friends. Lev cares about you so much. And…there's something else."

"What?" Marx, please don't tell me they're engaged and planning a wedding. I refuse to be her bridesmaid. I swear, "The Show Must Go On" by Queen was written about me. My whole life consists of pretending everything is okay. Know that dog sitting in a fire, *this is fine* GIF? Hello, my entire personality. Nice to meet you.

Thalia hesitates on the seam between the kitchen and hallway, her face crumpling like a paper napkin. "I worry about Lev sometimes. I feel…I feel like he isn't where he wants to be in his life."

My soul slumps with relief. Phew. No wedding. *Yet.*

She's right. Lev is trying to please his dad by playing college football, even though he's been dreaming of becoming a pilot ever since we were five or six. Lev's always been this living-on-the-edge thrill-seeker.

Does that mean he opened up to her? Told her about his weaknesses, his secrets? Is that worse than them sleeping together?

I am falling apart like a house of cards. That he would share his body with someone else was something I prepared myself for in the past few years. But his soul, I thought, belonged to me. Or at least, it did. When did he retrieve it? How hadn't I noticed?

"I'm not going to pretend I know him like you do, but that doesn't mean I don't want to help him." Thalia shoots me a sad smile. "Is it okay if I sometimes reach out to you? I know you guys were best friends growing up and I just wanna make sure we're both there for him."

I want to say no. It's too painful to hang out with Lev's girlfriend. Truth be told, it's too much to share a state with her. But this girl cares about him so much, she paid a visit to a complete stranger. And she *did* bring me cookies. Just because the situation is shitty, doesn't mean she is. She is opening the door to friendship, and I'm not gonna slam it in her face because of petty jealousy.

Forcing a smile that feels like a rubber band stretching across my face, I say, "Absolutely. You can come to me anytime."

And if I'm being honest, I could kinda use a few more allies right now.

In response, Thalia flings her arms over my shoulders and gives me a hug. She smells of jasmine, black cherries, and amber. And suddenly I hate all flowers and red fruit in the world.

We stand there for a few moments before I detangle from her and head to the door. She gets the hint and leaves. After I wave her goodbye, I watch through the dining room window as she struts her ass to Lev's house. This time the pain is so bad, I can't even breathe.

Lev opens the door for her. Tall, broad, chiseled everywhere. The definition of esthetic perfection. For the first time since I've known him, it truly hits me. Not just the idea that he is gorgeous—I always knew he was beautiful—but now I'm letting it all sink in. It's like I've always been aware of the ingredients for a delicious cake, but I'm sinking my teeth into it for the first time. Everything about him is alluring. His soot-black eyelashes—thick and curly and wrongfully placed on the eyes of a boy. His eyes that look like a capsule of entire rainforests. The carefully drawn planes of his jaw and cheekbones. I study with the most talented athletes in the world, and still, I've yet to meet a guy as cut as Lev Cole.

His shoulders—muscular, bronze, and Photoshop-smooth—are draped in a muscle shirt. A tattoo peeks through it on his ribs. The one I've brushed my finger over so many times—of a rose, made out of thorns instead of petals. A reminder that the most beautiful things need to be protected.

Okay, Bails. You're officially a Peeping Tom. Not a good look.

He gives her a half hug, but they don't kiss. He smiles at her, and it feels like he punched me in the gut.

Look away now, psycho.

She walks in.

Was he the one who sent her to check on me? Is he giving me the same silent treatment I'm giving him? Are they going to have sex?

They close the door.

They're definitely having sex. Probably right now. On the entrance floor. In front of Dean. Perverts. I hate them both. Have they no shame?

Lev has a girlfriend and he didn't tell me. Lev keeps secrets from me. What's more, I keep secrets from *him*. For the first time since we stopped being best friends, the consequences of what happened really hit me.

I need something to make everything go numb. To fall into the feathery, loving arms of numbness and feel like I'm floating through all this.

Mom's in her office, not in her room. I can get away with it.

I tiptoe my way to the primary bedroom upstairs, yank open the bathroom door, and retrieve the medicine they shoved to the back of Mom's cabinet, behind all the face masks she never uses. I slide three extra-strength Tylenols into my palm and swallow with some faucet water.

You know how the sky is looking today, Levy?
Like you're a fucking traitor.

————————

This is the point where most people would stop and ask themselves why Lev and I never happened.

He wants me. I want him. That much has always been clear. There must be a good reason for the devastation I caused and am still causing to both of us. And there is—Lev loves me, but he isn't actually *in love* with me.

Hear me out: I'm all Lev has ever known. I held his hand during his most traumatic experiences. Shared a bed with him throughout puberty. I slayed his demons for him, babied him to oblivion and back while we were kids, and taught him to depend on me to a point where we literally couldn't fall asleep unless we were in each other's arms. This wasn't Knight and Luna's sweet friendship. This was an all-consuming, jealous, possessive, destructive codependency.

It took me time to realize the amount of damage I'd caused to both of us, but eventually, I did.

Which is partly why I'm in this situation in the first place. Craving drugs. I'd spent so long wanting to know who I was without Lev Cole in my life that I didn't take into consideration that person might be a weak teenager who isn't good enough to make it as a ballerina. Running back to Lev now would be like running to a different kind of drug. I would slow him down, and he has enough people in his life doing that to him. Not to mention, I'm addicted to taking care of him. Obsessed with making him need me.

So even though there's nothing I want more than to be with him too, I have to turn my back on this thing. On *us*.

He deserves a clean slate. A fair chance at a healthy relationship. Not damaged goods with a side of bad habits.

They say if you love someone, let them go. If they don't return, they were never yours.

Lev took a semester and some change to find a girlfriend. He seemed happy before I arrived.

Pushing him into Thalia's arms will be doing him a favor, and I've always been the charitable kind.

He'll thank me later, and I'll smile through the pain. After all, that's what good ballerinas do.

CHAPTER SEVEN
LEV

Miserable Fact #357: More than 7,000 people die annually due to their doctor's bad handwriting.

Thalia: I forgot to mention, I spoke to Bailey yesterday and accidently told her we're a couple lol.

Lev: ?!

Lev: 1. Why did you speak to Bailey? 2. How did it come up? 3. We aren't.

Thalia: 1. I wanted to check on her. You don't OWN her, Lev. 2. We talked about ASH. 3. Just bc we're not official doesn't mean it's not a thing.

It's the beginning of football practice, and as captain, I'm leading the stretching and conditioning portion of the warm-up. Everyone is on the grass, watching me texting my girl-something instead of getting ready before Coach shows up to rip us a new one.

"Can we work on our hamstrings, not our fingers?" Mac drawls from his position in a deep 90/90 stretch.

"Yeah. He already jerks off three times a day. Those fingers get their workout." Finn throws a thumb Mac's way.

"Nah. Just from fingering your ma."

"Hey, Ballsy, when you doggystyle someone and your balls

hit the back of her pussy, is it considered BDSM?" Mac snorts. Everybody laughs.

Ballsy pounds his chest. "My balls may be big, but so is my heart. Besides, what's the alternative? Finn's yogurt-covered raisins?" More laughter. I wonder if the Air Force Academy is also full of idiots who think Emily Dickinson is a porn star. Probably not. But since I'm going to a legacy football college, I'll never find out.

"Remember when he shaved them before hooking up with that chick from Las Juntas? It looked like his dick was sandwiched between Korean buns." Ballsy cackles.

"Hey, hey!" Finn rips a wad of grass, tossing it at Ballsy. "Even Michelangelo's *David* was a grower. My dick is perfect-sized."

"For a hamster, maybe."

"'Kay, assholes. Time to snap into shape." I clap once. "Follow my lead." I start duck-walking across the field. Everyone joins me, grumbling that I'm a buzzkill. The less eye contact I have with these fuckers, the more I can concentrate on the epic shit show Thalia has stirred up especially for me.

> Lev: She's going through big changes. She doesn't need updates about my sex life.

Notice how I didn't call it my love life. Because there's only one person in it—Bailey.

> Lev: Besides, you know the drill. You and I are just having fun together.

I'm such a jackass, but right now I'm more concerned about Bailey's feelings than Thalia's. I told Thalia what was up before we hooked up. Never lied about what we were.

> Thalia: She took it fine. You're freaking out.

Thalia: She said she's happy for us.

Thalia: Besides you said we were exclusive. WTF??????

As if on cue, Grim joins me. You'd think duck-walking would make him look ridiculous like the rest of us. Nope. Assfuck is as graceful as a swan. "Thalia getting tired of being a placeholder yet?" My best friend tuts.

I swing my gaze back to my phone, ignoring his ass.

Lev: We are. Exclusive, not serious. Stop overreacting.

Thalia: Stop gasliting.

Lev: Stop misspelling gaslighting.

Thalia: LOL you're lucky you're cute.

As soon as I reach the end of the field, I turn around and bear-crawl. Everyone groans in frustration but follows suit.

Lev: I hate to be this asshole, but I'm going to be this asshole
    to avoid being an even BIGGER asshole down the line. I
    thought we had an agreement this would be casual. Chill.
    If this doesn't work out anymore, maybe it's time we go
    our separate ways.

She answers after a few minutes, when Coach emerges from the locker room to the field, his assistants in tow.

Thalia: Trust me, Lev, I'm not sending out wedding invitations
    or anything like that. I like Bailey and I want to be her
    friend. That's all.

Guess Bailey could use some company here to keep her mind off things. Though it still pisses me off to hear Bailey was happy I'm in a relationship. What the fuck? If she was hooking up with someone else, the only thing to make me happy would be drowning the dipshit's head in a toilet.

Lev: Okay.
Thalia: Love you.

My eyes nearly bulge out of their sockets.

Thalia: KIDDING.
Thalia: Omg look at your face.
Lev: You can't see my face.
Thalia: But I can sit on it l8r today 😊
Thalia: Meet me in the locker room after practice.
Lev: Busy day.

But I really should get my rocks off. My nuts are about to explode from the sexual tension with Bailey earlier this week.

Thalia: <sent an attachment>

The attachment is a naked selfie. I delete it before anyone can see it. Or at least, I think I do.

"Ask her for anal, dude. And to gag her. Her voice is awful." Grim makes a face, his head inches from my phone.

I punch his arm, growling. "Kwon, I say this as a friend—you're a fucking menace."

"Aww." Grim parks his head on my shoulder, staring up at me. "I love you too."

"Cole!" Coach barks, tromping toward me, his legion of assistants scurrying behind him. Gotta hate SoCal and its super-competitive high school football mentality. "Find anything amusing?"

"No, Coach."

"You sure? Because the shape of our team looks like a real

joke to me. St. John Bosco will annihilate us if you don't take this seriously."

"Yes, Coach."

He is in my face now, all six-foot-five former NFL player of him. What's with people pissing all over my personal space? I've never been closer to punching someone to a pulp than I am right now.

Happy for me, my ass. Bailey has to be jealous. She has to be.

Coach Taylor's nose touches mine. "You missed practice yesterday."

I shrug indifferently. "Had the shits."

"There's a lot more shit in your future when I throw you off the team." He steps back when he realizes I don't flinch. "Clear head makes for steadier legs. Ditch the phone, or I'm ditching you from my squad."

Blow me, asshat. I'm the best you've got and we both know it. The worst part is that I wish he'd kick me off of the squad. Then I'd have the perfect excuse to apply to the Air Force. Alas, I'm too chicken-shit to disappoint Dad and Knight.

"Yes, Coach."

Coach starts breaking us into groups for agility drills. Before I toss my phone into my duffel bag, I text Bailey, Fine. You win. Lunch?

I'm not doing this whole silent-treatment bullshit with my former best friend. Even after the clusterfuck that was our reunion.

I turn to join the team Coach assigned me to. My head's such a mess, I fall flat on my face, stumbling over my own legs. I recover quickly, back up on my feet, but people aren't blind.

"Oh, shit!" Austin booms. "Is the ground okay?" Laughter rings across the field.

"Do you want us to be the butt of every joke south of Huntington Beach?" Coach roars, stomping in my direction. "I miss your brother. He was a fuckup, high as a kite half the time, but at least he liked to play ball."

"Yeah, well, feel free to play with my balls if you're so inclined," I mutter, jumping up quickly and joining his group.

"I'm gonna pretend I didn't hear that, boy," Coach Taylor says.

By the time the school day ends, Bailey still hasn't replied.

At first, I accommodate Bailey's brazen ghosting. I get it. Everyone deserves a free pass. And technically speaking, she has every right to give me shit. Not about the drug inquisition. That, I would do all over again. The Thalia thing, however...that must've stung. We never really dated anyone seriously when we were good friends. I once beat a guy to a pulp for asking her out. He was a senior while I was a freshman. So I'm feeling pretty fucking two-faced right now.

After school, I head over to the Followhills' and let myself in. Bailey is probably waiting for me to pick her up to grab a bite like we used to. Her lack of response was general fuck-you-ness for telling her she's a junkie. Only, when I walk in, Mel announces Bailey went with her dad to Costco. She chose Costco over me. *Costco.* Bailey doesn't even eat the free samples. She likes bulk electronics as much as I like jerking off using hot cooking oil as a lubricant.

"That's fine," I bite out. "I was gonna work on the Chiron outside anyway. I'll just catch her when she comes back," I hear myself tell Mel. I tromp outside and pull the navy chrome Bugatti outside of our garage, pretending to change the oil.

I'm swallowing every piece of the humble pie she's serving me, crumbs included.

Happy now, Bails?

Finally, Jaime's Rover pulls into their garage across the street and I wipe my hands with a dirty cloth, sauntering their way. Bailey slides out of the passenger's seat. She's wearing a plaid green skirt, knee-high white socks, Mary Janes, and a cropped top. I shove the oiled cloth to my back pocket and give her a look as I stop in front of her in their garage. "Lookie here, now. You're alive after all."

"Disappointed?" An insolent smile tugs at the corner of her mouth.

I see I'm getting the Royal Bitchiness version of her today.

"Never." I unleash a charming Cole Man smile.

"I'm gonna go make myself scarce," Jaime mumbles, shaking his head behind boxes laden with food and drinks. Bailey juts one leg out, showing me that her new skirt is about six inches shorter than the one Old Bailey wears. Not gonna lie—New Bailey is a fucking hot new nightmare.

"Got your text, Levy," she purrs. "Sorry, I'm *super* busy. Let's try to get together later this week."

Later this week? This little shit needs permission from her parents to go to the bathroom.

I run a hand over my buzzed scalp. "Is this how we're playing now?"

"Oh, Levy." She throws her head back, laughing. "I'm not playing games. But if I were? You'd be the pawn. Ta-ta, now!"

She blows me a kiss, then blows me the fuck off as she darts inside. Her tone is so airy, so casual, so unlike her, I'm tempted to turn around and throw the towel. She's pretty but also horrible. No pussy is worth this kind of BS. But then I remind myself that somewhere inside this idiot is my best friend in the whole entire world.

On my way back to the garage, I calm myself down. If I were to find out she has a secret boyfriend, heads would roll. Of course, I'm actually in love with her, but that's beside the point.

When I get to the Bugatti, I kick it so hard I leave a dent on the front bumper.

Motherfucker.

Whoever invented love was one sadistic son of a bitch.

The same evening, I send Bailey a chain of unhinged text messages.

Lev: If this is about Thalia, may I remind you you BEGGED me to move the fuck on?

Lev: On your knees and shit.

Lev: Not how I imagined seeing you on your knees, btw. You
owe me a fantasy.

Lev: Something tells me these texts are not serving their
purpose.

Bailey: Is that "something" your singular functioning brain
cell?

Lev: Jesus, Bails. What are you addicted to? Witch potion?
You're a meanie when you're in withdrawal.

Bailey: This conversation is over.

And it is, because a second later, I hear a splash on my window
and see an egg dragging down it. She's *egging* my fucking house.
The girl who used to get riled up about TP-ing houses because
it's not environmentally friendly and can make squirrels choke
or whatever.

A glutton for punishment, I visit her the next day. And the next-next
day. And the one after that too. Not because I care about the twisted
version of her I'm seeing on the reg, but because I want to save the
Old Bailey from the girl who hijacked her body.

Dove is full of excuses. *And* bullshit. One time she's practicing
downstairs; the other she is online tutoring kids who struggle at
math. At this point, she'd rather eat a cake made out of all the dirt
under the Kardashians' fake nails than give me the time of day.

I want to grab her by the shoulders and shake her. Unfortunately,
Mel and Jaime are always around. And there's something else standing in my way—I'm not an abusive asshole.

I don't think she's using, but the truth of the matter is, she doesn't
look like herself. Something's off. Her eyes are glazed over, her skin
is gray; she's a static radio sound. A fuzzy-screened TV. Just because

you're drug-free, doesn't mean you're not an addict. Bailey is in some kind of limbo, and I want to help her, but I'm also growing tired of feeling like a pathetic puppy.

Actually, I'm tired of feeling, full stop. She makes me *feel*. And I cruised through the last several months being comfortably numb.

The St. John Bosco game comes and goes, and we actually win, albeit out of sheer luck. Coach is still pissy with my ass. I miss practices left and right, locked up in the attic with my aviation simulator and working on my cars with the garage door open in a bid to catch a glimpse of my neighbor across the street. Grim takes advantage of my absence and apparently leads warm-ups and acts like the captain.

I feel like Bailey's demise is going to be my demise too, and it pisses me off that she didn't keep her shit together for both of us.

Four days after Thalia told Bailey I'm stuffing her muffin, I catch Bailey in a compromising position. Unfortunately, a partially clothed one. Spot her through my bedroom window, sunbathing topless.

Since Bailey is not in the habit of showing her tits to her parents, I take it her dad is at work and her mom is away. At the sight of her tits, my dick gets so hard I have to squeeze it to relieve the pain. She's alone and this is her way of inviting me over. I know because she's been playing the sex-kitten game ever since she arrived here. I oblige, even if I'm not sure if I hate or love her at this point.

I amble through her front door, unlocking the cabana and stepping out to her backyard. She's sprawled over a sun lounger, a gym towel thrown over her face. Holy shit, her tits are just insane. Pear shaped, with the tiniest, little, pink nipples.

Feeling vindictive—not to mention ruthlessly horny—I grab the ice-cold bottle of water next to her and squirt it all over her tits.

She yelps, jumping to her feet and ripping the towel from her face. "Oh my Marx! Lev, what the hell?" She's running around in circles, her skin full of goose bumps.

"My bad. You looked hot." I pull her into a one-arm hug, her diamond-hard nipples pressing against my muscle shirt. "Still do, though."

"Get off of me!" She squirms, pushing me away. But this is the first time we've talked since the Thalia fiasco, and I'm not letting her run away. I step into her personal space, backing her up against the side of her house. Her bare back hits a wide window. We're flush against each other. I pin my arms on either side of her shoulders. Her tits are bouncing with her labored breaths and I can't decide if I want to devour her or punish her for what she's doing to herself. My feelings for her just got a whole lot more complicated.

"Been busy, Bails?" My mouth is so close to hers I can almost taste her. And I want to. Fuck, I want to. The new her. The old her. I'll take any version she is willing to give me.

"Not as much as your dick, apparently." She flashes a snarky smile.

If I were an optimist, I'd think she is jealous. Because I'm a realist, I know the reason why Bailey is bitter about Thalia is because she wants to mommy me to death and know everything about my life. Thalia caught her off guard.

"Really, Bails. If you wanted a taste, all you had to do was ask."

She barks out a choked laugh. "Not if you were the last guy on planet earth."

"Sure about that?" My eyes glide over her upper body, halting on her tits. Her nipples are rosy and hard and begging to be tugged. Her breasts swollen, her back arched to try and touch my pecs. "I could swear you'd let me suck this tit whole if I wanted to."

She licks her lips, her gaze dropping to her feet. If she can even see them behind my mammoth erection that's poking into her stomach. She is defiant but also interested. Problem is, I think the version of her that's interested is also the version who'd suck me off for a Xanax prescription. And it's breaking my fucking heart.

"What do you say, Bails?" I run the back of my fingers along her rib cage, going north. Her breathing picks up. She doesn't slap my hand away. My mouth is dry. I want this, but I also know I shouldn't do this. I stop when my index is almost at the curve of her breast. We're staring at each other silently. She is there on a silver platter. All I have to do is have my fill.

"Should I?" I whisper.

The tiniest nod. Barely visible. But I see it.

It takes everything in me to pull away and shake my head. "Jesus, Dove."

That makes her angry, and she stomps on my foot, all hundred and fifteen pounds of her, trying to push me off. "Oh, screw you."

I don't budge an inch. I am huge and she is little. Physics isn't her friend.

"What are you on, Dove?"

"Nothing, but you're currently *on* my nerves, so get off my case."

"You need to go to rehab. Just because you aren't using doesn't mean you're yourself."

"I *am* myself." She pushes me again, her eyes glinting in rage. "It's just a side of me I tucked away to make sure I fit into everyone else's life. Well, everyone can suck it."

"If you're sober, you wouldn't mind going to rehab." I bump my chest against hers, losing my patience. "Fess up or I swear to God, I'm ripping this entire house upside down to find your stash."

"Ew. Say it, don't spray it, Lev." *Lev? I'm Lev now?* She wipes imaginary spit from her face. "Took a leaf out of Vaughn and Penn's book? Trying your hand at being a big, bad bully?" She goads me, her eyes, blue like a frozen lake, narrow on mine. They're full of contempt. "I don't wanna hang out with your ass. Deal with it."

"You really that butthurt over the Thalia thing, or are you just out of your mind because you're always high?" I push her back, and we're both close to the edge of the pool.

"I'm not!" It's her turn to push me. "I don't care."

"You don't have to worry about Thalia."

She is frantic, but that seems to hold her attention. "Why?"

"Because she isn't you."

She shakes her head, looking tired all of a sudden. "I was never really good enough. Which is why now, when I'm being less than perfect, everyone is so upset. You included. Seriously. Just…leave."

I hate that she sounds sad. I hate that she is still topless and doesn't even realize it. She lost her pride. Or maybe it's something else she doesn't have anymore. Either way, it made her *her.*

Sighing, I say, "Look, I don't know what crawled up your ass, but if it's that big of a deal, I'll break up with her. Problem solved."

She tips her head back and laughs coldly. My intestines twist together into tight knots.

When her fake giggle subsides, she shrugs. "I don't want you to break up with Thalia. At this point, she is your only redeeming quality."

"What the fuck does that mean?" I scowl.

"I like her." She pouts, studying her fingernails with her arms folded over her chest. "She's a hustler."

"Are you guys BFFs now or something?"

"Why? Are you micromanaging her life and friendships too?" Bailey ducks under my arm quickly, snatching her cropped MTV top from the floor and slipping it on.

"Nah, Thalia's none of my business. But you are." And honestly, this sounds crappy, but I'm not sure I want them hanging out. Thalia knows some shady-ass people.

"Are you done spreading your toxic masculinity like a dog pissing on furniture?" She marches into the house.

"Still got the couch and kitchen table left," I growl, following her. Truth is, I *am* treading bully territory and don't want to overstep that line. I need to figure out a way to take care of her and still give her space. But first, I need to know if she is sober and can't relax unless… "I want you to piss into a cup, Dove."

She sighs. "Go home, Lev."

I snatch her hand a second before she goes upstairs, pushing our dove pendants together. They clack, and a shot of electricity runs through me. My fingers shake as I lace them through hers. We're doing this finger-play thing that used to soothe me when we were young. She gasps a little. Our eyes meet. The world falls back around us like walls collapsing. For one small moment, we're Bailev again.

"You said you would never turn me down. That you'd always be there for me." I feel stupid reminding her of that. "In the forest, remember?"

Her bottom lip shakes. She's about to cry. "And I will be there for you. But I never said anything about wanting *you* to be there for me. I don't want you to see me like this. Broken. Lost. Hopeless. I love you, Lev Cole. But I wish I could unlove you. Your mere existence is too much for my soul."

Her words cut through skin and muscle, cells and bones. Bailey stops midway up the stairs, holding the balustrade railings. She looks like a queen addressing her lowly citizen. "If I really am your dove, you'd let me fly away. Set me free, Lev. You have a girl who looks like me who adores you, and I can't afford this drama in my life. You're my sun. Lovely as you are, I can only admire you from afar."

CHAPTER EIGHT
BAILEY

Altruistic intentions aside, I'm not handling this whole Lev-Thalia thing very well.

Actually, I think it'd be fair to say I'm not handling it *at all*. I point-blank ignore Lev, even though I miss him like a limb. He's changed, and I'm only now seeing how far he's come from the kid I've coddled all my life. Lev is no longer the boy next door. Now he's the man in the mansion across the street.

A man who is working on his vintage cars outside in the sun, shirtless, grease marring his sweaty, tan six-pack, which is flexing deliciously each time he takes a breath.

For the first time in my life, my emotions override my logic. That scene two days ago in my backyard keeps playing in my head. Why did I say those hurtful things to him? Well, he *did* goad me. Said I was jealous of his girlfriend. Dared me to have sex with him. And I may or may not have found some leftover painkillers that same morning, so perhaps I was a teeny-tiny bit high.

Thing is, I have an INFP personality. I'm the mediator. The caregiver. I avoid conflicts at all costs and normally find it easy to forgive people, not that Lev owes me an apology for dating someone. It's just that the news hit me surprisingly hard. The idea of Levy holding someone else, kissing someone else, *loving* someone else…

The worst part is, I get off on the attention he gives me, even when it's negative. That's why I'm being so horrible to him. The way he seeks me out as I ignore, push, and punish him…it's a sick thrill and not one I'm proud of. But I can't stop.

A sound jars me from my position making snow angels on my bed. It's coming from outside my window and is faintly familiar. I charge up from my bed and fling my bedroom window open, poking my upper body out as I lean over the windowsill.

Lev is here. He positioned himself outside my window, standing in the pouring rain with a boombox on his shoulder. "When Doves Cry" is playing on full blast. I scowl at him.

"People are sleeping here!" I chide him. I don't know whether to laugh or cry.

He rolls his eyes, repositioning the boombox on his crazy huge deltoids. "At nine in the evening? I don't think so. Come on down, Dove."

"I can't." I bite down on my lower lip.

He nods, tapping his temple. "That's right. Now I remember. You're the only nineteen-year-old I know who's grounded."

I duck beneath my window, find something—a glittery pen—and toss it at him in retaliation. It is so first grade, laughter clogs my throat, but it's something I had never allowed myself to do before. Just be silly.

"We're playing like that, huh?" His eyebrows jump to the sky, and he puts the boombox down, shoves his hand into his pocket, and rummages for ammo. He finds a black credit card. "Hope you're ready for that papercut, Followhill!" He throws it at me.

He has a great throw—much to no one's surprise—and it hits me right in the forehead. I gasp. He laughs. I pick up the book I'm reading—an honest to Marx sacred *book*—and hurl it at his chest.

He throws a granola bar at me.

"Why do you have a granola bar in your pocket?" I yell.

"Why not?" It's still raining and he looks like a mess. A beautiful mess. "I'm a growing boy, okay? Always hungry."

"You're already too big for some houses."

"I'm just the right size for your body, though. Promise."

Something loosens in my chest. My anxiety uncurling some.

"Hey, I thought about what you said." He kicks the stereo to shut it up, because we can barely hear each other over the rain and music. "Maybe you're right. Maybe I'm the sun. But you're the sky, and I can't live without you. You know how the sky's been looking since you moved to Juilliard?" he asks. My heart is crumpled like a piece of discarded paper, an unimpressive sketch, in my chest.

He holds my gaze through the dark. "It is always dark."

When Lev suggested he break up with Thalia, I secretly waited for it to happen. But it didn't. Because here she is, three days later, in my basement, wearing a pink Alo Yoga sculpt bra and matching shorts and looking like a Pinterest-worthy It Girl.

Thalia is collecting her hair into a messy bun and grabs the ballet barre, extending her arms and dropping her ass to the floor. "Like, how am I even supposed to plan around Lev's college arrangements when he still has no idea where he wants to go?" She arches her back, exhibiting insane dexterity. "It's like he doesn't even want to talk about it."

My tibia, spine, and muscles are still sore and tender. But I push through, working day and night at the studio, dancing my life away. I join Thalia and start stretching, ignoring the persistent pain.

"Have you talked to him about it?" I roll my shoulders.

"Tried to. He gets really frustrated whenever I mention college."

That's because he doesn't *want* to go to college. He wants to go to the Air Force Academy in Colorado and become a fighter jet pilot. I shouldn't feel gleeful that I know things she doesn't about him, but I am. Katia, my college roommate, would be proud. I turned into a petty, mean thing after all.

"You need to be honest with him. Tell him you're worried about what the future holds for both of you guys." I slide my hands off the barre, doing a full seated forward fold. Thalia does the same. Her range of motion is much better than mine. She also has a rounder ass, more muscular legs, and fuller breasts.

Why am I comparing myself to her?

Because Lev has probably visited every hole in her body.

"Yeah, maybe." She sighs, descending gracefully into a pigeon stretch. "But I just got a letter of acceptance from LSU and it's a really good opportunity for me."

"You should totally take it," I say, and not because I want to break them up but because it really *is* a great school. I try to get into a pigeon stretch, but my muscles are killing me. *Dove my ass.* My spine is throbbing. Thalia leans deeper into her stretch.

Is she made out of frigging Play-Doh?

"Our love is like an addiction, though. Do you know what I mean?"

I swallow daggers. "Not really."

She studies me intently. "We can't get enough of each other."

The door to the basement slams suddenly, and my sister's voice pierces through it like a bullet. "Open up, Bailey!"

I press my finger to my mouth to motion for Thalia to stay quiet. She looks a little confused but doesn't argue. Daria, however, is in a hella confrontational mood. "Bitch, I made my way from NorCal because your ass embarrassed me. You better open up or we're gonna have a problem."

I swallow but don't answer.

"You know I can take you, Bailey," Daria warns. "I weigh more and these coffin nails are sharp at the edges. Don't try me."

Thalia and I remain still for a full minute, not even breathing. I feel so horrible doing this to my sister, but again, my anxiety doesn't let me face her a minute sooner than I absolutely have to. To see the disappointment on her face when she sees me...my injuries...my scars—I just can't take it.

"Oh, screw you, Bails. For real now!" She kicks the door in frustration. "Out of all the things you could've become, you chose to become a coward."

I can practically envision Daria throwing her hands in the air and trudging back upstairs. My eyes sting with unshed tears, and it feels like my inner organs are made out of lead, they're so heavy.

"Wow. Harsh words. Daria really is as bad as everyone said she was, huh?" Oblivious to my internal meltdown, Thalia does a backbend bridge, raising her feet up in the air into an unsupported candlestick, all the way up to a perfect handstand. She's in better shape than most people at Juilliard, and I can't stop staring. I feel like a pile of haphazardly arranged bones and cell tissue in comparison.

"No," I say quietly. "She's not bad at all. She's..." *the best.* "She's amazing. She's my sister."

"Sorry." Thalia slants her gaze my way, not even breaking a sweat. "What's up? Do I look bloated? Ugh, I feel *so* self-conscious. Lev hasn't touched me in over two weeks."

I want to vomit. No, I *need* to vomit. Not that I didn't know they were having sex beforehand. I mean, they're together. Maybe I should be happy because he hasn't done it with her since I've been back? My head is such a mess, I don't even know what I'm feeling anymore. The only thing I know is that this hurts even more than my body does.

Thalia glides to a sitting position, frowning. "Bailey, look at you, you're green. *Ohmigod*, I'm so stupid." She puts a hand over my back, rubbing in circles. "I totally forgot Lev is like a brother to you. It's probably so gross to hear about him doing the nasty with his girlfriend."

"It's fine." I attempt a smile.

"Kind of like hearing your parents having sex in the other room when they think no one's home. I mean, don't you call his dad Uncle Dean and shit?"

I hold my stomach, about to barf. "Yup. Point taken. We can change the subject now."

"Daria?"

I shake my head harder.

She looks around helplessly, trying to find a topic to sink her teeth into. "This studio is huge! Please tell me you're taking advantage and practicing here until your legs break, ha-ha."

She hops up, walks over to the edge of the room, runs into momentum, and does the Biles on the hardwood. Triple twisting, double back, perfectly executed. I'm still on the floor, malnourished and wilting. In a desperate attempt not to look completely useless, I try a simple front split. My lower back snaps loudly—crap, did I break a small bone?—and it feels like someone shot me there.

"*Ugh*," I grunt.

Thalia tilts her head in confusion. "Everything okay?"

"Yeah." I pull my legs into crisscross applesauce. "It's just…Marx, the pain is just *so* persistent. I thought I'd be way better by now."

Thalia huddles toward me, concern flooding her face. She puts a hand on my shoulder. "Maybe we should stop. Juilliard is not worth killing yourself over. It's a great prospect but at what cost?"

I nod, breathing sharply through my nose. "Yeah. You're right."

"Not everyone is cut out for competitive sports. I mean, Lev and I are kind of similar in that way that we don't let the pressure get to us. It takes a certain personality. Not everyone has one."

I stare at her blankly, feeling hot and cold and cloudy-headed all at the same time. She snaps her fingers, her eyes lighting up. "Hey, did I tell you about my friend Fern, who dropped out of Texas Christian University's ballet program? She became a Zumba instructor. I can't tell you how fulfilled she is today!"

But I don't want to become a Zumba instructor. I want to do ballet. And Juilliard is where you do it professionally, so it's a stepping stone I cannot skip. It's what I've worked for since the day I was born. I have no other identity. Being a ballerina is the only thing that matters. I clutch on to Thalia's arm just when she is about to stand up.

"I can't lose my spot there," I say desperately, as though she has any weight in the decision. Thalia looks a little sad. She pities me. Why wouldn't she? She got the boy, the talent, and the opportunity. I got nothing.

"Bailey." She shakes my touch off gently. "You can't even stretch properly. I think training is off the table right now."

"Oh, but I could train. If only I had painkillers." I suck in a breath. *Real* painkillers. And lots of them. Not the stuff I have found lying around home. Those feel like Skittles.

She sighs, looking away from me. I have a feeling she wants to say something more.

"What? Tell me." I dig my fingers into her skin. "Do you know somewhere I can get some?"

"Bailey, please." She heads for her bottle of water, swinging her hips lightly. "That's a terrible idea."

I chase her, limping on my busted leg. "Come on!" I beg. "I have to get out of here. Go back to Juilliard…" Then an idea pops into my head. A manipulative, horrible idea but one that might nudge her in the right direction.

"You know Lev'll stay here if I'm not okay, right? We've always held each other back. When one of us is in trouble, the other stops everything and goes to their rescue. It's totally toxic. He'll never leave here as long as I'm around."

That makes her stop. She closes her eyes, taking a sip of her water. "You're that close?"

"Dude!" I throw my hands in the air. "I was there when his mom died. You don't stand a chance."

I hate myself. I feel sick to my stomach. I'm using Rosie's death to score. I officially stooped to the lowest form of human I could become. I think. Thalia's face twists in horror.

"Look, I know you're not an addict. Sports injuries aren't

something new to me. Had them plenty of times. If you're really serious about getting back to Juilliard…" She trails off.

Hope blooms in my chest. "Yes?"

Thalia presses her lips for a moment, then sighs. "I know someone. He sells prescription drugs. They're legit, regulated; his dad owns the CVS on Soledad Avenue. But if I find out you're using dangerously, Bailey…" She shakes her head. "I'm telling Lev."

There's a fleeting moment of clarity where I realize I have an opportunity to kick the habit and turn my back on the drugs and that maybe I should tell her to forget the entire thing. But then Thalia grabs her backpack, takes out a notebook, rips a page out of it, and unlocks her phone. She starts scribbling down a number on the piece of paper. "His name is Sydney. He looks like a dork, but trust me, he's connected as fuck."

Thalia waltzes toward me, her movements agile and purposeful. The way mine were before I accumulated enough injuries to last an entire NBA season. She folds the paper and tucks it into the elastic of my leggings. "Just do me a favor?"

"Don't tell Lev?" I fight an eye roll.

She smiles. "You know how he is."

"Yeah." *Never trust a person who tells you to keep secrets from people who care about you.*

I walk Thalia back to the front door and close it behind her. My sister is upstairs, slinging her Hermes bag over her shoulder. She peers out the window, probably waiting for an Uber.

I put my hand on my sister's shoulder, not really feeling anything, and she jerks back, like I'm a stranger at a train station trying to grope her. She hikes her bag up her shoulder with a scowl, and it's all there in her eyes. The pain. The rejection. The confusion.

"You're really far gone, aren't you?" She scoffs. "I caught an emergency flight to have a heart-to-heart with you, and you locked yourself in the basement with this snake with a blond wig instead."

My jaw drops. "Thalia's nice."

She tips her head back and laughs humorlessly. "Thalia is a manipulator. Trust me, it takes one to know one. She's probably planning your demise right now, as we speak."

"How do you—"

"Heard enough through the door before giving up on you."

My head is spinning. I know I deserve her wrath, but I feel so sorry for myself that everyone isn't cutting me slack. "You've given up on me?" I choke out.

No matter how bad things were with Daria when she was a teenager, she always loved me. I was as sure of it as the sun rising in the east. My sister always had my back.

She opens her mouth, just when a luxurious BMW slips into the cul-de-sac to take her to the airport. "No, sweetie. You did that to yourself. If life has taught me one lesson, it's that you need to take accountability for the situations you insert yourself into. Let me know when I can help. Because that front-row ticket to your demise? I don't want it."

CHAPTER NINE
BAILEY

An entire lifetime passes in the days Lev and I are in the same town, *on the same street*, but not on the same page. Kingdoms rise. Empires fall. Somehow, I don't call Sydney. I don't throw away the piece of paper with his number, either. I let it burn a hole in the bottom of my nightstand drawer while I contemplate taking a swim in the ocean and never swimming back to shore.

I'm lying face down on my bed when Mom bulldozes into my room. She stopped knocking when I first came home from the hospital, and I know it's because she doesn't trust me with a boiled egg, let alone to not to try to get high on some innocent home supplies.

"Hello, Mother." My voice is muffled by my pillow.

"Darling girl." Her voice holds a note of exasperation. "Your father and I are taking leave of our roles as your bloodthirsty, tyrannical guards and will be attending the theater tonight."

They must be having one of their quadruplet dates with Baron and Millie, Trent and Edie, and Dean and (sometimes) Dixie.

"What're you watching?" I lift my head, pretending it matters and that I'm not completely numb and dead inside.

Mom sees this as an invitation to take a seat on the edge of my bed. My room, like the rest of my pre-drug life, is flawless. White, upholstered queen bed, pastel pink walls, fairy string lights clipped with Polaroid pictures of all my friends and family, an elaborate vanity and a shelf with my favorite poetry books—all hardcovers, customized sprayed edges, and in pristine condition. Once upon a time, the same could be said about their owner.

"*OKLAHOMA!*" Mom says. "All capitals, with an exclamation point at the end, in case you were wondering."

"Sounds…frenetic," I murmur. "What's it about?"

"It's a musical. Pretty well-known, actually. I can take you if you want." Mom is all dolled up. It occurs to me she and Dad haven't gone out once since my return. They usually went on weekly dates. I killed their social life, then shot it in the head for good measure in case it still had a pulse. They must hate me.

Join the club, folks.

"As lovely as it sounds, I'm beat." I force a smile. "But you go enjoy *OKLAHOMA!* in all capitals and an exclamation point. I'll be fine alone. Don't worry."

"I'm not worried," she says airily. "Lev will be staying here while we're gone to make sure your needs are met."

This makes me shoot up from my bed like it's on fire and stand in front of her, an angry porcupine, all spiked up and ready to stab someone. "My needs are to not see that douchebag's face right now."

"Oh." She hitches a shoulder up. "Well, *that* specific need won't be met, I guess."

"You're shitting me, right?"

Mom blinks slowly and retorts, "Actually, I had you vaginally. Not for your lack of trying to make me get a C-section. You were breech the entire last trimester. Dr. Shulman had to turn yo—"

"Not funny, Mom." I rake my fingers through my hair, shaking all over. "I'm not being babysat by Lev Cole. *I* was the one who babysat him, for chrissake!"

"You were different back then. And you were left together unsupervised because we trusted both of you not to burn down the house or do hard drugs," she says tersely. "Only one of you is still trusted not to do those things—and I thought you were still friends."

I want to scream. To announce Lev Cole isn't *that* perfect. That while I was a senior and he was a junior, I drove him home from parties plenty of times because he was too shit-faced to recognize the color of his own car. That he once broke Tyler Barrera's nose because he pinched my ass. That when he found out Travis Tran gave me my first kiss, Lev—then a freshman—dangled the poor guy from the roof of the mall and threatened to use Travis's spine as anal beads. That Lev has anger issues. Plenty of them. That he would bungee-jump without a rope if someone would let him and that he loves participating in illegal car races because fast machinery gives him a thrill.

Lev isn't some tortured hero. He is explosive, jealous, possessive, and more toxic than a straight shot of laundry detergent. He's just great at hiding it and can probably get away with a lot more because he is a boy. And boys will be boys, right?

Pointing a finger at Mom, I warn, "If you care about our relationship even a little bit, you will cancel with Lev and let me stay alone."

Mom stands up, smoothing her white-belted, feather-hemmed Miu Miu dress. "I care about our relationship very deeply, but I value your well-being above all else. Lev will be here any minute now. I'm not sure what the deal is between you two, but one thing has stood the test of time, and that is the fact that Lev loves you far more than he loves himself and will never let anything happen to you. So put on your big girl pants…*any* pants would be good, actually." Her eyes drop to my bare legs. "Swallow your pride and start taking the help people offer you."

She turns around and leaves my room. I stalk after her. Dad ambushes me in the hallway, blocking my way. He fills the space like a tank. Why is every man in my life either a past footballer or a current one? I don't deal with humans; I deal with industrial fridges. Mom hurries down the stairs while I scream at her that she is ruining my life. My entire adolescence I managed to dodge being a cliché only to get to *this*.

"Dad!" I growl, balling my fists. "What is this nonsense about Lev babysitting me?"

"I'm sorry our concern is an inconvenience to you, but you chose not to check into rehab, so we brought rehab to you." He opens his arms in a game-show host manner, and I want to throttle him, I'm so on edge. "Congratulations."

Folding my arms over my chest, I narrow my eyes at him. "You're being a helicopter parent."

"Bailey, baby, I'm a Boeing 777 parent and damn proud of it. I will destroy the world to keep my girls safe. Lev is not gonna take his eyes off you. Normally, that pisses me off. But nowadays, it's a good thing. I trust him to look after you. End of discussion."

He takes the stairs down. I'm bolting after him manically, barefoot and only wearing an oversized hoodie to hide my panties. I come to a screeching halt when I get to the landing. Lev is already here, in gray sweatpants and a black muscle shirt, looking fifty shades of orgasmic. Seriously?

Muscle shirt *and* gray sweatpants?

I have to stop finding him attractive. And being mean to him for no reason. *And* wondering what the tip of his tongue would feel like if it flicked my clit.

He glares at his phone, refusing to acknowledge me. It's been days since he came over with his boombox, and I'm starting to wonder if it's not because he is giving me space but because he legit hates the new me. If he does, I can't exactly blame him.

My parents wander off. Dad to the garage to start the car, Mom to grab her purse and phone. Welp, guess it's showtime. And since I have no idea who I am anymore, acting should be easy.

"Look what the cat dragged in." I amble over to him, tipping my chin up proudly.

Lev still doesn't look up from his phone, his thumbs flying across the screen. "Better to be a dragged cat than a drugged-up pussy."

"Hmm. Babysitting the kid next door on a Friday night. Tell me you're a loser without telling me you're a loser." I pout.

Lev smiles, lifting his eyes from his phone momentarily. "Aw, I like this game—how about a college dropout who needs a high school babysitter because her parents don't trust her to stay sober?" He winks. "How far up is this on the loser-meter?"

Okay. That hurt. Like a crash between a semitrailer and an airplane.

"I can't believe you just said that," I moan. New Bailey is definitely not a resilient one. "Take that back," I demand.

"Piss into a cup." He yawns. "And I just might."

Mom pops out of the living room, clutching her Birkin bag to her waist. "Have fun, you two. *Mwah!*" She kisses my cheeks. "Thank you so much, Levy." She pats his buzzed head, and a violent urge to run my fingers through the fuzz takes over me. I want to know what it feels like too.

"Anytime, Mel." He pecks her cheeks. *Kiss ass.*

The door closes behind us and we're alone.

"I'm DoorDashing some pho." He points at his phone.

"I hope you choke on it." I smile, batting my eyelashes.

"On soup? Unlikely. I'll order those shrimp rice roll thingies. With the peanut butter sauce. Those are a motherfucker to swallow."

"Kindly evacuate yourself from my line of vision," I grumble, trudging to the couch. I could go upstairs to my room, but this is *my* territory. I grab the remote with a huff.

A nasty smirk slashes his beautiful face. "Trust me, no part of me wants to be here any more than you do. I'm missing out on three parties right now. Unfortunately for both of us, I feel obligated to take care of you. Don't mistake my high morals for affection."

"High morals!" I splutter, aggressively punching remote buttons. "Is that what you call stringing Thalia along and asking your best friend to piss into a cup?"

"When have I ever asked Grim to piss into a cup?" he quips back.

One thing is for sure—Lev is no longer a fan of mine.

"You're not funny," I announce.

"And you're not dressed." He gets into my face, grabbing the remote from my hand. "Go upstairs and put some pants on. Until you piss into a cup, you're not my best friend, the great Bailey Followhill."

"Then what am I?" I ask, holding his gaze, hope almost resurrected at the thought of him calling me his current best friend. Or maybe he means I can be his future girlfr…

There's a beat. I feel like he swallowed all the oxygen in the room. His nostrils flare.

"You're just a stranger who, unfortunately, knows all my secrets."

———————

Just to spite him, I end up putting on pants so short, Lev could give me a vaginal exam without removing them. Then I go back downstairs and we both eat our takeout silently. Well, he eats. I haven't had an appetite in months. Lev puts a football recap program on TV, but I know he's not really watching. I move my noodles around the broth with my chopsticks.

"So did you lose the game tonight?" I ask derisively.

He doesn't rip his gaze from the TV. "Nope. Won."

"Aww. Did Thalia wear your varsity jacket?"

"Nobody wears my varsity jacket."

"Yikes. Ego trip much?" But of course, butterflies take flight inside my chest, telling me that there's hope.

He looks up from his food. "Giving a girl my varsity jacket is a statement of ownership. I don't own Thalia's ass."

The idea that Thalia tested me by giving me Sydney's number goes through my head. But I decide that I'm being paranoid, even if Daria said she is manipulative.

"We don't have to be enemies." I clear my throat. "I might've been…a bit harsh with my treatment of you."

He drops his spoon and chopsticks into his bowl noisily, aiming his stare at me like it's the barrel of a gun. "Piss into a cup right fucking now to restore trust, Bailey. Put me out of my misery, and we'll be best friends again."

Somewhere deep in the back of my head, there's a small voice that tells me Lev makes an excellent point and I'm just not ready to admit it yet.

"Know what? Forget it. I think our trust in each other has been irreparably broken."

"Yeah?" Lev leans against the table. Marx, he is beautiful. The outline of his lips looks pencil-drawn, it's so perfect. "And how exactly did I lose your trust? *Don't* say Thalia."

"You didn't tell me you have a girlfriend."

"I don't have a fucking girlfriend!" He pounds the table, making everything fly an inch above the surface. "I have a girl I have sex and hang out with. *Occasionally*. She knows the score. We're not serious. And really, what were my options here?" he asks calmly. "Sit around and pine for the girl I love who told me not to wait for her because it's never gonna happen between us? You said you didn't want me, then punish me for being with someone else. You said you'd never forget me, then move away and cut all ties. You called me in the middle of the night, *dying*, but now won't take a drug test. And you expect me to believe you're even related to the Old Bailey? You don't hold a candle to her. Not even a fucking damp match."

I bang my palms on the table, standing up. "She looks exactly like me!"

He stands up too. His high cheekbones flushed pink. "Bullshit and a half."

"Yes, she does! I—"

"She." He bangs his fist on the table.

"Does." *Bang.*

"Not." *Bang.*

"Look anything like you." *Bang, bang, bang.*

"Your beauty is unparalleled. You will always be the most beautiful girl in every room, in every country, in every goddamn continent, on every planet. You're endgame, Bailey, so it kills me that you don't want to play. Oh, and I cannot stop thinking about you, even when I know I'm better off forgetting you've ever existed."

This sounds like a love declaration, and the high I get from his words is unmistakable.

"Maybe I do want to play," I blurt out breathlessly from across the table. "Kiss me and find out."

He shakes his head, looking sad and a little disappointed. "Nah. It's not my best friend I'd be kissing. The person you are right now? Hot as shit but not my style."

Maybe because I know he's right, this pierces a hole straight through my soul.

"You were never in love with me, Lev," I choke out. "You were just confused because we were always together."

He holds my gaze steadily. "I *am* with every cell in your body. Admit it, Bailey. You fucking blew it. You ruined us because of your stupid insecurities. We could've been happy. Now look at us."

"You seem happy," I bite out.

He shakes his head, sighing.

Anger seizes my body. I toss the back of my palm against my bowl of soup and watch as it splatters against the credenza. Thick noodles crawl down the expensive wood. The fine china breaks. I storm upstairs like a toddler in a tantrum. I hear Lev quietly finishing his meal at the table, not bothering to run after me, to bargain, to apologize.

The boy I love just told me he loves me back and all I can feel is fury and despair. Because maybe he is right. Maybe I did ruin everything because of my insecurities. Deep down, I've always known I wasn't as beautiful or charming or engaging as my older sister. As talented as my mother. As badass as my dad.

I storm into my room and start opening all of my drawers, tossing clothes and underwear and knickknacks until I find what I'm searching for. Last Christmas, I got prescribed some heavy-duty painkillers. I never took them with me to New York because I figured I'd try to kick the habit during the semester.

Now? Now it's time to take the edge off.

I shove two down my throat and swallow. Then I start pacing.

Lev is in love with me. I'm in love with him. We should be together. I'm not even a real addict. I just spent weeks taking nothing other than low-grade painkillers, for crying out loud.

My phone pings on my bed with an incoming text. I tackle it, thinking it's Lev, asking me to come downstairs and talk it out.

> Thalia: Hiiiiiii. Whatcha up 2?

I like her, I do, but I also take her existence as a personal slight.

> Bailey: Bored. You?
> Thalia: Come to the beach. There's a party!
> Bailey: No can do. #HouseArrest, remember?
> Thalia: I thought your parents went to a play or something???

So Lev told her. She knows he is babysitting me. Now I'm determined to go meet her at the beach just to prove a point.

> Bailey: Yup. Your boyfriend won't let me leave the house, though.
> Thalia: If I distract him for a few minutes, would you be able to slip out?

Glancing out my bedroom window, I decide that yeah, I probably could. I did it for four years, after Lev lost Rosie and I snuck into his bedroom every night. Other than a few summer camps away and the odd sick day, we slept together for the entire duration of my high school.

> Bailey: Do your best, girl. 😈 💦

A few seconds later, I hear Lev's phone going off downstairs. He answers. I can tell he is in a crappy mood by the clipped tone of his voice.

Cracking my window open, I slide down the roof and make my way to the ground. Whatever sound I'm making is drowned by Lev's cutting words to Thalia.

"...unhinged if you think I'm going to leave Bailey and come meet you at some house party. What's wrong with you, T?"

She is covering her tracks, making him think she's somewhere else in case I get busted. Daria's words dance along my skin. *She's a manipulator. Takes one to know one.*

Daria used to wipe the floor with other mean girls. She was unmatched in the cunningness department.

"...no, I can't bring her with. She's an addict. There'll be alcohol there. And drugs. It's like bringing a gambler to Vegas, a sex addict to a whorehouse, a white, drunk chick to a karaoke bar—a recipe for disaster."

Whatever Thalia says on the other line calms him down because he lets out a sigh. "Sorry. I'm just...frustrated. You have fun, yeah?"

My sneakers land softly on the lush grass of my parents' front lawn. I turn around and bolt out of my street without looking back.

Fifteen minutes later, I'm at the beach. I pull my phone out of my pocket, about to text Thalia, when I spot her running toward me from a huge bonfire. The low grumbles of the bass shake the loose sand beneath me as "I Want to Start a Religion With You" by Fireworks blasts through a stereo.

Thalia is wearing a tiny, white cotton dress and has golden star stickers on her tan, freckled face and I want to die because she is so, so, *so* much prettier than me, and if Lev is the sun and I am the sky, she is every single shining star, and maybe one day he'll wake up and realize a starlit night is as beautiful as a clear summer day.

"Bailey!" She grabs my hands, tugging me to the sand. "I'm so glad you made it! You didn't tell Lev I invited you, right?"

"What? No. I'm not a snitch." *Not anymore, anyway.*

My body is humming with adrenaline from sneaking out. It's also trembling from pain after that spontaneous jog. Those two painkillers must've been placebo or something.

The doctor prescribed you placebo? Are you listening to yourself? Next you'll think there's a 5G chip in your annual flu shot.

On the sand, there's a bunch of people drinking and dancing.

She introduces me to some of them until she gets to the last one. A short, redheaded guy with shrewd eyes. "And this is Sydney," she coos, plastering a kiss on his cheek.

Sydney. Sydney. Sydney.

Is this a trap? If so, I don't want to admit it to myself. Not only because Thalia is my only company these days but also because I really, *really* need some painkillers. It was one thing to avoid calling him. But now he is right in front of me, probably carrying a ton of them.

I sit on the sand in front of the fire and accept an uncapped bottle of beer from Thalia with no intention of drinking it. Painkillers aside, I never consume alcohol unless I open it myself.

"I heard you go to Juilliard." One girl touches my elbow. She looks completely drunk, and something protective rises in me. Old Bailey would get her a cab home. "That was legit my dream. You must be so talented."

"Thanks," I mumble.

"She's amazing!" A muscle twitches under Thalia's eye. "I've had the honor of working out with her. Girl is *fire.*"

Fire? No. Fired? Maybe, if someone was dumb enough to give me a dancing job. I know I sucked the time we trained together, but it's nice of her to try to pump me up. Most of the girls I've been around are way too competitive.

"I go to Las Juntas." The other girl nods. "But I hang out with Thalia, hoping Lev would show up and bring his best friend, Grim, along so I can make a move."

Grim Kwon. I remember him. A dreamboat who speaks fluent sarcasm.

"I'm sure he'll turn up one day," I say.

The girl tilts her head to Thalia. "Even Lev doesn't show up for this girl, so I'm not holding my breath." *Ouch.* The girl hiccups, then proceeds to keel over and vomit between us. I nudge aside just in time, then put a hand on her back. "I'm calling you an Uber, dude. Time to go home."

"Can't afford one."

"My treat." I know she's going to ruin my perfect five-star score, but I can't chance anything happening to her.

Taking the girl up to the promenade and seeing her enter the cab of the Uber takes about ten minutes, and then I'm back by Thalia's side. Thalia puts her hand on Sydney's shoulder and yawns. "Ugh. I have a history test to study for. I'll need to pull an all-nighter."

"Those were the best for me," I squeak out lamely. I loved studying through the night. There was something romantic and wholesome about it. If I weren't destined to be a ballerina, I would have loved to study history or art. Somewhere cool and cozy in New England. Oversized sweaters and long nights at the library. There were so many alternate universes I've never even entertained because of ballet. Which is why I need to fight for what I've already achieved even harder.

Thalia and Sydney both look at me like I spurted two more heads and a tail.

Thalia turns to a doped-looking Sydney. "Got any Adderall?"

He shoves a hand into his front pocket and tugs out bags with dozens of pills. My eyes widen. Now I'm sure this is a trap—it's not very subtle, either. Thalia bringing me here. Surrounding me with people so much younger than me. My mom would call them riffraff. And frankly, Old Bailey wouldn't hang out with them either. I don't know if she is doing this to hurt me or as a scheme with Lev to show me that I really am an addict—I mean, *am* I an addict?—but it doesn't matter anyway because I can't stop myself.

As it turns out, something else might be stopping me—namely, *capitalism*.

"Get me three more and put it on my bill, okay?" Thalia pops an Adderall into her mouth and washes it down with beer. Lev's love interest might be prettier than me, but she sure is depriving some village of its idiot.

"Mixing alcohol and Adderall is a no-no." I pry the beer from between her fingers, tossing it into a nearby trash can.

"Wow, you really are a Goody Two-Shoes." Thalia laughs and clutches my shoulders. "Lighten up, Bailey."

"Anything I can get you?" Sydney glances my way, his corn-on-the-cob yellow smile on full display.

"Don't have my wallet on me," I answer shortly, trembling a little. From the cold, probably.

Thalia rolls her eyes. "I got you, boo. You can pay me back next time I come for a workout. Which should be soon, right? You said you were still gunning for Juilliard?"

"I...I don't want anything. I'm okay." I gulp. I don't want to confirm the gossip about me that I'm a drug addict. I'm not.

Thalia stares at me for a few seconds, then grins. "No, you're not. Come on. Let me help the pain stop."

My voice is barely a whisper: "Okay."

"What can I get ya?" Sydney scoots closer.

"Vicodin," I hear myself say. "And...and Xanax if you have it."

As soon as he slides the pills into my open palm, I shove one of each down my throat and swallow them dry. The rest I shove into my sneakers.

"That's it, honey." Thalia pats my back, grinning from ear to ear, and now I know for a fact that Daria was right about everything. This girl is mean. "All better now, huh?"

I don't stick around for too long for obvious reasons. I've no doubt Lev knows I snuck out by now. The sixty missed calls and five hundred threatening text messages are a slight clue.

Lev: Where the fuck are you?
Lev: You left the house?
Lev: YOU LEFT THE FUCKING HOUSE.
Lev: I swear to God, Bailey.
Lev: When I find you, and I WILL find you, drugs will be the least of your problems.
Lev: No need to piss into a cup. Just got my answer.

———

I'm finally not in pain anymore.

The high from the Vicodin makes me feel like I'm walking on cotton candy as I make my way back home by foot. There's a huge smile on my face. Lev said he is pissed and I believe him, but I have an idea how to make him forgive me for this inconsequential relapse.

I'm not even going to feel bad about Thalia because I just found out she's a snake.

Lev is an exceptionally resourceful guy, so I'm not at all surprised when his Bugatti blinks its lights at my back not even six minutes after I leave the bonfire. He accelerates, then makes an aggressive right turn and blocks my way with his car. He stops horizontally in the middle of the street. Drivers honk and shake their fists from their windows, creating a long line of traffic. Lev slips out of the car, moving like a summoned demon.

"Jesus, you're fucking freezing" is the first thing he says. He takes off his varsity jacket and wraps it over my bare shoulders. Am I? I didn't even notice the temperature, which should be a bad sign. And where's my hoodie? Where did I lose it? You're not supposed to strip off without realizing, right?

But I still don't like making a scene, so I say, "People are watching."

"They're about to get the show of their lives because I'm two seconds away from spanking your ass." He grabs me like I'm a potato sack, hurls me over his shoulder, and dumps me in the passenger seat. He snaps the seat belt against my waist. His jaw is clenched tight, and his eyes are a storm of thunder and hail. I'd be scared if I weren't higher than One World Trade Center (which happens to be the tallest building in New York, *not* the Empire State building). The drugs, however, give me strength.

He starts driving. Something occurs to me. "I'm wearing your varsity jacket."

His nostrils flare. "That just occurred to you? Fuck, you're high."

"No." I shake my head. "You said it's a sign of ownership."

Lev doesn't say anything. That's fair. Now's probably not the best time to fish for compliments. I bury my nose in his jacket, the singular scent of him hitting my nostrils. Ironically, Lev is the most addictive drug of all. When we reach a red light, he turns to me and snatches my phone from between my fingers—I expected it—and I know he'll look through my texts, but he's not going to find anything because I deleted the convo with Thalia.

"If you take my phone, does that mean I get to take yours?" I grin.

He tosses me his phone, eyes still on the road. "Unlike you, I have nothing to hide."

Shakily, I punch in his code—my birthday—and immediately go to his text messages. Thalia is the fifth conversation, which makes me pathetically happy. I get into their chat.

> Thalia: I miss you're a dick.
> Lev: Dude, for the last time, grammar is important.

Not exactly the stuff Romeo and Juliet were made of. Everything before that is just dry arrangements about where they should meet and where they are.

My next stop is his camera roll. If he has dick pictures or naked pics from Thalia, I will probably open the passenger door mid-drive and plunge to my death. My heart is a ball of anxiety in my throat as I scroll through his images, but it's mostly boring football strategy stuff and...*me*.

There are so many pictures of me. Like, hundreds. Most of them, I don't even recognize. I wasn't aware when they were being taken. There's a bunch from my going-away party, for instance. I remember that day very well, but in my head, it played out differently. I was unwrapping Daria's gift for me, a Chanel purse, or as she called it, "*A BBB. Bad Bitch Bag. Everyone needs one, Bails. Even girls like you, who are ashamed of being pretty and rich.*"

It was after the Bailev fallout. I remember Lev was messing with his phone and I was hurt he wasn't even looking at me when people presented me with going-away presents. Only he *was* looking. He was documenting every moment of it. Every smile. Every laugh. Taking pictures of my reactions. All zoomed-in, cropped, and focused on my face.

Oh Marx. This is so creepy. And adorable. *And* creepy again.

There's another set of pictures of me playing with the kiddos—Sissi and Den—and then a picture of me with my back to the camera, leaning against the kitchen counter, licking a spoonful of cake frosting when I thought no one was watching.

But I was wrong. Lev was always watching. There are maybe a thousand pictures of me just from that day.

"You done snooping around?" Lev drawls, eyes hard on the road.

My heart slides back to my chest, and I toss his phone in his lap. "All boring stuff. As expected."

I don't know why I'm so awful to him when he is literally the only person worth fighting to stay in this world for.

"I'd rather be boring than be a fuckup."

"You know, I really hate you." A rusty laugh escapes my lips.

His jaw flexes. "Doesn't surprise me. Hate is just a cheap substitute for love." He floors the accelerator, eager to get home. "And we both know why you're all drugged-up and numb now, Dove—you've always been afraid to feel."

———

Lev parks, opens the door, and storms inside without sparing me a glance. I take a deep breath and stare at my house. That wasn't so bad. He talked a big game for someone who decided to bicker with me lightly the entire ride home. Then I see the light flicks on in my bedroom on the second floor and realize through the sweet fog of euphoria that we've reached the clusterfuck portion of the night.

Because Lev is in my room and I know exactly what he's doing there.

I zip out of his car and fly up the stairs. By the time I get to my room, it looks like the FBI raided it. *Thrice.* Lev ripped apart every piece of furniture looking for drugs. My dresser is upside down, all my books and clothes are scattered on the floor, the sheets are torn, and one of my nightstands is broken.

"Stop, stop, stop!" I plead, trying to grab at his arms when he starts plucking my pillows. Feathers rain down on both of us, painting everything in white. "You're not gonna find anything, I swear."

But he keeps ripping linen, flipping drawers upside down, and ripping Polaroid pictures from my walls. He is like he was in the forest the day Rosie died, only about a hundred pounds heavier and ten inches taller now.

When my room is thoroughly destroyed, Lev turns to me, heaving. "Get naked."

"What?"

"You heard me. If there're drugs on you, I'm gonna find them."

"Oh yeah?" I snort. "Are you gonna check my rectum to see if I stashed them there?"

"Fuck yeah. Junkies do stupid shit to avoid getting caught. I have two former druggies at home, remember? You're not bullshitting your way out of this one, Dove." He sits on the edge of my mattress-less bed cockily, making himself comfortable. "Play stupid games, win stupid prizes. Start by losing the shirt. Then work your way down from there. You can dance a little if you're so inclined."

I stand frozen, giving him a disgusted look.

His eyebrows shoot up. "You need to get in the mood?" He slides a thumb over his phone and puts "Milkshake" by Kelis on. A stripper song. "Here. That should work."

"Fuck you," I spit out.

Lev smiles smugly. "Planning on it. One day. When you're deadass sober, and not a minute before." He checks the time on his phone. "Ticktock, Bailey. You're not getting any younger, and I'd really hate to rip the clothes off of you…no, wait. I'd actually enjoy that a lot."

Raging, I turn around and stalk out of my room, taking the stairs two at a time to escape him. He follows me, his feet pounding on the floor, making the entire house shake.

Adrenaline pumps through my veins, making my heart pound violently hard. I slide the back doors open. We have a long, narrow pool with round hot tubs on either side. Lev says it's the shape of a dick with balls and he's kind of right. I stop at the edge of the pool and turn to smirk tauntingly at the boy who gave me his favorite GI Joe binoculars so I could spot Halley's Comet.

"Since seeing me naked is going to be the height of your existence, and I'm actually in a *good* mood for once, here. Have at it." I clutch the hem of my shirt and pull it off, tossing it on a sunbed. I'm wearing a pink satin bra. Tugging at my scrunchie, I let my hair down. Thick waves of gold cascade down to the small of my back. I push my shorts down. Kick off my sneakers, careful to keep the plastic bag with the Vicodin and Xanax inside. I'm wearing matching pink panties. The satin is so thin, he can see the imprint of my slit. And he's looking. Oh, he can't tear his gaze off of me.

"Should I lose the bra and the panties?" I arch an eyebrow, feeling so high, so powerful, so *good*.

This is me taking control. Driving him mad. Giving him a taste of the dish I'd never prepared for him but wanted to so many times. *Me*.

His throat bobs with a swallow, but he doesn't answer, mesmerized. I can see even in the dusky night how every cell in his skin is risen to a goose bump. His eyes glittering with want. I've never felt so beautiful from the outside…and ugly from within.

I glide my gaze down from his sculpted face to his crotch, and I can see he is fully hard behind his sweatpants. It looks like he stuffed an entire bologna into his boxers.

"Wow, Lev, you're packin'." I can't believe I'm saying this to the boy whose tears I dried each night for months. Vicodin is hella potent. "How does Thalia take it?"

"Eagerly," he deadpans.

The thought of her fills me with fresh anger, and I decide to retaliate by unclasping my bra and pushing down my panties. I stand before him naked. He's never seen me like this. Completely bare. Ten seconds pass. Then thirty. Neither of us says anything. His eyes are roaming.

"Search me for drugs," I croak. *A dare.* "Just try not to come in your pants when you do."

Lev doesn't move. He looks somewhere between haunted and bored. "Just because I popped a boner, doesn't mean I want to touch your ass."

I take a seat on the edge of the hot tub and open my thighs wide. He can't stop looking. Based on the imprint of his bulge against his sweatpants, dude is so packed, he could fill an entire U-Haul truck. I want to crawl the length between us, slip his dick out, and blow him. It'd be a first for me, but I think I'd be good at it.

"Here." I create a V shape with my index and middle fingers, parting the pink lips between my thighs, showing him the inside of my pussy. His mouth hangs open. His eyes darken to a point they aren't green anymore. But he doesn't step closer. Doesn't take the bait. "See? No drugs inside."

His jaw sets, his thick brows slamming together. "Push a finger in, curl, and pull out slowly."

"Didn't know my best friend is a kinkster."

"Your best friend wants to see that pussy is as empty as your brain is right now."

Slowly, I push my index finger into myself and curl. I hit my G-spot and moan loudly. I hear Lev's breath catch as I pull out my finger slowly and erect it in the air between us as proof. It is glistening with my juices. "Happy?"

"You have no idea." He glowers under hooded eyes, his cuttingly sharp cheekbones bright red now, matching the tips of his ears.

We're both panting and moaning like our hands are all over each other even though we are at least six feet apart. I don't think I've ever been this wet and turned on in my entire life.

"I can do that again if you're still skeptical." I begin stroking myself in front of him, pushing my finger in and out, playing with myself. I'm wet. So wet he can hear the slurps my fingers produce. And the best part is, I'm too high to be embarrassed. "Should I stop?"

He doesn't answer. My nipples pucker. I'm almost there and it feels so good being watched by him. "Aww." I pout. "Not so mighty and holy now, are you, Lev? Everyone's best football hero likes watching his unrequited love getting off."

I keep on stroking, becoming wetter and wetter in front of him. He licks his lips, and I can tell he wants to step closer. Get a better look. I know I'm taking advantage of the fact he wants me, but I can't help it.

I slip a finger in and groan. I'm going to get off if I don't stop soon.

"Pussy's clean," Lev snaps suddenly, his tone ominous. "Mouth's full of filth but not drugs. Now turn around and show me your ass."

Marx, I love it when he is being mean and bossy. The opposite of his usual sensible aura. I'm probably going to be mortified when the high wears off, but right now it feels like I'm a dove cutting through the clouds with its wings, kissing the edge of the universe.

"For drugs, right?" I snort out, calling him out on his bullshit.

"Nah, I wanna see if you're hiding Flight 19 in there," he retorts dryly, rearranging his junk in his sweatpants.

"Sarcasm doesn't suit you," I murmur.

"A drug addiction doesn't suit *you*," he retorts.

"How do you wanna do it?" I huff.

"Bend over the hot tub and open your ass cheeks nice and wide for me."

Holy hell. He is serious about this. I do as he says, resting my breasts over the cold stone. My butt is wide-open, my skin stretched tightly around my tight hole.

I can hear him behind me sauntering toward me, and my pussy is throbbing, dripping down my thighs, I'm so turned on. Lev and I are going to hook up now. He is going to confess his love for me. He is strong but not inhuman. He's been fantasizing about this for years. Both of us have danced on the edges of explosive sex since we hit puberty.

He will dump Thalia, and we'll be together. I'll keep taking the pills until I'm better. Go back to Juilliard. We'll do long distance— what we should've done in the first place. He's always been the one.

My dove. My destiny. My final destination.

I can feel the heat of his body rolling onto my skin from behind now. The ripples of the hot tub bubbles and the crickets are the only sounds engulfing us. I turn around to look at him, but he seizes the back of my neck and turns my head back to the water. "Didn't give you permission to look at me, now did I?"

"You still need to check if I have drugs there," I moan.

I can actually hear him swallow. "I believe you."

"Why? I'm just a junkie, remember?" I'm begging him now, arching my back, rubbing my bare ass against his hard-on. Who even am I? What am I doing? I don't recognize myself in this moment. "About as reliable as a broken compass. I could be lying. You said so yourself."

"*Are* you lying?"

"Maybe. Maybe not. I'm a mystery wrapped in an enigma. Better check."

"Goddammit, Bailey," his voice cracks, and he is about to too. I can feel it.

"Come on, Levy. *Dare*." We never skip on our dares. Heck, Lev once licked a PE dodgeball just because I challenged him to.

He spits onto his fingers, and every inch of my skin blooms with goose bumps. He places his palm flat against the small of my back and eases one wet finger between my ass cheeks gently, wiggling it an inch. A groan escapes me. My clit is swollen and I sneak a hand to touch it, but he slaps my hand away. "This is not a hookup."

"But it could be."

"No, it can't. I'm with another girl and in love with a version of you who'd fucking hate me if I hooked up with *this* version of her."

But he's just feeding himself more lies because he slips in another inch. Then another. My ass is full of my best friend's finger. My knees are shaking. When his knuckles hit my ass cheeks and he is all the way in, my moans become soft whimpers of elation.

I'm coming.

I'm coming.

I'm coming.

He can tell I'm coming, so he is doing me a solid by not pulling away immediately. He lets me ride his finger, thrust myself backward as the warm waves of an orgasm crash through me.

"No drugs." He pulls out of me as fast as humanly possible. The wetness between my legs slides from my thighs all the way down to my knees. Lev notices because he wraps his fingers around my hair, tugging my head up until his lips are at my ear. "If you were sober, I would fuck this tight, little ass with my fat dick then come in your mouth, making you drink every drop of it. I want you to remember this moment, Dove."

His other hand finds my hip and he clutches my waist to keep me from falling.

"The moment I stole an orgasm from you?" I purr cunningly.

"Stole?" He chuckles darkly in my ear. "Baby, you missed out on the best dick you'll ever meet for a mere finger because you're high. But you *will* come down from this high you're on. Once you do, I want you to remember how the perfect Bailey Followhill, voted Most Likely to Become the First Female President, offered a guy she supposedly hates to fuck her ass bareback. How you came when I stuck my finger inside your ass to check for drugs like a desperate little slut. I want you to remember I rejected you. I want you to remember the sting. And I want you to remember burning for me, knowing you will only have me—all of me—when you're sober." His voice is low and husky. His breath leaves little earthquakes all over my skin. "Now, Dove, time for a cold shower."

With a lazy push, he throws me into the deep end of our pool.

I resurface quickly, gasping from the temperature. I slap the water angrily. "Do you want me to get pneumonia?"

He is standing on the edge of the pool, his face icier than the water. "Not particularly, but since you don't give a shit about your health, why should I?"

I'm tempted to tell him his precious Thalia gave me the drugs, but I don't want to burn this bridge in case I need more.

"So glad I didn't hook up with you tonight." I blow a raspberry. Because…apparently I'm five now?

"So glad you're rewriting the history of what happened." He reaches for the small beverage fridge and opens himself a soda, resting a languid shoulder against a palm tree trunk. "Don't worry, Bails. I intend on fucking every hole in your body until it is the size and shape of my dick. But not like this. I want it to be with my best friend. Not the volatile rando who hijacks her body whenever she's high."

"Stop saying that. I'm still me. I'm just—" My foot cramps, and I can't swim anymore. My body curls, folding in half, and the pain is so much it feels like something snapped like a wishbone in my foot. I begin dropping like a stone to the bottom of the pool. My head goes under. I swallow a glassful of chlorine water. My feet—heavy with painkillers—touch the bottom of the pool. Panic claws at my bones. I'm drowning and can't tell him. Then I see through stung, wet eyes a sharp splash. Lev slices the water like an arrow. He swims toward me, grabs me by the waist, and pulls me up. He rolls me to the edge of the pool, hops outside, then carries me to the cabana. He is still dripping water when he shoves me into a hot shower. Under the water spray, I grip the back of my neck and start crying hysterically. The anxiety is back, and with interest. I can barely breathe.

Lev wordlessly takes a sponge, squirts soap onto it, and lathers my back. His movements are circular and deep. He is massaging every inch of me, soothing, kneading, tickling. My sobs become louder, ripping through my chest savagely.

"Why are we crying?" he asks very softly.

"I was scared to drown," I sniffle. "And I was...you know."

"Tell me."

"*Under.*" The influence. Water. Everything.

"Okay," he says, tender again. "What did you take?"

"Painkillers. Xanax." I snort. "Marx, I'm such a loser."

"I'm sorry, Dove." He brushes wet strands of hair from my eyes. "Sorry I wasn't there to protect you when it happened. Sorry that it hurts. Sorry you're in this screwed-up cycle. But you have to get help. I can't watch you killing yourself. Every time you poison yourself, you poison me too. Only difference is I don't get to enjoy the high. For me, it's just the lows."

I'm too upset to produce any words, so I just let him take care of me. After he's done showering me, he pats me dry with a towel, puts me in a pair of fresh pj's, and brushes my hair. We're back in my room, or the room of the person I used to be before I changed completely. While he rearranges the mattress, he tries to take my mind off what happened tonight. "Remember when we used to do shadow puppets and I would throttle your shadow and you would stomp on mine?" He grins.

I smile tiredly. "Things were so simple when we were kids, weren't they?"

He nods, turning somber. "But some things still are."

"Yeah?" I sniff. "Like what?"

"Like the way I feel for you and the way you feel for me."

Lev lays me in my bed, then massages my foot to loosen the pulled muscle. My feet are on his steel-hard thigh as he digs his thumb into the center of the cramped foot. I whimper into a pillow I'm hugging, hiccupping as I descend the Olympus of euphoria to the mortal land of my disastrous reality. Lev was right. Now that I'm no longer high, I'm feeling all of it. Humiliation. Embarrassment. Mortification.

This is why I love the Xanax so much. It extracts me from my thoughts, my fears, my worries. It isn't a hedonistic pursuit of pleasure. It keeps the pain at bay.

"Levy?"

"Yes, Dove?"

"Did I really let you shove your…*you know* in my…*you know*?"

"Down to the knuckles," he confirms. "Like, I think I felt your pancreas."

Swallowing, I contemplate murdering him. Pros: he wouldn't remember what happened. Cons: I'm kind of attached to him.

"Don't worry, we'll get you cleaned up." Lev pats my knee like a fatherly T-ball coach. "I'm going to look for rehabs for you tomorrow. I can ask Knight what h—"

"Would you have…" *defiled me like a porn star?* I crinkle my nose as I stare up at him. "…*you know*, if I were sober?"

"In a heartbeat." He presses the pad of his thumb into my muscle and I feel the knot unfurling. "If you were sober, I would have grabbed your hips from behind and alternated between fucking your ass and your pussy until I came in both."

I feel myself blushing. "That would be very unhygienic for my vaginal health. A urinary infection waiting to happen. Just…" I clear my throat. "For future reference."

"—then I'd lick it all off and suck your clit until you passed out," he continues, ignoring me.

His words make me so shocked and aroused, I stop hiccupping. He throws a glance at me and chuckles. "You're so fucking cute, I could eat you whole."

"I see you've given it some thought."

"Eating you out? Nah. Maybe like once every second or so." He shrugs. I melt into his touch, lulled by the bliss of having him here. "You're all I think about," he admits. "Other than becoming a pilot.

And MH370. Like, it just vanished off radar, Bails. People still can't decide if it went to the South China Sea, Strait of Malacca, or freaking Kazakhstan. I know it's been well over a decade, but—"

"I can't believe you have a girlfriend." I flip onto my belly and bury my face in my pillow.

"A girl-*something*." He kisses the sole of my foot, tucking it under my blanket when I'm all massaged out and cramp-free. "Only because you told me I never stood a chance and I had to lose my virginity somehow."

"You could've just hooked up with her once or twice."

He gives me a sad smile. "Guess I'm not the type to screw around."

"You always had a chance," I whimper. "I was just…confused."

"We're not dead yet, Bails." He kisses the back of my head, sliding the blanket up my body. "And I'm not done trying to make you mine."

I don't know why it hurts so freaking much to know he gave Thalia his virginity. Especially considering I handed my own V-card to a guy who didn't even deserve my Sam's Club membership. A guy who saw me struggling with my performance and injuries and chose to exploit it.

"Well, now you know you have a chance." I sulkily give him my back.

"No, now you know *you* have a chance." He stands up. "If you get clean. Night, Dove."

"Night, Big Traitor."

He chuckles as he presses his pillowy lips against my forehead. Lev's forehead kisses are the best. He flicks the light off, hovering over the threshold to my room.

"Levy?"

"Yes?"

"You know what I love the most about doves?"

Pause. "Yes?" I can hear the smile in his voice.

My eyes flutter shut. "They're like human hearts. No matter how lost they get, they can always find their way back home."

CHAPTER TEN
LEV

AGE SEVENTEEN

Miserable fact #9,492: Left-handed people die three years earlier than right-handed people.

It's a week before Bailey goes to Juilliard, and I'd be shitting bricks if I had any appetite.

The term *now or never* has never been more accurate because if she turns me down *now*, it will *never* happen between us. She'll go off to her fancy dance school and meet fancy dancers and they'll all have fancy acrobatic sex, and now I want to break the legs of hypothetical faceless people with little derby hats. Awesome.

I honk in front of Bailey's house, which is also in front of my house, which is also in front of Uncle Trent's house. He's outside with his son, Racer, throwing the ball.

"Hey, Lev, you got legs?" Trent asks from his front lawn, tossing a football to Racer, who catches it effortlessly.

I sling an arm over my window. "Not the kind you're into. Why?"

"Use 'em and go knock on Bailey's door next time." He pauses, giving me direct eye contact. "And don't put yourself down, kiddo. Your legs are *fantastic*."

A chuckle bubbles in my chest. "Dude, you changed my diapers."

"Not in the last sixteen years." He deliberately winks at me, and I think my soul just detonated.

"Scarred for life." I pretend to gag.

Trent grins, tossing the football back to Racer. "Don't doubt it. Your dad is Dean Cole. You never stood a chance."

"Hi, Uncle Trent!" Bailey darts outside her door, waving at him.

"Hey, Bails."

She hops into the passenger seat and plasters a lip-glossed kiss on my cheek.

"Levy! I made us a slushie. Probably messed it up, but I know green grapes are your favorite, so I gave it a shot." She passes me a foam cup. I just stare at her. I wish she'd stop making my favorite slushies, my favorite cookies, my favorite *everything*. I appreciate her taking care of me, but I don't like how she treats me like I'm her kid. How am I going to move on if she rejects me? But I already know the answer: I won't. I'll be a hermit. I'll die alone. With, like, twelve dogs to keep me company. I'm not a cat person. They're actual certified selfish assholes. Science says so. Man, picking up dog shit twelve times multiplied by three times a day means thirty-six times. That's a ton of crap. The future stinks if she isn't into me.

No pressure, though.

To make shit even more awkward, ever since The Night We Don't Talk About, she's been pretty off me. Not cold, per se, but definitely keeping her distance. Like she's practicing how to not be friends anymore. Part of it is my fault for what happened, but I never thought my being shitty to her one night would result in a total breakdown of #Bailev.

I take the slushie wordlessly.

"Is everything all right?" She rubs my shoulder, an encouraging smile on her face. She's wearing a pair of denim cutoffs and a tiny white *Earth Liberation Front: You Can't Control What's Wild* shirt that shows off her tan abs. It occurs to me that if she ever gets married to someone who isn't me, I might go to prison for first-degree murder. At least California doesn't have the death penalty. Fuck, I hate needles.

We drive to our place in the woods. Neither of us talks. We haven't talked since The Night We Don't Talk About, and not for my lack of trying. Bailey completely gave up on us as friends, and instead she just treats me like I'm her flower project or some shit.

We get to the woods. I park. We drink our slushies on our hammock. Silently. Time is running out. So is my patience. My pulse hammers against my neck. Bailey is telling me proudly how she kept all of her notebooks and cheat sheets from senior year so I can use them—we both take a gazillion APs for credits—when I decide to go for it. There's no right or wrong way to confess your everlasting love to someone you've known since before you were potty-trained.

"I have something to tell you."

She puckers her cherry lips in confusion. "This is not about how you want to drop out of Human Geography, right? Levy, you need it for your Air Force Academy applica—"

"I love you."

Silence. Bird chirp. A river rippling in the background. Her face splits into a smile, and for a second, I'm so happy I can't breathe. Then she pats my shoulder and says, "I love you too, you silly goose! Goodbyes are so hard, but I'll be here every holiday. And if you ever have a question about how I do your laundry—"

Great. Laundry talk when I'm trying to be the man of her dreams. That's going well.

"Right. No. Take two." I shake my head. "I'm *in* love with you." Then, to bring the point home, I artfully add, "Like, I love you as a person, as my best friend, as my soul mate. But *also*, I wanna suck your tongue. And shove my dick into you." Pause. "Basically." Pause. "Obviously, when you're ready. *If* you're ready. At some point in the near…or far…future."

Yeah, that's not going down as the smoothest love confession on planet earth, but it came straight from the heart. In my defense,

I never had to talk my way into the fairer sex's good graces. Girls usually throw themselves at me. Not a week goes by without a half-naked girl ambushing me in the locker room, lab, or at a party. Unfortunately for everyone concerned, I'm Bailsexual. Meaning I don't find girls or guys attractive. Just Dove. Which significantly narrows down my hookup options.

She blinks rapidly. "I…Lev, thank you."

Thank you? Oh, fuck. Thank you is the opposite of what I wanted to hear. I was hoping for *I love you too* but would've settled for *I, too, want your dick shoved inside me.*

"You're welcome." I sprawl back on the canvas, dying from the inside. "Now put me out of my misery and tell me what it means for us?"

Bailey tucks her sunshine hair behind her slightly pointed ears—and yes, it is the most adorable thing ever, hands-down—scratching the pink nail polish off her toenails distractedly. She looks anguished. "I love you. So much it's hard to breathe sometimes. But…I think you're just confused. You look at me like a mom, like a sister. You always have."

I arch one eyebrow, refraining from reminding her about The Night We Don't Talk About, when she did *very* unsisterly things to me. Unless you're from West Virginia.

"Okay, not like a brother-brother." She rolls her eyes, pinking. "But I made a promise to Rosie to always be there for you, and I can hardly keep it if I go off to college and one of us cheats on the other and we have to break up."

That is the dumbest excuse I've ever heard in my entire life why *not* to be with someone.

"That person isn't going to be me, so unless you're planning to arabesque in someone else's bunk bed, I don't see the problem." I feel my nostrils flare. "Plus, in the last few months, there's not much left of our friendship, wouldn't you agree?"

She rubs her face, looking tired and frustrated, and this is not at all how I hoped this would go down. We were supposed to be dry-humping at this point. Her nipple was supposed to be in my mouth for God's sake.

"Look, it doesn't matter how we feel. Our families view us as siblings. They treat us like we're twins or something." She squirms.

"Fuck our families," I raise my voice, then add, "Not *literally*. We aren't blood-related in any way. Our parents are friends and we're neighbors. This is stupid."

"Lev, I've been taking care of you ever since you were a baby." Her tone is begging now. I can't force her to be with me. She looks as shattered as I feel, shrinking on the dirty canvas of our forest fort, and I'm torn between pressing her for a real answer and giving her some mercy. She grabs my hands and we're both so cold even though it's summer. "I tended to your wounds, dried your tears, slept in your bed. If we get together and you change your mind...if you wake up one day and decide you don't want me anymore..."

"I won't."

"You feel that way now. But I told Rosie—"

"Don't bring Mom into this. If she knew how I felt about you, she'd want us together."

Dove's mouth clamps shut. I feel like I'm losing her. Lacing my fingers in hers and playing them like a piano, I peer into her face. "Forget our families. My mom. What other people think. Forget about The Night We Don't Talk About. About the world. About expectations. How do *you* feel about me?"

And I can feel her wanting to tell me the truth. It's on the tip of her tongue. Our fingers curl and twist around one another. It's our thing. We always play each other like pianos.

"I...I love you," she chokes out.

But she already said that and I need more. "Love me or are in love with me?"

"I don't know."

NO, BAILEY. THE CORRECT ANSWER IS "BOTH."

"Do you want to *try* to figure that out?" My gaze clings to her face desperately.

She looks up, shaking her head with tears in her eyes. "I'm sorry," she whispers. "I think I'm the problem. I've treated you like a brother for too long to make you my boyfriend. I'm sorry."

I close my eyes and inhale through my nose.

Fuck. Twelve dogs.

Thirty-six shits a day.

This is gonna suck so hard.

A FEW MONTHS LATER

"Would you throw a fit if I hook up with Declan Abela?" Grim takes a pull of his beer as we sit on the edge of Austin's pool. To say the party is weird is the understatement of the century. "Victim in Pain" by Agnostic Front rages through the surround system, making the ground shake. Austin is balls deep in this anarcho-punk chick these days. He put her in charge of the playlist, and it's all Dead Kennedys and Anti-Flag and nobody is dancing and *everyone* is tanked, so he just feeds us more alcohol and weed so we'll forget about the music.

I don't even know why I'm here. I hate Austin. Maybe because everything tastes like nothing ever since Bailey left. At least when I'm surrounded by people, I can pretend I'm not alone.

I think I'm on my third bottle, which is way too much for me. But this is what happens when your heart is broken and the girl you love is not your girl nor your friend anymore.

"Stop flirting with me," I murmur into my beer bottle in a deadpan.

Grim snorts. "You wish. Answer the question, asshat."

"Why would I be mad?" I drawl, knocking back the last of my beer and accepting whatever's left of Grim's bottle. Grim came out of the closet to me two weeks ago. No, that's not true. He didn't come out of anywhere. It was me who barged into his shit with the finesse of a circus clown. I had stopped by his house to give him his wallet that he forgot in my car. When I walked into his room, I found him trying to scoop some dude's tonsils with his pierced tongue.

"Didn't see anything." I had tossed his wallet on the dresser, unsure if he was open about his sexuality or not.

"That's because I haven't dropped my pants yet. You know my dick is monstrous." Grim had laughed into his kiss with the dude. "I'm not in the closet."

"Oh." *File under: stupid shit that comes out of my mouth.*

Guess technically he wasn't, since he always made comments about dudes and girls. And I just thought he was being…I dunno, progressive? Edgy?

"I'm not gay." His hand slid under the guy's shirt and it was obvious he couldn't give half a shit about being caught.

I shifted my weight from one foot to the other. "Clearly."

He laughed. "I'm bisexual. And you're staring. So kindly get the fuck out."

Now he's asking me if I care if he hooks up with Declan like I'm the sex police.

Grim explains, "Because you never get ass. Not for the lack of All Saints High's population trying."

Months into the stinging rejection from Bailey, and I'm still hardcore abstinent. No one does it to me like she does, so why try?

I slap Grim's thigh. "I live vicariously through you."

Grim frowns at me. "You need to Band-Aid this shit, Cole."

Putting his beer to my lips, I down it too.

"I mean it. You're mentally blocked. Just get it over with. Fuck someone else. Sex is a carnal urge, not a marriage proposal. Just because you choose to play the field, doesn't mean your endgame isn't Bailey." He stands up and saunters Declan's way.

I watch them talk and flirt and do all the things I should be doing right now. I wrench my phone out of my pocket and text Bailey while someone miraculously puts a fourth fresh beer in my hand. We're barely on speaking terms these days. She mainly communicates with me via DoorDashing me food and vitamins. I text her weekly to check she's alive. She sometimes answers but mostly doesn't.

Lev: Doing something fun tonight?

Surprisingly, she answers after a few minutes.

Bailey: Neck deep in comparative politics of North Africa. You?
Lev: Balls deep in a boring party.

I'm a little drunk and a lot unbalanced, so I snap a picture of the pool party and send it to her along with: Ever go out over there?

Bailey: Sure. Maintaining a healthy social life is a huge part of one's mental well-being.

She is so fluent in nerd talk; it is so cute.

Lev: Yeah? You go to parties?
Bailey: Yes.
Lev: And hook up?

She types and deletes and types and deletes and types and deletes and my heart is in my mouth, clenched tight between my teeth, and I really shouldn't have asked a question I'm not prepared to hear the answer to. Too late now.

Bailey: Yes.

Yes. She does.

And maybe she is lying, but even if she is, that's a clear push for me to move the fuck on and stop hanging on to this stupid, improbable hope we are ever going to be together. I'm being unfair to both of us. I look up and suddenly realize *everyone* is paired up. People porking in the pool, making out on sun loungers, holding hands, kissing, grinding. I glance at Grim. He has a fresh beer in hand, and he is tracing the sweaty, cool glass over Declan's arm as he whispers into his ear.

I'm about to stand up and call it a night—watching others getting off is too depressing—but then my mind decides to melt into piss because suddenly I see Bailey. She is standing with her back to me, talking to a bunch of people from the track team. I rub at my eyes, blinking away the confusion, but she is still there. Athletic legs, long sunshine hair, tiny purple bikini.

I'm hallucinating now. Perfect.

She swivels her head in slo-mo and my heart sinks. It's some girl named Thalia who's been on my ass about tutoring her even though we have zero classes together. It's kind of mean to say, but I consider her a fangirl.

She catches me staring. Her eyes twinkle in surprise and she slices through the crowd, advancing my way. Great. Now I have to be social and shit. She plops down beside me and wipes invisible dirt from my bare shoulder. Her skin feels not-awful on mine, and maybe Grim has a point. Maybe it's time to Band-Aid Bailey out of my system.

"Hi, Lev! What's up?"

"All good. Thalia, right?"

"Aww, so sweet of you to remember!" She beams.

Talk about having a low bar.

My eyes dip to her cleavage. Bigger than Bailey's. But not better. Definitely not better. "You liking the party so far?"

"Loving it! Different kind of music for sure, but I enjoy trying new things!"

Jesus fuck, she can't finish a sentence without an exclamation point. But she does kinda look like Bailey too. My best friend has a similar kind of sunniness, though with Thalia, it's more glaring than warming.

"Aww, dope bracelet." She touches the dove pendant.

I pull away instantly. "Thanks."

"Sorry!" She bites her lip, looking mortified. "Is that…like… expensive?"

I massage the flimsy string, wondering how much to tell her—if at all—then decide it's probably best if she knows the truth. No better chick repellent than confessing my love to another, and I'm really not in the mood for chitchat. "Me and my best friend have matching bracelets. I like to think of it as something that connects us. Like the two people who wear these pendants in this world have a speed-dial to each other's hearts." As I listen to myself, I start chuckling at the dorkiness of it all. "As you can see, I'm shit-faced right now."

"How much did you have to drink?" She laughs too, and instead of filling my gut with something warm and fuzzy, I feel cold.

"Enough to drown the *Titanic*."

"That friend is Bailey Followhill, right?"

I nod. I don't think there's one person on this planet who isn't aware of how much I love her.

"Everyone says I look just like her," Thalia points out.

"Don't see it."

"Maybe you should take a closer look." She winks.

"My eyesight's fine." Damn, I'm a shitbag. I'm usually nice, but not right now. Not after Bailey just told me she hooks up with people.

The conversation comes to a halt before Thalia refuels it.

"Hey!" She lights up. "I heard Austin's parents have a waterfall Jacuzzi."

Subtle, she is not. It's basically a synonym for *Do you want to come on my face or in my mouth when I blow you?*

For the first time in my life, I give fooling around with someone who isn't Bailey some consideration. What am I proving by waiting here? Bailey doesn't want me. Do I want to die a virgin?

"Yeah?" I take a slow sip of my beer. "Bet you there are people doing the nasty there as we speak."

Thalia shakes her head, grinning from ear to ear. She produces a small key from her bikini top. "Austin gave it to me."

My eyebrows slam together. "Why?"

"I made a bet with him."

"That you could get him grounded until he's thirty?"

She laughs, and her laugh feels so wrong in my ears. "That I could hook up with you."

That's definitely a turnoff. "Pass. I'm a little tipsy."

"I'm dead sober," she says. "So I'm making the decision for both of us. We should totally check out the Jacuzzi."

I stare at her, unsure. She puckers her lips and shimmies her shoulders. "I have a new nipple ring, and I need you to tell me if it looks good on me. You'll be the first one to see."

Jesus. There's only so much a guy can take. And somehow, the fact it's so un-Bailey-like—and, okay, she does look a lot like Bailey—makes her suddenly more appealing.

We both stand up and walk up the stairs to Austin's parents' room. Seeing as they saddled the world with the human answer to a chia pet, I'm not feeling too bad about the prospect of having my jizz circulating in their two-hundred-grand hot tub.

Thalia unlocks the glass door to the waterfall tub. It's a big-ass white thing, surrounded by crème tiles, with a blue-LED cascade that makes it look like a giant toilet. Thalia hops inside. I slide in after her. She swims my way and starts kissing me and I let her. With her hair framing our faces and my eyes closed, I imagine she is Bailey, and maybe it's the beer and maybe it's because I've been fantasizing about my best friend since I was thirteen, but somehow, it's easy to pretend.

She wraps her legs around my waist and runs her tongue down my neck.

"I don't have a condom," I grunt. A last-ditch to stop this.

"I do."

"Why?" Maybe I *am* the sex police because what do I care if she walks around with a jumbo, Costco-brand variety pack of johnnies? More power to her.

She keeps kissing her way down my chest. I keep reminding myself Bailey is hooking up with other people. That stupid *yes* haunts my brain.

"Because I've been hoping to get together with you for two years now."

"Didn't you wanna show me your pierced nipple?"

"Oh, I lied just to get you here."

She pushes me back and pulls my trunks down. I sit on the edge and let her suck me off. I'm softer than Mother Teresa's heart. In my head, I hear Bailey tsking, *"Mother Teresa was an opportunist whose missions were in such poor condition, people compared them to concentration camps. Her heart wasn't that soft."*

Way to kill the mood, Dove.

Lips clasp around my balls, and I'm sucked into a wet mouth.

I run my fingers through golden hair. *"Bailey,"* I croak. "That's it, Dove. Just like that. Graze your teeth on them."

She freezes for a nanosecond. I suck in a breath. Shit, I'm an asshole. A hasty apology, followed by pulling my junk out of *Thalia's* mouth nearly escapes me, but then she pulls her lips in and does as she's told, moving her teeth over my balls. I'm about to throw up but also can't make her stop. I'm miserable and vindictive and annoyed and getting turned on all at once.

Thalia works me until I'm semi-hard, then stands up and reaches for her little purse and takes out a condom. I put my hand on her wrist before she rolls it on my dick. "I'm not looking for a relationship," I say gruffly.

Thalia looks up, and the more I see she isn't Bailey, the faster my dick wilts.

"Relax, no one's expecting a wedding ring." She rips off the condom wrapper with her teeth. "I'm not after a boyfriend, Lev. I have goals, dreams; I'm getting out of the shitty neighborhood I grew up in. No boy is gonna slow me down."

"We can fuck around but no hearts and roses," I add. Better to be a clear dick now than an asshole later. "I mean it."

She rolls her eyes. "I'll try to live through the heartbreak, Cole."

I park my elbows on the edge of the Jacuzzi, ready for her to ride my cock.

"I do have one condition." She presses her finger against my chest.

The word no is on the tip of my tongue, but because we're already deep into whatever this is, I say, "Yeah?"

"Exclusivity." She bats her fake eyelashes. "I want every girl at school to know the *only* girl you fuck is Thalia Mulroney."

No problem there. I doubt I'm even going to dip into *her* twice.

"Word," I nod.

She rolls the condom on me and plants a knee on either side of my waist on the surface of the water, wanting to ride me cowgirl-style. But her face is in front of mine and it's hard to imagine my best friend when the eyes looking back at me don't hold all my secrets, memories, and darkest desires.

I know she isn't a virgin because I know at least two guys who've been with her. Which is fine. But that means I don't necessarily have to be extra careful.

Thalia leans in for a kiss, but I break away, pick up her tiny waist, and turn her around so all I can see is her hair. Then I drive into her in one go, hissing when I'm balls in.

"Bailey."

Thrust.

"Bailey."

Thrust.

"Bailey."

From this moment on, we slide into a routine.

Me, pretending she is Bailey.

And Thalia, pretending we're not a complete and utter mess the rest of the time we're together.

CHAPTER ELEVEN
LEV

PRESENT

Miserable Fact #1,188: The Egyptian pyramids were created to prevent grave robbers from stealing jewels and treasures that were buried with the royals.

After Mel and Jaime come back from the theater, I drive straight to Thalia's place to break things off with her. There wasn't much going on to begin with, but I'm no cheater, and I did make a promise to T that we'd be exclusive. And even though I'd have loved spilling the beans to Bailey's parents, I'm still holding on to the stupid hope she and I can figure this out together before I have to become a snitch.

Every time I think about my finger up Bailey's ass—which is every second since I got out of there—my body full-blown shudders and precum trickles out of my stone-hard dick. I think I had seven mini-orgasms in the time between then and now. I give my cock a hard tug, trying to snap it out of it. *Down, boy.*

When Bailey said she and I have a shot together, I wanted to believe her. But she was so out of it, I knew it was the drugs talking. Plus, getting into a relationship with a spiraling addict is a huge, fat no. She needs to prioritize her sobriety, and as much as I want to be with her, I want her to get better more.

Man, love sucks. I hate that people hype it up like it's a chicken-and-waffles combo. Speaking of shit that sucks—why are smart people so prone to forming an addiction? Like, I know. Life's trash. Most humans are dichotomous, single-digit-IQ morons. I get that. But for real. Bailey's addiction leading me into hoping she might be into anal play is crueler than animal abuse.

I park in front of Thalia's house and stomp my way to her front step. She lives in a ranch-style fixer-upper between Encinitas and Poway. It's by no means glitzy like Todos Santos or even Carlsbad. A small inland town, no glamour or frills. I know her folks won't be home because her mom is a nurse who works night shifts and her dad's a truck driver who pulls weekends for extra cash. Thalia's older sister, Tiff, had bone cancer when she was younger, so her parents got into crazy medical debt paying for an experimental and successful treatment. They've been paying it off for over a decade. Tiff's a sophomore in college now, so it was obviously worth it, but I get why Thalia is so messed up about money. She grew up with people who had a ton while she had none.

I knock on the door. When she opens it, my jaw drops because holy crap.

She looks *exactly* like Bailey.

She has the same makeup as Dove today (peachy eyeshadow, mascara, pink lip gloss). And the same clothes (Burberry skirt, white cardigan, and a big hair bow). She's even wearing the same perfume.

"Hey, sexy!" She balls the collar of my muscle shirt with her fist and tugs me inside. "Thought you'd never come."

"What made you think I'd show up?"

"Oh, just a feeling you'd need some TLC tonight." She winks.

Because you were at Bailey's, Grim's voice mocks in my head. *And she figured you'd be too horny not to fuck now.*

Oh well. The least Thalia deserves is a breakup conversation. We walk over to her backyard, which is basically a patch of turf and plastic furniture, and she lights up a joint and cracks open two tall boys. She looks a little high herself.

"We need to talk."

She tilts her head, licking a path up the side of my throat. "Cool. Can we have sex first?"

Definitely not.

I place my untouched beer between us, drawing an invisible line. "I think our time has run out."

"What? Why?" Her eyes are two pools of hurt. Even though we'd agreed it would be casual, I feel like a jackass. They call it catching feels because emotions are like the flu. Nobody ever asks for them, and they show up at the most inconvenient time.

Instead of stating the obvious, I say, "Things are a little complicated for me right now."

"Is this because of Bailey?" Her lower lip trembles.

Yes. But I pride myself on not being an asshole, so I shake my head. "Not just her. I have to figure out where I'm headed after I graduate, get a plan in place." This is not a lie. Thalia clutches my muscle shirt, tugging me to her desperately.

"She doesn't want you. And she's in a very bad place now. It's not like you'd be able to hook up when she's in this state."

Gently, I pry her hands off my shirt. *"Thalia."*

"It's true." She dumps her joint on the ground, tramping on it, glancing at me through red-rimmed eyes. "Aren't you tired of being strung along? Of wasting your time chasing a girl who doesn't get you? Me, I *get* you. I accept you as you are. I'll never give you trouble."

Whatever happened to exclusive fuck buddies? This veered off route and is currently not even in the same state as casual.

"She scored drugs today. I have to focus on getting her help." I grab the beer between us and down it in frustration.

"H—how do you know? Do you know who sold them to her?" Thalia splutters, looking panicked. "Ohmygosh, that's cray!"

I shrug helplessly, softening that Thalia cares for Bails too. I've no idea how Bailey scored drugs in Todos Santos. Must be someone who doesn't know me, as no one is stupid enough to cross me that badly.

"But this isn't about her spiraling. I don't understand," Thalia screeches, looking slighted. "I'm tailor-made for you. She's nothing! Just a nepo baby who can't even keep her shit together."

I stand up, ready to leave. She clutches my arm, then falls to her knees, wrapping her hands around my ankle. Honest enough to recognize this is all my fault, I spare her the colorful words for talking shit about Bailey.

"Look, it's not you. You're amazing. Fuck-hot, easy to get along with, sweet. You'll find someone else. You *deserve* someone else." I shake her off my ankle like she's a stray cat. "It's impossible not to fall for you," I lie.

"But you still managed not to." She buries her face in my sweatpants, still clutching tight. "Because you're already in love, aren't you?"

I incline my head, wordlessly admitting as much.

"Ugh. I hate that I fell for you." She sniffles, rubbing at her arms. "No point in asking you to try to do the same, huh?" She rolls back to sit on her backyard's deck, regaining her composure.

"We don't choose who we fall in love with. That's what makes love so fucking great, T. It's like a present. The surprise is the best part."

She bites her lip, jerking her foot impatiently, thinking all of this over.

"What're you thinking?" I ask.

"Now I'm just worried about my reputation. It's gonna look sus, Lev." She rubs at her chin, frowning. "People know Bailey's in town. It'll be extra humiliating for me when word comes out. Everyone s-speculated you would ditch me as soon as she set foot back in Todos Santos." She wipes at her red nose. "Never mind. This is a me problem, not a you problem."

She isn't wrong. I'm trash for Bailey Followhill, and that is the worst kept secret in SoCal.

"I'll tell them you dumped me," I volunteer. Big egos are for people with small dicks.

She snorts, shaking her head. "As if anyone's gonna believe *that*."

An idea pops into my head. Thing is, it's actually not a bad idea for Bailey to think I'm still attached to Thalia. It would make her focus on her sobriety and less about manipulating my pussy-whipped ass to be her partner in crime.

I screw up my nose. "What if we don't tell anyone we've broken up?"

"What do you mean?" She perks up, looking intrigued.

Shrugging, I explain, "What if we forget telling people we've broken up for a month or two so they assume we're still together? You can set the ground. Tell people I'm a self-involved jerk or whatever—not a lie—for when you dump me." And that way Bailey won't get any ideas and I won't be tempted to take her up on her salacious offers.

"Oh, Levy." Thalia rises up and flings her arms over my shoulders. She buries her face in my shoulder. "Thank you, this means the world to me. You're so thoughtful."

I pat her back awkwardly, wondering if I just made a deal with the devil. She pulls away.

"Just tell me one thing." Her fingers curl around the lapels of my varsity jacket that still smells like Bails. "If Bailey never existed, do you think we'd have had a chance?"

And because my life is a recollection of white lies strung together by good intentions, I tell her what she wants to hear, not anything remotely true.

"Yes."

I wake up with a stiffy from last night's scene with Bailey and a headache from my bargain with Thalia. I flip my phone on my nightstand and check my text messages.

Thalia: Thanks for agreeing to do what we talked about last
night. <3

Thalia: When do u wanna hang out?
Bailey: I know what I want for my birthday.

This last one from Bails makes me smile. Her birthday isn't until December. I immediately yank my phone from the charger and text her. What do you want?

Bailey: For you to undergo selective memory suppression to forget last night.

A laugh bubbles up my chest.

Bailey: Hear me out.
Bailey: The procedure has been tried and tested. I calculated the success rate and it's only 28%. But 28% is still better than nothing.
Bailey: You'll have to go under drug-induced amnesia, where they basically fry your neurons, and there may be lasting damage.
Bailey: Sold on the idea yet?
Lev: Shockingly, not really.
Bailey: It IS the big 2–0 so I feel strongly that you should step up your game.

I can't stop laughing because she is back to being Normal Bailey and Normal Bailey is my favorite thing in the whole entire world.

Lev: I'm never getting rid of that image. It is locked in my spank bank, in a 22-ton blast vault, with machine gun wielding guards, armed artillery, and surveillance cameras.
Bailey: I hope you know eye contact is out of the question for us.
Bailey: For eternity and beyond.

Lev: Why would I need to look at your eyes when your ass
is so fine?

I'm flirting with her because I can. Because Thalia is no longer
my girl-something. And because yesterday, it was clear that Bailey
and I are done being platonic. Forever.

Bailey: I'm talking if-we-ever-meet-in-heaven-I'll-pretend-I-
don't-know-you.
Lev: You weren't you.
Bailey: Is it too late to tell you I have an evil twin sister?
Lev: Your evil twin sister is fun.
Lev: Mind if I hook up with her?
Bailey: Lol. What's wrong with you?
Lev: Mommy issues, separation issues, trust issues, and I
think I'm too much of a people pleaser. Your turn?
Bailey: I love too hard.
Bailey: Stay away from my sister, Cole.
Lev: Come on. Daria isn't that bad.

I put my phone away, adjust my hard-on, then go to the
bathroom to brush my teeth and wash my face. Famished, I make
my way downstairs. The house is a total graveyard in the mornings,
since it's only Dad and me and Dad jogs ten miles every day. Which
is why I'm surprised to see a silhouette of long hair and a pencil skirt
standing in the kitchen, sipping coffee.

Dixie? She spent the night here?

Don't get me wrong, I'm loving the idea that Dad's getting
some action. It's been four freaking years. I love Mom and miss her
every day, but Dad needs to move on. Mom was hell-bent on the
idea of Dad marrying again. She said he was too young and too
hot to stay single. I don't know why he is keeping Dixie a secret.
It's not like they aren't going to restaurants and movies together,

or spending holidays together. Dixie is like family. Ridiculously fuckable family.

I'm about to enter the kitchen and make myself known when she checks the Cartier on her wrist (a birthday present from Dad), sucks in a quick breath, and drains her coffee in one gulp. *My goodness, Dixie. Pull yourself together.*

She plucks her jacket from the back of the stool and hurries out the door, closing it with the softest click.

Dixie spent the night here. *Damn.* How often has that been happening?

They were counting on me to never find out because on weekends, I usually wake up at sunset. But somehow, I still can't imagine Dad moving on after Mom.

I tug my phone out of my pocket and call Knight. He answers, drowsy and irritated. "This better be good or I'm decapitating your ass."

"Holy anger issues." I roll my eyes. "Are you talking to me mid-sex? Because gross."

"Morning sex is a luxury people with toddlers don't have. Den finally let us sleep in today for the first time since he was born." Den—or Cayden—is Knight and Luna's three-year-old. He has more energy than a nuclear weapon. Causes about the same amount of damage too.

"Well, this is actually good. Or maybe just weird. Dunno yet." I throw the fridge open and grab some milk, gulping it straight from the carton.

"Hit me."

"I'm aiming low, so prepare your nuts."

"Lay it on me, motherfucker."

"Dixie spent the night here."

Beat. Silence.

"When I said motherfucker, I wasn't being literal. That's my biological mom. What the fuck kind of joke do you think you're making?"

"With *Dad*, you dumbass." I slam the fridge door shut.

A callous laugh escapes Knight's mouth. "Get the fuck out."

"Yup." I pop the *P*, my eye catching the ghost of a lipstick smear on the mug Dixie left behind. I didn't imagine it. She really was here.

"You think they're bumping uglies?" I can hear Knight scratching his stubble.

"Why else would she spend the night here?" I ravish a granola bar in one bite. "But then why doesn't Dad just fess up? It's not like we'll be mad at him."

"Nah, but he'll be mad at himself." I can hear Knight gurgling toothpaste and water in the background. "Hate to say this, but I think there's an innocent explanation to her stayover."

"He needs to move on," I mutter.

"Yeah, like somebody else I know." *Touché.* "By the way, how's Bails doing? Heard she's back in town, but Mel said she isn't accepting any visitors."

Releasing an exhale, I admit, "I guess you know why too."

He groans. "Painkillers, right? That shit is the *worst*. Easy to get your hands on too."

The door swings open and Dad waltzes in, plucking his AirPods out of his ears. He's shirtless and sweaty, in running shorts only.

"Breakfast should be delivered in about five minutes. Get the door, will ya, Levy?"

He breezes past me but not before brushing his sweaty shoulder against mine *deliberately*. I slam the fridge shut and roar, "Dad! Gross."

"That's rich, coming from someone who is literally an evolution of my spunk." He evil-laughs on his way upstairs.

"Talk later. I gotta go barf, then find a new family," I murmur to my phone.

"Too late!" Dad yells, his feet pounding the stairway. "You're eighteen and not all that cute anymore."

Knight cackles on the other line. "Never have I been happier to be adopt—" But he doesn't finish the sentence because I hang up on his ass.

Ten minutes later, Dad is all showered and we're both unpacking the breakfast we get every Saturday from the bougie bakery down the street. They have the best coffee, hands-down. The table is laden with pastries and fresh kiwi juice when Dad initiates a conversation about his favorite subject in the whole wide world besides Mom—football.

"Saw my buddy Jim while I was out last night. Guess what? He says Nebraska is desperate for quality QBs for next year. I think they're gonna have an offer for you, along with Notre Dame and Michigan, probably."

"Dad, I'm not moving to Nebraska."

"Don't be a snob. It's a good team."

"It's in *Nebraska*."

What drives me nuts is that I'm one of the few people in this country with the physical ability, GPA, and SAT scores to make it into the Air Force Academy. Of course, Dad is going to go nuclear if I mention I wanna join the military. Heaven forbid a Cole pursue a "blue collar" profession—or worse yet, risk spilling blue blood by dying prematurely. Even though Dean Cole would deny this through his teeth, I know that's what he thinks. No one at school is contemplating applying. It's what the *others* do. Those without cushy trust funds and a timeshare in St. Regis Residence Club.

Dad thinks I can make it to the NFL. Knight almost did, and I'm his last chance at fulfilling that bucket-list dream two generations of Cole men failed to do.

"I'm surprised you haven't received any acceptance letters so far." Dad sucks his teeth in, taking it as a personal slight.

Shrugging, I take a bite of my bacon and brie-covered, scrambled egg-filled croissant. "All Saints High is ranked fifth in the country. They're probably making offers to the kids from Bosco first."

"You're in better shape than all of them combined. We've played them, remember?" Dad leans across the table, fire dancing in his eyes. "There's no 'see' about it. You're in a league of your own. Any college team would be lucky to have you."

"Which is why I should be applying to the Air Force Academy," I can't stop myself from blurting out.

I want to swallow the words back.

Dad looks up from his croissant, his face whiter than a '90s boy band member. He is scared. And that's when I remember it is not really my blue blood Dad is worried about—it's his own blue heart. He lost a wife. He sure doesn't wanna lose a son too. And being a fighter jet pilot guarantees I'd be putting my life at risk on the reg.

I've only broached this subject with him once before, and he basically dismissed it as a childish dream, like I told him I wanted to be a cowboy astronaut. He told me to get real and to take my life seriously, and to plan for things that make sense, then moved on to the next subject.

He never asks me about my aviation simulator. About volunteering at the airport. Any of those things that bring fire into *my* eyes.

"Not this again, Lev." Dad's jaw nearly jumps out of his skin, and his emerald eyes darken. "Look, I get the appeal. But aside from supersonic rides and the fact the Cole ass definitely looks bomb in a flight suit, military life is tough. Boatload of stress, being hurled from one place to the other every couple years, no permanent residence, whacky schedule, family on the go. Not to mention being sent to war zones. Tell me when to stop."

"Now's a good time." I violently stab my food with my fork. "I get it, being a fighter jet pilot sucks."

"Not to mention, as I said, having a heart attack is gonna throw my schedule way off."

"Nothing'll happen to me," I grind out. But I can't really promise him that, can I?

"True that because you aren't enlisting."

"You can't tell me what to do."

"You're right, I can't. But I can tell you what would kill me. Do with it as you wish."

As I said—the pressure is on.

Anyone else would probably tell their dad to take a hike all the way to Dante's seventh circle of hell. I turned eighteen in February, so it's not like I need his permission to apply to the Academy. But I have this intense sense of responsibility. Leftovers from being the Good Kid. Knight's addiction nearly ruined this family. Mom dying buried it under rubble of suffocating depression. I'm not gonna be the one to deliver the final blow. Knight begged me not to apply. And my inclination is to put my happiness behind Dad's, even if it kills me.

Knight would murder me, then resurrect me just to murder me again if I tell Dad I'm thinking of applying, never mind actually applying, so I decide to change the subject. "Knight and I vote you start dating again."

"Oh yeah?" Dad slaps his newspaper open with a deep frown and decides to let the military stuff rest, for now. "Well, I vote you stay out of my business. In fact, I veto that shit."

"It's cool if you move on. Mom would be pissed if she knew you were sitting here regrowing your hymen."

"That's not... Wait, what are they teaching you in sex ed?" He scowls.

I toss a grape into my mouth. "You mean, other than the Pop Rocks blow-job trick?"

Dad laughs and picks up his paper again. "Mom's not here to bitch-slap me for regrowing my hymen, so unless you know a medium to contact her in heaven, no harm done."

"Don't you want to have sex again? Go on dates? I dunno, *live*?"

He shakes his head. "Living is an invitation people without jobs made to justify their existence."

"Be serious for a sec," I groan.

Dad lowers the *Financial Times* and glares at me with annoyance.

"Look, this is probably a terrible life lesson to pass on to your kids, but it's not gonna happen, okay? I'm not gonna magically get over Rosie LeBlanc. I'm never getting over her, I'm never moving on. There won't be a second chapter because the minute I met this woman, my epilogue was already written. I've accepted my fate and find my pleasures elsewhere. I have you. Knight. Cayden. *Football*. Plenty of friends. I have big family vacations. I love my job. Taking it one day at a time is manageable for me."

"I'm going to move out at the end of the year when I graduate," I remind him. Just the thought of going off to some college to break my back playing ball makes me wanna punch my own face.

"I know." He works his jaw, touching it like I slapped him with my words. "I'll survive."

"Look." I sit back, huffing. "You can cut the crap. I know Dixie spent the night here. I saw her taking off this morning. Knight and I are happy you're getting some."

Dad chokes on his chia seed pudding, grabs his coffee—four shots of dark roast, basically tar with some Stevia—pops the lid, and chugs it. "You think I'm hooking up with Dix?"

"Why else would she spend the night?" I fold my arms over my chest. "And can you please stop calling her that? Every time you do, I imagine a bouquet of cocks squeezed together into a pencil skirt."

"First of all—*great* imagery." Dad wipes his mouth with the back of his hand. "Really selling me the whole Dixie idea. Second of all, dating is not on the menu for me."

"You messing around with her?" I eyeball him, surprised. "Look, if you wanna play the field, maybe don't do it with your best female friend? Kind of a fuckboy move. I'll introduce you to Tinder. It's a—"

"Sit down, boy. I ruled Tinder when you were still swimming in my nuts." Dad balls a napkin and tosses it at me. "I'm a widower, not a boomer. And I'm not fucking Dix…*Dixie*. Or anyone else for that matter."

"What about self-love?"

"Rarely," he grumbles into his food.

"Dude, you have no sperm circulation. Your spunk must be so stale."

He cocks his head, frowning. "You *do* look a little crusty."

"I am getting emancipated," I gag dramatically.

He reaches to steal *my* coffee, and I'd be mad if I wasn't sad for him. No sex for four years straight sounds brutal. "Dixie stayed here because her apartment is getting repainted. She's selling it. She'll be crashing here tonight too. Tomorrow she goes back to her place. *Where she belongs.*"

"Don't you like her?" I press.

"Love her." Dad takes big bites of his food to keep his mouth full. "I also like this chia pudding, and I don't wanna fuck it."

"The temperature's a little off-putting."

He doesn't say anything.

I sigh. "Gotta be honest, I'm disappointed."

"Why?"

I don't want to make it even more cringy for him. He's allowed to lead his life in whichever path he chooses, even if it's straight to the arms of blue balls, so I lighten the mood by slumping my shoulders. "I just…"

"You just what?" Dad frowns, leaning closer.

"I…"

"Out with it, Lev."

"I just really wanted a new mommy."

He stares at me in confusion, before he sees the smile creeping on my face.

"You little shit." He sits back, kicking me under the table. I cackle. "I almost had a heart attack for failing you in a whole other way." That only makes me laugh harder.

"So. Dumped Thalia yet?" Dad pops a strawberry into his mouth.

"Am I that obvious?" My laughter dies.

Dad shrugs. "It was a question of when, not if, once Bailey set foot across the street. It's the Cole curse."

"To be in love with women who don't want our asses?"

"To try to substitute our heart's desire before we wear her down."

"I don't think I'll ever wear Bailey out."

"You can always wear her skin, then. You seem obsessed enough to do that." But when he sees I'm not in the mood for jokes, he tilts his chin down. "Look, our vacation in Jackson Hole next week will be a good opportunity for you two to reconnect."

"She hates me now," I rasp. "I mean, Sober Bailey still likes me, but the one hooked on painkillers thinks I'm an asshole."

"She doesn't hate you. She hates what the drugs are doing to her. The cravings. The lack of control. She's a good kid, Lev. She'll figure it out, but it might be a long journey, and I'd advise strongly against seeking love from someone who is struggling to love themselves right now. Keep her safe. Don't take advantage of her situation— and don't let her slip. If anyone can help her, it's you."

I don't know if I can, but I know I *must*. Bailey saved me when I needed her the most.

I'll die before letting her down.

CHAPTER TWELVE
BAILEY

The comedown is brutal.

I'm not going to pretend I'm handling any of it well. Not when the Vicodin and Xanax wear off, or the haze over the memory of what I did when Lev babysat me.

Who, by the way, is undoubtedly a *very* bad babysitter.

The memories flooding my brain make me want to crawl under a rock and hibernate until everyone in my life dies. I can't believe my best friend shoved his finger up my butt. *Upon request.* That I tried to seduce him. And failed. That Lev, who normally looks at me like I hold the answers to all of the world's mysteries in the palm of my hand, finished the night washing me off in the shower with pain and pity in his eyes.

Which is why I refuse to see him, despite our friendly exchange. He visits me every day, leaving my favorite Froyo outside the studio door in the basement and small boxes full of…nothing. I don't know what the point behind the boxes is, but I keep them. It feels wrong to get rid of something Lev gave me. Even if it's technically…well, *nothing.*

"Bailey, open the fuck up." He bangs on the door, and it rattles like the thing inside my chest.

"Busy," I moan.

"Busy being full of shit?"

"That too."

"Dove." I hear him plaster his forehead over my basement door, groaning in pain. *"Please."*

"I'm not your problem."

"You're right. You're my solution. My salvation. So open up."

I never let him in. Can't look him in the eye after Anusgate, also known as the Buttmageddon.

Even if I wanted to look him in the eye, I couldn't on account of my pupils are currently the size of a poke bowl. I'm popping Xanax like they're Mentos. The only reason my parents are missing the signs is that I'm on house arrest with the drugs hidden, so technically, they think there's nothing here to get high on and aren't looking...at all.

There's no point in denying what is starkly obvious at this point—I *am* an addict.

I'm dependent on painkillers, and I let my reliance run the show. But that doesn't change the fact that I still need to train if I want to remain at Juilliard.

I just need to prove to my professors that I can do this. Once I ensure my spot is secure for next year, I can lay off the pills and really start taking care of myself. I'll detox. Drink plenty of water. Meditate. Push through in more sustainable ways.

Since I don't accept any visitors, I have plenty of time to work out. I stretch, dance, rehearse, and stay on top of my academic schedule. For all intents and purposes, I'm still a Juilliard student. It's not like they officially kicked me out.

Mom is the definition of worried sick. She's literally been coughing and sneezing nonstop. Psychosomatic, my dad tells her when he thinks I'm not listening. She throws judgy looks my way when I go to the basement every day, pushing plates of food to my chest, begging me to stop.

"I don't understand why you're pushing yourself even harder when you're on a *break*." This, from the woman who had me training in the studio five days a week since the age of six.

"First of all, it's for my mental health." I pull my hair into a bun and storm down the stairs, Mom at my heels, holding a vegan power bowl with extra passionfruit. "Second, if I'm a so-called painkiller addict, exercising is actually one of the best ways to detox. Flush the hydrocodone and acetaminophen out of my system."

"You know what's better than exercising? Going to meetings every day." Mom shoulders the door open when I try to slam it in her face. We're in the studio now, standing in front of each other like in a duel. Her weapon is an organic breakfast and mine is a wrathful glare.

"Three times a week is plenty." I roll my eyes.

"Three times a week is nothing when you overdosed less than a month ago. Now eat." She thrusts the bowl to my chest.

"I have to start working." I fold my arms, taking a step back. The pills are killing my appetite. I live on handfuls of nuts or high-calorie energy drinks throughout the day.

"On *what*?" My mother treads deeper into the studio, and is it just me or is she hogging all the oxygen in the room? "All you do is harm yourself even more. Don't think I wasn't listening when they told you in the hospital about your tibia and spine injuries."

"Of course you were listening." I shake my head. "It's not like you have a life of your own to focus on."

I'm being super mean right now. Mom dedicated her entire life to Daria and me. Turning this against her is disgusting, but the Vicodin is running the show right now. I'm so raw, I feel the shallowest paper cut could make me bleed out. I'm exposed. A lie told and detected. A fraud. A nobody who deserves to be alone, so I am pushing her away.

"They're probably not even going to take you back!" she snaps.

This lands like an iron fist straight in my gut. I keel over at her words, and Mom slaps a hand over her mouth, letting go of the fruit bowl with a gasp. It shatters between us, just like our trust. I can feel the shards in my mouth. All the unspoken words that sat between us for weeks and months and years.

Bailey is different.

Bailey is so talented.

She has what it takes.

"I didn't mean it that way." Mom shakes her head, tears rimming the edges of her pale eyes. "Bails. I…I…"

"You *what?*" My voice is unrecognizable to me. Cold as the goose bumps blossoming along my gray skin.

"I just want my daughter back." Now the tears are all over her face, her neck, running down the collar of her tennis dress. White-hot anger zips through me. She has to be kidding me. *She* is why I'm doing all this. She is why I keep pushing through the pain.

"I *am* your daughter." I hit back, spreading my arms wide, putting myself on display. Every inch of marred skin, battle scars, and hard-earned bruises. I'm a kaleidoscope of purples and blues, of pain and suffering. "All I ever wanted was to make you proud. I still do, Mom. Pathetically, all I care about is making you and Dad happy."

I clutch on to a pointe shoe and hurl it against the wall. It lands a few inches above her head, but she doesn't even twitch. It's like she's hypnotized by me.

"I'm your little ballerina, remember?" Tears run down my face. The anxiety is back again, like deep, thick tree roots shackling me in place. "Just talented enough to make it, unlike Daria. All I have to do is work a little harder, stand a little straighter, be a little more like you."

Mom's jaw drops. "I thought you wanted this. You asked me if I could put you in ballet, and I guess—"

This. This is why I need the pills. So I can control the overwhelming fear of failure. The pain of not measuring up. Before she can finish the sentence, I grab my other shoe and fling it at her too. This time she dodges.

"*Of course,* I wanted to do ballet! It runs through your veins, and you run in mine. Just admit it, Melody. You fed me to the wolves. You mourned your short career at Juilliard, your own career-killing injury when you were a student. You never recovered. Not from the broken leg—and not from the broken dream. Remember how you told me your parents never supported your dream, which was why you were going to make sure I made it?" I pant like I just ran a marathon. "Well, your over-supportiveness meant I knew I couldn't fail. At first you thought Daria would fulfill your dreams, but she was as wild as weeds. Unruly and disinterested in being squeezed and shaped into your perfect daughter. Now, me? I was your winning ticket. Obedient and hardworking. I became the prized daughter. The apple of your shrewd eye. *You* introduced me to this cutthroat world. Willingly inserted me into a life of never-ending auditions, grueling physical work, injuries, heartbreak, sacrifice, and rejection. Now you need to live with the consequences of your own doing. Even if they include a junkie child whose drug of choice is standing onstage, doing pas de deux with an acclaimed ballerino."

The words hit her so harshly, she bucks and staggers backwards. Her knees lower, her head slumping down. I hit where it hurt. Bull's eye.

"Please quit." Her words come out as a pant. "You're right. I pushed too hard. But I changed my mind. It's not worth it. The ballet. The school."

A rusty laugh bubbles out of me. "It's not about you anymore. This is who I am. Whether I wanted it or not, I'm hooked for life."

I turn to storm out of the studio. It's only when my foot hovers over the debris of glass beneath me that I remember Mom dropped the bowl. My mouth falls open even as my foot falls. Mom's killer instincts snap her into action. She pounces forward, pushing me out of the way so I don't step on the glass. The shards beneath her feet make a terrible crunching sound.

We both wince, looking down. She is barefoot. Blood spreads beneath her foot, pooling like a never-ending lake.

Oh, fuck. Fuck, fuck, fuck.

"Mom!" I rush around the glass and pick her up even though

she is about twenty pounds heavier than me. I bolt upstairs, shaking, crying, screaming.

"Dad, help! Mom's hurt!"

My body strains to get her up the stairs. She weeps into my neck, boneless and hopeless. I slip over her blood on the stairs and yelp. My injuries are burning, reminding me how broken I am too.

I hear the thrashing of feet hitting wood as Dad rushes to meet me halfway on the basement stairway. He takes Mom with frightening ease. Red paints our feet like lipstick kisses. It looks like a crime scene.

She saved me, even after all the horrible things I said to her.

"Holy sh—what happened? Is she okay?" I don't think I've ever seen Dad as pale as he is right now. His face is a mask of terror.

"She has glass in her feet." I chase after him. "She needs to go to urgent care. They'll suction it out."

"What did you do?" he growls, and I've never heard this tone from him before.

"No! I…I mean, I fucked up, but she dropped a bowl. It was… not really…"

His deathly glare makes me shut up. He studies me for a fraction of a second before saying, "Stay here. Don't you dare leave this house, Bailey."

I follow him to the front door. Mom is still crying. I don't know how much of it is the glass and how much of it is us. We've never fought before.

The door slams behind Dad. I'm all alone. It's eight thirty in the morning, and my parents have left me alone for the first time since I got back. There's a lot of blood to clean up. I need a pick-me-up. I *need* to stop feeling like a failure, because right now? Breathing is too much of a task.

I go downstairs and tug my drug bag from behind the mirror. Only one more Xanax. Crap.

I hesitate only for one moment before I pull the mangled note with Sydney's number from the bowels of my drawer and make the call.

"Sydney? It's Bailey. Wanna come over?"

Of course, he says yes.

There's no steadier client than an addict.

———————

Three hours later, my parents are back from urgent care. Mom's foot is bandaged securely. She looks tired and miserable, suckling on Jamba Juice. I wait for them in the kitchen, head hung low and hands in my lap. After Sydney popped in to sell me more drugs, I cleaned up all the mess in the basement and stairs. I made lunch—herbed salmon and broccolini—folded the laundry, and put fresh flowers in Mom's office upstairs. I'm sick with guilt and as high as a kite. My body is lax, relaxed, and pain free. My mind is clear, like my thoughts are cruising through fluffy, white clouds in the sky. As soon as Dad places Mom on a seat at the dining table, I drop to my knees and take her hand in mine. I can't even feel the hardwood floor beneath my banged-up kneecaps, which means the pills are doing their job.

"I'm sorry, Mom. I didn't mean to—"

"You're checking into rehab." Dad cuts into my words, pressing a hand over Mom's shoulder behind her. Like I'm going to hurt her or something. "I've already paid the down payment."

My head snaps up. "Why? Because Mom and I had a fight?"

"Because you're acting like a stranger and one I don't want under my roof," he says matter-of-factly. "And because you invited over another stranger when we were at the hospital, which means I'm gonna cancel all my meetings for the rest of the day so I can play hide-and-seek with a bag of pills."

I brick up, press my lips together, and sneer. "Sydney is a friend from high school."

"We said no guests when we aren't around," Dad snarls.

Dad's not gonna find anything. I'm smart enough not to hide drugs where they'd look.

I hide them in the studio in the basement, where I lock myself up. In the one-inch slit between the floor-to-ceiling mirror.

Mom grabs my fingers, bringing them to her lips. My eyes follow to where her mouth brushes my fingertips. "I'm sorry I pressured you into becoming a ballerina. Seems like I am full of good intentions and bad decisions where my daughters are concerned. I know an apology isn't a magic eraser for everything that happened, but I'll try my best to make it up to you. Please, I'm begging you, check into rehab. You are not *you* right now, and *you* are one of my favorite people. Juilliard isn't important. It's—"

"I'm not going." I bring her hands to my mouth. Kiss them. Tears running down my cheeks. I can't lose Juilliard. I can't go from Perfect Bailey to Pathetic Bailey. "If you want me to go live somewhere else, I will respect your wishes. I can crash at a friend's house. You and I both know that if I go to rehab now, my Juilliard dream is over. I'll never make it. The school is not going to wait for me. I'd have to drop out. Tell me it isn't true, Mom. Tell me I'm exaggerating."

The silence curls its cold fingers around my neck, cutting my oxygen supply. My greatest fear has been confirmed. If I enter rehab—which, let's admit it, I probably should—it's game over. The kiss of death to the thing I have lived for my entire life: ballet.

I drop my forehead in Mom's lap, squeezing my eyes shut. I want to get better. But I will have to get clean without going to rehab.

"Bailey, I—" Dad's phone starts ringing. He frowns at the screen. "Fuck. It's Vicious. I just missed a huge presentation."

Dad cursed. Dad never curses. This house is falling apart, all because of me.

He walks out of the room, and we're left alone. Mom and me. A tour de force turned tour de crap.

"So this is what my child looks like when she's high." She peers into my face. But she doesn't know. Not really. Only assumes because a stranger was in the house. I'll convince her otherwise. Lie through my teeth if need be. "I didn't know you'd look so…happy." Her face almost crumples before it goes blank.

I look away instinctively, my cheeks burning with shame. My eyes stare at the door hard, and I make a wish that Lev would walk through it and save me.

He doesn't.

CHAPTER THIRTEEN
BAILEY

The day keeps hitting all the checkmarks to becoming the world's crappiest.

Thalia shows up at my door. She smells of Miss Dior and wears a green plaid minidress, a big hair bow, and a bracelet with a sparrow on it. *Subtle.* She looks like she is wearing a costume of *me*. I'm all about Daria's hand-me-downs and high-fashion knockoffs I find at thrift stores.

"Come on in." I smile, not sure how to feel about her anymore. On one hand, she hooked me up with Sydney knowing—or highly suspecting—I have a problem. On the other, she must feel like a third wheel, which is terrible. She never asked for me to come back into town. I rolled in and ruined all she's worked for.

"Bailey, you look radiant!" She checks me out from behind orange opal sunglasses. Liar. I'm as presentable as a bag of hair. Probably just as lively. "Is now a good time?"

Never would be a great time, but we're gonna have to talk sooner or later.

"Yeah. How about we hang at the pool?" I suggest.

"Totally, if you can give me a bikini?"

Sure. You took the boy I love. Why stop there?

"Follow me."

We climb upstairs and I hand her my lettuce-edge floral bikini. I slip into a white handkerchief piece, trying not to stare at her nause-atingly flawless body. I finger my dove bracelet. Thalia catches the gesture, releasing a sigh. "I'm so bummed I can't come with you all to Jackson Hole."

Every year our families go skiing together. Uncle Vicious has a mansion there. Thalia is implying Lev invited her—and that invita-tion is active... But that can't be true. He was going to dump her. I officially gave him the green light to go after me. You know, right before I started ignoring him again.

"Why aren't you coming?" I swallow, trying to recover from the surprise.

"My gymnastics schedule is brutal." She pouts. "Plus, we won't be able to keep our hands off each other, which would be so cringe." She giggles.

"Ho ho ho, Merry Cringemas," I say dryly. *Literally kill me now.*

She twists up her nose. "Oh my God, what's that smell? I can't breathe."

"Sage." *And that's because you're a succubus.*

"Aw. Guess I'm not a fan."

I'm actually burning sage so Mom doesn't smell how I haven't washed my sheets in days, maybe weeks. "I'll keep it in mind for next time you come."

I won't. But my dang manners won't let me say anything else.

We go downstairs to the pool and occupy two sun loungers.

"I was *so* worried for you when you left the bonfire the other day. Did you get home okay?" Thalia lathers her legs in enough baby oil to drown one.

The question is so backhanded and manipulative that I can't help but let my inner Daria do the talking for a second, "Oh, yeah. Lev looked for me all over town. Found me pretty quickly, though."

"He is great, isn't he?" Thalia smiles brightly, reaching to pat my arm. Feels like a snakebite. "He came to my place right afterwards."

What?

My rage is so potent it feels like there are lava bubbles burning through my veins. He was supposed to break up with her. If he is so-called in love with me, why does Regina George over here think she has an invitation to *our* family holiday? There's so much anger and frustration and despair in me, and I have nothing to do with them. Nothing but wait for her to leave so I can pop more Xanax.

Thalia notices me flinch. She presses home with a dreamy moan. "Oh, don't be nervous, Bailey! I totally kept our little secret." She winks. "Let's just say I found a way to distract him, if you get what I'm saying."

Barf fills my mouth, and I force it down my throat. No way am I letting her see how much it hurts.

Slanting my gaze her way, I ask, "Have you spoken to him about college yet? Are you guys sticking it out?"

Lev might be knocking boots with Daisy Douche over here, but he is not taking her seriously.

I know because he is all heart and she is all venom. But Thalia seems serene as she folds her bikini bottom an inch to allow the sun to evenly tan her groin. "Not yet. But things are looking up. I'm starting to see he truly cares for me. I think we're super bonded over the fact he lost his mom and I almost lost my sister to cancer, you know? We *get* each other. Thanks for the advice, Bailey. You're such a good friend!"

It hurts. Hurts so much I can't breathe. Hurts that I can't make one good decision lately. Hurts that I'm addicted. Hurts that I'm injured. Hurts that I'm hurting others. My entire universe seems to be pain, and for the first time in my life, I wonder if the world is going to be better if I just…leave it.

"You're so welcome." I smile.

"High-school sweethearts! Imagine if we end up married!" She squeals.

Thanks, I'd rather imagine being devoured by hungry sharks in the open ocean.

I fling a towel over my head to signal the conversation is over.

———————

I shove Thalia out my door as soon as decorum allows and trek downstairs to the basement to pop a few pills. Only after my mood is somewhat leveled, I decide to launch *Operation Make Lev Dump Thalia*.

Not the catchiest title, but it's safe to say I'm not at my peak right now.

I'm doing this out of purely altruistic reasons. She is obviously a terrible influence. She gave me drugs when I tried to kick the habit. Lev deserves better, even if that better isn't the drug-addict ballerina next door. If he dumps her without realizing she is the one hooking me up with drugs, I can get both my drugs and happy ending with my best friend.

Standing with my back to the studio mirror, I pull out my phone, stick my butt out, and drop my bikini bottom, snapping a semi-naked picture of myself and sending it to Lev.

I'm not sure what I expect to get back from him, but it isn't the deafening silence that greets me, so I decide to give him another nudge. Sexting is the bread and butter of the twenty-first-century civilization—how hard can it be?

I lie on the floor, pulling my bikini top down, and snap a selfie of me topless, swimming in the shimmering gold of my hair. My nipples are taut, my lips pink and parted, and now it is no longer a hint. It's an open invitation. Old Bailey would say ten million Hail Marys just for *toying* with the idea of sending a nude pic. But my normal self isn't home right now.

This time, I send it with a caption: Still settling for the knockoff, or are you ready for the real thing?

A minute passes. Then five. Fear trickles into my gut like acid, drip, drip, drip. What if he's had enough of my mood swings? What if he hates this new me? Normal Bailey texts him fun ballet and aviation facts, not pictures of her nipples. How much longer can he be kind and understanding before he finally snaps?

The door upstairs swings open, crashing violently against the wall. I jump in surprise. Upstairs, Dad is growling, "What the hell, Lev? I'm gonna send your old man a bill for that crown molding."

"Where is she?" Lev demands savagely, ignoring Dad's threat. He doesn't sound horny. He doesn't sound happy, either. He sounds… *murderous.*

Yup. There's definitely room for growth in the sexting department for me.

Quickly, I slip back into my bikini and hastily tie my bottoms over my hips.

"Practicing downstairs." Mom's voice is barely a whisper. "She had a day."

"Yeah? Well, it's nothing in comparison to the evening I have in store for her."

I run to the mirror and pinch my cheeks to look half-alive, noticing my eyes are glassy, blank, un-mine. Not only do I not look pretty, I don't look like myself, period. I'd been hyperfocused on my body in the selfies, not my face.

Lev bursts inside still in his gear. His white football pants are muddy, his buzz cut dirtied, streaks of sweat and mud contouring his godlike face. He is shredded to perfection, all bronzed, glistening skin and smells of freshly cut grass, warm summer nights, and sex.

"You are so fucking dead, Bailey Followhill," he sneers, getting right in my face.

I take an involuntary step back, my ass hitting the ballet barre. My shaky fingers curl around it. My unsteadiness is the result of adrenaline and desire, not fear. Lev would never hurt me. If he makes me scream, it'll be from pure pleasure.

"Ignoring my ass for days and weeks, making me worry sick about you, then sending me nudes." His roar bounces off the walls. "Where're the drugs?" His breath skates along the column of my neck, hot and citrusy. Chills nip at my flesh, and my breath becomes shallow and fast.

"What drugs?" I bat my lashes innocently. "I just want to have some fun." I buck my hips forward, rolling them over his pelvis. A small moan escapes me.

"Searched your room again when you went to your support group yesterday, since you wouldn't let me see you." His jaw tics with fury. I want to lick a path through the sharp slope of it. "Went through all the bathrooms and Daria's old room too. Should've known you'd do a good job. You're smart. Fucked-up, but still the smartest person I know."

Holy hell. He went through my entire room and I didn't even notice? How high was I? For the first time I'm questioning my grip on reality.

Old Bailey would know if someone moved her markers an inch.

"Maybe I'm sober." I trail a fingernail down his chest.

"Old Bailey would never send me nudes."

"Old Bailey sounds like a bore."

"Hey." He coils his fingers around the front of my neck, angling his chin down. "Don't you dare fucking badmouth the girl I love."

"If you love me so much, fuck me!" I toss my hands up in the air.

Ho. Ly. Heck. What did I just say? Weirdly, I can't bring myself to take it back.

I need him to do this. To treat me like the subject of his darkest desires, not some holy nun. Lev is no cheater. If he touches me inappropriately now, he'd break up with Thalia. His conscience wouldn't let him two-time us.

"Never said anything about loving *you*." His eyes rake my body with noticeable boredom.

I rub myself shamelessly against his pelvis. The chafe of my bikini bottom's fabric against his rock-hard bulge makes my clit swollen and sensitive. Heat swirls in my stomach.

Lev bares his teeth. "Feel free to stop humping my jockstrap whenever you're ready. I can't feel jack shit through it."

His words are like freezing-cold water over my mood.

Then he adds, "Even if I were hard, I wouldn't fuck you."

I plaster on a smile and purr, "Too bad. I might actually cooperate if you get me off. Tell you where all those bad drugs are."

A spark of something sinister ignites behind his pupils. There is a domineering element to Lev, and I don't know how I haven't noticed it before. Maybe because I always considered myself his security blanket, his person, his *home*. Now when I'm clearly not all those things to him, I'm hard-pressed to come up with a more alpha, controlling…man.

"So it's like that?" His free hand grabs at my hip bone, and with an effortless tug, he pulls one of my legs to wrap over his waist. The dove on his tattered bracelet brushes over my outer thigh and a strangled grunt rolls past my lips. His tongue swipes at his full bottom lip, and his eyes hood farther.

"That's exactly what it's like." I pinch my shoulder blades together to display my chest. "What are we doing now, Lev?"

"Foreplay." His hand hikes farther down my waist, drawing at the string keeping my bikini bottom together deliciously slowly.

I gasp with pleasure. "My parents could walk in any second."

Or maybe not? It's hard to tell because, lately, they've been trusting me with nothing. But they do trust Lev. Trust that he would always make the right decision for both of us.

"Let them see," he answers, his lips tracing my own, and it's not exactly a kiss, but it's not exactly *not* a kiss, either.

I want him to devour my mouth until I can't breathe. Jockstrap and cup or not, he is affected. He groans into my mouth, and for a moment, I'm not high anymore. I'm Old Bailey, and he is my Lev, and we're pressing our lips together like children practicing what we saw on TV, breathing each other in. Our hearts beat in the same rhythm. Our fingers lace together. It's quiet. It's romantic. It's everything. My eyes flutter shut and my lips clasp over his so seamlessly, we're like a lock and a key. A match made of kismet heaven.

"Lev…"

"No. Shut up. Let me pretend you're her." My heart squeezes for a second, and I can't breathe. Her? Her who? Thalia? But then he adds brokenly, "*My* Bailey."

He glides his hand from my neck to my jaw and squeezes, opening my mouth forcefully. I welcome his tongue as it chases mine, licking, flicking, exploring. He swallows my little pants of appreciation with greediness. With my bikini bottom half-undone, he presses his hot palm against my pussy until he hits bone. My nipples pucker and I shudder, rolling my hips relentlessly, hunting his touch.

I want him to bend me over the ballet barre and fuck me raw. I want him to tell me I'll be fine, that we'll get through this together. I want him to come inside me and watch me drip. To lick the inside of my thighs from behind and whisper sweet nothings that would soak into my skin.

I open my legs wider, giving him access to me.

Lev *tsks* into my mouth, his tongue stroking mine skillfully. "You're gonna have to use your words, Dove."

"Finger me," I whimper. "Please."

His mouth rips from mine, and he drags his nose down the side of my neck, leaving hot, sexy kisses everywhere his lips land. These kisses are a drug more powerful than anything they can create in a lab.

"Where're the drugs?" he repeats.

I don't answer, taking his hand and jerking it desperately between my legs.

The asshole laughs into my collarbone, hand limp between us, as his tongue draws lazy circles around the tip of my shoulder. "Answer me."

"Finger-fuck me first," I groan. "Don't pretend like you're not curious to know what I feel like inside."

Lev hisses into my skin, a mixture of pain and guilt swimming in his tortured expression when I feel his digit skimming my slit. I'm so wet it slicks the tip of his finger instantly. We both stop everything and take a moment to tremble in each other's arms. Our heads drop forward and we watch as his finger strokes back and forth along my entrance. My breasts feel full and heavy, and my belly bottoms out. Our eyes meet, and Lev plasters his forehead against mine, closing his eyes. "Where are you hiding those pills, baby?"

Baby. Oh Marx. I love this nickname in his mouth. I shake my head. I'm never gonna tell him. I can't. "Please give me some relief. Please, Lev, I need it."

"It's wrong."

"Then do something wrong anyway. Even if you don't like it. For me. For once."

He buries his face in my shoulder as he pushes his finger deep inside me. I clench around him instantly, so wet and turned-on he meets no resistance from my body.

"Oh, fuck. You're so tight. You'll milk my cock dry when I fuck you."

When. He said when.

"Now seems like as good a time as ever." I rotate my hips, riding his finger like a cowgirl when he adds two more to the party. I'm so close I can practically feel the edge of an orgasm before it overtakes me. He glides in and out of me, his dirty, sweaty fingers still smelling like cowhide and grass from football practice. With three fingers inside me, he massages my clit with his thumb, flicking it teasingly. My knees are trembling and I drop my head back. Stars dust along the ceiling, a thousand tiny supernovas, as my vision blurs and my climax crawls up from the tip of my toes up my legs. Warmth spreads along my limbs. It's happening. I'm coming.

"Where are the drugs, Bailey?" Lev repeats, his teeth grazing the tip of my chin.

"I'm not on drugs." I clench around his fingers.

"You're a liar." He keeps thrusting his fingers into me, manic, hungry, fueled by desire. His other hand is holding me by the front of my neck to keep me from falling. I'm pressed against the mirror. He's handling me roughly, just like I want him to. And I can't get nearly enough of this.

"And you still love me," I taunt.

"Tell me where."

"Keep dreaming, Levy."

"Fuck, Bailey!" He tears himself away, running the hand that was inside me over his scalp.

My orgasm comes to a screeching halt, and my ass hits the floor now that he is not there to hold me. I stare at him from my spot on the parquet, my limbs knotted together like a newborn fawn.

He paces back and forth, swiping his hand over his mouth in frustration. He stops. "Last chance, Bail. Where are the drugs?"

"Screw you. You just cut my orgasm short." I reach between my thighs to play with myself. But the moment is gone and so is the promise for climax. The wetness inside me feels cold and empty. I have a moment of clarity where I see myself from the outside. Through his eyes. This wretched, long-limbed creature trying to reignite something that is long dead.

As if confirming my suspicion, Lev drops to his knees beside me.

"Look at yourself." He ties my bikini back together hastily. "Fuck, Dove. What would it take to make you get some help?"

Smiling, I try to gulp down the ball of tears forming in my throat. "Just because I'm no longer perfect, doesn't mean I'm not perfectly me. Anyone ever told you you're a fair-weather friend?"

And then, something awful happens. He stops helping me. Stands up. Flashes me his megawatt, crooked, '90s-heartthrob smirk. The one I see him giving his rivals on the field before he wipes them out and finishes their season. Lev doesn't have bedroom eyes. He has bend-you-against-the-kitchen-counter-while-your-parents-are-*literally*-in-the-next-room-and-fuck-your-brains-out eyes. And right now, this drowsy, sexy, long-lashed stare is looking at me like it is trying to measure me up. Which part of me he wants to break first. The answer is clear, by the way—the heart.

"Fine. You wanna act like a loser, Bailey? I'll treat you like a loser. Have fun with your drugs."

He advances to the door, and I chase him, grabbing at the edge of his shirt. "You're just gonna walk away from the conversation?"

"What more is there to say?"

"Break up with your girlfriend. For me."

I always thought that if I were to channel an Ariana Grande song, it'd be "Dangerous Woman." This is definitely not my month.

Lev turns to glare at me. I never thought I'd see the day when he looked at me like I'm a bug he wants to crush under his shoe. "For you?" He arches an eyebrow, giving me a slow, patronizing once-over. "Nah. Let me know when my best friend is back."

CHAPTER FOURTEEN
LEV

Miserable Fact #2,200: After being decapitated, the average person remains conscious for an additional 15–20 seconds.

I leave the Followhill residence without saying goodbye, their daughter's juices still all over my hand. I storm across the street to my house, throwing the door open. Dad and Dixie are sitting in the living room watching *Parks and Rec* like the most wholesome couple on planet earth. They seriously need to pork already.

"Hey, Lev." Dixie twists her head, smiling at me from the couch. "I made some steamed eggrolls if you—"

"Yeah. Thanks. Later." I shoot up the stairs to my bathroom like I just downed a bottle of laxatives.

"Manners!" Dad barks from the couch. Like he gives two shits about those when Dixie isn't around.

In my bathroom, I begin dumping my football gear on the floor. I get to my jockstrap. I pull it off, then grimace as I peer inside. Yup. I came in my pants like a goddamn rookie. My jockstrap is superglued to my junk by spunk.

With a hiss, I dump the jockstrap into the trash and squeeze the edges of the granite counter, staring at myself in the mirror. I felt like a shithead, fingering Dove. Not because it didn't feel good. It felt *fantastic*. But because she was under the influence and I genuinely thought she'd tell me where the drugs were if I brought her to the brink of coming and denied her.

My dick is hard again—fuck this shit and fuck being an eighteen-year-old. I drop my gaze to the hand that's still coated in Bailey's juices. It's all sticky and dry now, but I can still smell her. *Taste* her, if I ran my tongue over my palm. But I can't. I can't jerk off using her juices. It would be wrong. The guilt would kill me.

Leaning forward, I close my eyes and tap-tap-tap my forehead against the mirror, willing myself not to headbutt it and send it crashing.

I love Bailey Followhill to death.

But the girl she becomes when she's high…

I hate that chick. With a passion.

———

"So, anyway, thanks a lot for blue-balling my ass, Mom." I sit next to Mom's grave, snapping twigs distractedly. "Bailey said she didn't wanna start something together because you made her promise she'd always be there for me. She took it to mean she had to friend-zone my ass into oblivion. Now she's in trouble and I'm not sure how to help her."

How do you help someone who doesn't want to be helped? I bet Mom would have wise words on that.

"Okay, fair," I groan. "It's not your fault that things are messed up. But I'm allowed to vent, all right?"

Shaking my head, I shove my hand into a bucket of warm water and dish soap, pull out a sponge, and start washing her grave. Dad, Knight, and I come here every Sunday to hang out with her and take turns cleaning her gravestone and decorating it with fresh flowers. Then we all tell her about our week. It's probably the only place Dad doesn't bring Dixie.

Today is my turn to clean and put flowers. Dad and Knight said they were running a little late.

After I'm done drying the gravestone with a microfiber towel, I slip flowers into the vase that's on top of it. Roses for Rosie. Pink and white. Her favorite.

"There, Mom. Looking like a million bucks, as per usual." I stand in front of the stone, winking at it.

"Stop hitting on Mom, Lev. She's taken," I hear Knight chiding playfully from behind me, gravel crunching beneath his boots.

I feel him clap my back, drawing me into a bro-hug, and I hear Dad's car locking automatically as he joins us. Knight kisses my head to piss me off, because it makes me feel like a kid. "You look good, baby bro."

"Yeah? Well, I feel like crap."

"Smell like it too." Knight's nose twitches, but he's just pulling my leg. "Bailey still giving you trouble?"

Before I can answer, Dad crouches down to the gravestone and rearranges the roses with a frown. He is so meticulous and particular about everything Mom related.

Maybe it's best if Bailey and I part ways. There's nothing sadder than living your heartbreak every single day after you lose someone you love.

"Boys, can you take a little walk? I need to talk to your mom."

"Uh-huh." Knight presses two fingers to his lips. "Someone's gonna get his ass handed to him. What'd you do? Mom, don't go easy on him!"

Dad pins him with a *really?* glare. I shake my head and tug Knight down the green lawns toward a bunch of whitewashed granite benches. Knight slings an arm over my shoulder and tilts his chin to Dad. "What do you think that's about?"

"Dixie, probably."

"Word. Did you ever find out if he's giving her the ol' selfie stick?"

"Jesus, Knight. What did the English language ever do to you that you abuse it so badly?" I shake off his touch. "Annoyingly, Dad claims they're just friends."

"Maybe he's asking Mom for permission to move on?" Knight raises his eyebrows hopefully, peering over his shoulder at Dad earnestly conversing with the gravestone.

"Hope so because apparently Dad hasn't porked anyone in *four* years."

"*Oof.* Fun conversations happening in the Cole household these days." Knight flicks his aviators down his nose. "Well, that's sad." He pauses. "Not as sad as you still being a virgin, but close."

"I'm not a virgin." I don't know why I'm scowling. Maybe because even though Knight is chronologically my big brother, usually I'm the responsible, mature one.

"Right. Thalia." He snaps his fingers. "The knockoff version of Bailey. *Mailey.*" He chuckles. "You broken up with her yet?"

"Kinda, yeah." I suck my teeth, again wondering what the fuck I was thinking with this whole pretend act. Now Bailey thinks she got fingered by a dude who's attached. I don't want *any* version of her to think I'm a dick. "So let me ask you a question. As a former addict—" I start.

He cuts me off. "Addict, just addict. I'll always be an addict. Keeping shit under control is a daily struggle. I still attend meetings weekly, you know."

"As an addict, tell me how I can help her. Get through to her. She doesn't want to admit she's using painkillers. But she must be using a ton because she's always high."

"That's not a thing." He kneads my shoulder. "You can't force someone to get better. They have to hit rock bottom first, then take a little nap on that bitch for a few weeks or months. It's not like in the movies, where she has a light-bulb moment and boom, everything's fine. She still has so much to lose, and my advice? Let her take those hits. Just don't give up, okay? Be there for her *as soon as* she's ready and not until then." He tilts his chin down, holding my gaze. "I'd have been so fucked if Luna had decided I was too much work and walked away."

"I'm never gonna give up," I say. I still place an empty box by her bedroom door every day. Unfailingly. Hopefully she gets the meaning of it. Otherwise, I just look like a weirdo with a boner for cardboard. "I can't just let her lose everything. She's worked so hard for it. I'll never just sit back and watch as her world burns." And there was another thing—a selfish need to prove to myself that I could save her like she saved me.

"Good. Good. Hey." Knight wrangles me into a brotherly headlock. "How's football? Still kicking ass? I expect you to ask me to be your agent when you go pro, yeah?"

I am about to answer him that I won't go pro but, thankfully, get distracted.

"All right, boys. Ready to grab lunch?" Dad walks over to us. His eyes are red, but he actually looks like they had a good talk. One thing my mother's death has taught me is that people die but the love you feel for them stays alive. And that love? It is the most precious memory you can have. More than photos, videos, or any kind of inheritance.

"Are we gonna meet Dixie there?" Knight pokes as we all head over to our cars.

"No." Dad makes a face. "She doesn't always come."

"That's why you should always start with foreplay and oral." Knight winks.

Dad flicks Knight's back. "That woman *birthed* you. Do you have no moral lines?"

"Clearly not." Knight makes a face. "No, but seriously, is Dixie coming?"

"No," Dad groans.

"Aww, but I want my new mommy." Knight pouts.

Dad and I both shove him forward in unison, which only makes the three of us laugh harder.

Sometimes, it's okay to not be okay.

CHAPTER FIFTEEN
LEV

Miserable Fact #98: Most people die within a five-mile radius from the place where they were born.

I slam my locker shut, and Grim's head pops up on the other side, a shit-eating grin on his face.

"Stop looking so happy. It's ruining my day." I hoist my backpack over my shoulder and trudge my way out the doors. He follows me, wiggling his brows.

"How could I not when Thalia is going around telling people you guys are gonna miss each other like crazy when you go to Jackson Hole?" He cackles. "Which, by the way, is probably the only hole you'll be enjoying for the foreseeable future, knowing your track record with Miss Followhill."

Dipshit. Also, what business does Thalia have saying stuff like that? We're supposed to be fake dating. This is *real* annoying.

"We're not together anymore," I mutter under my breath, waltzing out the doors toward the parking lot. "Just saving face so people keep their mouths shut."

"Shocking." Grim falls into step with me.

"Keep your mouth shut about it, yeah?"

"Hold on a moment, gotta cancel the press conference."

Swear to God, this dude is made out of pure sarcasm. He

probably bleeds one-liners. I get to my car and unlock it, tossing my backpack in the passenger seat, getting ready to climb in.

Grim blocks my way. "Not so fast. We need to talk."

Alarm bells blast in my head. Grim is not a talk-it-out kind of person, so it must be serious. I fold my arms, slowly raking my eyes over his face. "Make it quick."

"I wanna do another vote for team captain," he says matter-of-factly. "You're slipping, your mind's not in the game, and you're missing practices left and right."

"The team has already voted," I say blandly. *Unfortunately.* I didn't want this, but I can't walk away from this, either. I'm not a quitter, and being an All Saints football hero is my family's legacy.

"I was next in line by two votes."

"Well, shit, Grim. I forgot the rules have changed and second place now gets the cake."

"You're already the president of the debate club, have a thousand AP classes, and three volunteer stints. Your résumé is fucking sick."

"I worked hard for all of those things." I grit my teeth. "Spat blood, mind you."

"Look." Grim sticks his hand through his hair. "You don't even attend every practice. Your mind is off the game. I actually *want* this. My parents are gonna strong-arm my ass into a life of billable hours and never-ending fucking arguments on behalf of rich people. I haven't gotten any offers yet. I need the airtime. Do me this solid, Cole."

I want to. Fuck, there's nothing I want more than to dump this football bullshit and go my merry way. But *Dad.* It's the only thing giving him joy these days. And there's also something else—the high I get out of being hot shit. The best in school. In the zip code, really.

This is the only real place I'm getting any validation these days, even if that makes it even more narcissistic.

Grim sees the answer on my face. He sucks his cheeks in, then spits on the ground beside me. "This is my dream," he croaks, and I've never seen him more serious in my life. His nostrils flare, and he looks like he is holding his breath. "I'm not asking you to hand it over, man. Just let the team vote again."

I wish I could turn my back on my dad's dreams. On Knight's expectations. But they're all I have, and it's important to them, so I have to make this captaincy important to me. Somehow.

"Dude, I'm sorry," I groan, slipping into my car.

I get back from school to an envelope in our mailbox. That's pretty rare, since we pay our bills online and all the junk is thrown out by our housekeeper. I pull the letter out of the box and take it inside, flipping it over. My throat is dry. It's from the University of Michigan.

Shit. Shit. Fuck.

Tearing the envelope open, I can already make out the words I don't want to see. *Committee on Admissions* and *acceptance* and *congratulations* and *extraordinary achievement.* Bile hits the back of my throat because I just officially got into a crazy good football college, and if Dad finds out, my Air Force Academy dream is about as attainable as dinner with Marilyn Monroe and Jesus Christ. I glance at my phone. Dad will be home soon. He can't see this. He can't find out I got in.

Shaking my head, I stomp my way up into my room. There, I go to the one thing no one ever touches—not the cleaners, not our housekeeper, not Dad—Mom's portrait, which is hung on my wall. I move it slightly to the left and tuck the letter of acceptance in a rubber band, along with the other letters of acceptance I've ignored. Five so far. All from leading colleges. *Duke included.*

I return Mom's picture to its original position and take a step back, watching her staring at me, wondering what she'd have thought about what I just did if she were here.

Probably that I've become a liar. A cheat. A cop-out.

The same faker Bailey has become. Caving under the pressure and making people miserable in the process.

Maybe Bailey isn't perfect anymore.

But neither am I.

CHAPTER SIXTEEN
BAILEY

We're all crammed inside a Bombardier Global on our way to Jackson Hole. Dad co-owns a hedge fund company, Fiscal Heights Holdings, with his friends. The firm owns the jet, which is about as environmentally friendly as setting dumpster fires in a rainforest, but I'm too tired to launch into a save-the-planet speech right now.

It's the first time I'm seeing the entire cul-de-sac clan since I got home from New York, and I'm self-conscious to say the least. My skin is gray, my eyes are sunken, and I'm hiding my frail body under an oversized pair of Costco pj's. Not exactly the symbol of beauty and sophistication.

Even though everybody is trying to act normal, I know they're curious. Why wouldn't they be? Bailey Followhill—everyone's standard—overdosed and now looks like she's spent the last year taking a lengthy vacation in hell.

Uncle Dean and Dixie are on a love seat, locked in an intense conversation. Uncle Vicious and Auntie Emilia are semi-making out, which would be awkward if they weren't still mega-hot. Uncle Trent and Auntie Edie are sipping organic juices, glancing my way with raw interest. Racer, their son, is playing with Cayden. Knight and Luna are studying me too, waiting for a heroin needle to drop out of my sleeve or something. Then there's Vaughn, Lenny, and their newborn twins, Auggie and Maggie. Lenny is tandem-feeding them while Vaughn sends violent, demonic glances at everyone, as if this entire trip were a ploy for the chance to look at his wife's breasts.

Daria, my sister, is also here with her husband, Penn, and their almost-two-year-old, Cressida. We haven't spoken to each other since she tried to see me that day with Thalia. Not for her lack of trying. And now that she is right in front of me, the guilt is so much, I can hardly breathe.

Lev is in the cockpit and hasn't said a word to me the entire plane ride. I keep thumbing the dove bracelet, trying to convince myself we'll get through this, but I'm not sure anymore.

Daria is the first to penetrate the tension in the air. She tosses a hand, rolling her sapphire eyes. "Is everyone going to pretend Bailey isn't the current bane of our existence? For Marx's sake, she is still a Selena, even if she pulled a Hailey!"

"Was that in English?" Uncle Trent turns to Auntie Edie.

Edie sighs. "Pop culture reference."

"Daria," I whisper, horrified. "I'm sorry about...*you know*."

Daria grins. "Apology accepted. It's time I break the ice. Missed you, sissy!" She lunges in my direction, butting into my narrow seat.

I coil into myself, pressing my nose into my Rupi Kaur paperback. My socked feet dig into the plush crème leather.

"Here! Ice broken." Daria holds me as passionately and tightly as she usually holds a grudge. Which is to say I am being suffocated to death right now.

"More like you *Titanic*-ed right into the iceberg." Knight sucks on his Smoothie King beverage. He literally made us all stop in Utah to get it. "Nice floats, by the way."

"I'm going to make kirigami out of your ass using the charcuterie knife if you make another boob joke about my wife," Penn announces sunnily. "Make it extra bloody too."

"Mind the beige carpet," Uncle Vicious snarls.

"You guys, can we focus on how Bails has mastered the RBF? I never thought I'd see the day." Daria sniffs.

"What's RBF?" Mom frowns. My insides turn inside out because my sister only has filters when she uploads a photo to Instagram.

"Resting Bitch Face," Knight provides, at the same time sweet Luna singsongs, "Running Barefoot Foundation!"

Bless her.

"Do you mind? I'm reading." I scowl at my older sister. I hate that Lev is in the cockpit. I always feel calmer when he's around. I hate that too, right now.

"Whatever, bitch. It's poetry. You don't have to follow the plot." Daria rolls her eyes. "Also, Sissi wants to say hi."

Cressida, her not-so-secret weapon, stumbles into my lap, smashing through my mental barriers. I adore my nearly two-year-old niece. A mass of blond curls tickles my chin. Sissi climbs up my body, pudgy fingers and ruddy cheeks drawing me close. She tries to grab my nose with her dimpled hand. "*Bayblee!* I thteal your nose."

"Oh no! I can't breathe now!" I put the book down and snuggle her close to my chest. She giggles, pretending to screw my nose back onto my face.

I don't know how something so innocent came out of someone so devious. My sister is the epitome of the smoke-show villainess. Fresh-faced and long-legged, her bombshell body is swathed in a pink tennis dress, her shiny, canary hair arranged in a high, sleek ponytail. She always looks like she just finished shooting a double spread for *Vogue*, and she never apologizes for who she is and what she wants.

"How's it going, Bails? You've been ghosting my ass like I'm a dating app date who asked you to split the bill after one drink." Daria wraps a dainty arm around my shoulder, and I roll my lips together to prevent myself from bursting into tears. If nothing else, she doesn't hold a grudge for how I treated her the past few weeks.

"I really am sorry, Dar." I start braiding Sissi's out-of-control curls just to keep my hands busy. "I've been swamped."

"Doing what, rearranging all your poetry books alphabetically?" Daria arches a fluffy, perfectly shaped eyebrow.

"No." They're already arranged by spine color, author, and date of publication. *Duh.* "I have a ton of schoolwork to catch up on."

And there it is again—the look of pity and concern.

She shakes her head. "Never mind, I'm not here to lay into you. I'm sure Mom and Dad are ripping you new ones every single day."

"What are you here to do, then?" But I don't want to know. Because I *already* do. It's written all over her face. Laced into her elegant features.

"You don't want to go to rehab, and I totally get it. You don't want to give up Juilliard," she says matter-of-factly. "Which is why I came up with a better idea."

I sit straighter, a glimmer of hope flickering like a broken flashlight inside my chest. The prospect of being treated without going off-radar tempts me. "Yeah?"

"A live-in sponsor!" She opens her arms wide. I finish braiding Cressida's locks and send her on her way to show Cayden. Daria grabs my poetry book and uses it as a fan, beaming. "Someone to keep you on the straight and narrow, be with you twenty-four seven. I spoke with this friend from college—she was a *total* cokehead; you could make a snowman with the amount she snorted a day—and she told me her parents had refused to send her somewhere at the time because her dad was running for senate or whatever." Daria rolls her blue eyes. "Anyway, I zoned out—honestly, people who take longer than twenty minutes to tell their life story are so high maintenance. *Hello, you're not Jennette McCurdy; no one wants to read your autobiography*—but she mentioned she had a live-in sponsor and that they work with doctors and cardiologists and whatnot to ensure you don't go all cold turkey while you're in withdrawal. They're professional. With degrees and all that jazz."

I'm digesting her words, which keep on coming at the speed of light. "It's not cheap, but Penn and I have decided to give you a very early birthday present. Or maybe you can call it an extension of your last birthday's present. That Miu Miu skirt did *nothing* for your knobby knees, honey." She pats one with a patient smile.

"Didn't that Miu Miu skirt make her look like an English schoolboy about to run away from his prep school to join a dark-magic academy?" She twists her head to look at her husband.

"Uh-huh, absolutely, Skull Eyes," Penn agrees. He'd agree if she said I looked like the Loch Ness Monster.

"Daria, I—"

"No, don't shut it down. It's going to be so much fun, I promise. A nice and easy rehabilitation. It'd be like having an au pair, but for—" She sinks her teeth into her lower lip.

"Junkies?" I pop an eyebrow.

Daria huffs, giving me an exasperated look. "People who need help overcoming their addiction. *Anyway*, most agencies get their personnel from overseas. We can get you an Italian stud, Bails! A Magic Mike. *Ohmymarx* or we can get someone from South Korea. They have the hottest men." She wiggles her brows.

"Pretty sure you're not supposed to dance the horizontal tango with your sponsor." Butterflies flutter their delicate wings inside my stomach. It *is* a good idea. I want to get better, I truly do. I just don't want the stigma and setback of rehab. "I mean, why not? I can try the at-home thing."

Having some kind of plan makes me feel better. Plus, if I say yes to a live-in sponsor, I'll have to binge on all the pills I packed up for this trip to get rid of them. Of course, Mom and Dad thoroughly checked my suitcase. Turned it upside down and shook hard. And *of course*, I hid them in a small, inner pocket I sewed with my own two hands. I grew up to be way too resourceful for my own good.

"Really?" Fire ignites in my sister's eyes, and I can see my parents glancing our way hopefully, on high alert. This is not an intervention; this is a full-blown coup. They all planned this. I nod anyway, trying to feel grateful instead of railroaded and trapped.

"We've got a green light, folks." Daria stands up, sending two thumbs-up my parents' way. "Excuse me while I go find you the hottest sponsor possible so they can start next week!" She claps excitedly.

"I don't know why you're so happy, seeing as I'm gonna make sure you're never gonna meet him." Penn pins her with a look.

"Aww, someone is jelly." Daria struts toward her husband, landing on his knee with a giggle.

"I may be jelly, but he's going to be straight up liquid if he ever looks at you the wrong way."

"Please choose a woman." I rub my face tiredly. "A calm, collected, friendly-looking one."

"Party pooper." She pouts. "Whatever, your funeral."

After Daria is off to start the research on her laptop, I get up and walk into the lavatory. I pull my jammies down to pee. When I finish my business and stand up, a sharp pain slices through my spine.

Shit. Tears spring into my eyes. My spine injury is worsening because I keep on dancing and using painkillers, pushing myself to the edge, and not stretching or recovering. I'll have to take some serious time off if I want to get better. I wobble to the sink, mentally happy-talking myself into this new sponsor idea. I mean, I have to start somewhere, right?

When I finish washing my hands, my phone pings. I look down, and my breath catches in my throat. An email from Juilliard.

I open it so fast I can't even make out the words at first. But then they focus back into coherent letters, informing me that I am formally invited to retake my practical exam four weeks from now.

I'm getting a second chance.

This is kismet, right? A sign from above.

I'm so happy, I clamp my elbow over my face and joy-scream into my hoodie. I'm going to kill it onstage. Reclaim the narrative. I'm back in the game, baby.

How, exactly? a voice asks in my head. *You're going to get a sponsor and get off the painkillers, remember?*

But maybe accepting this kind of help has been premature. What's four more weeks in the grand scheme of things? I'll survive. Painkillers aren't crack. It's not even oxy. And Xanax is a recreational drug that literally every famous person I know has used. I just need to pull through. And *then*, I'll get a sponsor. Actually, moving out of my dorm room to an apartment with a live-in sponsor next year sounds like a perfect plan. So it's not like I'm rejecting Daria's idea; I'm simply *postponing* it.

With a cheek-splitting grin on my face, I get out of the bathroom and waltz back to my spot.

"Dude, what'd you do in there for twenty minutes?" Knight narrows his eyes at me. Marx. He thinks I took drugs?

"Number two." I smile sweetly, determined not to let them get to me when I actually didn't do anything.

"Bullshit." He laughs.

I shrug.

"Thanks for killing the mood," Penn mumbles into my sister's lips, trying to make out with her while she's on her MacBook. Can everyone just get a room here? And some manners to go with it?

Vaughn screws his nose up in distaste, his arm slung over Lenora. She's holding a sleeping Auggie, and he is embracing a half-awake Maggie. "Speaking of shit—Knight, how's your football team doing?"

Knight coaches middle school football and is also a model. Spoiler alert: He and Luna just bought a five-bedroom beach house with a private ADU and a pool because of his Armani contracts, *not* his coaching side gig.

"We actually just won an away game, thanks for asking. How 'bout you, bro? Still sticking needles in Play-Doh and calling it art?" Knight coos.

It seems like I managed to get away from a public conversation about my bowel movements. I tiptoe to my seat, silently thanking my lucky stars.

My sister decides to unglue her lips from her husband's and yelps, "Bails, I found you a live-in sponsor! She's a woman, middle-aged, with a bunch of degrees, and looks about as fun as filing your tax returns. You're going to *love* her!" She winks, trying to seem flippant when really, the way her right eye tics tells me she is nervous. "Aww, and guess what? She is available to start this Monday, as soon as we get home."

Everyone congratulates me, other than Lev, who is still in the cockpit. I put a stop to it before they get their hopes up.

"Actually, I think I'll wait a few more weeks. I just got an email from Juilliard. I have a bunch of academic work to catch up on and the setup at Mom and Dad's is just gonna throw me off. It'd be *majorly* crowded. She'll just be standing in my way."

The entire airplane goes quiet. Uncle Vicious gives me a don't-bullshit-a-bullshitter scowl. I want to duck under my seat and hide out the rest of the journey. Mom blinks rapidly, and I know she's trying not to cry. Dad can't even look at me. By the way everyone is looking at everyone, I know what just happened here was an orchestrated intervention.

Mom says, "Juilliard emailed you?"

"Yeah, they did."

"They usually send letters."

There's nothing I can say to that, so I shrug feebly as my own plan feels like it's crumbling beneath the weight of their stares.

"But a sponsor...a one-on-one person—" Edie clears her throat.

"I think Jaime and Mel should probably broach this with Bails privately once we land, don't you?" Auntie Emilia coos in sympathy. "This is a lot to take in, in a public setting."

But I won't change my mind. I won't miss this chance.

Then I hear a familiar voice behind my back. A beautiful voice that right now feels like a blade licking down my spine.

"She's still in the contemplating stage." *Lev.* He is talking about the five stages of recovery. "Hundred bucks says she didn't take a dump because she's still full of shit. Don't worry, *Dove*." My nickname sounds like blasphemy rolling off his tongue, and I feel his arm hook around my neck. His lips skim over my ear, and I know everyone is looking, so I try not to show him how much his touch affects me. "I'll make sure you kick the habit this trip, whether you want to or not. You saved me, Bailey Followhill. My turn to repay a favor. Get ready for a fucked-up vacation because I'm not letting you relapse again."

CHAPTER SEVENTEEN
BAILEY

Lev wasn't kidding.

He's been shadowing me everywhere ever since we got off the plane. The 7-Eleven. Ski equipment store. The slopes. The cabin. Even the bathroom. None of the grown-ups like him running the helm, but he gives major head-biting vibes when anyone tries to pry him away from me.

He was there when I unpacked, then dragged me to his room to watch *him* unpack, then patted me top to bottom before and after I got into my ski gear. He also makes me chug enough water to fill a pond. Every time I finish a bottle, another one magically appears in my hands. I think I've peed fifty times since we've landed. My bladder is one water bottle away from filing a restraining order against him.

My parents seem on board with Lev's Soviet-prisoner gig, which means I can't blow him off and spend an intimate, romantic vacation with my Vicodin and Xanax.

I am bullied into skiing. Not only am I not a good skier, but my body is broken, which means my injuries are bothering me even more. At the end of day one, I'm so wiped, my body feels like I've been run over by a motor grader. Thrice.

"Remind me how I'm supposed to go for a number two with you always on my ass?" I mumble as I get out of a steaming-hot shower, squeezing my hair dry above the sink.

"Whenever nature calls, Dove." Lev is slouched on the edge of the clawfoot bathtub, watching porn on his phone so I won't think his boner is from my general nakedness. "I've changed Cayden's diapers dozens of times. Nothing you can do I haven't already seen and smelled."

"I'm not a baby." I yank my hair straight with a brush.

"Debatable." He doesn't raise his head from his phone screen.

"And when will *you* take a shower?" I drop my towel and start slathering myself in body lotion. His throat bobs as he hikes up the volume on his phone, filling the bathroom with moans and grunts.

"Any second now. Your mom's gonna spot for me while I get washed and tug one out, then everyone is going out for a drink and I'm on babysitting duty." He finally looks up from the phone, clicking it shut.

"Thanks. I really needed to hear that you're going to masturbate."

"Don't pretend like you didn't want to the entire time you were taking a shower. We have that effect on each other."

Lev stands up, sashaying until he is toe-to-toe with me. I'm naked. He is...*not*. We hold each other's gaze. He looks predatory, menacing, and sadly—delicious. I'm not high, but I *am* irritated and flustered enough to ruffle his feathers.

"Go ahead. Take a peek." I smile sweetly, stepping back to allow for a better view. "See what you're missing. What you'll never get your hands on."

"Big words from someone who begged me to fuck her ass with my fingers not even two weeks ago."

Snorting, I murmur, "I was high. Now I'm sober, so all your flaws are on display. And there are many, Lev Cole."

Rather than verbally spar with me, he leans back, having his fill. His jade irises skate down my body slowly, halting everywhere they land. I can almost feel him clasping his teeth over my tight nipples, grazing them along my stomach. The way his tongue swirls around my navel and dips south, to the holy triangle between my thighs. I'm shivering all over, and I know he can tell. Finally, he opens his mouth and says, "Your body is full of blues and purples."

My heart somersaults to the pit of my stomach. This is what he noticed?

Huffing, I answer, "Welcome to college sports. That's what your reality is going to look like unless you get the balls to apply to the Air Force Academy."

He doesn't say anything. Just swallows. And now I'm embarrassed because Sober Me remembers Lev has a huge problem on his hands—his *future*—and instead of helping him, all I do is sulk and give him whiplash.

Our hands find one another—mine wet, his dry and rough—and our fingers lace and play with one another, doing the soothing thing we used to do when we were BFFs. Somewhere between a thumb war and piano playing.

"Come on," I whisper, stroking his thumb with the pad of mine. "If you won't tell Uncle Dean he is overstepping, I will. You were born to become a pilot. Your résumé is flawless."

More staring. I don't know what he's thinking, and that scares me because I *always* know what Lev's thinking. Used to, anyway.

"Marx, point taken. I look haggard." I disconnect our hands, grabbing the towel from the sink and wrapping it against my body to hide it. "Anyway, about the Air Force Academy—"

"You don't look haggard." His voice comes out thick and gruff. Honey soaked.

My throat dances with a swallow. "I don't?"

He shakes his head.

"What do I look like, then?"

"You look like the love of my life, who I'm scared to death of losing."

My heart. My dang mangled heart is about to be vomited out of my mouth and onto the floor. Lev is telling me he is in *love* with me.

I open my mouth to confess the truth. That I've always been in love with him.

That I want to get better. But as soon as the first syllable slips out of my mouth, loud bangs fill the bathroom. The door shakes on its hinges from the force of a fist.

"Bailev!" It's my dad, and he sounds exactly like what a dad should sound like when he knows his naked daughter is locked in a bathroom with a sexy football captain who spends twenty-five percent of his awake time watching porn. "Get your asses out, pronto. I thought Mel was watching Bailey."

"No. She is taking care of Sissi while Penn and Daria show the sitter around," I shout back.

"Well, *evidently*." Dad sounds pissed. "Open the damn door before I break it, then use it as a weapon against Lev."

Hurriedly, I put on panties, a pair of Lululemons, and a 49ers hoodie. Lev adjusts his hard-on before opening the door. His sharp cheekbones are stained pink, and his Adam's apple is rosy.

Dad is wearing a death glare, standing on the other end of the threshold with his fists curled.

"Bails, did he act inappropriately?" He is asking me but staring at Lev.

I sigh. "No, unfortunately."

Lev gives me a *really?* look. I give him a private grin only he can see..

"Did you take a look?" Dad thunders at Lev.

"No, sir."

"Are you lying to me right now?" Dad's eyebrows shoot up.

"Yes, sir. Sorry, sir. It's not my fault you make good-looking kids."

Dad shakes his head with a sigh. "She okay?"

"She's right here," I say through gritted teeth. "Still capable of answering a question, thank you very much."

"Bitching and complaining but sober." Lev ignores me.

"Good. Enjoy your *very* cold shower, Lev."

"You're welcome, Jaime."

"Apparently, *you're* welcome," Dad bites out after Lev's back. "Also, what happened to *Uncle* Jaime?"

"With the things I want to do with your daughter, safe to say we're not family." Then he whispers, almost inaudible, "*yet*," and again, I want to kiss this guy hard.

Dad starts after Lev with every intention of shaking him but then thinks better of it when he realizes I would be left alone for a few minutes.

I rearrange the hoodie to cover my wet hair and skulk out of the bathroom. Dad follows me. He looks dapper in a striped navy suit, his blond-gray hair pulled back into a bun.

"Where are you guys off to?" I toss today's clothes into the laundry basket, incredibly aware of how close I am to my suitcase—and the drugs inside it.

"Drinks with this *Yellowstone*-type bullshit cowboy." He blocks my way to the closet. My fingers itch to rip the seam of my suitcase and take my pills out. Marx, can't I have one moment for myself?

"Do you want me to stay and keep you company?" Dad suggests. "We can catch a movie. Veg out in front of the TV like we used to."

"Lev and I have some stuff to talk about." I shake my head. "Thanks, though."

"You're sure he isn't overstepping?" Dad studies me intently. "Just because you grew up together and he means well, doesn't mean kid's got any idea what he's doing."

"Yes, Dad, I'm sure. If he were bad for my psyche, I would tell you."

"I love you, Bails."

"I love you too, Captain Rando."

"You'll get through this." His voice is steady, solemn. "*Impossible* is basically possible with some redundant letters."

"Um, this is not how language works." And then, because my head is a jumbled mess and I truly do feel lost in these bones I grew up in, I say, "It just feels so stupid that I made it this far without any issues, and at age nineteen I'm about to lose everything I worked for."

"It's not the years that age us, baby. It's the experience that comes with them." The look he gives me is disarming. "You're evolving, honey. And every up has a down. Smart people turn those downshifts into learning curves."

Dad studies me for a beat, then shakes his head. He fishes his phone out of his pocket and puts "Be Alright" by Dean Lewis on, and now I *really* want to cry because he remembers. Remembers this was the first slow song I ever danced to. With *him*. He was a chaperone at a freshman ball and the song came on and I loved it so much, but no boy wanted to ask me to dance in front of my father... so *he* did.

Dad did it right too. No shortcuts. Walked over. Asked me gingerly. Timidly. All my girlfriends *swooned*. He spun me on the dance floor, dipped me down, making me laugh, and told me I was the most beautiful girl in the room. And I believed him. Because to him, I knew I was.

Dad opens his palm in my direction, a humble smile on his face. "I know you're a professional dancer and I'm just an old man with his heart on his sleeve, but would you do me the honor?"

Wordlessly, I put my palm in his. He drops his phone on the bed, and I press my head to his chest, burrowing into his warmth. I close my eyes and move to the rhythm of the song, feeling so heavy with emotions, the moment so bittersweet it takes my breath away.

"Are you mad I stole your first dance?" His breath tickles at the baby hair fanning my forehead.

"Are you kidding me?" I squeeze him tight. "What a privilege, to have your first dance with the one boy you'll always love the most."

"What about Lev?" he asks after a beat.

I think about my first kiss. My first *time*. All with people who weren't Lev. "I think my destiny is that Lev will be my second every-thing." I sigh.

"Second," Dad says. "And if you wanna know my prediction—*last*."

For one moment—just a brief one—there are no painkillers. No pain. No Juilliard. No Thalia. No anxiety, panic attacks, crippling expectation, and confusion.

There's only Dad and me.

And the silent promise everything will be okay.

Everything is not okay.

Everything is far from being okay. In fact, *okay* is not currently even in the same universe.

My entire existence is in pain, my mouth is dry, and it must be a hundred thousand degrees in this place.

"Is it just me, or is it superhot in here?" I'm stomping across the landing of Uncle Vicious's Jackson Hole mansion. Cayden, Sissi, and the twins are upstairs with their nannies. It's just Lev and me, and Lev has been trying to get me to watch *Everything Everywhere All at Once*, but I keep wandering off from the couch.

I just wish he would give me *one* moment alone so I could pop a few pills and breathe normal again. I'm on the verge of a panic attack from the overwhelming emotions slamming into me all at once now that the Xanax and Vicodin are out of reach.

Lev stands up slowly, leaning a hip on the wall, eyes hooded. He's more cut than shredded lettuce, in a white V-neck and black sweatpants. "It's sixty-eight degrees according to the thermostat." He runs his tongue over his upper teeth. "Good number, don't you agree?"

"I'm *roasting*." I pull my hoodie off, standing in front of him with nothing but a sports bra and leggings. Outside, snow is falling down onto mounds of white. It looks like we're nestled inside a marshmallow bag.

I discard my hoodie, wiping off my sweaty face. "The thermostat must be broken. I feel like I'm inside a marathon runner's tanga."

"Yeah, Bails. It's called withdrawals," he says sadly.

Rolling my eyes, I walk over to the kitchen, fling open the glass door of the Sub-Zero fridge, and stick my head inside, groaning. I'm burning alive over here.

"This isn't even helping." I bang my forehead against one of the shelves.

Lev's arms wrap around me from behind, his chin resting on top of my head. "Come on, Dove. I'll fill you a cold bath and you can soak in it. I'll make you some lemonade too, okay?"

"Hmm." I turn around to hug him, and he squeezes me close, dropping kisses to my forehead like a top-grade book boyfriend. "That sounds good. You go fill that bath, I'll make us lemonades."

His chest rumbles against my ear. "Nice try. I'm not leaving you for a nano-fucking-second."

"Ugh, I hate you."

"I *love* you."

"You say that a lot."

"I mean it completely." He stands still, studying me under a thick fan of eyelashes. "Fuck it, I'm turning off the thermostat. The babies are swaggered or whatever it's called."

"Swaddled," I correct. "Yup."

"They'll survive," he mutters, then scowls. "They *will* survive, right? Baby Killer is a great rap name, not so much a title I wanna acquire for myself, though."

Sighing, I push off of him. "They're bundled up nicely. Plus, one of the suspected SID causes is overheating."

"Fuck. I'll turn it off but just on the first floor." He flicks off the device, then starts making us lemonade, all while keeping an eye on me. He's doing it the elaborate, overachieving way. *The Lev way.* Squeezing lemons, mixing sugar, crushing ice cubes. I pace back and forth. Sweat drips down the tip of my nose over the floor. *Drip, drip, drip.* It's hot. Too hot. Hot enough to do something reckless.

Wildness takes over me. I peel off my leggings, tug my hairband loose, wrench the door open, and run straight into a pile of snow. I dive into it. The snow melts around me, biting into my feverish flesh.

I rub my face against it, opening my mouth, my legs, my arms— letting it sneak into my bra and my panties. I moan and laugh and cry and promise myself that if I ever kick the habit, I will never *ever* use a painkiller again. Not even if I have surgery. Or a C-section. Or *both*. At the same time.

Muscular arms wrap around my waist from behind. They yank me from the hill of snow I'm perched over. Sleet tumbles off every crease in my body. I moan in protest as Lev chucks me over his shoulder as if I weigh less than a wristwatch and tramps back into the house, oozing dark energy. His back is a triangle of bulging muscles, and I rake my fingers along the slopes of his latissimus dorsi. His skin pebbles wherever it's exposed—elbows, forearms, even his fingers.

"Let me down. I said I'm hot."

"You don't have to say it," he mumbles, kicking the door open and making way too much noise. "I have eyes, and my dick is in complete agreement."

"I'm roasting, Lev. I need the snow."

"You'll catch pneumonia." He is going up the stairs, leaving the half-finished lemonade behind. My face is dangling dangerously close to his ass now, and I'm tempted to sink my teeth in for a cheeky bite.

"Actually, there's no scientific evidence linking cold, wet weather to respiratory infections. It's a myth," I point out.

"A myth, huh?" His fingers dig deeper into the back of my thighs, and my insides clench deliciously. "Consider me a Hellenist, then."

Lev drops me on the edge of my four-poster bed. He turns his back to me and throws my closet open, sifting through my stuff. I watch him, dread filling me. Is he searching for drugs again? I hope he doesn't go for my suitcase. But he comes back a few seconds later holding my...*pointe shoes?*

"Planning to work on your rond de jambe?" I bite out sarcastically. Apparently, I'm back to being shitty again. It's hard to keep up, though.

"Why'd you bring these along?" he asks, pulling the ribbons apart from the shoes callously.

I gasp. "What are you doing? It's so hard to resew—"

"Answer me," he cuts in, and I don't know why, but I'm kind of scared of him right now.

"I thought I might squeeze a practice or two in!" I snap. "Is that a crime?"

With the ribbons ripped from the shoes, he makes his way over to me with death in his eyes. "Arms up, Dove."

"You want to *tie* me?" If my eyes are as large as they feel right now, they must be taking over the entire state of Wyoming.

"Gotta leave you alone for a couple minutes and I don't trust you," he says dryly.

"What if there's a fire?"

"I won't be gone long enough for that to come up."

"Are we gonna open the trust issues Pandora's box?" I laugh coldly. "Because last I checked, you were the one who—"

"Arms up," he bites out again.

"Fuck you!"

"Trust me, baby, it's on my agenda. Your smart mouth will be the first to be full of me. Your pussy will be next, and finally, that perfect ass. Don't think I forgot about that pool scene. I'm going to fuck *all* of you and soon, but first, you'll be sober, willing, and of sound mind."

He scoops both my wrists and slams them above my head, using the satin ribbons to tie me to one of the columns. Uncle Vicious bought one of those vintage nineteenth-century poster beds with a wooden canopy, so there's no way I can wriggle myself out or drag the bed with me.

Also, is it just me, or is Lev *freakishly* good at restraining people?

"Is that why you're dipping your junk into a cheap knockoff?" I spit out as Lev double and triple ties the satin around my wrists while his jaw flexes with irritation.

"Thought you liked Thalia."

"Well, I don't."

"What made you change your mind?"

"Her fucking the boy I love!" I buck back and try to kick him.

He steps back to admire his handiwork. His face is blank and serene, as though my love declaration didn't register at all. Lev hooks his finger into the satin to loosen it a little around my skin, then exits the room. A few moments later, he returns with a bowl laden with snow. It reminds me that I still feel as overcooked as a Thanksgiving turkey, and I whimper in self-pity.

"I'm going to run a cloth with some snow along your body to take care of that fever, all right?" He crouches down to my eye level.

I nod. Swallow. "Lev?"

"Yes, Dove?"

"I need a distraction."

"It took Leo Tolstoy six years to write *War and Peace*." He moves the cloth up and down my body. "And the same amount of time for me to read it."

I groan in frustration. I can't concentrate on anything or bring myself to laugh.

"Let's see what else...oh!" Lev says. "Abraham Lincoln was also a professional wrestler. He had a 299 and 1 record. Only one loss."

"*Armph.*"

"Also, Reagan helped Barry Manilow write 'Copacabana.'"

"Are you making all those things up?" I seethe.

"No! Google it." Lev lifts two fingers in a scout's honor. "Okay, don't Google that last one. But everything else is legit."

"Untie me," I demand.

"Nah, it makes my job easier."

"The ribbon bites into my wrists," I lie.

"Oh." Lev, being the most considerate man on planet earth, quickly loosens the tie, tossing it on the floor. I let my arms drop to my lap and massage at the tender part with a wince.

Lev grabs a chair from a desk nearby and takes a seat in front of my bed, redirecting his attention to the stupid, snow-covered cloth and pats it across my belly like a midwife in a '50s movie. I'm only wearing my bra and panties and would like to be treated like an irresistible femme fatale, not a lady who is about to perish during childbirth.

"More fun facts?" he suggests charmingly.

I produce a sound from the back of my throat.

"How does this feel?" he asks, focusing on my face as he brushes the cloth up and down my torso. I fall backward on my elbows, spreading my legs in front of him.

"Like we're reenacting *Jersey Girl*. Can you put some snow down here too?"

"*Bailey.*" He gives me a pleading, please-don't-do-this-to-me look. His erection can be seen from neighboring planets. He is obviously turned on and wants to do the right thing by me.

"Oh, come on. We both know you and I are going to fuck each other's brains out now that I'm no longer uptight and you're no longer my lovestruck sidekick. Might as well take advantage of our time together before I go off to Juilliard and you go off to play college football because you're too much of a pussy to stand up to your dad."

Wow. Withdrawal-suffering Bailey is a bitch. Lev doesn't fail to notice that.

He grabs my foot and places it on his hard thigh, running the cold cloth down my inner thigh, teasing me. "First of all, I was never your lovestruck sidekick. You wanted someone to baby—someone to practice your nurturing nature on—so I humored your ass." He stops right at the junction between my thigh and groin, knowing he is driving me crazy with need. "Second of all, you're high if you think you're going back to that school. Since you and I both know that you're currently sober, might as well admit it's time for a plan B."

"What!" I shriek. "Of course I'm going back. I have a practical exam in four weeks."

"Uh-huh."

"I *do*!" I thrash and kick at his chest.

He catches my ankle and squeezes. "Stop moving."

"No, you stop talking! Why did you say that?" And then, because apparently, I have left my faculties back in California and have zero self-control, I start sobbing uncontrollably. I jerk away from him, roll around on the bed, bury my face in my elbow, and cry. I'm not being quiet about it, either. I'm wailing and howling, and I'm pretty sure the kids sleeping in the other rooms can hear me.

Lev confirms my suspicion when I feel his hand rubbing at my back. "Shhh. Bails, you'll wake up Den and Sissi." The twins are down the hall, but my lungs are showing good capacity to wake them up too.

No matter how low I've stooped, I still care about those kiddos. So I stifle my sobs by biting into a pillow. I'm bawling even harder now, but the linen swallows my tears and snot and saliva. I wonder if I finally hit rock bottom.

"Bailey. How do I make you feel better?" Lev asks desperately somewhere above my head, still stroking my back with the damp cloth. "Tell me what to do."

But I'm too stuck in my own head. In my paranoia of failing. In the scorching, torturing arms of withdrawal. In all those feelings I have been trying to keep at bay.

I ball into a human knot of emotions, my whole body shaking.

Suddenly, I feel something weird happening. I swallow a hiccup before I can decipher what it is, my face still plastered to the pillow.

Did he just…?

Yup. Lev shoved snow into my panties. Took a handful of white fluff and rubbed it into my core. My whimpers stop, and I hiccup once. The tantalizing damp and cold feeling between my legs is spreading to other regions and my nipples harden.

"Is this what you need right now, Dove?" His hoarse tenor licks at my spine. Confident fingers stroke the slit of my ass all the way down to my pussy from behind through my wet panties. When he gets to my clit, he pushes the fabric aside and pinches the bundle of nerves with a dusting of snow on his fingertips. I buck my ass backward. "Does this help?"

My only response is a loud, desperate groan.

Lev is distracting me. He is doing what I asked him to. Taking my mind off the withdrawal even though we both know that this is torture for him. He didn't want to claim me tonight. He wanted us to do this differently. A part of me wants to stop this for him. So he'll get the chance to do it right. But I'm too selfish right now. Too needy.

On my knees and with my back to him, I back toward him, awarding him access.

"No," I hear him drawl like a brusque king. "Use your fucking words. I'm not your *lovestruck sidekick*." Welp. I'm going to pay for that one for eternity.

"You want my words?" I peer at him from over my shoulder, locking my gaze with his. There's a blaze behind those emeralds. It promises to burn down everyone and everything in his way to have me. "Fine, I'll give them to you. I'm sober right now—unhappy but sober nonetheless—and there is nothing I want more than for you to taste me, fuck me, use me, and come inside me. You're right. You were never my lovestruck sidekick. You were the boy I was deathly scared of because I knew you had power to destroy everything I've worked for. And when I got into Juilliard…" I hesitate, my breath catching. "I was too afraid I'd actually choose to stay just so I could be near you, so instead, I broke both our hearts. Happy now that the truth is out? How's that for words?"

"Sufficient," he clips out.

He's never been more beautiful than he is right now. Erotic and powerful, all corded muscles and hungry eyes. Lev flips me on my back, grabs the back of my knees, and drags me along the mattress. He stops when my ass is on the edge of the bed, hovering in the air, and spreads my legs wide. I hear the scrape of his chair over the parquet. He hoists my legs over his shoulders. I'm bare before him and he can see my entire pussy, only the fabric of my underwear between my lips.

Lev paws some snow from the bowl and shoves it into one of my bra cups. I drop my head back and hiss, the delicious chill over my warm skin sending tremors up my spine. I'm leaking all over the linen and I don't even care.

"Lev," I rasp, pushing my bra down to expose my nipples. "Please, I—"

"Shut up, Bails. If you don't talk, at least I can pretend it's a fantasy and I'm not really doing this to you." He grabs my jaw and pushes snow into my mouth—lots of it—to keep my mouth shut. I could spit it out, but I moan around it, my teeth sensitive to the cold, when he claws the rolled sports bra and yanks me forward. He wraps his mouth around my snow-covered nipple, sucking on the cold with his hot mouth.

I fall apart into a trillion pieces at the sensation. He grabs more snow and starts playing with my nipple. One moment he rubs snow over it, the other he licks it better. I hump the air as he works my tits.

"I feel so empty," I groan.

He shoves snow into my pussy.

I'm trembling all over, about to experience the most violent orgasm to be recorded on planet earth. A sound other than our panting penetrates the air, and when I open my eyes, I realize the chair Lev was sitting on is askew on the floor, and he is climbing on the bed atop of me, covering my body with his huge frame. His lips crash over mine. An unrestrained snarl ripping out of his chest.

"Bailey."

"Lev."

He grabs the back of my neck and tongue-fucks my mouth in a way that is entirely too dirty from the boy who helped me figure out how to clean my braces when I was younger. The tip of his tongue is cold, but the rest of his mouth is hot. And with this kiss, he sucks my heart out of me—whole, clean, arteries included—so that all that's left in me is empty space and useless information they taught us in chem class.

"Daria saved Penn all of her firsts…but you, I want you to have all my seconds. All my lasts. All my everything."

"They're mine," he growls.

I almost gag when he thrusts his tongue deep into my mouth, rolling his hips between my legs, letting me feel what I do to him. He is thick and hard and *huge*, and I cannot wait for him to fuck my face.

"Distracted yet?" he rasps into our kiss, pulling my bra all the way down. It pushes my boobs up, and he takes a break from my mouth to trail his tongue along the outline of each of my nipples. He bites my pale flesh, leaving a dent of his perfect teeth.

"Very." I peel his white shirt off, then clasp my thighs around his waist, turning us over so that he's flat on his back and I'm straddling him. I splay my fingers over his chest. Over the Rosie tattoo on his ribs. And the compass on his chest—an homage to his love for aviation—when I notice something I've never seen before. Right atop his heart.

"What's this?" I run my index finger along the ink. He hisses, like it's still fresh, then looks away, blushing.

"You know what this is," he grumbles.

"Two doves," I choke out. "Us?"

There is a brief silence before he inclines his head. "Us."

"When did you get it?"

"On the day you turned me down." Our fingers find one another. "And I knew that it didn't matter because I'd still always be yours."

His dick is still throbbing and twitching between my legs.

"Well, I love it." I lean down and roll my tongue over it seductively. "Thalia has seen it?"

His nostrils flare. "She did. Even if she hadn't, d'you really think she needed to be clued in to how I feel for you?"

No. Because Lev and I were always endgame. We were both too proud, too scared, too much of perfectionists to blow it. We both know every single person we messed around with was nothing but a pawn. A collateral time-waste.

He reaches between my legs, pulling my panties so that they disappear inside my slit. The pain is delicious, and my toes curl around the crisp sheets. "Every second inside her, I thought about you."

He lets go of my panties, and they *thwack!* over my skin.

"Now, come on my fingers and tell me how much you want me."

He pushes two fingers into me, and on demand, I start convulsing and jerking, squeezing him inside me in a death grip.

"That's my good little lovestruck sidekick," he growls. "Had enough of me yet?"

Not nearly enough.

I drop to my knees between his thighs and start working.

CHAPTER EIGHTEEN
LEV

Miserable Fa…ah, screw it. Nothing is miserable about what's happening right now.

I should stop this. I know I should.

Not because Bailey doesn't know what she's doing—she does; she's completely sober—but because she is in a vulnerable position and I would do anything to take her mind off detoxing from drugs.

Temptation was designed to be yielded to, especially when it comes to the woman I love. *Especially* when the woman I love is on her knees between my legs, tits out and pushed together by her rolled down bra, looking at me like a lamb waiting to be slaughtered.

"You shouldn't do this if it feels wrong." My voice is thick and husky and *lying*. I want to be a gentleman, but I also want this girl to vacuum my cock into her mouth like the country's welfare depends on it.

Luckily for me, Bailey doesn't give me time to play hero. She curls her graceful fingers around my wrist and shoves my hand into her panties. She's slippery with juices and snow, still pulsating around me.

"Does this feel like I'm unsure?"

My command of the English language evaporates, along with my IQ when she reaches to lower my sweatpants. I help her, rolling my ass up, and my cock bobs out of the elastic. It is painfully dark and hard. The crown is purplish, the shaft engorged. I'm as thick as a fucking Smartwater bottle. Fuck my life and best of luck to Bailey. Because once she welcomes me into her mouth, I am going to fuck it until she can taste me for years to come.

Bailey reaches to hold me by the root before her blue eyes widen comically. "A Prince Albert?" She looks up, her sweet mouth falling open. "Plot twist!"

I shrug, mumbling, "You like shiny things."

"You did it for *me*?"

Who else? Other girls weren't even on the menu until recently. And the one that did manage to become a snack was tossed away promptly.

"Well…" I shift uncomfortably. "Yeah. Remember that one time you said you love jewelry on the body?"

"I was fourteen!"

"I have a good memory."

She lowers her head and swipes her tongue across the precum decorating my crown. It's a simple hoop with a small diamond. I'd actually seen Bailey wearing similar earrings—and yes, I'm aware this is all completely twisted.

"Does this feel good?" She flicks her tongue back and forth, tossing the piercing from side to side on the tip of my cock. I gather her beautiful face in my rough palms.

"Baby, you could bite this shit off and it would still feel good. I'm such a goner for you."

She grins with the tip of my cock inside her mouth, and I swear it is the most gorgeous smile I've ever seen. If I could snap a picture of this moment and put it as my screensaver, I would die a happy man. Unfortunately, I would also die a young one, once Jaime found out.

"Okay, now, sweetheart." I stroke her hair, and it feels so good, being here, with her. The subject of all my desires. "Don't worry about the length. Just suck on the tip a little, all right?"

She does. She only sucks on the crown, batting her lashes at me, nibbling like the good girl that she is. I don't expect the head she's giving me to be mind-blowing. To be fair, I don't even care what she does as long as she does it to me.

Apparently, though, I'm not the only one with the plot twists. She sheathes the base in her fist, then slowly brings my dick into her mouth an inch at a time until I feel the warm texture of the back of her throat. My balls immediately tighten, and I let out a hiss. She slowly tautens her lips around my dick, measuring her breaths to control her gag reflex.

God, she feels so good. So right. So *Bailey*. I don't know if it's the new her or the old her, but I know that it's her, and for now, that's enough.

"You don't have to do this if you don't..." I startle when I see tears leaking from her eyes, but I stop myself, because she looks up, a *shut your fucking trap* expression stamped over her angelic face.

Alrighty, then.

I start lazily thrusting into her mouth, already dangerously close to coming. In an ironic twist of fate, maybe I *should* be imagining someone else so I don't blow my load before she even gets accustomed to the size of my dick.

"Marx, Lev. What were they feeding you? Why is it so big?" Bailey complains as she starts jerking and sucking me off at the same time. "There's big dick energy, and then there's this. This is *Royal Pipelines* territory."

I choke on her name, concentrating on not blowing my load. She is so good at this. She is going down on me like it's her favorite thing to do, spitting and sliding her hand up and down my cock, then taking me in her mouth again and letting me hit the end of her throat.

"Dove," I groan, running my fingers through her golden hair. "Whose dick are you sucking, baby?"

"Yours."

"That's right. Your smart, 152-IQ mouth is wrapped around *my* dick. How many hands you got?"

"Two."

"Take the spare one and play with your nipples for me."

She does. I can ask anything I want from her and she'll do it. And maybe this is the wrong time and the wrong place, and I will *definitely* regret the way it happened in the morning, but she needs a distraction, and fuck, I need *her*.

Bailey angles her mouth sideways so my dick hits her inner cheek, then she sucks on it so hard I tilt my head back, stars exploding over my eyelids. My crown is all tingly, and I swear I'm about to detonate in her mouth before I even get to fuck it properly.

"Who taught you to do that, baby?"

Do you really wanna know, fucker?

"You think you're the only person in the world who watches porn?" she moans. "I've seen this done before—online."

Should've known she was going to make sex her bitch, just like every other aspect of her life: research, practice, and nail it.

"I'm going to come, so if you don't want me to…" I trail off, hoping it's not too late and I still have time to pull out.

"Come in my mouth," she prompts. My stomach bottoms out, the climax clenching my balls, and I feel the thick strings of cum coating her mouth. The linen beneath me is damp and all I can see is Bailey, sucking every drop out of me like a pro. Holy shit.

She doesn't stop sucking for twenty seconds after I come, making sure I'm all juiced out. Then she tips her head back and smiles at me.

"Did you swallow it all?" I ask throatily, stroking the hair out of her face softly.

She opens her mouth, and it's pink and clean. "Can you fuck me now?"

"I wish I could," my voice breaks. I hate to deny her. Deny myself. Deny *us*. "But I'll never forgive myself. I have another way to distract you, though."

She smiles. "As long as it's not fun facts, I'm in."

CHAPTER NINETEEN
LEV

Miserable Fact #611: Some prehistoric societies defleshed the bones of their dead.

I wake up with Bailey's taste still in my mouth.

Last night I found out my best friend's pussy is my favorite dessert. Screw red velvet cupcakes—I want Bailey on my tongue for breakfast, lunch, and dinner.

Our one-way ticket to Orgasmville last night came to an abrupt stop when we heard everyone filing back into the house just when she was riding my face, her ass bumping on the headboard while she was jerking me off. We both dressed in the nick of time. When Jaime and Mel burst in without knocking, they immediately asked why her bed was soaked—fortunately so was Bailey and her hair. I explained about the withdrawals, and thankfully, they were too panicked about her condition to suspect anything.

Still, Jaime seized the tip of my ear and dragged me down the hallway to my room, a fake smile plastered on his lips. He spoke through clenched teeth.

"My daughter is going through enough as it is, so if you complicate shit for her, I am going to be *extremely* unhappy. I've extended a lot of trust so far… Have you ever heard stories of what happens when I get extremely unhappy, Levy boy? It's rare but quite the sight."

"Yup." I refrained from wiping my brow. Everyone had heard the story of what he did to All Saints High's former principal, Mr. Prichard, for his inappropriate relationship with Daria, though I never got the exact details. "Trust me, if anyone here is going to break a heart, it's gonna be your daughter breaking mine."

"That, I'm okay with." He threw me in my room, dusting his palms off for good measure. Good for Jaime, man. For an old man, he sure had some juice in him.

Now, here I am, with morning wood the size of a french baguette and a stupid smile on my face, eager to start the day.

Mel spent the night in Bailey's room, so I *know* she is on her second day of not using. For a moment, I allow myself to indulge in cautious optimism.

I brush my teeth, comb my hair, and put on a pair of black insulated pants and a khaki crew shirt. On my way to the breakfast room, I stop at Bailey's. I hear the shower running in the en suite and open the door to surprise her. Not only have I seen this girl naked, I can write a dissertation about every beauty spot and blemish on her body.

What I don't expect is seeing Mel leaning against the vanity, filing her nails while Bailey is in the shower.

"Oh, sorry." I have the good manners to lower my gaze and make a move to close the door.

Mel pushes off the vanity, unimpressed. "I'm giving you five minutes. Spend them wisely. *Fully* clothed."

"Mom! You shouldn't let me replace one addiction with another," Bailey shrieks, and for one, perfect moment, she's the Old Bailey.

"You're not gonna get addicted to sex, honey. UTIs run in our family."

Melody leaves, and I turn to look at my best friend through the glass, arching my eyebrows. "Not sure that was meant for my ears."

"It definitely was, mainly to embarrass me." She rubs a coal soap bar on her arms. "Is this off-putting to you?"

"You could swim in barf every morning and I'd still not find you off-putting."

Bailey turns off the water and I open the glass door of the shower and she's in my arms. We're kissing, the water sweet on her lips. Actually, Mel wasn't far off. I *am* hoping if I give Bails enough pleasure, she'll forget about the drugs and settle for me.

I grab her hips and kiss my way down her neck, licking her tits, her nipples, sucking her side boob into my mouth. Pancakes and bacon can go fuck themselves. This is the tastiest thing on earth.

"Sleep well?" I kiss my way down her body, and she hooks her leg over my shoulder when I'm on my knees, leaning her back against the wall and falling open for me as my tongue flattens over her pussy and I start going down on her.

"Uh-huh." She fists my hair in her palm, tugging me here and there when I start licking and sucking and adding fingers. "Once I stopped feeling like I was in a furnace, it got better."

"Proud of you, Dove."

Then I give her a sobriety present, as I finish what I started last night, and make her come on my tongue.

Twenty minutes later, we're sitting at the table with the entire cul-de-sac clan, and everyone, and I mean *everyone*—including the goddamn catering staff, housekeepers, children, and decorative plants—seems to know what Bailey and I did in her room.

The first clue was us being fifteen minutes late. The second one was that orgasmic glow on our faces when we assumed the two empty seats at the table. Now, all the grown-ups are staring at us, while the toddlers hurl mini-waffles at one another.

I know they're judging me, but considering every motherfucker in this room has their own less-than-pristine happily-ever-after story, I'm not about to sweat about what people think.

"Have a good shower, sissy?" Daria makes a kissy face Bailey's way, popping a red grape between her glossy lips. "You look *uber* refreshed."

Bailey moves smithereens of scrambled egg on her plate with her fork, her face the picture of innocence. "I had to choose what to wear carefully. I run hot these days because of my, *um*, withdrawal."

Daria's smug beam vanishes. I disguise my chuckle with a cough.

"Try not to bite your toes off with that foot in your mouth," Vaughn drawls. The only reason Penn doesn't come to his wife's defense is because he missed Vaughn's taunt while trying to extract raspberry pieces from Sissi's hair.

"What about you, Lev?" Vicious takes a swing at me because making people uncomfortable is his lifelong passion. "Do you also run hot or just horny?"

Everyone chuckles, other than Cayden and Sissi, who snap their heads up curiously. "Who's hormie?"

"Homer," Racer corrects, deadpan. "Simpson."

"Wow." Knight takes a bite of his pastry, sitting back. "This is not uncomfortable at all. Keep going, everyone."

"So now I'm getting trashed for staying behind and taking care of my best friend while everyone else went out and got tanked?" I arch an eyebrow.

"You're not old enough to get tanked," Dad points out.

"Racer is not old enough to get tanked, either, and he tagged along," I quip back.

"Can everyone please stop using that word in front of the children?" Auntie Emilia flinches.

"Sorry." Daria sighs. "Old *is* a triggering word. Which is why I already started on Botox and Juvéderm. Minimal but makes a world of difference." She winks.

Our families are nuts. No wonder we all ended up coupling with one another.

"You heard my wife. The next shithead to say the T-word gets booted," Vicious announces.

"*Shit!*" Sissi tosses star-shaped cucumbers in the air, cooing eagerly. "Shit, shit, shit!"

"Well, this went great." Knight gives Vicious the thumbs-up.

"Mama and Dada go on a shit," Cayden says.

"*Ship,*" Luna coos. "Mama and Dada went on a ship."

Uncle Vicious throws daggers through his pale blue eyes at everyone at the table, toddlers included. "Everyone in this room is about to be sent packing. If it makes my wife uncomfortable, it goes."

"Should've given your seventeen-year-old self the same advice." Jaime chugs orange juice, and he and Trent fist-bump each other.

Daria laughs and picks a fussy Sissi up from her high chair. Trent turns the TV on and flips to the sports channel on the grounds that "we need a segue more than I need a stiff drink."

Small talk about drafts and college football ensues. *Of course,* Penn, Dad, and Knight all turn to look at me, with Trent and Racer jumping in eagerly.

It's not long before the conversation turns from football to *my* football. After all, Penn is a 49ers star, and everybody at the table is eager to know if they're going to have another NFL hero in the gang.

"So, did you get any offers yet, Lev?" Penn lounges back, crunching a piece of bacon between his straight, white teeth.

"Nope," I lie, feeling my chest constricting as I do. I'm just delaying the inevitable. I *will* go to college and play football. That's what Dad wants, and I want him to be happy. "Sure they'll come soon."

"That's weird. I was sure Michigan was gonna make an offer for you." Penn's hair flops over his forehead. He gives Leo DiCaprio in *Titanic* a run for his money. "Spoke with a pal of mine who knows the coach. He's been pining for your ass since freshman year. Said it was a done deal."

Fuck my life sideways with a pair of scissors.

"Maybe we should call the school. Find out where it stands on their end. The USPS is unreliable these days," Dixie chirps. First of all, way to blame the postal service for my own doing. Second, now Dixie is playing mommy? Screw that.

Dad snaps his fingers. "Dixie's right."

"Dixie isn't my mom—no matter how hard she fucking wants to be—so I won't be taking suggestions from her," I announce cheerfully.

Everyone's heads snap my way. Stunned faces scan mine. I've never spoken like that to anyone before, let alone Dixie, who is a pretty awesome chick. But I don't want to get caught on my lie. If Dad finds out about the Michigan offer, I'm toast. *And* I still haven't filled out the application to the Air Force Academy, even though the deadline is fast approaching. My oxygen levels seem to drop when I think about it.

"*Whoa*. What crawled up your ass?" Dad scowls.

"Language!" Mel tosses her hands in the air.

"My business is mine, and I don't want it discussed at the breakfast table." I drop my utensils.

"We're talking about your college plans, not your anal hygiene," Penn points out. "Chill, dude."

Bailey bumps her thigh against mine, signaling that now is a good time to confess my plans to apply to the Air Force Academy. And I should, I really should. But I can't. Not with Knight's eyes boring into mine from across the table. I know this look. It's a look that says, *Dad has been through so much and barely made it. You can't do this to him. I won't let you.*

Overall, Knight is happy with his life. But there's one point of contention between us—he says I always look for creative ways to die, between the fast cars and pilot dreams, and *I* say it's none of his business.

I hope my face can convey my answer to him, which is, *Part of the reason why Dad is so fucked-up is because you were high on everything you could crush into powder while Mom was taking her last few breaths, so don't make me atone for your sins, pal.*

Did anyone say fun times? If this is my tribe, I want to be a lone wolf.

"No, that's all right. Lev's right. I'll mind my own business." Dixie smiles apologetically, putting a hand over Dad's to calm him down. "I didn't mean to overstep. I hope you know that, Levy."

"No, fuck that." Knight snorts out, standing up, his chair scraping the floor. "Don't apologize to him. You were just trying to help."

"*Language*," Edie singsongs.

"I'm about to throw everyone but my wife out." Vicious sounds as serious as a heart attack.

"The children you can put down carefully outside our door," Emilia suggests. "They didn't do anything."

I shoot up to my feet. Bailey is upright in an instant, beside me. I shift my weight onto my knuckles, which are flat against the table. "I suggest you shut your trap, Knight, since the entire reason why we're all having this conversation is because *you* weren't good enough for the NFL."

"I opted out." He yawns, feigning boredom.

"Yeah." I snort. "But you won't let me do the same, right? Someone has to appease Daddy dearest, and we both know it's not gonna be you."

That sets Knight off. "It's not about football, dumbass. For all I care, you can go get a liberal arts degree in feminist knitting and never play ball again. It's about the dangers."

Dad frowns, looking between us. "What dangers?"

"Lev wants to become a fighter pilot," Bailey supplies, and I shouldn't feel embarrassed and self-conscious, but I am.

"Lev *can't* be a fighter pilot," Knight says decisively.

"Why not?" I snarl. "Because all *you* can do is coach a little league team and take pictures with man thongs?"

"First of all, they're called *thonginis*." Knight's outrage at the mistake is written plainly on his face. "Second, *as previously stated*, I don't give one crap about your footba—"

"I do," Dad pipes in. "He's got talent. Why not use it?"

"Because I don't want to!" I toss my hands in the air.

Dad looks surprised. Offended. His laser eyes are aimed at me. "What are you talking about? I thought you loved football."

"That's because you're so busy mourning your dead wife, you don't look up and see what's right in front of you!"

Uncle Trent sighs and takes a sip of his orange juice, slanting his gaze to his wife. "I told you we should've gone to the Canary Islands, just us and the kids."

"Knight, you need to calm down." Luna puts an arm on my brother, and he immediately sits down, the pussy-whipped asshat that he is. "This is not the time nor the place."

"Sorry, Moonshine."

Dad's eyes are still on mine. "Got anything to say to me?"

Let me make my own decisions.

Stop hanging your hopes and dreams and happiness on me.

But the words don't come out. They're stuck in the same black hole inside me where I keep all my secrets.

Instead of gently releasing them, I turn around and storm off like a little bitch.

CHAPTER TWENTY
BAILEY

Seeing Lev chastised and unhappy makes me want to blow up the entire world. To mix hydrogen azide and potassium chlorate and put my chemistry studies to terrible use.

But I'm Bailey. Nice. Sweet. Nonconfrontational. Only recently, this girl is a total stranger to me. Like I shed snakeskin and dumped it when I boarded the plane back from New York to San Diego. Ever since I stopped with the Xanax and Vicodin, I started feeling. *All* the time. Sadness. Confusion. Anger. Jealousy. Love.

I try to pretend I'm focused on skiing and not on Lev looking like a kicked puppy, but it's hard. He is the most talented, capable, funny, smart person I know. His only crime is loving his father and brother too much. Letting his family control the narrative of his life. Kind of like how I let mine do to me.

I know Knight and Dean mean well. They're good people, trying to look out for their own. Dean is petrified of losing his sons, and Knight wants to compensate for years of putting his parents and brother through hell. They'd both take a bullet for him in a heartbeat. Problem is, Lev is currently the one bleeding for them.

After a few warm-up sessions on the green trails, Uncle Vicious announces he and Emilia are taking the aerial tram to the pro trails. The entire gang decides to join them. Last Christmas, Vicious bought his wife an unorthodox gift. Amongst the black, advanced skiing trails on the mountain, he bought a trail that belongs only to her. The Pink Trail. Pink to his black, I guess.

Everyone I know ranges from a capable to an amazing skier, Lev included. Over the years, when they were eagerly hitting the snowy mountains, I was busy curling up with a good book back in the mansion while on a break from competitive ballet—and that was pre-injury and pre-overdose. So when I announce I'm sitting this one out, no one is surprised or suspects a thing.

"I'll take Bailey home," Lev volunteers, stepping forward.

"No, I can do it." Daria flicks her ski glasses up, bundled in her huge, pink attire. "I'm sure you need some time off."

"From her?" Lev slides his gaze over my body with a smile that doesn't reach his eyes. "Never. Let's go, Dove."

"I saw the look you gave my daughter," Dad calls out to our backs when we turn to take the main road back to the resort's exit. "You're supposed to be taking care of her, not taking fucking liberties."

Lev's jaw clenches. "She means more to me than her body."

"Her body shouldn't be something you even think about with what she's going through."

We make our way down the entrance, where Uncle Vicious's driver awaits in an Escalade.

"Thanks for volunteering as tribute." I elbow Lev, initiating contact so he'll finally pounce and cover me with kisses.

"Yeah, course," he replies tersely. He seems deep in thought.

I want to help him sort through whatever's going on in his head, so I say, "You have to tackle your beef with Knight first, explain to him that your aspirations and life goals are a need, not a want, then break the news to your dad."

"I don't wanna talk about it." Lev shakes his head.

But I'm a problem solver. The one with all the answers. So I add, "Or you can skip the whole Knight routine and just go straight to—"

"Enough!" Lev snarls, halting his strides. "I said I don't wanna talk about it."

"Hey, I'm just—"

"You're just about the last person I'll seek advice from, that's who you are."

Rolling my lips over my teeth, I keep my head down the remainder of our journey to the car. The sting morphs into a full-blown burn. How dare he talk to me like this when all I tried to do was help? Somewhere in the back of my head, Old Bailey points out that Lev is still raw from the breakfast showdown. But Current Bailey—the one still experiencing mood swings and withdrawal symptoms—demands constant reassurance. Which is probably why I hear the next words leave my traitorous mouth: "You better break up with Thalia when we get back home."

This was the wrong thing to say. Lev is no pushover. He resumes his steps toward the Escalade, which rolls into view in silhouette, with white-tipped mountains and wooden inns behind it.

"Or else *what?*" There's a perilous edge to his voice. But he is not the only one who is raw right now. If he wants a fight, I'll give him one.

"Do you have a creative way to explain to her why you spent this trip volunteering your face as my rodeo horse?" I look away so he doesn't see the red on my cheeks or the tears in my eyes.

Lev sneers. "Who says I'm gonna tell her?"

"If you won't, I will," I snap. If she means as little to him as he claims, why can't he let her go?

Lev shrugs in my periphery. "I can fuck the entire zip code and Thalia would still say 'thank you' when I give her an STD for Valentine's Day."

Nausea hits the back of my throat. "Wow. You're disgusting."

"You're the one who's been fucking around with a taken man."

Whoa. Someone needs to hold my earrings. "Who even are you?"

"I'm the product of too many expectations and not enough fucks to give," he replies sourly, before adding, "This is not the start of something, Bailey. Not until you get your ass in a serious rehab program. I'm not gonna willingly chain my destiny to that of an addict."

"I'm not an addi—"

"Yeah, you are. An addict. A liar. A good, tight cunt to be sure—but not good enough to ruin my life over."

And this is it. The crazy train has officially left the platform. Wave your handkerchiefs and toss your flowers. The gloves are off and I'm about to murder him with my bare hands.

"At least I went after my dream. Fought for what I care for. You're a coward, Lev. A coward and chickenshit. You are going to die miserable and unfulfilled just because you're too scared to stand up to your daddy. You're just jealous because I did what you never could: went for what I wanted."

His jaw flexes under his taut, golden skin. "You should focus on your sobriety, not hooking up."

"Hadn't realized all we did this weekend was a casual hookup." I let out a humorless, joyless laugh.

"Yeah, well, it was."

He's lying, isn't he? I am usually so good at reading people—Lev, especially—but I don't trust my own judgment anymore. Not when it comes to us, and not when it still feels like I'm floating on a cloud of acid.

"Why don't you go back to skiing with everyone else? I know my way home," I suggest. Just in time, since we're right in front of the Escalade. I expect Lev to reject the idea, channel his inner caveman, and tell me he would never leave me alone right now. But he surprises me by hitching a careless shoulder, glancing at his watch.

"Yeah, good idea. See you around. Or you know, not."

With an icy smile and impeccable demeanor, he turns around and walks away.

It takes me five whole minutes to unglue myself from the pavement and slip into the car. I'm way past shocked and well into dazed territory. I spend the car ride stewing in my own rage. The overpowering, acerbic tang of betrayal coats my tongue.

Lev isn't going to break up with Thalia. Maybe he never meant to. He's a player, and I got played. He didn't just do a number on me. An entire calc book is more like it.

When I get into the Craftsman mansion, the only people present are the nannies and children. Neither can judge or stop me. And that's when it hits me.

I'm alone. Truly and fantastically alone. Left to my own devices.

I take the stairs two at the time, flying like a bullet toward my room. My hands are shaking when I flip my Dior suitcase and pat the black fabric along the horizontal zipper. I sewed a secret pocket on the right-hand side. I feel for the stitch, itching to rip it apart, only to find it is already loose. It's unlike me to half-ass a job, but maybe my sewing is a little rusty. I push my index and middle fingers inside, feeling for the pills. Instead, something else hits my fingertips. Some sort of…paper? I pull it out slowly, finding a yellow note. I unfold it, my eyes wide as they scan its content.

GO TO REHAB, BAILEY.

L

Lev found my drugs. He found them and got rid of them. I want to scream. Correction—I *do* scream. I kick and rip things apart. I open the toilet seat to see if maybe I can salvage some of the pills—he must've thrown them there; when'd he do that?—and I realize that two things are true at once: 1. He is right. Rehab isn't just calling to me—it is screaming my name in capital letters. And 2. I would die before becoming *him.* Before giving up my dream to appease my family. Juilliard is not the Air Force Academy. It is not interchangeable.

I go downstairs to the kitchen. Find a stray bottle of whiskey and polish it off. It is awful and not at all like painkillers. I end up barfing most of it. The minutes chase one another, transforming into hours. The alcohol soaks into my system. Dying doesn't seem like a horrible idea right now.

Then—*plot twist!*—as I lie head-down on the couch, head spinning, I feel a cool hand over my sweaty back. "Oh, Bailey."

It's Lenora. She stayed behind. She is breastfeeding the twins. *Duh.*

She thinks I'm asleep—or maybe she knows I definitely don't want to talk about it—because all she says is, "It's okay to have demons. We all do. But it is not okay to let them win."

The day darkens, and the house fills with yellow, warm light. Everyone starts filing in after a day of skiing. I somehow managed to drag myself to the shower and brush my teeth twice before they got here, so I don't think anyone can tell I've been drinking. Maybe just Lev, who has my soul on speed-dial and can read me like an open book. Luckily—and I use the term loosely—he isn't paying attention to me. Breezes right past me like I'm air on his way to his room.

We eat dinner. Have small talk. Pretend like everything is hunky-dory. Dean, Lev, and Knight heatedly discuss movies that are so bad they're good, bodily functions, and the NFL. They're acting like they didn't have a nuclear showdown just a few hours ago over almond-flour waffles and bacon. Then we all retire to our rooms. Mom is on night watch with me. She doesn't say anything to me when she sees how I wrecked the room. Just mutters something about how Uncle Vicious owes my dad some favors and he better not have a tantrum about it.

I fully expect Lev to contact me. He doesn't. Not during the night or the morning after it. Not when I am dragged to one of the green trails by Racer, Knight, and Luna, who try to teach me how to ski. And not when we all sit down for another dinner.

The night before we're scheduled to board the plane back home, I blink first and break the silence. I text him under the covers once Mom is asleep.

Bailey: Congratulations on finding them.

Bailey: The pills, not your balls. Those are still MIA, as your family can attest.

Aaaaand we have reached the truth-bomb portion of the evening, ladies and gents.

Lev: You seemed to know exactly where they were when you sucked nice and good on them the other day.

Bailey: That was before I knew you were a cheater, a scumbag, and a narcissist.

Lev: Check into rehab, Bailey.

Bailey: I'm actually glad you didn't apply to the Air Force Academy. Our country needs people with ACTUAL courage. Not a spoiled brat who wants to play Top Gun.

Lev: Check into rehab, Bailey.

Bailey: Don't bother contacting me ever again. We're done.

Lev: CIRB. Good night.

CHAPTER TWENTY-ONE
BAILEY

AGE SEVENTEEN

It's been seven hundred and forty-six days since Rosie died.

Seven hundred and forty-six days since Lev and I have started sleeping in the same room. In the same bed. In each other's arms.

Seven hundred and forty-six days since our scents began mixing together into a perfume called love.

Seven hundred and forty-six days since I promised to never leave, to never betray him, to never disappear.

Humans are adaptable creatures. Designed to mold themselves into shape even in the harshest conditions. You'd think things would get easier for me. You'd be wrong.

The complications keep piling up. The warm, inviting morning wood that keeps bumping into my flesh under the blankets. The way I notice things about him I had been blind to before. Like his cheekbones, that have recently chiseled into perfection. Or the way his hair turned from straight and silky to coarse and floppy over last summer. The way his body filled out everywhere—biceps, abs, shoulders, back. Biology is doing a number on me.

Shut up, evolutionary psychology. I'm trying to do the right thing here.

But it's terrifying. To see a hot-as-hell man spurting out of your cute, unassuming BFF.

I see the way he looks at me. With unapologetic hunger. I want him to eat me whole. To gorge on his forbidden fruit, seeds and all.

But I'm stuck in this stupid, boring role. I'm his best friend, his saint, his salvation. I cook his favorite meals, hug him to sleep, and send him reminders for important games and homework that's due.

Like right now, I am sitting on the bleachers, cheering him on as he wins the state championship against St. John Bosco, making history for All Saints High.

The game is over. The crowd is on its feet, cheering. I jump the highest and shriek the loudest. Uncle Dean grabs me by the jacket and pulls me into a hug, ecstatic. I have tears of joy in my eyes when his brother points at Lev and roars, "That's my brother over there! What a freaking legend!"

Happiness alters into pent-up sexual frustration as Dean, Knight, and I make our way down the bleachers and I catch the sight of Lev peeling off his shirt, exposing his abs, every ridge and curve so defined he looks Photoshopped. His skin is golden, glistening, and demands to be licked to its last inch. His hair is a mess and I want to comb it with my fingers. I stop a foot away from him and wait patiently as he spits out his mouthguard and hugs his brother and father. There's a bottle of his favorite iced tea in my hand. Then he turns to me.

"I'm so proud of you!" I exclaim, opening my arms wide, expecting a hug.

"Screw your polite hugs. We just won the state championship!"

He picks me up by the back of my thighs and hoists me in the air, spinning around. I laugh and shriek as he tickles me, elated, and there's a good chance I've never been this happy my entire life. Not even during my own victories.

"Lev!" I squeal as he tosses me in the air like I'm a toddler, grinning, his eyes coated with tears. I know those tears are there not only because he brought his dad happiness but also because his mother couldn't be here to see it.

Lev keeps his hands firmly on my waist when he brings me

down, tucking my head under his chin, nestling me close. "Couldn't have done it without you. Thanks for being the ground beneath my feet...or, you know, some shit." He winks.

"Are you calling me flat?" I scrunch my nose.

"I'm calling you gravity."

"Sounds like a stripper's name."

He laughs so hard, his dad thinks he's choking.

I urge him to go celebrate with his friends and promise him a thousand times that I'm okay, that I don't mind we're not spending time together, that I have homework to do anyway.

But as I drive home, for the first time, a selfish thought pops into my head. The idea of him partying it up with hot girls right now makes me nauseated. And the fact that this bothers me is a huge red flag. I cannot afford to be jealous. Jealousy leads to impulsiveness. Impulsiveness to chaos.

I do my homework, clean my room, read a book, and glance at my watch every two seconds. I do that until two in the morning, which is also when I check my phone. No texts from Lev. Still out, partying. I'm not sure if I'm more worried or jealous about it.

Let him be. He literally just won the state championship.

Trying to keep busy, I go outside to get the mail. I pull out a fat envelope, my heart racing in my chest. Could it be? How long has it been sitting there? Holy best news ever.

I rip it open in the stark darkness, aiming my phone's flashlight at the words. And there it is. The acceptance letter I've been waiting for since I learned how to walk.

Juilliard. I'm in.

One of the seven percent of applicants who actually gets accepted. Up against the most talented people in the world. A piñata of emotions bursts inside me. I want to announce the news, but Mom and Dad are asleep and Daria and Penn are in Paris, doing hot-couple shit. I could call one of my friends, but it feels wrong sharing this important news with someone random.

My fingers quake when I type the text message.

Bailey: Guess what?
Lev: Chicken butt.
Lev: So apparently I Benjamin-Button into a six-year-old after
    a few beers. Sorry about that. What's up, B?
Bailey: Can I call?
Lev: I mean, it's super noisy here at Finn's. I'm about to head
    back home in about an hour though if it can wait.
Bailey: It can't.
Lev: Uh-huh. What is it?
Bailey: I GOT ACCEPTED TO JUILLIARD!!!!!!!!!!!!!!!

My grand announcement is followed by big, fat nothing. One
minute turns into four, which turns into fifteen. No response. I go
back into our chat to see if maybe my last message didn't go through.
It did. I stare at the screen until it dies. Then blink, realizing for the
first time, I'm still outside my house, engulfed by the night. Weird
things are happening in my body right now. The piñata that just
burst inside me? It was full of rusty nails.

A century and a half later, a reply finally pops up.

Lev: That's great news. Proud of you, B.

I don't know why, but his message sinks into my skin and spreads
like a lethal injection.

After my undying support, my undivided attention, serving as
his human alarm clock every morning so he'd never miss practice,
cooking his chicken breast the way he wanted because he was super-
stitious about eating it before big games, when it was time to be
happy for me...he wasn't. He *isn't*. My big life news, my celebration
isn't even worth a FaceTime...

I take the stairs back to my room and curl inside my bed, facing the wall and closing my eyes. I really don't feel like waiting for him in his bed tonight. Hot tears roll down my cheek and into my mouth. I cry myself to sleep.

Sometime later, I feel my mattress dipping under familiar weight. A muscular body presses against mine from behind. He's warm and delicious and smells like home. That unique Bailev scent we both carry, mixed with a tinge of alcohol.

His arms circle around me and I'm helpless against his pull. I curse my inability to resist him when Lev nuzzles his face into the crook of my shoulder. Tears sting the backs of my eyeballs. Is there such a thing as loving someone too much? I suspect there is. I think he steals my sunshine. Swallows my light. I might be feeding myself mean stories to convince myself to leave for New York and not stay here with him, but seriously? Maybe we both need to find out who we are without each other.

"Dove." He burrows against my skull, sending shivers down my spine. "Fuck. What am I going to do without you? I need you. You're not supposed to leave. You're supposed to…I don't know. Be a good girl and stick around for me. Put me first."

He is drunk and I'm heartbroken and this is not a good combination for either of us. He also thinks I'm asleep, which is the only time the truth tumbles out of his mouth so easily.

"I should be happy for you, getting into Juilliard. I always knew you would. But my selfish ass can't see past the idea that you won't be close to me anymore."

He swallows audibly and I wonder if the universe forgot we are young and stupid and decided to descend every wrathful punishment God has in store on us.

"I used to lay awake with you in my arms for weeks and months and years, praying that you would break a leg. Tear a ligament. Get injured so you have to stay back here." Lev chokes on the admission, talking into my hair. "I'm so fucking awful, but I still hoped that. Hoped something would stop you. Because that someone can't be me. I can't do that to you."

A storm brews inside my body. He keeps talking, growing stiff in his briefs between my ass cheeks, which are clad in a pair of boy shorts. And I can admit it to myself now. How we haven't been platonic friends for a long time. Sex has hovered over our relationship for the last few years. We've been skimming the line of dry humping wordlessly every night. Accidentally brushing each other's abs, and nipples, and *everything*. He came close to the edge a few times. So did I. And we never spoke about it. We've been playing with matches for months. Now? We're drenched in gasoline. Soaked to the bone.

It's time to set this lie between us on fire.

We lie there for a long time, until I'm sure he's asleep. For one thing, he stops talking. Pouring all his secrets, about all the times he not-so-accidentally got off while we were in bed together. How he scared off all my potential suitors at school, how he once beat a guy from Las Juntas to a pulp for following me home when I didn't pay attention.

His breaths even out. I mull his words in my head all night. *Bailev*. Best friends. Thick as thieves. Always have each other's backs. And it's all bullshit. We're not friends. We're two people obsessed with each other, holding each other back. He doesn't want me to become a ballerina, and I don't want him to ever find true love. If we stick together, we'll end up resenting each other, then hating each other...

I know what I need to do and how I'm going to do it.

The sun slinks up from between fluffy, marshmallow clouds. The sky is painted pink and blue, and the moon is as thin as a fingernail dent. I gather my courage like the hem of a ballroom dress, turn around from the wall, and make a move to kiss Lev. To ruin everything.

I'm startled when I see he is already up, wide-awake and staring at me.

By the red spiderwebs on his eyeballs, I can tell he didn't sleep at all.

"Stay." His throat bobs with a swallow when he says, "Please, Dove. Just…just stay here. One more year. Then we can go together to New York when I graduate. Please don't leave me."

"Lev," I say. "You don't… You wanna go to Colorado for school."

But what I really want to say is *how dare you?*

What I really want to say is *I'd never ask you something like that. How can you do this to me? You know how serious I take my promise to Rosie to always take care of you.*

"Yeah. I know. You're right." He licks his lips. "Look, I got you something."

He turns around and rummages in his jeans on the floor. I hear rustling, my eyes focused on his corded, muscular back. In a few moments, I am going to ruin us—if he hasn't already. Lev turns back to me, plants something in my fist, then brings the fist to his mouth and kisses it. "Whenever you're ready, Dove."

I uncoil my fingers to find…a bracelet? No, two of them. With little wooden dove pendants. They're identical, with a simple black leather string.

"Carved it myself at the party. That's why it took me so long," he admits, blush creeping onto his cheeks. I thought he was hooking up with girls…when this is what he did? I'm speechless. "That way you'll never forget about us in New York when you become a superstar." He winks.

The smile on my face feels hollow. I gently rest the bracelets on the pillow between us. "Where did you get the wood?"

"Is now a good time to make a boner joke?"

"No."

"In that case, let's just say Finn's house has a credenza in need of replacing."

"Well, thank you," I say primly. "It's beautiful."

"That's it?" He quirks an eyebrow. He's used to my constant cooing and praising.

"No, that's not everything." We are so close, I can feel every inch of him, and I want to laugh that I told myself we were ever just friends.

"What else?"

I swallow hard. "Kiss me."

Lev's mouth falls open. "*Kiss* you?"

Nodding, I trail the tip of my fingernail along his neck. My fingers are trembling. I'm ruining us together, to save us individually. To give us a chance to blossom apart, not just together. "Isn't that what you've always wanted?"

"Yes." His pupils dance frantically, searching my face. "But I have a feeling this is a punishment, not a reward. Is this about my asking you to stay?"

It's about our entire relationship. It's about sacrifice. Redemption. About us finding who we are without being attached at the hip.

"It's just a kiss, Levy. Don't read too much into it. I just want to feel good."

He slides his long fingers through my hair, bringing my face close to his, and he is arrestingly beautiful—always but now especially. "I was born to make you feel good, Bailey Followhill." His breaths are slow, his heartbeat fast. "But I won't take a kiss from you. Not right now."

"Why not?" My lips curl in annoyance. Seems like he is very good at denying me everything I want.

"Because I don't want our first kiss to be like that."

"Like what?"

"Tinted by my anxiety and your anger." He brushes the tip of his nose over mine, holding my shoulders in his big bear palms. "When I kiss you, you will believe every unspoken word the kiss will say. You'll believe the *I love you*, the *It was always you*. You will see that I mean the *You and I are forever*. There will be no second-guessing."

His lips slant to the edge of my jaw, then move down to skim the column of my neck. The initial touch is an electric shock, and the world is thrown out of focus. The entire room is holding its breath—walls, furniture, ceiling. Then his lips move back up and close in on mine. It's a perfect lock-and-key match. His lips taste divine, but it's not them that make our kiss a once-in-a-lifetime event. It's the fact that it symbolizes the complete destruction of what we were until now. Best friends.

"Bailey?" Dad asks from behind my bedroom door. I gasp into Lev's mouth, panicked, but all he does is pry my mouth open and slip his tongue into my mouth, slowly and sensually exploring the area.

Dad presses. "I heard noises from your room."

Lev is chuckling into our kiss. I try to bite him, but that only makes him laugh harder. *Bastard.*

"Um, yes, Dad!" I call out, voice muffled. "Everything's fine!" More than fine, to be honest.

"Everything okay?" Marx, so rude. Why can't I have a neglectful family that leaves me to my own devices when they hear random whimpering coming from my room?

"I...was...crying?"

Awesome job, Bails. Nothing screams certainty more than finishing a sentence with a question mark.

Lev is nibbling on my lower lip before returning his attention to the inside of my mouth.

"Why were you crying?"

Who died and made you the Spanish Inquisition, Dad?

"It's...happy tears."

"You fucking bet," Lev mumbles into the side of my mouth, kissing and biting and teasing. As my father drones on about his patience running thin with my shenanigans, I focus on the magic unspooling between me and my best friend. The way he holds me in his arms.

"Why?" Dad insists.

"I'll tell you when I come out." *Thank you, Juilliard, for giving me news to break to him and inadvertently saving Lev's life.* "Just give me a few minutes."

"All right, baby."

Lev stops snacking on my skin and pops his head far enough for us to look each other in the eye. He is pressed on top of me. We're both grinning like lunatics. Then I remember what caused all of this, and my heart drops.

"I thought you said you weren't going to take a kiss from me?"

"This wasn't a kiss." He shakes his head. "This is a foreplay for a kiss. A declaration of intention. When I kiss you—yes, just kiss, nothing more—you won't be able to think straight for weeks."

We both grin like two idiots.

"You may stop crushing me to death now," I whisper, patting his shoulder awkwardly.

"Not before you tell me this changes nothing."

"It changes nothing," I lie.

"Why don't I believe you?" His eyes—green with a drop of hazel around each pupil—scan me.

"Because you're paranoid?" I offer with a sweet smile.

"I didn't mean what I said about Juilliard. I want you to go."

"Good, because I'm going."

Reluctantly, he rolls off of me.

I put the bracelet on. He dons his too.

"How's the sky looking, Dove?"

"Clear as day."

CHAPTER TWENTY-TWO
LEV

Miserable Fact #2,016: The human body is reduced to between 3 and 9 pounds once being cremated.

The blowup with Dad and Knight in Jackson Hole changed something in me. Made me snap out of my autopilot existence.

It is time to do right by the people I love.

I started out with Dove, by redirecting her attention to getting sober, as opposed to getting dicked. Yeah, we messed up a little by fooling around, but she's managed to do so well. I don't want her to switch one obsession with another, so I'm giving her space.

And Bailey was right. I *am* jealous of her passion for what she does. I *am* cruising. I play ball and don't apply to the Air Force Academy because of Dad and Knight. I don't move on because of Bailey. I fake a relationship with Thalia because I don't want her feeling embarrassed or used. By trying to please everyone, I end up pleasing no one, so maybe the answer is doing what's right for myself.

Maybe being authentically yourself spares everyone else around you a whole bunch of pain.

The next person on my to-do good list is Grim Kwon. He wants to be captain. And I want to…be left the fuck alone. And that includes never playing football again after high school. This is the one resolution I decided to do for myself. Grim is right—I'm not the right man for the job. I never was. Passion *is* merit.

Maybe I can't follow my dream of becoming a fighter pilot, but I'm also not going to break my back playing football just so Dad can have something to talk about with his buddies at his country club. And I'm certainly not going to cock-block Grim's actual dream to do it.

So here I am, in the locker room after practice, ready to corner Coach Taylor and tell him I'm stepping down as captain but will still fulfill my commitments as a player for the remainder of the year. Everyone is still in the showers.

"Dude, personal space," I hear Mac telling Ballsy in the showers while soaping his own ass. I'm clean, dressed, and ready to leave. My duffel bag is hung over my shoulder. Bet they all think I've already left. "If I can see each individual hair on your ball sack, that means you're too close."

"Or in Ballsy's case, in the same town," Finn quips. I should probably give them one more warning about being assholes to Todd before I pass the captain title along. I'm about to walk from behind the row of lockers and do just that when Austin's voice makes me freeze in my spot.

"Seen Bailey Followhill at the beach yesterday."

What was she doing at the beach? Who was she with? How did she find her way out of her house?

"Yeah?" Finn asks. "Is she still hot?"

"Bro, flammable is an understatement. Bitch must be pissing lava or somethin', she's so hot. She wore a tiny yellow bikini and looked like she ran out of a Victoria's Secret catalog. She's more bangin' than ever."

"And just as unattainable, I'm sure," Grim drawls. *Atta boy.* "She didn't notice your existence when you both attended the same school for three years. Doubt she changed her mind now that she's in college and you still look like what happens when steroids and my left nut decide to procreate."

I'd make him captain of the Miami Dolphins if I could right now.

"Au contradictoriany." Austin takes a stab at French…and murders the entire language in the process. "I'm hearing she is, indeed, a tweaker, so there's a lot of room for error on her part. Easy prey."

The only thing stopping me from popping his kneecap off with my Swiss army knife right now is that I want to hear more about their meeting.

"For real? She gave you tweaker vibes?" Ballsy gasps.

"She isn't a tweaker," Mac grunts. "Her rich parents would detox her ass in some 5k-a-night Swiss village if she was doing anything harder than weed."

"She's on something, all right," Austin snorts out, stepping out of the stream of water, toweling himself. "Apparently, she's been grounded or some shit until a couple days ago. Her parents are now testing her for drugs, and as long as she's clean, she's allowed to go out. That's what she told me anyway." *She confided in him? Why?* "Needless to say, I invited her to *all* of the parties this weekend." Austin flashes a shit-eating grin of the douchebag variety. "Including the one going on in my pants."

My head feels woozy. Are Mel and Jaime kidding me? They're making her piss into a cup and letting her do her thing?

Yeah, why not, asshole? Because you love the idea of Bailey locked up where no one can reach her or hit on her? a voice inside my head scoffs. It's been real easy for me not to pretend Thalia and I are still an item since I knew Bailey wasn't in a position to revenge-fuck someone else. But that's no longer the case, and Bailey has never been more volatile and vindictive in her entire life.

"Mark my words." Austin steps into his chino pants and J.Crew shirt—the international *I am a mediocre white man* uniform. "By the end of this week, I'm going to be balls deep inside Bail—"

"Shut the fuck up, Austin." My tone is acerbic enough to cut his face to shreds. "Or I'll fuck *you* up and finish the job Grim started last year."

We don't talk about it, but last year Austin called some freshman a slur for holding hands with his boyfriend or whatever, and Grim went so batshit crazy on his face, it took three of us to unplaster him from Austin. We only did it because we didn't want Grim to get arrested. I've met STDs more lovable than Austin.

"You got the balls to come here and say it to my face?" Austin bares his teeth, looking flustered. He didn't know I was still here.

"I thought I did. Damn, your ass looks uncanny."

"Speaking of ass." Austin's lips stretch into an ugly sneer. "Bailey's—"

He doesn't get to finish the sentence. I slam him against the floor. I'm on top of him, straddling his waist, plowing my fists into his face. I hear the crack of bones shifting but don't stop. There's blood everywhere. It splatters over the sleek, wet tiles. Over the flawless track record I maintained the past twelve years at school. Who cares? It's not like I'm headed where I want to be. Austin is screaming, trying to raise his arms to wrap his hands around my neck, but I'm bigger, faster, stronger, and I have the most potent weapon of all—anger.

Finn, Mac, and Antonio try to pull me off of him. They're grabbing at my arms, tugging me away, pleading for me to stop before I kill him. Ballsy and Grim each grab one of Austin's arms and haul him to the other side of the room. Austin is still protecting his face with his hands. His designer clothes are soaked scarlet, and I'm pretty sure I broke a few small bones in the process.

We're both pushed to opposites sides of the room. Mac and Antonio nail my arms to the wall, blocking me from getting in his face again. I'm panting, rage oozing out of me in currents.

"Do you have a death wish?" I'm genuinely curious because trashing Bailey in the same zip code as me is nothing short of suicidal.

Austin laughs, his teeth pink from blood and saliva, the bruises under his eyes swollen with my punches. "You think so fucking highly of yourself, Cole. Just because you like a girl doesn't mean she's off-limits for the rest of us mortals."

"What's your problem with me?" I demand. Austin has been a pain in my ass ever since we met. As far as I can tell, I'd never done anything to deserve his constant ire. Freshman year, I even helped him with calc and tossed ball with him ahead of scrimmages.

"My problem with you," Austin spits blood and maybe even a tooth on the floor, "is that every Cole man I've met is a total ass face."

I stare at him vacantly, momentarily confused. "There're only three of us." Four with Cayden, but come on, kiddo is barely potty-trained.

"Three more than there should be," he snarls. "And your brother, Knight, just happened to steal the captain title from *my* brother. Stole his girlfriend too."

"Luna?" I ask, surprised.

Austin shakes his head. "Poppy."

Holy blast from the ice age past. Poppy—Lenora's older sister—dated my brother for two seconds. Maximum. And I don't even remember who Knight competed with for the captainship at All Saints High. Which I guess cements that the resentment Austin is feeling is tribal and not personal right now. His family was pretty much invisible to mine.

"What's your brother's name?" I ask. I don't know why.

"Alvin."

Eh, shit. He even has a chipmunk name. Can't help but feel bad for the guy.

"Alvin is a bookkeeper in a real estate office by the way. All because your brother stole what was his," Austin accuses. "He could've been big."

My jaw works from side to side. "Listen. Sorry, but…this has nothing to do with Bailey. Stay the fuck away, yeah?"

Austin shrugs off the hands around him, flashes me a bloody smile, and shakes his head as he walks off. "If you want something, you better fucking know I'm going to beat you to it and get it myself. Consider this payback, Cole. The thing about turning everything you touch to gold…" He trails off, stopping a few inches from me. "Is that you end up with a bunch of soulless, lifeless shit."

———————————

Next on my list is Thalia. I've given her a few weeks of fake dating in which we haven't really met or communicated. I think it's time to cut the cord. I know she was hoping for a bit more time, but I can't do this to Bailey. Can't do this to Thalia, either. Giving her false hope is cruel, and I have a feeling that's exactly what's happening right now, based on the trillion text messages she bombarded me with while I was in Jackson Hole.

> Thalia: how's jacksonhall?
> Thalia: miss u.
> Thalia: <sent attachment> Nuddies for my baby lol.
> Thalia: call me when u get the chnce.
> Thalia: Lev where r u? 😨

So now I'm shouldering past a sea of acned faces, about a foot taller than everyone else, trying to find my fake whatever-the-fuck-we-were.

I leave no rock unturned. The gymnasium. Her homeroom. Her friends. I even walk into the girls' restroom and cause a small fire (*literally*. Not my fault, though. Who brings a hair straightener to school?).

I'm losing my mind. *And* patience. Where the hell is she? A few days ago, she seemed to be everywhere I went, popping up in the cafeteria, the locker room, football practice. Something is definitely up. She did ask me to call her a few days ago. And I *did* forget to answer that text message, which is epically shitty, I guess.

"Hey, Birdie, seen Thalia?" I corner her bestie in the hallway. Her back slams against her locker and she clutches her textbooks to her chest, biting down her lip. Her eyelids droop when I get all up in her face. Pretty dramatic, but these girls live for this shit. For that *Riverdale* effect.

"Uhm…Thalia?" She squints like she is unfamiliar with the name.

"Yeah. The girl you basically live with and have on your screensaver." I jog her memory, snapping my fingers between us so she'll stop staring at my lips. Birdie is fifty shades of red, and all of them tell me that she's hiding something.

"Oh…I don't know."

"You don't *know?*" I have a great bullshit meter, and right now it's dinging so hard I'm going deaf. "When was the last time you didn't know where Thalia was at any given time?"

"L—listen, I'm sorry. I don't know what to tell you. I haven't seen her today."

It is obvious I'm not gonna get anything but a headache from this chick, so I decide to cut my day short and pay a visit to Bailey. Ideally, I'd have given her a bit more time to take a chill pill. But I need her to know she won't be prancing around in little yellow bikinis. As I head to my car, I text Thalia.

Lev: Tried to find you at school. Where are you?

She answers after three seconds.

Thalia: sick at home 🤕
Lev: I'll swing by with some Gatorade. We need to talk.
Thalia: If it's about breaking up, don't bother.
Lev: ?
Thalia: Not ready yet.
Lev: Well, I am.
Thalia: Well…….if you don't do as I say…

What. The. Fuck. This sounds a lot like a threat, but what could she threaten me with? I've always been on the straight and narrow, for better or worse. And then it hits me. It's not *me* she is threatening to hurt if I put a stop to the charade.

Lev: You wouldn't.

Thalia: I don't know what we're talking about! Bailey is lovely

<3

Time to go Boomer on Thalia's ass. I do the undoable: I pick up the phone and call her. *Call.* Unprompted. She doesn't answer. I text her again. She doesn't answer. I send smoke signals, pigeon post, fucking telepathic communications—nada. Thalia isn't picking up. She's letting me stew in her last text message because I let her broil for days when I was in Jackson Hole, busy juice-tasting every hole in Bailey's body. And yes, I'm done with the liquid metaphors. For now, anyway.

The ride home is a blur. I have no recollection of parking the Bugatti in front of our eight-car garage, but somehow, I manage it. My mind is solely focused on the fact that my life just potentially got a whole lot more complicated. Thalia wormed her way into Bailey's good graces, and the latter's judgment is not amazing these days.

Staggering to Bailey's doorstep—why does it feel like she lives on the other side of the continent?—I push the door open, all but crawling up to her room. I'm not usually an anxious person, but the idea of something bad happening to her, of not marrying her, starting a family with her, lacing my life in hers like we're roots of a very old oak, makes me woozy.

"Gotta stop doing that," I hear Jaime calling out from his home office. "Walking into my house like you're the one paying the mortgage."

Doubt he can even spell the word mortgage, let alone still pay one. When I reach Bailey's room, the door is ajar. It is empty. I stand there like an idiot, waiting for the sound of her. For music to curl up from the ballet studio. But all I can hear are the keys of Jaime's mechanical keyboard and the chirp of doves sitting on a branch outside Bailey's window.

Don't rub it in, Mom. Didn't have to send reinforcements. I know she needs my help.

Then I see a note on her nightstand—yellow and simple and folded neatly—and I know it is directed at me. It pisses me off that she anticipated I'd seek her out, be the first one to break. She is getting back at me for flushing her drugs down the toilet. If only she knew I might've flushed my life out with it too, for a few sloppy fucks.

I pick it up and open it.

Oops. Sorry, Lev, your balls aren't here either.

B.

CHAPTER TWENTY-THREE
LEV

Miserable Fact #5,522: Washington Square Park in New York used to be a graveyard, and it is believed that about 20,000 people are still buried there.

I hit every single motherfucking party that week, worried about Thalia putting drugs in Bailey's hands.

I attend those I'm invited to and those I'm not invited to because it's clear that on a normal day, my ass wouldn't grace these fuckers with my presence. All to make sure Bailey isn't in attendance. By Saturday night, I think I'm out of the woods. There's only one party left, by a guy named Donnie. A total dudebro who thinks acting like a dick would somehow make his bigger. Donnie is a fan, so I'm not worried about crashing his party. Or, you know, burning it to the ground if need be.

What I *am* concerned about when I slip out of my car, parked in front of Donnie's house, is Thalia. She skipped school the entire week and wouldn't answer my messages *or* open the door for me. Something's up with her, and if I wasn't so pissed, I'd be worried.

Donnie's parents are both architects, which means his house has twenty-foot ceilings, a handcrafted fireplace, and a swim spa the size of an Olympic pool.

As soon as I walk through the door, people clamor to

congratulate me on another football win. "Hotel" by Montell Fish plays through the surround system coming from the ceilings, floors, and fuck-knows where else. I spot Austin doing a keg stand—still fully committed to being a waste of environmental resources—and Grim leaning against the glass doors overlooking the pool, holding a red Solo cup and talking to Mac and Antonio. I've been meaning to tell him I spoke to Coach about the captainship, that I'll be stepping down soon, but between Bailey and Thalia, didn't get the time.

Birdie hangs on my arm like we're friends or something, pressing her lipsticked mouth to my cheek. "*Ohmygod*, Lev! You made it."

"Superb observation skills, Birdie. Is Thalia around?"

Someone bows their head and slips a beer bottle into my hand silently as I stride deeper into the room full of people dancing, talking, and making out.

"No." She makes a sad pouty face. "She's really under the weather."

And *I* will be under house arrest for breaking and entering if she continues dodging me. I shake her off me. "Let me know if you hear from her."

Waltzing straight to Grim, I butt into his conversation with the guys. "Seen Bailey?"

Grim turns to give me an ice-cold look.

"*Hi, Grim, how are you doing? I'm doing good, thanks. How are you, Lev? Yeah. It is indeed a fine evening,*" he sarcastically plays out the conversation we *should* have had were I not on edge and if we weren't in the fucking twenty-first century.

"You sound like a Rosetta Stone tutorial for learning English." I take a swig of my beer. "Where is she?"

"On my dick." Antonio points his hand to his groin, in case anyone had any doubts as to its whereabouts. I impale him with a deadly gaze. He laughs into his beer. "Damn, Cole. Look at your face. Someone have any anal bleach? I know an asshole in need of lightening up."

Shouldering past these idiots, I descend the stairs to the pool. Some people are playing water volleyball, others are making out on sun loungers, and I'm immediately relieved when I can't spot Bailey anywhere in the water.

Then my relief turns into rage when I *do* spot her in the corner, perched on the same lounger as Austin, laughing and smiling and *existing* in full color, her new, sexy persona on full display.

What. The. Fuck.

She is wearing a see-through fishnet minidress with a tiny black bikini underneath. Guess she is pissing into cups and coming up clean every single time.

I hate the dysfunctional, drug-addict version of her, but I can't deny she turns me on. There's something dangerous, wicked, and unhinged about her, and help me God, I want to tame her so that she's bad only for me.

Austin is beyond eye-fucking her. I'm there to see the foreplay, the oral, and the spooning afterwards. The whole damned show. Austin snakes his arm around her, placing his palm on the small of her back as he dips to yell into her ear through the music. I can't figure out what he says, but he fishes something out of his pocket. A wad of tissue with what appears to be pills in it.

Bailey sees them and I swear her eyes look like a slot machine jackpot sign. *Ding ding ding.* He uses his knuckles to gently push her hair away from her face, murmuring into her ear, and she nods and stands up.

My pulse is through the roof as she tosses her head back, her sunshine hair running free down her back and tan shoulders. There's not a trace of shame or embarrassment as her muscular, lean thighs clasp Austin's knee and she begins moving seductively, throwing her arms in the air and giving him a lap dance.

At first, I'm too stunned to realize what's happening. My dick applauds her courage, stiffening in my pants, while my brain is plotting to cut Austin scrotum to groin and sell his inner organs to the highest bidder. Once I digest what's happening, I force myself to stay still, knowing damn well I could really, genuinely, *literally* kill the prick.

As if on cue, someone changes the song to "Freak Me" by Silk. I whip my head to see Grim standing next to the phone connected to the Bluetooth, giving me a cheesy grin and a thumbs-up. *I'm going on a fucking killing spree in about two seconds.*

Bailey is oblivious to the fact all eyes are trained on her. She's in her own little world, a prisoner to the music, rolling her hips over Austin's thigh, her gaze locked with his, riding and dry-humping him to the rhythm like she was born to do it. I can't stop looking. Watching this stranger dancing for Austin for drugs. Yeah, she isn't perfect, sweet, funny, and smart like Old Bailey. But she is sexy, daring, carefree, and frankly, fucking infuriating. She isn't safe and I'm starting to see I like that she isn't. How fucked up is that? Very.

Austin plucks a pill from his palm and puts it between his teeth, half pushed out. Bailey takes the bait, leaning forward to kiss him and steal the pill. That's when my self-control crumbles like a stale-ass cookie. I white-knuckle the beer, toss it back in one go, and head over to them. I'm not sure on what authority I am acting right now—I'm not her boyfriend—so I feed myself a bullshit story that Austin is going to hurt Bailey, even though Dove will sooner get her heart broken by a lukewarm cup of piss than this shit-for-brains nobody.

"Show's over, everyone." I grab a handful of her lousy excuse for a dress and pull her off of Austin, slinging an arm over her to protect her modesty. "Grab your shit, change the song, and get the fuck out."

Austin swivels toward me, his face a map of scars and broken blood vessels. My handiwork. "Enjoyed the view, Cole?"

He doesn't have a pill in his mouth right now so I take it Bailey already swallowed it. Does she even know what it was? Does she even *care*?

Ignoring the asshat, I turn to Bailey. "I need a word."

She smiles sunnily up at me, while jerking away from my touch. "I'll give you two, then—*fuck off.*"

A few weeks ago, I'd be stunned that she cursed. Now I'm low-key happy she didn't knife me to prove her point.

Austin slaps his thigh, cackling like a hyena. "Man, what a humbling experience, huh, Cap?" I swear he is coming in his pants, he looks so happy. "Always wanted to see someone bringing you down a notch or two. But that's a whole damn skyscraper you've fallen from."

Keeping my gaze focused on my best friend—and yes, she's still that; she will *always* be that—I drawl, "The way I see it, you have two options, Dove. Either you come with me willingly, or I call your parents and tell them to pick up the trash because the bag is almost broken."

Her mouth hangs open in shock. "Are you calling me trash?"

"Sweetheart, you treat yourself like it. Why wouldn't I call you that?" I *tsk*, then look around me, adding, "Plus, this place is full of drugs."

She looks around, confused. "No, it isn't."

I produce a bag of weed from my pocket, a borrow from a pothead skater dude I know here, and dangle it in front of her. "Sure 'bout that, Dove?"

She can't win this argument, and she knows it. I can see it in her eyes. They burn with hatred toward me, and I can't help but suck my bottom lip and wish she were the one to do it. Because Passionate Bailey is my newest addiction.

"*One* word," she hisses. "Wait here, Austin."

"Baby, you don't have to ask twice."

I turn around and make my way upstairs, to a secluded bedroom. Bailey follows me. In the upstairs hallway, I catch a glimpse of Maria, who is both on Power of the Pen and Model United Nations teams with me. She also happens to be one of the other girls at school whose lifelong mission isn't riding my dick. "Maria, can you come with us real quick?" I ask.

She frowns, ripping her attention from the group of her nerdy friends. "What for?" she asks. "I'm not having a threesome or whatever."

"Crushed," I deadpan. "Follow me."

"What's in it for me?" Maria thunders. I can feel Bailey's glare burning a hole through the back of my shirt, wondering where all of this is going.

"A hundred bucks," I say.

"Two hundred." Maria folds her arms, tilting her chin up. "Inflation, Cole. Oh, and I want Todd's number."

Ballsy? I suppress a snort.

"Why not?" Her face falls as she reads my reaction as a dig at her. "You think he's out of my league?"

"Nah, I… Never mind. Not my story to tell. You got yourself a deal. Come."

The three of us file into one of the rooms. It looks like a guest room by the sheer lack of personality, but come to think of it, it could easily be Donnie's.

I close the door behind us. The two girls in front of me look pissed.

"Switch clothes," I order.

Bailey offers me her vacant, dopey stare. "Drop dead."

"I will, probably soon from the heart attack you're gonna give me from looking like a slut, but you'll switch clothes with Maria first."

"Excuse me?" Bailey screeches. "You're wearing a white dress shirt with the sleeves rolled up to the elbows and a thumb ring. You're the epitome of a male slut."

"I'm actually uncomfortable with this word in general," Maria mutters, glancing between us in confusion.

"Bailey, change your fucking clothes," I growl impatiently, shoving my hands into the front pockets of my dress pants. I'm overdressed for sure, but I came here from a country club dinner with Dad for one of his big investors.

Maria and Bailey glance at one another. Maria wrinkles her nose. She is wearing a pair of baggy jeans and a plaid long-sleeved shirt. I can tell Bailey doesn't want to make her feel uncomfortable. At her core, Dove is still a considerate person.

Bailey turns to me. "No," her voice is resolute. "There's nothing wrong with my outfit."

"Yes, there is," I counter. "It's torn."

"What are you talking about? It's not—" But before she can complete the sentence, I step into her personal space, grab the collar of that stupid fishnet dress, and tear it from her body. It falls behind her back in a tattered pile. "See? A total mess. You should be more careful next time."

"What am *I* supposed to wear?" Maria shrieks. "Now that you destroyed her *Pretty Woman* costume?"

I unbutton my Brunello Cucinelli shirt and toss it Maria's way. "It's long enough to reach your knees and worth five Benjamins. You're welcome."

"And you're delusional," Maria growls in frustration.

Bailey whimpers, "Sorry," to her. Then adds, "I'll wear his shir—"

"No, you're not," I cut her off. "Be thankful I'm not wrapping the entire bed linen around you."

Then I turn around to give them some privacy. After a couple minutes, Maria announces, "We're done." I turn around, give her a couple hundred bucks and a promise to connect her with Ballsy, and send her and her soon-to-be crushed vagina on their way. This leaves me with Bailey, who is currently two things:

1. Modestly dressed.

2. Fucking fuming.

"What are you doing here anyway?" She collects her yellow hair into a high bun. "Austin said you don't even like Donnie."

"Fun, in case it isn't obvious." My voice is dryer than David Duke's wife. "What are *you* doing here?"

"None of your business," she informs me. "As long as I'm sober— which I unfortunately am—I can do whatever I want."

"And the pill you shared with fuckface?" I arch an eyebrow.

She shakes her head. "Gummy bear."

Even after everything and all that was said and done, this still makes my heart dance in my chest.

"I'm happy to hear that," I say softly.

"Is Thalia here?" She looks around the room, like the latter could crawl from under the bed and ambush her. I know what she's really asking, and there's nothing I want more than to assure her Thalia and I aren't involved anymore. But maybe it's best to clear things up with Thalia first.

"Not that I know of," I answer, hoping, wishing, *praying* she can read between the lines and see that she has nothing to worry about. Thalia isn't competition. She never was. The only thing ever standing between us was fear of losing one another.

Bailey nods somberly. "Can I go?" She sniffs. "I really don't want to talk to you right now."

I can't blame her, and I'm not even sure what to tell her right now, so I just gesture for the door, letting her know she is free to leave.

An hour later, I'm playing beer pong in the game room. *Shirtless.* Grim and I split the football squad into two teams and are competing against each other. If that's not the height of irony, I don't know what is. My team is winning, even though I got paired with Mac, who is just a little less capable than a wet fart. Bailey is in my periphery all throughout the game, sipping from a can of Diet Coke and talking to her girlfriends.

"Wanna make this interesting?" Austin, who is on Grim's team, asks.

"Strip beer pong is not a thing," Finn chides him flatly. "And not everyone wants to see Ballsy's two beach ball testicles."

"Well, this is disappointing," I hear Maria mumbling from the crowd.

Austin doesn't miss a beat. "If we win, Cole gives Grim the captain badge."

The entire room falls silent. Grim stares at me, blank-faced. The stakes are nonexistent to me, as I already told Coach I'm stepping down. I just needed to officially loop Grim in, which I'd been meaning to do officially on Monday. Why the fuck not?

But I can't be too obvious, so I ask, "And if I win?"

"You won't win." Grim doesn't miss a beat. "But on the off chance that you do, I'll give you a blank check. An open favor. Anything you want. Anytime. No questions asked."

I shrug. "Sure."

"All right." Ballsy claps, then rubs his hands together. "Shit just got a whole lot more interesting."

The entire party gathers around the beer pong table, which is actually an air hockey table I'm pretty sure we're destroying. The Solo cups full of beer float left and right to make it difficult for us.

It's Mac's turn, and he misses the beer cup, and everyone hoots and cheers and laughs. I spot Bailey from the corner of my eye drawing closer, peering at the game curiously.

"My turn!" Austin steps forward. "Bailey, give us a good luck kiss, baby."

He shoves his cheek to her line of sight, and she grins, making eye contact with me before giving him a peck. Austin slides the ball effortlessly into a floating cup. I'm shaking with rage.

When it's my turn, I put the ball in.

Grim misses and curses. He is agitated and sweating. I wish I could break the news to him right now, but to be honest, I think he would draw much more joy from it if I win this game, quietly step down without anyone knowing, and have it appear like he one-upped me on the field and was given the captainship directly from Coach Taylor.

I'm three points ahead, losing steam from my initial edge on Grim, when Bailey props a hip against the air hockey table. She is right beside me. I don't look at her, already bruised from the verbal whiplash from earlier.

Grim slam-dunks the Ping-Pong ball into a cup, and everyone roars in ecstasy. He just might win after all.

"You can do it, Grim," I hear Dove say, reminding me of the good times when she would cheer on every game of mine. Home field and away. How I took all we had for granted, and still, greedy me, wanted more. Now she is on whoever-isn't-me's team.

"Stay close, Bailey. He loses his mind every time you breathe in another guy's direction," Grim instructs her, popping another ball into a beer cup.

Bailey grins at him, perching her ass on the hockey table, her back to me and looking at Grim. "How've *you* been, Grim?"

"Yeah, not bad. How's Juilliard?"

"Awesome."

Awesome my ass. I bite my tongue and breathe through my nose, popping balls into cups.

"You look good," Grim flirts. "Even dressed like an aging cowboy from a bad eighties flick."

"Hey!" Maria protests from the back of the room. "I heard that."

"Good," Grim barks back. "Now you can do something about it. You're welcome." He redirects his attention to Bailey. "Is Lev giving you trouble?"

"What else can he give a woman?" Bailey scoffs.

The little liar. I could bring her to climax without laying a finger on her.

"My patience is running thin," I warn both of them.

"Aw, that makes one of you." Bailey examines her pretty nails with a pout. "Because your ass sure isn't moving faster than a jog on the field."

"Burn!" All the football squad laughs in unison. "Holy damn, Cole!"

"Bailey, move away," I clip out.

"You're not the boss of me." She's in rare form. She might be on one of her post-withdrawal mood swings. I read those can last for months after. And normally I'd be sympathetic to her situation, but not when she's grilling my ass and I'm already raw.

"Maybe not, but we both know I still own your ass, so you better listen."

"Buuuuurn!" People laugh and crumple their Solo cups.

"At least I pay my way through most of my stuff," she taunts back. "Remind me how much your car costs?"

"Less than the rehab you're headed to," I bite out.

The insult lands straight where it's supposed to, and her breath catches. Her cheeks turn red. We stare at each other for a second.

"Someone just lit a bonfire in Donnie's backyard!" a stoner from my class hollers from the terrace. "It's pretty awesome guys, come see."

"Sorry, the best show in the state is right in front of us." Grim laughs. I swallow hard, doing what I've never done before—I lose on purpose. Pretend to aim the ball in front of the cup. Swallow hard. And throw it slightly to the right.

It misses by at least three inches.

People roar and holler in excitement. "Yo, Grim is the new football captain, everyone!"

Grim is legit jumping up and down he is so happy, and though I pretend to be a sourpuss about it, I'm actually pretty happy.

"Oof." I puff my cheeks, spinning the Ping-Pong ball on my finger like it's a basketball. "Always thought losing was a part of your DNA makeup. But apparently there is a ball game you're good at."

Grim's nostrils flare, and I know I deserve to get my ass kicked for the bullshit I spewed out. He keeps it classy, though, smiling wide and big again to show me that he doesn't care.

"See, kids? That's what happens when you live your life as a coward. Too chickenshit to claim the girl you love, too scared to tell Daddy you don't wanna play ball." He takes a step toward me, the tip of his nose almost touching mine. "One day you just…" He snaps his fingers between us. "*Explode*. I'm going to let you detonate, Lev Cole, so that in the end, you'll be left with nothing but ruins."

Before I do something I regret, like beating the crap out of him, I turn around and stride outside to find Bailey. Time to deal with my own personal natural disaster—Hurricane Bailey.

I remember the stupid fire outside and walk straight over there. It is next to a hilly curve that stretches over the land Donnie's parents own. There is a group of people dancing to "Boom" by X Ambassadors. Among them, I spot Bailey. It's her hair that gives her away. The dazzling yellow that sprawls like a sunflower over a varsity jacket.

An All Saints High varsity jacket.

One that isn't my number—sixty-nine—an homage to Knight back when he played.

Austin's.

She's now sitting in his lap, giggling at something he says. There's no way on planet earth a girl of Bailey's IQ could laugh *with*, not *at*, guys like Austin. This is the same idiot who asked in class how old Leonardo DiCaprio was when he painted the Sistine Chapel. She's definitely getting back at me for our little exchange during beer pong. And it's working. Shit, Austin must be having a field day, having the girl I love perched on his thigh like that.

I slice through the crowd, straight to where they sit by the fire. I grab the back of that stupid jacket and hurl Dove up to her feet, letting her back fall against my chest so she doesn't trip. She yelps in surprise.

"Didn't I say show's fucking over? I'm taking you home."

She swivels and pushes at my chest. "Get off of me, you two-faced douche!"

"Take his jacket off." I'm so nauseous seeing her in this thing, I'm surprised I haven't vomited yet. She knows what varsity jackets mean at ASH. I *told* her.

"I'm cold."

"I'll give you my jacket."

"You don't even have a *shirt*, Lev."

"I'll let you wear my fucking skin. Now take the jacket off before this trainwreck derails into a cliff."

Pouting, she hisses, "If you want me to lose it so bad, beg for it, Levy Boy."

Everyone *aww*s and *ohhh*s. My ears go deaf for a few seconds, like I'm underwater. She lost the plot, and I'm about to write her into a painful thriller where Austin would be lucky to survive. Asshole looks so smug right now.

"Yeah, Levy," he coos. "Get your knees dirty for a change."

Rolling my lips, I turn to Bails again. "Grab your shit. We're leaving."

"No, really." She throws her hands in the air, laughing throatily. *Sexily.* She is not Normal Bailey right now, but that Bailey is still stuck inside of her somewhere. "If you want to order me around like I'm your little lap dog, then it's only fair you should be mine too, right? *Crawl* to me, Lev Cole. Come on. It's only, like, what? Three steps?" She steps back a little, putting distance between us. "Beg me to come with you."

In this moment, I swear I could do something really dumb and really violent to the person who first introduced her to drugs.

"And if I don't?" I ask in boredom. There's not one eyeball in SoCal that isn't staring at us right now.

"If you don't"—she licks her lips, her eyes leveling with mine— "I'm going to screw Austin tonight."

Austin howls and laughs in the background, and I know she's not lying. She will one hundred percent bang him, and there would be nothing I could do to stop her. Even if I hurl her ass to my car—which I technically can do—she'll find a way out and do it just to spite me. She's not being herself, not thinking clearly. The demon inside her wants his pound of flesh, and I'm about to tear a chunk off my goddamn heart and feed it to its satisfaction.

Or am I?

I've never begged anyone and not about to start doing so. I'm setting a dangerous precedent. But then Bailey sees my inner struggle, the pure hatred in my eyes, and sighs. "Got a rubber, Austin? Actually, I'm not picky. Anyone else with a condom will do too."

She is deep in the arms of a withdrawal spiral. I can tell from how she is sweating, how her eyes are empty, sad.

No one is actually *that* dumb as to take her up on her offer. Saying yes here in front of me is a sure way to an early grave. But I know the temptation would be too much for Austin when I'm out of sight. And I can't have that. I can't let Dove be with someone else. She's mine.

Slowly, I lower myself to my knees. Her breath hitches. I bend my head so I don't have to see anyone's face.

Then I begin to crawl in her direction.

I know this is screwed up and that word will get out to Thalia. I know people are recording this with their phones. I know I've done more damage to my reputation in the two months she's been here than I have my entire existence.

My knees brush the dirt, the ground hot from the fire. People are laughing and whispering and *fuck*, I am never going to forgive her for this. Not Sober Bailey and not Drugged-up Bailey. All versions of her are mixed together into a person I really should fall out of love with.

When I finally get to her feet, I lift my gaze to meet hers. I can tell she has somewhat sobered from her initial request—maybe she never thought I'd go along with it—because suddenly she looks full of remorse. Her eyes are wide, red and tinted with sorrow.

Ignoring her unspoken apology—*un-fucking-accepted*, by the way—I rise up to my feet and pin her with a death glare. "Happy?"

She swallows but doesn't say anything.

"Good. Now get out of his goddamn jacket."

She does as she is told, shaking and trembling. I should be more self-conscious about what's happening, but maybe Grim is right. Maybe I am imploding. As soon as the jacket isn't on her anymore, I snatch it from between her fingers and chuck it into the fire. The flames devour it before it even hits the ground. Austin snivels, "What the shit, Cole!"

Tackling Bailey's midriff, I throw her over my shoulder and march right out of this stupid place. Donnie trails behind us. "C'mon, Cole, the party's just getting started! More kegs are coming, and I'm about to open my dad's Macallan!"

Everyone follows us with their eyes as I get out the front door. Bailey erects two middle fingers in no particular direction, laughing tiredly. "Yup. Take a good look at the perfect Bailey Followhill. Not so perfect anymore, huh? Don't use drugs, kids."

Jesus Christ. She is more unhinged than Austin's jaw.

"How'd you get here?" I bark.

"Mom gave me a ride, and my friend Avery vouched she'd keep an eye on me. I'm still not allowed to drive."

"Shocking. I'm taking you back home."

I shove her into my car. It's only when the engine roars to life, and the air-conditioning blasts out arctic air, that I remember I'm shirtless. I back out of the parking spot and start driving. Dove doesn't say anything, and thank fuck for that. I'm still processing tonight. She humiliated me publicly. I guess I did the same to her too, in a way. In all of our time together as friends, we've never crossed these boundaries before.

We're both messing with our bracelets. I'm about to rip mine off, I'm so mad.

"Sorry abo—"

"Shut up, Bailey."

"I…um…" She scratches her cheek nervously, staring into space.

"You *what*?" I bark impatiently.

"Before we went to Jackson Hole I, um…borrowed some of your RCs from your collection to pay for…uh…"

"Drugs," I finish for her. My remote control planes are my pride and joy. She knows it more than anyone else. She bought me some of my most expensive pieces with her hard-earned money.

"Yeah," she says quietly. "Mom keeps tabs on everything I own because she knows junkies steal and sell things for drugs, and as you know, I refused any of their credit cards and wanted to be financially independent..." She trails off.

I close my eyes briefly when we reach a red light. I just hope she didn't sell one of the really good ones. Knowing her, she didn't. But still. What a shitty thing to do.

"How do you pass their drug tests?" I demand.

"I...well..." She looks around, doing anything other than meeting my gaze. "I'm not actually taking anything anymore. Which is why I'm being so horrible to everyone. Sobriety sucks."

"You're clean?"

She nods. Then starts crying. *Hard.*

I bite my lip until blood oozes out. Well, at least it explains her behavior tonight.

"Lev, I'm sorry," she hiccups, sobbing harder. "For everything. For tonight, for your RCs—"

"Please, *please*," I growl. "Just shut up and let me drive before I hurl us both off a fucking bridge."

The rest of the journey is spent trying to calm myself and *her* down. I keep reminding myself she is suffering. In pain. One of her legs is so swollen I'm pretty sure her bone is about to poke out. I have to give her a little leeway here.

We're almost at the cul-de-sac when Bailey opens her mouth again. "Take me to the woods."

"No can do. I'm planning to take Austin there after I tear him limb from limb and make his family play scavenger hunt to put-together his body."

She doesn't crack a smile. Just turns to me, her eyes pleading. *"Lev."*

As always, I can't deny her.

I start driving toward our secret spot. I'm so confused, my head's about to explode. Yet I always knew we'd be here. In this moment. On the seam between enemies and lovers.

"The pills..." Bailey clears her throat. "I didn't start using because of the pain and the injuries. Back at Juilliard. I mean, of course, they played a part. But it wasn't just about that."

"No?" I ask. She is opening up to me. Explaining how she got from being the nerdiest person I know to a drug addict.

"No."

Her head drops to her hands, and her back is shaking. I instinctively put a hand on her arm, trying to comfort her.

"The drugs were a coping mechanism. It was mainly the pressure to be perfect. Honor student. Prodigy ballerina. Prized daughter. I felt like I didn't have room to fail. At anything. Ever. I thought I could handle it...but the smallest thing ended up tipping me over the edge."

The silence between us sits like a ten-ton wall, and I want to break it with my fist until it bleeds out.

"I wanted to forget something that happened to me. And some things that didn't happen but maybe should have. Everything just reached a boiling point. I spent my entire life being perfect and working hard for it, and at Juilliard, my best wasn't enough. So I was constantly grinding, working harder, 'turned on.' I had to start supplementing with Xanax to keep myself alert and energetic and motivated. And then the injuries happened, and Xanax wasn't enough anymore. Enter benzos and Vicodin."

"Perfect is overrated," I croak. "It's unrelatable, unsustainable, and boring."

One question plagues my mind now—what did she want to forget?

WHAT DID SHE WANT TO FORGET?

WHAT DID SHE WANT TO FORGET?

I park on the edge of the woods and kill the engine.

"You said you wanted to forget something." My voice is pure gravel. "What was it?"

Her lips part and the world stops spinning.

"I'm no longer a virgin." She stares down at her thighs, digging her shell-pink nails into them. "The way I lost my virginity...it wasn't ideal. I think a part of me had always believed we were gonna lose it to each other, no matter how pathetic that sounds."

"It doesn't sound pathetic at all." I pull her hands away from her thighs before she makes herself bleed. "I believed that too. Some days, it was the only thing that kept me going."

"Remember the night you asked me if I partied? If I ever hooked up with people?" She sniffles.

"Yeah," I say. "It's the night I gave up on us. Kind of. Temporarily."

When I made the biggest mistake of my whole damn life.

"Then I achieved my goal." She licks her lips. "That night, I really was studying. But earlier in the afternoon, something happened."

That something better not be a someone forcing himself on her, because there's no bail sum to convince a judge to release me after what I'd do to that person. Bailey reads what's written on my face because she shakes her head fervently. "No, nothing like that. He had my consent."

"Okay." *Breathe. Breathe. Breathe.*

"He was a ballerino. Talented. Funny. Charming as heck. And he was accepted, Lev. Everybody liked him. You know how much I crave approval. And I was angry with you."

"Angry with me?" My brows shoot up. "Why?"

We'd drifted apart by the time she moved to New York, but I never figured out why. It couldn't have been because I semi gave her head that day we won the state championship. Because we were giving each other semi-orgasms long before.

"Because you seemed unsupportive about Juilliard. And then when you confessed your love for me...I thought it was another ploy to keep me here. To deprive me of my dream. I resented you for it."

I rub my palm over my face, groaning. She had every reason to be upset with me. I robbed Bailey out of her childhood in a sense. She put all of her emotional capital in me, so I wouldn't grow to be a fuckup after what happened to my mom. And when it was time to reciprocate, to celebrate Bailey and *her* achievements, I failed. But I'm not failing her now. I'm here, and I'm going to push through tonight's humiliation because she's finally opening up to me.

"So this guy. Payden—"

"Argh." I grind my teeth. "He even has a made-up name. Who names their kid Payden and thinks they'd grow up not to be a mega douche?"

A miserable smile grazes her lips. "We went out a few times. I wanted to forget all about you. He was also the campus's designated drug dealer. But I never touched anything, not really. Well, maybe a Xanax here and there. I told myself everyone was doing it. That it was time to lighten up.

"That afternoon, we got a little drunk in my dorm room. He said all the right things. That I was beautiful. Born for greatness, an amazing ballerina. That he wanted something real. Flattery and Xanax are a lethal combination. So…I fell for it."

"He got you high on his supply," I say matter-of-factly, feeling my jaw clenching tight. *"Addicted."*

She presses her lips together. "I knew what I was doing. One thing led to another, and…" A whoosh of air leaves her lungs and she stares down at the crescent-shaped dents she left on her thighs. "Next thing I know he's on top of me. *Inside* me. And he doesn't sound like you and he doesn't smell like you and his weight feels too light, too casual, too not-Lev. Then he pushes deeper, and it hurts. It felt like he was stabbing me. But I was too embarrassed to stop him." Tears begin streaming down her face. "And I already had a certain reputation. Cold. Frigid. Too uptight. So I just laid there and took it—I wasn't fucking him; I was fucking my reputation, if that makes sense. And…and when he was finished…" She starts hiccupping, crying and upset. "I said my head hurt because I wanted him gone. So he gave me some painkillers."

"He used you," I repeat.

She licks her lips, dropping her gaze to the floor. "Did he, though? Because I came back for the drugs even when he shoved that night in my face over and over again. Maybe it was my way of punishing myself, showing myself just how far I'd spiraled. Every time he'd stop in my room to give me drugs—which was weekly— he'd offer more. He wasn't subtle about it, either. He'd touch me sometimes in an inappropriate way. But my love for drugs always won the battle against my hatred toward him. I know it's not some great trauma, that I'm being silly—"

"You're not being silly. You gave your virginity to someone who didn't deserve it. It's like…it's like donating to a charity for people who you find out were drowning kittens…or something."

The grief that impales my heart threatens to drown it with sorrow.

My out-of-character awkwardness makes her snort out a laugh. "The problem wasn't him." Her stare swings and our eyes lock together. "The problem is he wasn't *you*."

I reach to grab her waist and she hops between the center console. She is on top of me and we're hugging and my face is in her hair, and for a fraction of a second, I can breathe deep and clean and feel like myself again.

I rub her back. Kiss her tears away.

"Can we just…make our seconds count?" she asks, lips shuddering against my skin. "Second dance. Second time making love. Second everything."

I rear my head back, so she can see me. "The second time is more important. First times are overrated. They're often just mistakes."

"What?" She wipes her eyes with the sleeve of the plaid shirt, confused.

"Thalia didn't count. Padlock didn't count. Our first times were diversions. Not the real deal."

"It's Payden."

"Still not a real name," I say tonelessly. "Let's have a do-over. *This* will be our first time. Nothing else counts."

"It doesn't work that way." She shakes her head sadly.

"Says who?" I buck, giving her my disarming smirk. "There are no universal rules here. One of the best parts about being in our own minds is we get to make the rules."

And as I lead her out of the car, I internally bleed to death because I'm starting to see that Bailey's wounds are much more than skin-deep. She'd been hurt and betrayed by her peers. Used by other students. Pressured by her family, her friends.

Her troubles are not a phase. They're distractions.

And unless she treats them…they'll destroy her.

CHAPTER TWENTY-FOUR
BAILEY

Lev's hand is sweaty and rough against my palm as he leads me to our huge canvas bed, still shirtless. He doesn't even notice that I cleaned it. I've been coming here ever since my parents loosened my leash. Feeding our doves, tending to our little corner of the world. But it's dark, and we're desperate. The entire world could burst into flames and we probably wouldn't even notice.

My heart is pounding in my ears. I'm glad I didn't tell him the entire story. How I lost so much more than my virginity to Payden—I lost my trust in men too.

"Hey, you. Eyes on me. Remember where you are." Lev pulls me out of the thick fog of misery I'm surrounded by, giving my hand a squeeze. He laces his fingers through mine and plays with them. "Let's rewrite our past, Bailey."

He takes his phone out and starts browsing through his music app.

"What are you doing?" I ask.

"I've always wanted to dance with you to this song." He tosses his phone onto the canvas and opens his arms for me to walk into them. And in I walk as "It Ends Tonight" by All-American Rejects sounds off his phone. The song is so final, so sad, I try not to read into it, but it's hard not to. Tears prickle my eyes. I don't want us to end, but I also don't know how to save us.

I rest my head on his shoulder and close my eyes, getting lost in the lyrics. Our hearts are pressed together. Our souls lacing into one another seamlessly, like two cats' tails. I'm glad that I'm sober to be present enough for this moment. When the song ends, I wait a few more seconds, just standing there, and Lev allows me this time to gather my thoughts.

Finally, he speaks. "We don't have to do anything you don—"

Pressing my finger against his lips, I shake my head. "I've never wanted anything in my life like I want this."

"Are you the real Bailey?" he chokes out. "The one I fell in love with?"

I bow my head in half a nod. "I am, Lev. I promise."

He lowers me to the canvas, which is damp with dew, and kisses every inch of my body. Every bruise. Every blemish. Every beauty spot and tear. He starts from my forehead and works his way down. My breasts. My stomach, then lower still, to the place between my legs. He worships me, and in this moment, I let him. I let go of my constant need to please. I stop giving. I start taking. I tell him what I want, where I want it, and at what pace. First, he kisses me with our clothes on, and then, he undresses me, item after item, mumbling into my skin, "You're so beautiful" and "I can't get enough of you" and "You're it, Bails. My beginning, my middle, and my end." Every inch of my skin blooms with gooseflesh. His head is between my thighs, his thumbs pushing my inner thighs apart, and he swipes his tongue along my center. I shudder all over, fingernails digging into his shoulders. Then he slips two fingers into me, and there is no mistaking the sound of my desire as he pushes in and out of me, sucking my clit.

"Lev..." My knees give in, and I'm trembling all over as the pressure builds and he slides his fingers into me faster and deeper. "I'm coming."

"Come on my tongue, little dove." He glides his tongue into me as wave after wave of warm pleasure slam into me. After my shudders subside, he looks up, his lips swollen and glistening, his hair a mess from my fingers, which played with it. "Hello." He grins.

"Hi." I feel my deep blush taking over my face. We're naked as he kisses his way back up. Our skin sticks together, glued by sweat. I'm choking with feelings, swept away by desire. Then he's on top of me, strong and protective. The guy who would never let me down.

"I don't have a condom," he whispers, rolling the crown of his dick over my pussy. "I wasn't expectin—"

"I'm clean," I say hurriedly. "And have an IUD to regulate my hormones and manage potentially heavy periods, so...you know, I think we're good." I don't want there to be any barriers between us. We've had enough of those over the years.

He slants his head sideways, giving me a hooded, sexy look. "Fuck, Dove. Your dirty talk is unmatched."

I shrug. "Guess I'm just full of surprises."

His lips descend, claiming mine in a sloppy kiss full of saliva and tongue, and he gathers me in his arms, bringing all the parts of me together. The good and the bad. The ugly and the beautiful. "I'm clean too."

Our eyes meet and I offer him a slight, barely visible nod. He closes his eyes, takes a deep breath, and sinks into me, inch by inch. And there are a *lot* of inches. My body stiffens and I hold my breath, pleasure and pain battling it out inside my body. "Let me know if I should stop." Lev's voice is strangled, his own desire barely contained.

"You're good." And I mean that in more than one way.

When Lev is all the way inside me, I'm surprised by how much it hurts. I'm not a virgin, am thoroughly wet, and have been fingered and tongue-fucked by him. Why does it feel like he just inserted a tennis ball canister into me?

"Is this okay?" He strokes my hair gently, his eyes full of tenderness and anxiety. *I got the best one*, I think to myself. *Out of all the delicious men I know, all the footballers, millionaires, dry-witted alpha-holes, I somehow bagged the best one.*

"Hurts a little," I admit chokingly. "But pain from you is better than pleasure from anyone else."

"No one should cause you pain, Dove. Least of all a person you love."

He spits onto the pad of his finger and snakes his arm between us, massaging my clit, not daring to move inside me. He's letting me get used to the size of him, drawing my attention to the delicious pleasure gathering between my thighs.

At first, I think my clit is too stimulated for me to come again. But he flicks, teases, and massages it until an orgasm rushes through me. My legs fall open and I feel myself stretching, my body opening up like a flower to accommodate him.

This is the moment I turn from a wallflower into a wildflower.

Lev starts thrusting. Softly at first. Then, when he peers down at me and sees me panting and groaning, following that second release, his movements become jerky and uncontrolled. We're one unit, moving in perfect harmony, and elation sweeps through me because nothing that feels this good can be a mistake.

"Dove, I can't take this anymore. Being inside you feels too good." A bead of sweat falls from his forehead straight into my mouth. I lick it, shuddering with an intense orgasm just as I feel warmth spreading inside me, letting me know that he finished too.

We're gripping one another, clutching hard like the tattered canvas beneath us is on the verge of ripping apart, an endless abyss beneath it with a path straight to hell. Our foreheads stick together. Our labored breathing calms down. We stay like this for seconds. Then minutes. Neither of us wants to pull away. To break the spell cast on this moment.

Eventually, I pull away. Lev is the one who has been shirtless for hours, shielding me from the frosty bite of the night, growing cold atop me.

"We should go." My lips move over his.

"We should," he agrees, closing his eyes. "But I'd rather run away with you."

"I'm tired of running away. One thing college doesn't teach you is that your problems always outpace you." I push him off softly, kissing the edge of his shoulder when he rolls on his back next to me. "Besides, I don't know if we can ever be together now, Levy. You're fighter jet pilot material. I'm damaged goods."

He turns to me sharply, the thundering ferocity of his scowl telling me he's in complete disagreement. He grabs my jaw, angling it so I look into his eyes. "Damaged goods are still goods. It's the dents that make them special. That make them *them*. Survivors. Molded by their experience. Be proud of your scars, Dove. Because where you see hardship, I see opportunity. Where you see imperfections, I see growth. Where you see failure, I see effort. Where you see despair, I see hope." He sucks in a breath. "You aren't just good enough—sometimes you feel *too* good to be true."

In that moment, on a dirty, old canvas, in the middle of the woods, in the arms of the boy I love, I realize that eventually, at the end of all this, no matter what happens, I will survive.

And that maybe, that will be enough.

CHAPTER TWENTY-FIVE
LEV

Miserable Fact #9,228: People are more likely to die by suicide than by homicide in New York City.

I stare at my laptop screen, snakes slithering under my skin. I'm trembling, even though I have no reason to be. I'm wearing a hoodie, it's a thousand fucking degrees outside, and I'm one hundred and ninety-five pounds of pure muscle. Still, my guts are twisting inside out. Because I can't bring myself to click on that little blue button. The one that would send my application to the Air Force Academy.

APPLY

It's the day of the deadline. My last chance. I've filled it out carefully, uploaded all my shit—SAT, grades, résumé—all I have to do is hit send. Then why can't I?

It was last night's encounter with Bailey that gave me the strength to even *think* I could do this. She was strong, resilient, open, hopeful. She's a true fighter—and who knows? Maybe so am I.

Click on the apply button.

"You should do it," a feminine voice encourages me behind my back, and I almost hit the fucking ceiling jumping in my seat. I'm in the kitchen. Dad is at Uncle Vicious's place, so I figured I had a few hours to myself. Of course, Dixie is here. Dixie is *always* here, on a silver platter, in case Dad changes his mind about getting his dick sucked.

Fine. That's not fair. She's good people. I just wish she'd stop the recent trend of shoving her nose into my business.

I minimize the browser, shooting her a sideways glance. "No idea what you're talking about."

"The deadline." She produces that egg-shaped moisturizer from her bag, running it over her lips. "Isn't it soon?"

"Today," I grumble. Guess she already saw the website. No point in being coy.

"You're going to miss it if you don't apply now." Captain Obvious breezes past the door to the kitchen table, which is when I see she has a tray with two cups of coffee from that bomb-ass bakery down the street. She slides one to me from across the table. "Three shots, two sugars, a dash of half-and-half. Did I get it right?"

"Yeah." I bring the coffee to my lips and take a sip, frowning suspiciously at her. Why does she know my coffee order? "Do you have a crazy wall with my fingerprints, saliva sample, and surveillance footage of me in your office?" I squint.

She shakes her head. "No, no." Then, after a pause. "I keep it at home. I'm not an amateur."

I force out a laugh.

"You're Knight's brother, and anyone who's important to him is important to me," she explains.

"I see we reached the cheesy Hallmark-speech portion of this visit." I lean back in my chair. I really ought to stop being such a tool bag to her. It's not her problem I have unresolved mommy issues brought on by anxiety about my best friend.

"I'll wrap it up quickly." Dixie drums her burgundy fingernails over the table, smiling brightly. "As I said, you should do it. Your dad will understand."

"Like hell he will," I snort. "You heard him yourself. He said—"

"Who cares what he said?" she interrupts, surprising the crap out of me.

"Umm…you?" I smirk tauntingly.

"It is your life, not his. You'll be the one who has to live with the consequences. Trust me when I say, the burden of your decisions will always squarely fall on your shoulders, nobody else's. I should know. I gave up my son, and every day, the pain of missing out on moments with him chases me."

"It hasn't been just about Dad and Knight recently." I lick my lips. It feels good, talking about it with someone. Dixie tilts her chin down, studying me. She is low-key hot. I really don't understand what Dad's problem is.

"Tell me why," she says.

"First off, there's Bailey. I have to keep an eye on her. Until she's in an inpatient rehab center, I can't just fuck off knowing she's still using."

"Helping someone—even the person you love the most—should never come with the price tag of ruining your own life," she says simply. "If you're starting to think about ways of sabotaging your own dreams in order to keep hers possible, you're heading in the wrong direction for you both. If Bailey was truly ready for help, I know it would be available to her."

All the things she says are making sense, but she doesn't have the full context. Bailey made all these sacrifices for me when I needed her the most.

"I'm worried someone will sabotage her efforts. Someone like…" I take a big gulp of the coffee. "Thalia."

"Why would she do that?" Dixie makes a face.

"She kind of threatened to if I don't stick around with her. Not sure what the big-picture endgame is."

The room falls quiet. The only sound audible is my heartbeat as the fucker tries to rip its way through my rib cage and skin, and run to a non-extradition country to assume a new identity.

Dixie nods slowly. "I know exactly why Thalia wants to stay

together. You're too much of a catch to lose. But going back to our original topic." She leans over the table, tapping her finger over the edge of my laptop screen. "All you've given me are *potential* problems. Not actual obstacles. It's now or never. Choose now, or regret forever."

I stare at her blankly. "You need to stop sounding like a bad Hallmark movie."

"It's stronger than me. They're just so wholesome. Especially the holiday ones." Her laughter floats around the room like a ray of warm sunshine. She stands up. "If you need to talk, you know where to find me. I'm gonna go get the keys to your dad's 1964 Ferrari."

"You *what*?" I growl. I've been trying to get my hands on that puppy since I got my license.

She shrugs. "He said I could borrow it for an open house that's going for thirty-four million. The garage is on the roof, so it's gonna look supercool."

"He's letting you borrow *Fifi*?" I'm surprised my eyes aren't rolling on the floor. Hot damn. Dad won't even let Knight and me *touch* Fifi. As the legend goes, he and Mom used to have crazy, dirty sex in there (thanks, Daria, you gross reptile), and we're not allowed to taint it. Dad barely uses it himself, other than a drive around the block to keep it running.

"Didn't realize he is so pussy-whipped." I laugh to myself.

"It's not like that." Dixie does her best impression of a beetroot. She actually touches her burning cheek, suppressing a smile.

"It can't be any other way. He wouldn't even let me clean dust from the interior. Fifi is holy to him."

"He just wants me to sell the house so I can get the commission. There's a place I've got my eye on and I could use the bonus as a down payment."

"Why aren't you asking him for a loan?" I frown.

Her expression darkens. "I'd never do that. It's bad enough I enjoy going on vacations with you guys on private jets and in fancy mansions."

She is too modest for her own good. Dixie does a shit-ton for this family. She is not some freeloader.

I stand up and grab my car keys. "All right. I'm heading to Thalia's. Maybe if I ambush her, I can hammer the point home that I'm not one to be blackmailed."

"So romantic," Dixie coos. "Hey, you haven't pressed the apply button yet!"

I pretend not to hear her as I walk out the door.

My future can wait. I need to be present for Bailey.

"Wake up, sleepy pants. You've slept in." Dad places a tray of breakfast on my nightstand. I curl my fists and rub my eyes.

"You seemed a little under the weather yesterday, so I let you sleep in even though you had practice this morning."

Holy shit. He let me miss practice? He is usually on my ass if I wake up after six o'clock on training days.

"Thanks," I say gravelly.

Dad loiters at my door, glancing at me behind his shoulder, like he wants to say something.

"Dad, I'm naked." I point at my duvet, arching an eyebrow.

"So?" He arches an eyebrow. "Nothing I haven't seen, you know."

"Not after I grew pubic hair, you didn't. Kindly evacuate yourself from my personal space."

"Do you want to talk about anything?" he insists.

Giving him a blank stare, I reply, "Like what?"

"Football? College?" he asks anxiously. But he doesn't have to be anxious at all. I already fucked up my one and only chance at happiness. "Wanna show me that aviation-stimulator thingy upstairs?"

"Simulator," I correct. "And no." It is only after he leaves when I allow myself to grab a pillow, press it against my face, and let out a scream.

I missed my deadline.

The dream is gone. The Air Force Academy is a dud. I've never felt so empty in my life, and I'm starting to understand Bailey for going to extreme lengths to chase her dream.

Eighteen fucking years of love, devotion, laser focus, and an RC jet hobby that had me spending all my pocket money since I was three—down the goddamn drain.

When I was five, my dad's friend from college came to visit us. He flew a fighter jet and had all these videos on his phone. The jaw-dropping stunts and maneuvers. He was supercool, super chill, super...I don't know, content. By the end of his visit—which lasted four days in which I pestered him with a thousand questions a day—he asked my dad to subscribe me to all those YouTube channels where I could learn more about aviation. Left me his aviator glasses too. I've been an addict since.

I'm so destroyed, I don't even bother to be angry at Thalia for avoiding my ass when I came knocking on her door yesterday. She was there. I saw her ducking and rushing into an inner room through the window. She looked like a mess, and I'm beginning to think there's more to her weird behavior than she lets on.

I drag myself to school. The only thing keeping me on my feet is the memory of Saturday night. I make it just to the tail end of football practice, when Coach Taylor gathers everyone around in a circle.

He tips his baseball cap down. "Got an important announcement for y'all."

"Ballsy's getting a nut-shrinking surgery?" Finn shrieks. "Is he donating the rest to the Nut Growers Association?"

"It's a medical issue!" Todd kicks the grass, fists curled tight.

Grim spots me from the corner of his eye and jerks his chin my way. "Lookie here. Sleeping Beauty's awake."

Coach turns around, pinning me with a frosty look before going back to his clipboard. "As I said, I have an announcement. It's been a long time coming."

Thankfully, no one makes an orgasm joke. I stand next to Grim.

He ignores me. He's about to have his little victory dance, though. I know because even though I wasn't here for the head count when they reelected the captain, I know he annihilated me in votes.

"For the past few weeks, we've shown resilience, excellence, and longevity as a team. Our game is good—but our morale is weak. To make this team invincible, I decided democracy isn't best after all."

Everyone looks at me, shifting uncomfortably. Coach soldiers on. "Lev Cole has outperformed on the field as a player. As a captain, however, he's shown zero enthusiasm and scored minus ten on commitment."

If this is the part where I'm supposed to get offended, it misses its target by a few states.

"He and I both agreed we need someone with boots on the ground who will be here ten minutes early for every practice and stay the extra time afterwards. Someone who will take the time to talk to each player individually, offer encouragement and guidance. Someone who doesn't have players looking like they got into a fistfight with a backhoe under his watch." Taylor's eyes land on Austin, who still looks like a slapped ass with a wig.

"The backhoe was about to put out," Austin mumbles. "But someone threw a hissy fit. Not naming names or anything."

"He deserved to get his ass kicked," I grit out, folding my arms over my chest.

"Problem is, it's his face you wrecked." Coach Taylor sighs.

"My bad. They look the same."

Coach Taylor pretends he didn't hear that and smacks his clipboard over his assistant's chest. "In short, we reelected the captain, and the person you chose is Grim Kwon. He won the majority of votes, so I trust you'll be happy with the decision. Congratulations are in order, buddy, it wasn't even a competition."

Keep rubbing it in, ass face.

Grim stiffens. His Adam's apple rolls before his mouth cracks into a hesitant smile. It's the first time I've seen him smile with teeth. Or emotions. Prior to today, I wasn't sure he possessed either.

"Holy shit, Coach. Are you serious?" His ears darken with a blush.

"No, I'm joking. This is my laughing face," Coach Taylor says flatly.

Everyone turns to look at me, as if asking for permission to celebrate. So I jerk Grim into a hug, ruffling his hair. "Come here, fucker. Congratulations."

"Stay the fuck away from me," he hisses into my ear, pushing me off. "You're a day late and a dollar short. You held my dream hostage for three years just because you didn't have the guts to chase yours. If this is how you treat your best friend, I don't want to know how you treat your enemies."

He bumps his shoulder into mine, moving on. The squad gathers around to clap Grim's shoulder and applaud him. I'm about to remind him football is not a fucking kindness competition—that I was chosen because I was better—but then I catch her from the corner of my eye. A lithe body clad in the gymnastics team varsity hurrying from the parking lot and toward the gymnasium.

Thalia.

I've never run so fast in my life. I'm practically hovering over the ground before I get to her. She notices me coming. Panic mars her face.

I catch the hem of her jacket, pull her back, and pin her against the wall. She is trapped between my arms, looking like a cornered animal.

Leaning forward, I bare my teeth at her. "Sorry, sweetheart. If you drop a bomb, expect some casualties. You owe me some answers. And I'm about to get them now."

"I was actually going to call you." Thalia is all over me like a nasty rash after a shady hookup. Her hands are on my chest and she puckers her lips, waiting for a kiss that isn't coming. It's like she did a one-eighty as soon as I caught up with her.

I would call her on her bullshit, but I've more pressing issues to deal with, so I appreciate her cooperating, on a level.

"What's going on?" I demand, removing her hand from my cheek.

"What do you mean, Levy baby?" She blinks up at me innocently.

"I mean about the threat you made against Bailey," I growl, adding, "I mean you insinuating if I make this breakup official, you're gonna hurt my best friend. I don't take well to threats. In fact, I'm in the business of destroying the people who make them."

"Aww, again with your precious Bailey," she hisses back, and there it is. The pain she promised I'm not going to be able to inflict on her. All over her face, like scars.

"Tell me what's happening." I don't flinch. "Where is this shit coming from? Why don't you wanna break up?"

She slams her mouth shut. Stares down at the floor. "Oh, you big moron!" She rolls her tear-filled eyes skyward, shaking her head. "I've never wanted to break up with you. I was always in it for the long haul, waiting for you to wake up and realize how good we are together."

My jaw clenches, and she presses forward, tossing her head back. "Remember the scholarship I told you about? The one I've been given?"

"Yeah?" I ask.

She shakes her head. "Well, it's gone. As in, not happening anymore. They withdrew their offer. Academic dishonesty." She drops her head down so I can't see her face, and something in me immediately goes out to her, and I put a hand on her shoulder.

"Shit, T. I'm so sorry."

The shoulder I'm holding is shaking as she continues, "There was a discrepancy between the grades I gave them and the ones All Saints High sent them. It's done. I'm not going to go to any college. And…and…I needed a plan B. And I guess you were it."

Even though I'm still angry at her, I cannot not-understand where she's coming from. She doesn't have the means to get the future she wants. I press my forehead against hers, shaking my head. "You should've said something. I could've helped you. We could still make school work. You could still apply—"

I notice that her suddenly happy gaze is drifting elsewhere behind my shoulder, so I turn my head to see what caught her attention.

From across the street, I spot Bailey standing next to her beat-up car. She is staring at us, and I know what it looks like. *Shit, shit, shit.*

And *now* I recognize the truth for what it is.

Thalia might've lost her scholarship, but she also lost her fucking plot. This was a trap, designed to show Bailey we're still an item. Thalia called her here. Expected her. She timed her arrival for when football practice was over. She doesn't even have practice now. The gymnasium is closed. And we look intimate, close, touching each other, having an emotional talk.

I whip my head back to Thalia because I need to finish this mess with her before I extinguish the fire she started with Bailey. "Jesus Christ, you're vile."

I can see the moment she contemplates denying what's obvious and trying to justify herself. She chooses the latter.

"She's not right for you, Lev. You deserve so much better. She's deadweight!" Thalia grabs the lapels of my varsity and clings to it like a lifeline. I shake her off. "You're just confused because you grew up together. You and I…we're both top athletes."

"And this matters because?"

"We want the same things."

"No. I want *her.*"

"She's a junkie!" Thalia snaps, and this is when I lose the remainder of my goddamn patience for her.

"Better a junkie than a loser. It's not like you have your shit together. Bailey is a good person in a bad situation. You, on the other hand, are a menace to society and such a waste of oxygen, I'm surprised the government didn't declare you a fucking global warming problem," I spit out, losing my cool. "Don't try comparing yourself to her. You'll always come out short."

Thalia forces herself to smile, even though she'd probably love nothing but to slap me.

"You'll never understand a survivalist—a person who fights for their existence. Your instincts are too dull, Lev Cole." She licks her lips, hanging those empty, generic-blue eyes on my face. How could I ever have compared them to the tranquility and solitude oozing from Dove's arctic blues? "You may have a six-pack, but for all intents and purposes, you're a fat cat. Satisfied, content, spoiled." It's amazing how much she doesn't know me. My journey. My struggles. But maybe that's not on her. I never did let her in. Thalia pouts seductively, running a manicured finger over my chest. "But I'll still give you a chance to change your mind, because you have all the power here, and I still think what we have is salvageable. The offer still stands, but not for long, Lev. Call me when you get a clue." She tosses her hair over one shoulder.

Turning around from her, I'm about to haul ass to Bailey and explain everything, but by the time I make a move, she's gone. Her car is gone. She left before she witnessed this fight.

She probably thinks Thalia and I are together, and for an addict trying to stay on the right path, that's a big fucking problem.

Skipping school isn't even a question of if but how fucking quickly I can sprint my ass to my car.

It takes me ten minutes to get home—five less than it normally does when I refrain from pissing all over every driving rule in existence—and I barge into her house, panting. I run up to her room, and it's empty. I rummage the house for a sign of her, then notice the rocking chair outside is moving rhythmically up and down. *Bingo.*

Pushing her balcony doors open, I start, "Bails, I can explain—"

"Please don't," Jaime responds laconically, just as I round the chair facing the pool and realize he is the one occupying it. He's holding a fizzy pink lemonade and a copy of *The Economist*, his aviator shades on. "My teenage drama days are long gone—just the way I like 'em."

Standing up straighter and trying to resemble someone he might consider as his son-in-law one day, I say, "Hi, Mr. F. Have you seen Bailey?"

"I have, plenty of times. But not in the last couple hours. She's dropping some of her old clothes off at Goodwill. You're welcome to wait for her here."

"I'll come back in an hour," I mutter.

Jaime looks up from his newspaper, smiling. "If you say."

What the fuck is that supposed to mean? "I *do* say."

"Watch that tone, Levy boy."

"What's the problem?"

"The problem is, there's saying and then there's doing. Like, if you say, *tell* everyone who is close to you how much you wanna go to the Air Force Academy but in practice continue playing ball to appease your father even though it would kill him to know he clipped your wings like that, your word ain't worth much. You feeling me?"

Jaime has always been like a second father to me—came with the territory of being so close with Bails—so this cuts deep.

"Dad doesn't—"

"Oh, he does. Bailey had a word with him," Jaime says. *Fuck.* That's why he questioned me this morning about colleges. I misread that whole thing.

Also: Bailey stood up for me? *Bad. Ass.* No wonder I want all of her seconds.

"He was so against it," I say, barely audible.

"Yeah, well, my kid has a knack for persuading people to do stuff."

True that. Bailey is the best. She made Dad see reason. But how?

"This neighborhood is way too fucking small and nosy," I mutter, turning around and marching toward my house.

His laughter rings in my ears all the way to my door. "Youth is wasted on the young, buddy."

CHAPTER TWENTY-SIX
LEV

Miserable Fact #15: In one version of the telegraph code, "LOL" means loss of life.

Glancing at the time on my phone, I decide to drive to Goodwill. I can probably catch Bailey still. But when I arrive there, she isn't around. I go to every charity store downtown, texting her whenever I'm not driving, before the evening rolls in. Better to go home, take a shower, make myself presentable, and continue my groveling later.

When I push the door to my house, the sound of laughter comes from the kitchen. I barely step inside when I see Dad standing in front of me, looking like a ghost of himself. Wide-eyed and distracted.

"Hey, bud. Heading out now. Call if you need anything." He shoulders past me and disappears inside his car, like a burglar in the middle of a heist.

What the shit?

Dad never leaves without stopping for a few minutes of conversation (read: interrogation about football and how my day has been). I'm barely able to recover from the shock when I step inside and find something even more disturbing—Dixie sitting at the dining room table with her back to me, her face covered with her hands.

She is not laughing, like I initially thought when I walked in. She is bawling her eyes out.

The scene unfolds in front of me, and I realize what I just stepped into. The table is laden with home-cooked food. Seeing as it isn't a burned omelet or in a restaurant container, I'm pretty sure it was Dixie who made it. There are candles burning in the middle of the table. Soft, old-ass elevator music is playing in the background. Perfect for boring, missionary-style sex. Dixie is wearing a tight red dress, and her hair looks like some kind of a fancy dessert. Shit, this was a seduction dinner date.

Or was *supposed* to be one before Dad lit outta here like Julia Roberts in…well, any '90s movie I can think of.

Holy shit. Dixie decided to go for broke, and in return, Dad broke her heart.

And I just stepped into this whole mess. Honestly, I should be filing for a restraining order against my luck today.

I'm about to step in and offer some kind of comfort, but then I hear her talking.

"I tried, Brooke."

Last time I checked, my name wasn't Brooke, so I take it she is on the phone. I tilt my head sideways and notice that one of her hands is pinned to her ear, her phone tucked inside it. "I gave it all I have. Everything. The dinner. The sexy dress. The pitch."

I'm now torn between tiptoeing my ass out of here, making myself known, or continuing to watch this train derailing not only off of its tracks but flinging itself right off a cliff.

"I told him I loved him. He said he only sees me as a friend. I can't do this anymore. I have to move on. If I want to have a baby— and God, there is nothing I want more than having a baby—I have to give up. I'm cutting it close as it is. If I want to get pregnant, it needs to be this year."

Dixie wants Dad to be her baby daddy. That means Dad would have a kid younger than his grandson. That *I* would have another sibling. Though, judging by the look of horror on his face when I arrived, sending baby shower invitations is premature. Ya know, as an understatement.

My phone pings with a message and blows my cover. Dixie twists her head, her mouth opening in surprise. "Um, I'll call you later, Brooke." She hangs up and hurries up to her feet. I check the text message, in case it's Bailey. Even though I know today is too trash to deliver any sort of good news.

Thalia: Fixed everything with your little girlfriend yet?

My gaze snaps back to Dixie, and I raise my hand. "It's okay. I…" Didn't hear anything? Bullshit. She knows I was here for the entire conversation. So instead, I say, "I know what it's like. I'm the president of the Unrequited Love Club, remember?"

Dixie sniffles frantically, busying her hands with gathering the delicious bowls of food. "Sorry! I'll clean up here and get out of your way."

"No. You can stay and eat." What the fuck am I saying? Why would she want to sit here and gnaw on disappointment and heartbreak in the house of the man who just denied her?

She inhales. "I know you don't like me…"

Hold on a minute—*what?* "Hey, that's not true." I scowl. "I like you a whole bunch."

"I don't blame you. I know I can be annoying, the way I butt into your business—"

"Yeah, you do. So does Dad. And Bailey. Knight. Jaime. Vaughn. Grim. And pretty much everyone who gives a shit about me. I still love them. Look, who cares what I say? I'm a sulky teenager. We know jack shit. It's your job to civilize us."

She snuffles and chuckles and cries at the same time. There's a lot going on, on her face. "Well…if you're hungry…"

"I'm always hungry. Let me call Knight. I bet he's hungry too."

A look of pure horror crosses over her face. It is one thing for me to know that she is pursuing Dad, but she isn't sure how Knight is going to react to it. I step toward her, touching her elbow. "Knight knows you're in love with Dad."

"How?" Her red-rimmed eyes flare in alarm. "Did you tell him?"

"Um, no." I give her a look. "You aren't very discreet about it. I mean, you look at him like he found the cure to cuntiness."

"He probably could. For your mom." A twinge of disappointment touches her tone.

I smile ruefully. "Probably, yeah. But since she isn't here anymore…"

She looks up, looking miserable and hopeful at the same time.

I smile. "It's time for plan *D*."

———————

Two hours later, Dixie is long gone. Knight and I hugged her and comforted her and told her she is pretty. Now my brother and I are sitting in the second living room, knocking back beers (Knight's is alcohol-free), arguing about who was hotter, Yasmine Bleeth or Tiffani Thiessen (you'd be surprised to learn they are not, in fact, the same chick). The front door slams shut and Dad enters the room, looking like he ran a fucking marathon in his three-piece Armani. All in all, I live in an extremely normal family, as you can see.

"Did you go jogging in your work suit?" Knight snorts into his beer bottle.

"Yeah," Dad answers matter-of-factly, falling into a recliner and pushing his wet hair off his forehead. "Yeah, I did."

"Great!" Knight says cheerfully. "That's not strange at all."

"We need to talk." I put my drink down.

Dad looks between us, scowling. "Why do I have a feeling I'm about to be grounded by two people whose credit cards I foot the bill for?"

"Because you are," I say at the same time Knight wags his finger.

"Now, this is fake news, Pa. I'm financially independent."

"Only because there's a billboard of you in a thong in Times

Square, showing a high-definition imprint of your erection," I remind my older brother.

"Please." Knight tosses his head back, laughing gravelly. "That was half a chub, max."

Dad turns to Knight. "You done licking your own balls?"

Knight sighs dreamily. "I wish. No matter how many yoga classes I attend with Luna, I can never quite get there. Can you imagine the freedom in doing that, though? Endless possibilities. And Luna could sleep in too."

As you can see, TMI runs in the family.

Dad snaps his fingers in front of both of us now, becoming increasingly agitated. "Focus. Anyone gonna explain to me why this looks like an intervention?"

I turn to look at Knight. Maybe he should start this topic, since he's closer to Dixie.

"You're being shitty to my mom." Knight throws him a level-headed, deadly serious glare.

Okay. Maybe not.

"Watch your mouth, Son." Dad's expression bleeds ire now. He's no longer confused—he is pissed. "I gave your mother everything I had. I sacrifi—"

Knight cuts him off, "Not Mom-mom. My birth mother."

Dad stares at him like he's crazy. *"What?"*

"I overheard Dixie talking on the phone after you ran away." I lean forward in my seat.

"I didn't ru—"

"Don't even, Dad." Knight brings his palms up, shaking his head. "You look like the Ridiculously Photogenic Marathon Guy meme. Sans the inner light. Ever since Mom died, you have the aura of dry cement."

"Em, thanks." Dad narrows his eyes at him.

"Look." I sigh. "She's in love with you. Doesn't take a genius to see that. She wants to have a baby, and she's…what? Forty-two? Forty-four?"

"Thirty-eight." Dad squirms in his seat like a schoolboy in trouble. "She still has time."

"Yeah, but you seem to be an expert at making her waste it on your ass." Knight stands up, sauntering over to Dad. Dad shoots up to his feet. They're almost toe-to-toe now. This looks way too confrontational, and I realize Knight actually likes Dixie a lot. Maybe even loves her. And that Dad does too. In his own unromantic way.

Knight raises his hand. Dad doesn't flinch. I suck in a breath, but Knight just wipes lint off Dad's jacket. "Don't be a douchebag, Dad." His voice comes out soft, calm. "She wants your happily-ever-after, while you aren't even sure there *could* be a post-Mom. Either you man up and give her what she wants or let her go. Give it to her straight—she has no shot. It's never gonna happen. Have you ever told her that?"

By the way a muscle jerks in Dad's jaw, I can tell the answer is no. He's never rejected Dixie outright. Just kept her at arm's length. Knight continues.

"Don't give her false hope just because it's nice to have someone to take to charity galas and dinners. Either you take the plunge or you leave the pool. Dipping your toes every once in a while is damaging for both of y'all. Stop wasting her time. She spent most of her life missing out."

I've never seen Knight stand up for Dixie like this before. It's kind of touching. Suddenly I'm filled with screwed-up jealousy because at least he still has *some* sort of mom.

Dad rubs the edge of his jaw, staring at the floor. "I'll take nothing."

It's my turn to jump up to my feet. "Mom made you promise you'd move on."

"Well, no one measures up," Dad barks out, looking between us wildly. Like we're ambushing him. That's when the penny drops. He's lonely. Lonely in rooms full of people. At work, and parties, and vacations. His soul mate is gone. His only flashes of normalcy are my football moments. Things that anchor him to his shared past with Mom. The good ol' days. Instead of my usual anger, I feel sad for him. He never meant to suffocate me with expectations.

"Besides, what's it to you?" Dad's eyes narrow. "You should be happy I love your mom so much that I don't jump back into the dating pool, catching every floating STD out there." We should definitely put the pool analogies to bed.

"Love*d*," I correct him quietly. "Loved, Dad. Mom's gone."

"It's been four years." Knight's eyes are twinkling with tears. "We miss her so much, Dad. We do. But her legacy was making sure we're happy. Fulfilled. Choosing life over grief isn't betraying her—it is honoring her."

"And your love for Mom was never put into question," I add. "You paid your dues. We want to see you happy. Actually…"

This is my perfect in to tell him about my own hopes and dreams. How he is standing in the way to all of them. The Air Force Academy is not in my cards for this year, but who knows? Maybe the next one.

Knight and Dad cock their heads, zeroing in on me.

"What?" they ask in unison. Knight gives me a *don't you fucking dare* glare.

But I'm done living for other people.

"Actually, Dad, the fact that you put all of your happiness chips in our corner puts a lot of pressure on us. Well, on *me*. I…well, I hate football."

He stares at me but doesn't say anything. I think he knows. I think he might have been actually paying attention the last few days.

"Despise it. As a game. As a concept. As a fucking hobby. And I mean…" I rub the back of my neck. "The Brits are right. Soccer *is* football. Football is…handball, I guess?"

"Very catchy," Knight mutters.

Dad stares at me like I just announced I'm in love with the kitchen sink and we're running to Vegas to elope.

"I've never liked it," I continue. "I mean, yeah, in elementary and middle school it wasn't so bad, and it brought the family together so I didn't mind so much. But when it started getting serious…well, I only kept doing it because I knew it made you happy. That you liked coming to games and dreamed that one day I'd get drafted."

The look on his face makes me want to vomit. He is grief-stricken. Horrified.

"Look." Knight steps between us, trying to diffuse the situation with a chuckle. "No harm done, okay? All Lev's saying—"

"Bullshit." Dad worms out of Knight's embrace, stepping in my direction. He is deep in a trance. "You mean it, Levy? You really only played football because of me? Because Bailey told me I was clipping your wings the other day, but I figured she was just…" He licks his lips. *"Overreacting."*

She wasn't. She was spot-on. Dad believed what he wanted to believe.

I shrug helplessly, staring at my socked feet. "I love you. I wanted you to be happy. Playing football made you happy."

"Fuck, how far were you going to take this?" He threads his fingers through his hair.

I think about it for a moment before walking over to my bedroom. When I return to the living room, Dad and Knight are exactly where I left them. I hand Dad the letters of acceptance held together with a rubber band. He snaps it off, sifting through them. "TCU. Michigan. Ohio State. Clemson. South Carolina. Holy shit…"

Knight turns his head to look at me in horror. I feel like a fraud. And supremely stupid. What was God thinking, giving me this talent? Should've given it to Mitchell Schwartz.

Dad balls the letters in his fist. There are tears in his eyes.

"If Rosie were here, she'd kill me. What have I done?"

"Mom's not here, so your secret's safe with me." I take a step toward him. I'm not going to pretend everything is dandy, but there's no need to be an ass about it, either. "Actually, I don't know about Knight. He has a big mouth, he might spread the news." I tilt my head in my brother's direction. The three of us chuckle. "The important thing is that I'm done chasing other people's dreams. It's time to chase mine. I'm going to become a fighter jet pilot."

Dad doesn't say a word, only pulls me into a hug. One where he uses all of his muscles, including the one in his chest. One that says *I'm sorry* and *I love you* and *I'm going to fix this, you'll see.* I don't expect him to, but I feel like six tons of deadweight just dropped off my back. He squeezes me so close to his shoulder he nearly cuts off my oxygen supply. "You have my blessing, Son."

When we disconnect, he thumbs away a desolate tear from my cheek. I'm not even embarrassed. Boys don't cry, but men do. The good ones anyway.

"Coach know?" Dad runs his fingers through my hair to fix it. Old habits die hard.

I nod. "I retired as captain."

"How do you feel about it?"

The question gives me pause, because I'm not used to being asked how I feel about things when it comes to football. Only to keep doing my best, to push harder. "It feels...right."

Dad sucks in a breath. "It's the end of an era."

"More like an *error*," I murmur. We grin back at each other.

He rolls his eyes. As supportive as he might be, it's still too soon to joke about the One True Sport. But even his most sardonic scowl can't hide the pride lingering at the edges of his mouth. Even if I don't end up fulfilling his dream, at least I've finally shown I'm capable of standing up for what I believe in. Perhaps that's all he ever really wanted.

"Sorry to interrupt this Oscar-worthy performance," Knight drawls, looking between us. I'd be mad at him if I didn't see the relief on his face. "But can we get back to the topic?"

"Your erection commercial?" I blink.

"*Tom Ford*," Knight corrects. "And I maintain it was barely a semi."

Dad pats his back. "It's okay that you got a little excited, Son."

"What are you gonna do about Dixie?" Knight growls.

Dad's face falls. "Undecided."

"Well, decide in the next week, or I'm telling her to cut off all communication with you, myself," Knight threatens. I believe him too. And if there's anyone who could attest to Dixie's loyalty, it is him. "One week, Dad. That's all you're getting."

He nods solemnly. Dad raises the acceptance letters in his hand. "Can we burn these in the backyard?"

"HOW DID YOU KNOW!" I'm laughing because that's what I've been wanting to do each time one came in the mail.

Dad locks my head in his arm, ruffling my hair as he leads us out. "Burning shit down is a recreational activity in this cul-de-sac. Just ask Uncle Vicious."

I show up at Grim's doorstep the same night, a knot of nerves in my throat. He lives in a Spanish colonial revival mansion with palm trees, a kidney-shaped pool, and all that jazz. I know on his door. His mom flings the door open within seconds, wearing a full-blown Hermes suit and a slight frown. She looks deathly serious, and again, I'm reminded how he's under so much pressure from his family to take over the family business.

"Mrs. Kwon." I smile and nod. "Is Grim around?"

She gives me a quick once-over, toes to face. "Why, isn't he expecting you?"

"No," I admit. "Actually, I'm not sure if he wants to see me. Which is exactly why I'm here."

"Weird logic. Let me ask him if he's accepting visitors." She slams the door in my face, and I can't help but chuckle a little. No wonder he's such a hard ass. It runs in his DNA.

Somehow, I know he'll see me. Grim is no cop-out, and even

if we have our disagreements, he meets every challenge head-on. Which is exactly why he's the right owner of the captain title. The door opens again. This time, I see Grim, wearing a No Fear hoodie and a tie-dye sweatpants, like it's the nineties. He frowns at me. "Thought I took the trash out earlier."

"Bro." I raise my palms up in surrender. "A few words?"

"Actually, there's only one I need to hear." He folds his arms over his chest. "And you know what it is."

"I'm sorry." The words slide out of my mouth easily. I know when I fuck up, and I definitely screwed up with Grim. "I put my ego before your happiness, which is a shitty thing to do to your best friend. I was so high on being golden, my principles turned to rust. I knew how much you needed this win to be able to unchain yourself from your family's grip, and still, I did the wrong thing."

"Then why did you do it?" Grim's eyes narrow. He's not letting me off the hook. Not yet. Hell, he didn't even invite me in. "Why'd you put me through all this crap?"

I let out a breath. "Because I wanted to make my dad and brother happy. Their approval meant more to me than my own dreams. Being an All Saints High football captain was a family tradition, and I didn't want to break it. But it turned out that it broke *me*." I rake my fingers over my head, looking at my feet. "I did it to make other people happy, and I ended up making everyone miserable. You and I included."

Grim sucked his teeth, considering my words. "Yeah, well, you're gonna have to make up for that."

I look up, frowning. "How?"

"Let's start with you not fucking up the Bailey situation. You know you need to clean up this mess."

"Already on it." I nod.

Grin rolls his eyes. "Wanna come in?"

"Can't," I say. "Got lots of fires to put out."

"Well." Grim smirks. "Consider mine done."

CHAPTER TWENTY-SEVEN
BAILEY

I'm carving a dove-shaped cut on my skin using a boning knife I stole from the kitchen.

If Mom ever finds out, she'd blow a gasket. But she's not here to chide me. I'm in the sanctuary of my studio. Just me and my demons.

Blood trickles through the fresh scar on my flesh. I chose my hip bone for this DIY tattoo, to keep it hidden from view. I'm not only cutting because I caught Lev holding Thalia like she was a precious, rare thing. I'm also doing this because my injuries are making my eyes water with agony. The endorphins numb the pain of my injuries. Plus, life these days is just a string of little Lev breaks callously sewn together by disappointment.

I could really use some painkillers and Xanax right about now to numb all the pain. The anxiety that's clogging at my throat. But Lev flushed them all away. *Asshole.*

Once I'm satisfied with my handiwork—the dove looks small and tiny and red—I dump the bloodstained knife on the floor. I pick up my phone and scroll through Lev's messages from yesterday.

Lev: It's not what you think. Me and Thalia.
Lev: I can explain.
Lev: I'm coming your way right now.

Lev: Your dad said you went to Goodwill. I looked around but couldn't find you.

Lev: Sorry. Got caught up in a homemade episode of Dr. Phil(th). I'm under your window. Throwing rocks.

Lev: OKAY THROWING STONES NOW. Don't tell me you aren't hearing this.

Lev: Fine. Will try you again tomorrow. I just wanna make one thing clear: I'm NOT with Thalia. You are my one. You are my only. You're my forever.

Lev: <3

Lev: (This was my heart, not my dick. Though you're welcome to both.)

Lev: For reference, this is my dick: <<<<<<<<<<<<<<<<<<<<<<<3

But it's four o'clock *tomorrow* and still no sign of Lev. I came down here hours ago to practice, but I'm struggling to care anymore. About Juilliard. About my relationship with Lev. My hunger for success is gone. It's replaced by a hollowness only drugs could fill.

The doorbell chimes. I stay where I am, spread like a snow angel on the floor, staring at the ceiling. Lev wouldn't knock. He's a barger—my heart can testify.

I close my eyes. A tear rolls down my cheekbone, slipping into my ear. Quietly, I can admit to myself that I'm not okay. I'm not getting better. I'm not on top of things. I *don't* have a plan. Maybe I've finally hit rock bottom. Because right now, I feel like I'm pancaked to a hard, jagged surface.

A perky, high-pitched voice impales my sanctuary from above.

"Hi, Mrs. Followhill! Is Bailey around? Thought I'd check on her!"

Thalia.

I scramble to my feet and zip up the stairway to the living room. She can't come down here. I'm not sure what's going on between her and Lev, but I'm positive her version of the story isn't good for my psyche *or* sobriety right now. Plus, she was the one who called me to come to All Saints High yesterday, under the guise that we'd be training in the gymnasium. I should've known it was a setup. Hindsight is twenty-twenty.

I'm halfway up the stairway when I hear two sets of feet pounding on wood. Thalia materializes in front of me, Mom standing behind her. Thalia is grinning like the cat who got the canary. Or in my case, the turtle dove. For the first time in a long time, she doesn't look like the 2.0 version of me. She looks pale, dark circles shadowing her eyes.

"*Ohmygosh*, Bails! Where were you yesterday? I thought we were gonna practice together!" She smacks my shoulder, air-kissing my cheeks. Mom is studying us acutely. Her bullshit meter is probably dinging so loudly, she's going deaf.

"Honey, are you accepting visitors? Thalia was very adamant you were expecting her." Mom looks like she's about to cut a bitch. Speaking of cutting, she absolutely *cannot* get into my studio, or she'll see it looks like a mini crime scene. *Ugh.*

"Right now's not a good time." I force a smile. "I'll call you later?"

"Why don't you walk Thalia upstairs?" Mom suggests. "I'll get into the studio and grab some of the empty water bottles—"

"No!" I shriek. "You can't go in there."

The muscles in Mom's face go rigid. "Why not?"

Because apparently, whenever I can't get high, I stoop so low I have to cut myself.

"I'm going to throw them into the recycling trash today. It feels wrong that you have to take care of it."

"Don't be silly." Mom squeezes my arm. "It's no trouble at all. You cleaned the whole house yesterday."

She slips past me, and it's better Thalia see than my mom. I have to stop her, so I find myself blurting out, "Thalia and I need to practice there now."

Mom rotates her head, scanning Thalia's attire, which comprises of two-inch heels, a skirt that barely covers her private business, and a shirt my dad likes to refer to as a shra—a shirt-bra. Mom is about to argue, but then Thalia shrugs off her backpack and lifts it in the air. "I've got training gear in my backpack."

"I need to check your bag for drugs," Mom says matter-of-factly. I'm about to die of humiliation.

Thalia tosses her bag into Mom's hands, the picture of nonchalance. "Be my guest, Mrs. Followhill."

She flips the bag upside down and goes through each item meticulously. Rummaging through textbooks, a box of tampons and an array of fruit-flavored ChapStick. Finally, Mom takes a deep breath and nods. She goes back upstairs, and I reluctantly lead Thalia into the ballet studio.

Thalia closes the door and leans against it, a wicked glint twinkling in her eyes. I don't *actually* think she's evil. Very few people are. Normally, people don't finger their ultra-thin moustache and *mwahahaha* when they see others suffer. But some people have no boundaries and very little healthy judgment, and I feel like Thalia falls into that category.

"What do you want?" I pick up the bloodied knife and clean it with the hem of my shirt.

Thalia looks around. "First of all, what the heck happened here? Why is there *blood* on the floor?"

"Aunt Flo's in town," I mumble, picking up a paper towel roll I keep here to wipe sweat from the floor and clean it. "I'll ask again—why are you here?"

Thalia pushes off the door. "Well, because we didn't practice yesterday like we planned, silly! Why did you leave all of a sudden?"

"You know why I left." I dump the sullied paper towels into the trash can. The metallic scent of blood tinges the air, prickling my tongue.

"Not everyone's a brainiac, doll. Spell it out for me."

"You wanted me to catch you with Lev."

"How can you *catch* me with my own boyfriend?" She gasps in shock. I've met fantasy books more believable than this girl. "So what if we had a moment? It's not like we noticed you."

"Are you still together?" I choke out the question. She stops a few feet away from me, giving me a once-over. I know I look terrible.

Suddenly, I regret asking her.

Her innocent expression breaks into a delighted, shocked smile, and my heart sinks further. "He hasn't spoken to you? Oh. *Of course* we are." She eats the space between us, gathering me into a hug. "And all thanks to you. Your friendship and your advice helped me so much."

I'm stiff in her embrace. My heart is pounding like crazy. I want to make this stop.

The truth pours out of my mouth like a gushing wound. "I had sex with him on Saturday."

Now it's Thalia's turn to become a pillar of salt.

"*What?*" she whispers.

I nod into her hair. "I'm not saying this to hurt you, I swear. But either you're lying about the fact you're together or he's cheating on you. Either way, you deserve the truth."

She pulls away from me like I'm fire. "I mean, things aren't perfect, but we're working on it. Especially now, after what happened."

"What happened?" My throat turns dry. Her perfume—*my* perfume—clings to my lips, the bitter taste of it exploding in my mouth. And I know in this moment that I'm never going to wear it again. It is ruined for me forever.

"He didn't tell you the good news?" She bats her lashes. "I'm not going to college. I'm joining him wherever he goes. I've a feeling he is going to propose."

The entire world tips over like a bowl of hot oil. The burn scorches through my inner organs, turning everything into ash. I stumble backward. My back hits the mirror. I glance behind my shoulder. Look at my face. Find strength. And remember who I am.

The words fall out of my mouth on their own accord: "You're lying."

That serene grin on her face spreads wider. I'm woozy. "Aww, I know it's shocking. *Totes* unexpected! But I mean, all of your families marry young, right?"

Yes. To people they're in love with. Lev is not in love with Thalia.

Turning around, I pick up my phone from the floor and scroll down to find his name.

"What are you doing?" Panic laces her voice.

"Calling him to ask if you guys are still together."

"P—put the phone down, you wacko."

I hit send instead. Screw her. So far I have been easily manipulated because my head is a mess, but one thing is clear to me—Thalia has been playing a game all along.

Thalia pounces on me, ripping my phone from between my fingers. She hurls the device across the room. It hits the opposite mirror, which cracks noisily. A large chunk of glass collapses to the floor, blanketing my phone. Thalia grabs me by the shoulder and pushes me onto the sea of broken glass. She is trying to *hurt* me. My survival instincts kick into high gear, and I raise my arms, pushing her back. She tries to catch my shirt, but I dodge, running toward the door. She is faster, though. And she reaches there first, blocking my way out with her body.

I open my mouth to yell for my parents, and she slaps a hand over it, her eyes manic.

"If you want to get out of here alive, you better not fucking scream, Bailey." She removes her hand from my mouth slowly.

I stare at her in horror. Her eyes are filled with tears. She's shaking inside her skimpy clothes. "Let him go."

"*What?*" I sputter. "I'm not the one clutching on to him, Thalia. I have no ownership over him."

"Stop being so greedy." Her voice spikes up. "You are surrounded by many rich, handsome boys. All of them can make you happy. I only know one. I only have a chance with one. And you're ruining it for me."

Is this what it's about? Securing a cushy future for herself? I'm not trivializing poverty or struggle, but Lev is more than a paycheck. He is my entire world.

I shake my head. "No can do, Thalia. I will fight for him with everything I have in me."

"How lucky for me that your everything is not much," she hisses out.

With a growl, she grabs on to my dove bracelet and rips it from my wrist. It's torn and tattered on the floor between us, a fatal blow in one shot. I drop to my knees on a gasp, frantically looking for the pendant between the shards. My heart is pounding in my ears. Where is it?

"You're a silver-spooned princess," she accuses, standing above me, glass crunching beneath her, while I'm searching for the unspoken love declaration Lev gave me. "No wonder you were perfect all the time. It's easy to be when you have the entire world in the palm of your hand. As soon as shit started becoming real, you fell apart. Look at you." An icy laugh bubbles from her throat. "A scrawny, purple mess. Just because Lev is confused, doesn't mean he isn't going to realize he made a mistake. We will get back together."

"Jesus." I heave out a sigh. "You're the one who is high if you believe that. Lev would have never fallen in love with you, with or without my presence in his life. He is a kind person. An expansive thinker. Your souls are oil and water. Mix them together, and they still won't stick."

Thalia towers over me, a scorn painting her face. "Look up, Bailey."

I do. And that's when I see the pendant dangling from between her fingers.

"Our souls don't need to match. Love is a story they sell privileged idiots and you eat it up and ask for seconds. The only thing that needs to fit is his dick between my legs, and we have no problem in that department." She lets out a manic laugh.

I stand up before she kicks me while I'm down—*while* kicking me while I'm down.

"Plus, now that I have this, maybe I can convince him I'm his true love." She puts the pendant to her heart, grinning. "Like Cinderella's slipper…"

"You're nuts," I whisper.

"Nah, you're just slow to catch up on the plot. I guess every good story needs a villain." Thalia's mouth hooks in a miserable smile. "And I'm the villain in yours."

"Why are you doing this?" I ask, even though I know. Why do we do things we shouldn't do? From pain. From desperation. From anger.

The question seems to sober Thalia, who actually responds in earnest.

"I wanted the fairy tale for myself, and with you gone to the East Coast, I thought I could have it. I wanted hearts and roses. Love declarations and neck kisses. I wanted the glitzy life, the nice cars, the year-round vacations. And I watched from the sidelines, seeing how all the Coles and Followhills and Rexroths and Spencers married young. Married *well*. You all seem so happy, so fortunate. I wanted that for myself. To write my own destiny. Lev is extraordinary. And you? You're as ordinary as they come."

"Ordinary and extraordinary aren't antonyms, Thalia," I say sadly. "They coexist beautifully. You cannot have beauty without ugliness. Love without hate. A rainbow without the rain. Being special is nothing special. The things that make us great are the things that we control. Our choices. And you?" I shake my head. "You're not a good person. He could never love you."

She looks left and right, as if searching for hidden cameras. A horrible feeling crawls all over my skin. She is planning something foul.

Thalia pushes a hand inside her bra. She takes something out and throws it into my hands. I catch it instinctively and hold it in my fist. I can feel what's inside it without even opening my hand.

Pills.

Tranquility.

All in a small, square transparent bag.

Heaven.

I shove it back at her chest. "No. I'm done."

"You *need* it," she insists.

Someone bangs on the basement door loudly. Mom's voice filters in through the crack. "I heard something crashing. Is everything okay?"

Thalia and I are locked in an unwavering stare-off, but she no longer feels as dangerous. I drop the bag of drugs between us. It's at our feet. Every cell in my body wants to bend down and pick it up. But I can't. I want to do better. To *get* better. So I remind myself of all the people I cannot disappoint. My parents. Daria. Lev. *Myself.*

"Bailey? Bailey, answer me!" Mom bangs louder.

"Take them," Thalia hisses, her eyes turning into slits. "You won't get another chance. Sydney is going out of town tomorrow. Do it."

"Mom!" It takes everything in me to turn around and yank the door open. I fall into Mom's arms, crying, crying, crying. I'm full of glass and blood and demons.

"You should leave," Mom clips out to Thalia, my head nestled in her hands. I feel like the most fragile thing in the world right now. A tissue paper ripped to shreds.

Thalia picks up her stuff and scurries her way out.

Mom doesn't ask about the mirror.

About the blood.

About the state of me.

She just kisses the crown of my head and tells me, "I love you. I love you. I love you."

And in that moment, in the arms of a mother who loves me unconditionally, I know the meaning of true wealth.

Mom encourages me to take a shower. Perhaps because I look like the post-bucket *Carrie* scene. I don't argue for a change. I sit curled up under the showerhead, letting the water whip at my paper-thin skin. When I hear the front door open downstairs and Lev announcing himself, I bark out a bitter laugh. Of course, he is finally here when I'm unavailable. But this time, he says he'll wait. I turn off the faucet, sitting naked and shivering in the shower, and listen to broken crumbs of his conversation with my parents.

"...not going anywhere. Your kid is harder to pin down than the president."

"When did you try pinning down the president?" Dad asks conversationally. "You know his address is public knowledge, yeah?"

"She isn't in a great place today," Mom admits faintly.

"A great place for her would be rehab," Dad interjects. "Kid is less than a hundred pounds. She's a ticking time bomb."

No, I'm not. I frown, huddling toward my mirror to take a good look at myself. And then I see that maybe I *am* less than a hundred pounds after all. My cheeks are sunken, my skin is pale, and you can see the outline of every bone in my torso clearly.

"Well, what do you suggest, kicking her out?" Mom barks at him. Mom and Dad *never* fight, so of course, I'm filled with fresh guilt. Ever since I came back from Juilliard, I've caused nothing but trouble and heartache. I made my parents miserable. Destroyed Lev's life. And caused Daria pain and sorrow.

"If her sobriety is at risk, heck yes," Lev spits out. I don't know who I'm mad at, but I'm fuming. Maybe it's at him for selling me out or at myself for this gigantic fall from grace. Or at the world, for making me believe for eighteen years that everything would be okay, just for me to crumble out of the safety net of my parents' house in less than a year.

That's it. I'm gonna go downstairs and shove it in their faces that

I actually refused drugs just today, when Thalia tried to give them to me.

I step out of the shower and slip into a bathrobe. My skin is ice-cold and I'm trembling from withdrawals. They continue arguing downstairs when my gaze halts over my hip bone. The carving of the dove has somewhat healed, and the jagged skin sticks out. I run my finger over it and shiver. A gust of wind. Like the window is open, but it's not. It's crazy, but I feel like something's happening. Like Rosie is here somehow.

Downstairs, Lev says, "Where's the draft coming from?"

I press my lips together, fighting tears. "*Thank you, Rosie*," I whisper.

There's a glimmer of hope in the sea of darkness I'm drowning in. A small hope that Rosie is watching over us and maybe she has a big, good plan how to get us out of this.

"What draft?" Dad asks. I start putting my clothes on, walking over from the bathroom to my room, listening to them as I get dressed. "Anyway, I'm not feeling comfortable sending her back to Juilliard before she completes some sort of program. She's been slacking on her support group meetings."

"Well, Juilliard is no longer something we need to be worried about, for better or worse," Mom says decidedly.

My heart grinds into miniscule smithereens. I can't move.

I.

Can't.

Breathe.

"What do you mean?" Lev echoes my thoughts. There is silence, so much silence, too much silence. Marx, *say* something. *Anyone. Anything.*

"We got the letter in the mail yesterday," Mom sighs, finally. "I hid it from Bailey. I know it's horrible—it was addressed to her. But I couldn't risk her finding out tha—"

"What's in the letter, Mel?" Dad's voice is urgent.

"She is not going back." Mom's voice cracks in the middle, like a twig. "Juilliard has a strict no drug abuse policy. They're extremely diligent about it. What happened to Bailey is no secret, and it's horrible optics. Plus, they want her to get better. She's not a risk they're willing to take, and frankly, I don't blame them." There's a beat of silence before she really hammers it home. "Bailey is not going back to Juilliard. They decided for her. And that's final."

I fall down on my knees, a feral cry escaping my lips. My mouth is dry and my ears are clogged, full of white noise.

The dream is dead.

Her dream is dead.

My dream is dead.

This makes no sense at all. They sent me an email asking me to retake the practical exam. Why did they change their minds? But then I remember what Mom told me on the plane to Jackson Hole. Juilliard doesn't usually send emails about things like that.

She is right—they sent snail mail. But someone *did* send me an email. It just wasn't authentic. Who could push me into working harder for an old dream, into taking drugs?

Thalia.

I grab my phone and get into the email again. Sure enough, the email address looks suspicious. thejulliardschooladmin@yahoo.com.

How did I not pay attention? A freaking yahoo address. And Juilliard is spelled *wrong*.

Is this amateur hour? I should've seen this right away.

But of course, it slipped past me. I was drugged up, in pain, and too jaded to focus on the details.

I don't deserve Juilliard. Or Lev, for that matter. I'd only slow him down. He is destined to greatness, and me? I'm below average.

From the corner of my eye, I notice something sitting on my nightstand. It's the drugs Thalia brought over today. She must've put them here when Mom was comforting me, before she slithered her way out. They're here, in plain sight, waiting to be consumed. How could I have missed *that*?

The same way you missed so many things these past couple months.

No Juilliard. No future. And...let's admit it, after the confiscated dove pendant, maybe no Lev, either. That bracelet was our lifeline. The one thing that bound us together, even when we were torn apart, each of us living on another coast.

Those things on my nightstand? They could make me shut down and forget who I am.

Rather than walking, I crawl my way to my nightstand. My knees hit the floor. I push three pills past my lips and swallow without water. Then I take the rest of the pills—I don't even know what they are—and shove them down my throat. I slacken against my bedframe, head hanging in shame, and stare out the window.

To the doves sitting on my tree.

To the sun twinkling in the sky.

To what very well could be the last day of my life.

CHAPTER TWENTY-EIGHT
LEV

Miserable Fact #75: Though the etiquette guide for Victorian mourning varied, widows grieved for two and a half years, while widowers for three months.

"I don't mean to be rude, but is there a chance Bails drowned in the shower?" I turn to Jaime and Mel. I've been sitting in their living room for forty fucking minutes, waiting for Bailey to come down. I know she's a chick and that there's an unspoken universal agreement where women are allowed thrice the time to shower than men. But forty minutes extra is a stretch. In this time, she could wash her hair, put on a fancy face mask, flick the bean twice, dry up, blow out her hair, and try on three sets of clothes.

Jaime stares into his whiskey, and I can tell he wants to hurl it against the wall. "Mel?"

Melody shakes her head. "I don't want her to feel like we don't trust her."

"Why not?" he asks. "We *don't*."

"I'm going to check on her." I stand up.

"Sure, in the same fantasy you're both going to attend a Playboy mansion party and scuba dive with unicorns." Jaime rises to his feet, shoving me back down to the couch by the shoulder.

I roll my eyes and grab my La Croix. "I've seen her naked before."

He shoots me a look before trudging up the stairs.

Mel turns her attention to me and smiles. "You know, her friend Thalia was here earlier. They seemed to have had quite the fight. Do you think she might be upset?"

My jaw is on its way to drop on the floor when Jaime's choked roar comes from upstairs. "Mel, come up here right now! Call an ambulance! JESUS FUCK."

———————

I'm only pretending to be alive.

I'm sure my heart is as flatlined as that of a plastic straw. I can't think straight.

I can't see straight.

I can't…

"You're going to get all of us killed if you don't watch the fucking road!" Dad hollers at me from the passenger seat, slapping my chest to snap me back into focus.

"Shit. Sorry." I rub at my eyes.

"Let me drive," Knight demands from the back seat.

"No, I can do this."

"You violated every traffic rule ever recorded on earth and some that haven't been enforced yet," Dad points out.

But we need to get to the hospital. *Fast.* That's where the ambulance took Bailey when Jaime found her unresponsive on her bedroom carpet. I darted upstairs and saw her. Saw everything. How she lay there, pale and angelic and *dead looking.* The PTSD crashed through me like a freight train. I had avoided seeing Mom like this in her coffin only to see the girl I love looking very much unalive.

"You need to calm the fuck down!" Knight shouts from the back seat of my speeding Tesla. Because that always helps things.

Ignoring him, I turn to Dad. "Can you call Mel and ask her if there's any news?"

A part of me is scared there's bad news they don't want to share with me.

I'm trying to remind myself this isn't about me, but it *feels* about my sorry ass. It's unfair that I have to bury my mother and the love of my life four years apart. And it seems *supremely* unfair that said love of my life brought this shit on herself.

Dad puts his phone on speaker and shoots me a look. "Eyes on the road, Levy."

I'm cutting past cars on the right lane, beeping people, stealing red lights.

Mel picks up, breathless. "Dean."

"Any news?" His voice is apologetic. "Sorry for pestering, but Lev…" He doesn't have to complete the sentence.

"She's in ICU. They're putting her in a medically induced coma. Dean, I can't… I don't know if I can survive this. Twice in two months. I'm not that strong. I'm not."

"Mel…" Dad's voice breaks.

In the background, I can hear Jaime yelling at someone, "She is my daughter and I want some answers, goddammit!"

Somehow, we make it to the parking lot of the hospital. I trudge my way to the corridors of the ICU. Dad and Knight have their arms on me from either side. They expect me to collapse any minute now.

When I reach the end of the hallway, where a couple blue plastic chairs are positioned in front of a closed door, I spot Jaime on the floor, his face in his hands, his back shaking.

"No!" I shoulder off Dad's and Knight's touch, rushing to him. I fall to the floor, grabbing Jaime by the shoulders and jerking him upright. I'm shaking him frantically. "No, Jaime. Tell me it's not true."

He doesn't say anything.

I've read this script before. Tragedies happen. Every day. And the author of my life, they killed Mom already. Why the fuck stop there when they can throw another curveball?

"Jaime, no."

"Lev, he needs a moment," Dad says.

"NO. Fuck that."

"Get off of him, Levy." I feel Knight's hands on my back. I slap them off. I go wild. Kick. Flail. Scream. I feel arms. And hands. And tears raining down on me. People are carrying me away from that door.

But I don't relent.

I stay.

CHAPTER TWENTY-NINE
DIXIE

THE DAY OF THE AIR FORCE ACADEMY DEADLINE

Lev leaves, a trail of his expensive aftershave lingering in his wake. I hear the door slam behind him and loiter in the kitchen for a few more seconds. I know he told me not to butt into his business. Several times, in fact. I heard him loud and clear. But I can't stand here and watch this bright, beautiful, overwhelmed kid make the biggest mistake of his life.

Take it from me—opportunities have the tendency not to knock on your door twice.

I know Dean doesn't want Lev to join the military, become a pilot, put his life on the line. But that stems from Dean's inability to move on. To embrace risks, new prospects, and changes. If Dean chooses to be stuck in the same place forever, that's on him.

And on you, for dallying around, waiting for the leftovers Rosie left behind.

Point is, none of it is Lev's fault. He deserves a shot at happiness. At devouring the world greedily, sinking his teeth into it like it's a juicy fruit rather than a bite of something he never wanted to sustain another man's vitality. He's worked hard for it. But he'll never go against his father's will.

Pushing the hesitation and self-doubt to the back of my mind,

I swiftly make my way to the laptop sitting at the table. I slide into Lev's deserted seat and double-click on the browser again. The Air Force Academy website pops in front of me. There are only a few more seconds before the browser will automatically refresh and everything Lev put into this is going to disappear. It is now or never. And never is a terribly long time.

Not your circus, not your monkeys, Dixie.

Leave the kid alone; he's dealing with enough.

Dean is going to kill you. Violently. Gradually. And eagerly.

Maybe I *am* ready for motherhood this time around. Because instead of thinking about the man I'm in love with, I think about his son, who I cannot bear to see sad. And about his late wife, who brought me here to take care of her family. And that includes Lev.

Squeezing my eyes shut and turning my face from the screen, I click on the apply button.

When it's all done and dealt with, I'm not even sorry for overstepping this red, shiny boundary. The tension rolls off my shoulders. The room becomes warmer, lighter. It's a new dawn. At least for one Cole member.

When Rosie died, Dean's heart died with her.

But Lev? Lev can still live.

PRESENT

I find Lev in the backyard, working on one of his many RC planes. He's flying it, making impressive loops, nosediving, then picking it right up inches from the ground. The kid has some serious skills, and I'm mad at Dean for overlooking them all these years.

I still haven't spoken to Dean since he walked out on me. I have nothing to say to him, actually. I came here for Lev.

Pushing the back door to the Coles' patio open, I close it silently behind me and wait until Lev notices my presence.

With his back to me, he asks, "How'd you get in, Dixie?"

"Your dad gave me the key back when my apartment got repainted." A blush creeps up my cheeks. I could've waited with the paint job. But I had wanted an excuse to lodge here, hoping it would bring me closer to Dean. In reality, we only drifted further apart. His uncanny ability to see through me, like I'm air, wounded me beyond words.

I'm starting to come to terms with what Dean told me three years ago, the first time I drunkenly almost kissed him, only a year after Rosie died.

"Don't waste your breath and hopes on someone like me, Dixie. I'll never be yours. I can be your friend. But never ever your partner."

Sticking around was a mistake. I thought he'd change his mind. Figured we were bound to have some sort of a relationship, anyway, because of Knight.

Back in reality, Lev uses his remote to shoot the RC high up in the sky, then have it loop around three times in perfect circles. His eyes are laser focused on it, not me. "Figures. Dad's not here."

"I'm not here for your father."

He doesn't say anything.

"How is Bailey feeling?"

Lev shrugs. "Dead-ish."

"Lev."

He lands the small airplane safely on the manicured lawn, sets his remote down, and turns to look at me. "She's in a medically induced coma. They're not sure when they're going to bring her back. And they aren't sure what she's coming back to. Like, they don't know if there's any neurological or intellectual damage or whatever. Oh, and her leg is apparently fucked forever or something." He pauses. "Just as well she's in a coma, since I have nothing to say to her."

I've never seen him behave this way. So lethargic and yet angry at the same time.

"You're at the hospital twenty hours a day," I point out. "You don't even go to school."

"I don't want her dead, yeah, but...I'm pissed."

"Why?" I ask.

"Because I'm still stuck somewhere between *I'm so fucking glad you're alive, and by the way, extremely in love with you* to *I hate your guts for what you're putting everyone through.* You know?"

I do. I know better than he can ever imagine. I plop on the edge of the hand-carved white wooden swing Rosie left behind. Her favorite reading spot. It is strange to be so familiar with the possessions of a woman who is no longer with us, but strangely enough, I miss her every day. I am so grateful that she gave Knight the life I couldn't give to him at the time. All through fighting her own battle.

She was the one who called me into Todos Santos. It was as though she was putting placeholders in her loved ones' lives. And what do you know? I fell in love with her entire world. Dean. Knight. And...yes, Lev too.

Guess Rosie LeBlanc had a talent for making the men in her life extremely easy to love.

Lev stares at me sitting in his mother's spot. For a moment, I think he is going to bark at me to get up and leave. But he takes a deep breath and joins me. My shoulders sag with relief.

"How do you feel about missing the Air Force Academy deadline?" I ask tentatively.

He tugs at his bottom lip, scowling at the grass. "Doesn't fucking matter, does it? I have bigger fish to fry."

"Like what?"

"Bailey," he says. "I know Dad says he is fine if I go—this does me little good now that I missed the deadline—but if she...*when* she wakes up, I still have to take care of her."

"You shouldn't," I blurt out.

He rears his head back. "What did you say?"

"I said you shouldn't." I shrug. "Take care of her."

A storm brews in his eyes. "You have no idea. She's done so much for me. When Mom died—"

"It was out of your control," I interject. "You didn't choose to lose your mother. Bailey has—will have a choice now. *When* they bring her back, she is going to have to make some tough decisions. And if she wakes up every day knowing you are there, by her side, babying her, I'm not sure she is going to make the right ones. You're enabling her. Putting pressure on yourself by constantly trying to save someone who might not want to be saved. You're setting both of you up for failure. It's one thing to help someone through a journey. It's another to willingly strap yourself into a vehicle with a deranged driver veering off the road—which is *exactly* what you're doing." My face is heated, my voice is high-pitched, and I'm pretty sure I'm half screaming at the poor kid. And still, I'm in a can't-stop, won't-stop trance. "You have to stop living for other people. It's not only being kind to yourself; it's being kind to them too. Let Bailey go. Be there for her—always one phone call away. But don't cancel your entire existence to nurse her. You will only fall out of love and happiness with her, the more of yourself you abdicate for her."

He stares at me blankly, blinking. I feel like he can see through me. Like he is reading every single thing that's on my mind.

"You speak from experience," he says gently, kicking his feet back on the ground to give us a push on the swing. The afternoon breeze caresses my face. I close my eyes, the faint scent of the ocean hitting the back of my nostrils. I don't know how I survived all those years in Texas. Living next to the ocean is truly magical.

"I do." I try to swallow the lump in my throat. "Yeah."

"Yet you're not letting Dad go."

Smoothing an invisible crease on my pencil skirt, I say, "I am letting him go, actually. This morning, I signed up with a sperm bank website. I also decided to extend my lease on my apartment, so I'm not buying the place next to yours anymore. How is that for do-as-you-preach?"

The sympathy in his eyes makes me so uncomfortable, I have to look away.

"It's...unfortunate." He clears his throat. "I'm sorry it didn't work out for you."

"Yeah." I smile. "So am I."

We both stare ahead, at the orange peaks of the mountains bracketing the town. I'm the first to speak again.

"So how do you feel about me right now? From one to ten. One is *loathe the sight of you*, and ten is *love you like a mother*."

He frowns. "Between seven-and-a-half to eight."

Am I blushing? It feels like I'm blushing. I was bracing myself for an average five. "Yay me. Well, get ready. I'm about to knock it down to around minus thirteen."

Lev's face hardens. "*Dixie*," he is already chiding me. "You overstepped again, didn't you?"

I wince.

He kicks the ground again to give us more momentum. "What'd you do?"

"I feel like I might have to stand up and put some distance between us before I tell you."

"Oh, shit." He looks down. "You're wearing sneakers. You *never* wear sneakers. You know I can catch your ass if need be, right?"

Chuckling awkwardly, I plant my feet on the ground, stand up, and walk over to a spot near enough to the patio door. Lev stares at me from the swing like I'm crazy. I probably am. I mean, who signs up a kid who doesn't belong to her to military school? Against his father's wishes? This idiot. Nice to meet you.

"I couldn't help it." I raise my palms in surrender.

"What did you do?" He stands up. Stands right in front of me. "I..."

"Spit it out." A few more steps in my direction. I'm sweating. He is not going to murder me, is he? The Coles are all teddy bears. Big on the outside but mushy within.

"I applied to the Air Force Academy. Uh, on your behalf. Obviously."

He freezes, his mouth hanging open. "*What?*"

I squeeze my eyes shut, bracing myself for a hit. "You left. The laptop was there. Everything was filled out. Mistakes were made."

Silence. Shock. Panic. Not enough oxygen. I push through with my explanation.

"I'm sorry. I didn't think. I…I just… You deserve this win. You earned it."

"Dixie." He blinks in confusion. "It wasn't even… All the documents…" Good news is, he seems more speechless than… *murderous.* Small victories. "I didn't even finish attaching all the… I mean, I don't know if they'll even *have* me."

Then something wonderful happens. Well, wonderful and a bit disturbing. Lev throws his head back, his shoulders shaking with glee. He is laughing, I realize, because he is relieved. Because not all is lost. Because he's probably regretted not applying every single moment since he walked away from his laptop.

He picks me up in his arms and spins me around, looking at me with a twinkle in his eyes. It is the first time I've seen him happy since Bailey came back. I smile back at him. His smile dissipates as we both remember why we're here.

Bailey. Dean. Heartbreak. *Right.*

He puts me down slowly on the porch.

"Thank you," he whispers.

"You're welcome, honey." I press my palms over his cheeks, squishing them like he is a toddler.

The noise of something being dumped on the counter comes from the house. I snap my head to where it comes from and see Dean looking like a feral predator, ambling toward us.

I instinctively take a step back. Lev doesn't move an inch.

"What's happening here?" Dean looks between us.

"Just hitting on Dixie, is all." Lev flashes a hedonistic smirk and, in that moment, looks like a carbon copy of his father. *Sheesh, those genes.*

Dean rushes over to us. I've never seen him like this before. Alert. *Alive.* I can't believe he actually thinks this isn't an innocent, loving moment. What's wrong with him?

"He is kidding!" I narrow my eyes. "You really think I'd make a move on your son?"

"I don't think you're making a move on my son, but I wouldn't be surprised if he makes a move on you to prove a point."

"And what point would that be?" Lev folds his gigantic arms over his chest, amused.

"That Dixie and I should be together," Dean spits out.

"Yeah, I stand corrected. This is *entirely* not a childish display of jealousy." Lev's chest rumbles.

Dean's eyebrows furrow. "Dixie, can I speak to you for a second?"

I glance down at my watch and frown. I have a showing in thirty minutes. I really didn't think my moment with Lev would turn into almost an entire hour. "Actually, now's not a great time."

Dean looks like I just kicked him in the face. I don't know if I want to laugh or cry. I've never denied him anything. But the truth is…now *isn't* a great time. And maybe I should be taking my own advice. The one I just gave Lev, about not being dragged down with the people you love.

"Okay…" he says slowly. "Tonight, then?"

"Oh, man." Lev puts his fist to his mouth, chuckling. "This is painful."

"Shut up." Dean squints at him.

"Tonight's no good, either." I shake my head, a blush creeping over my face. "I'm filming this realtor show in LA, remember? Our office is taking part in one of those parties. Good for PR, they said."

"Yeah. Uh-huh." Dean rolls his tongue inside his cheeks. "Guess

I'll call and schedule an appointment with your assistant, since you're so busy all of a sudden."

"Perfect." I ignore his sarcasm, feigning cheerfulness. "Jessica has access to my calendar. While I have you in such an accepting mood, I should also warn you that I sent an application on your son's behalf to the Air Force Academy." I deliver the news matter-of-factly and lethally. Dean stares at me with an odd expression. One I've never seen on him before. Somewhere between wonder and awe. I think I see some hate thrown in too. But I manage not to cringe.

Ignoring him, I rise to my tiptoes to pinch Lev's cheek. "I think he is going to get in. He's more than qualified."

For the first time, I leave the Cole residence not feeling like I've been sent away shamefaced after trying to steal something that isn't mine.

Dean Cole's heart may not be beating again quite yet…

But I think we all heard a faint pulse.

LEV

"Dad, you left the trash out again," Knight hollers, using the tip of his boot to roll me over on our backyard lawn. I'm holding a bottle of beer in my hand, but I'm not drunk. Not even a little. In fact, most of the liquid soaked against the ground when I popped the bottle open. Because apparently, I'm too fucking depressed to even take a sip now. Great.

"You're funny. And he is not home," I say in a deadpan, squinting up at the sun, like it's a staring contest. Like I might win.

"Hit rock bottom yet?" He half-squats, placing his palms on his knees and peering down at me.

"Think so," I murmur into the bottle, taking a pull. The pool lounger is two feet away. I can't remember why I didn't sit there when I walked out the porch doors.

"Great!" Knight smiles sunnily. "That means you're ready for some hard truths. I'll get myself comfortable."

He takes a seat on one of the loungers on the ledge of our pool, grabs me by the back of my shirt and perches me on the lounger next to him. I sometimes forget I'm not the only motherfucker in this house that can move a tractor just by breathing directly at it. Knight's a beast.

"You have to break her heart," Knight announces.

"I know," I say, because I do. Because *fuck*, mine is already broken, but at least I know what I have to do now. Glue it back into something functioning.

"You do?" Knight leans forward, side-eyeing me. His shades slide down his nose.

"Yeah. She needs to hit rock bottom. Dixie told me."

"Well, Dixie's smart. But it's not just that." He runs his tongue along his bottom lip. "You need to do this to regain who you really are again."

"And who am I?" I cock an eyebrow, putting the beer bottle down on the pool ledge.

"Not an asshole."

"Am I an asshole now?" I ask, but I already know the truth. I've been acting like a shithead throughout all this. If anyone told me six months ago that I'd be fingering, fucking, and sexually exploiting someone who is high on drugs I'd have laughed in their faces. And yet I did all those things. Crossed all those lines. I tasted her pussy, knowing it wasn't mine to taste. Kissed her lips, knowing they weren't mine to kiss. I gave myself plenty of excuses. Bought all of her lies and then some to convince myself that she is sober. That I had her full consent. But I knew the truth.

And still, I lie to my brother, because owning up the truth is apparently too much for my ass right now. "If you're referring to my hooking up with Bails while she was on drugs, she hit on me."

"She wasn't herself either, and you know it." Knight shoots me a *nice try* look. "You didn't have her full consent, bro."

I bury my face in my hands and shake my head. I didn't. And I'll have to live with this fact for the rest of my life. "I know. It's killing me."

"Yo." Knight puts a hand on my shoulder, snapping his fingers with his free hand. "That doesn't mean that Old Bailey would've chosen differently, okay? Facts suck because they don't bend to our will, but sometimes we have to face them."

The guilt consumes me from the inside, festering on my internal organs. Bailey and I started out all wrong. Our fairytale turned into a goddamn nightmare. And I'll have to live with that for the rest of my life.

"Since when are you smart, anyway?" I lift my head, giving Knight's shoulder a push.

"Luna makes me read books and shit." Knight sighs. "They don't even have pictures. Can you believe that?"

"She's a good influence," I say.

"The only influence I'm in, on, and otherwise don't mind consuming." He winks, grinning at me. "Hey." He grabs the back of my neck, pulling me close to him. Our foreheads are touching. He stares right into my eyes and it's kinda creepy, but I think he wants me to pay full attention for what he is about to say next. "It gets better, bro."

"How do you know?"

"I've been where Bailey is right now."

"And?"

"What doesn't kill you? Sometimes it revives you."

CHAPTER THIRTY
BAILEY

The first thing I hear is the steady rhythm of the EKG machine.

Beep. Beep. Beep.

Calm and comforting, it lulls me in and out of consciousness. I'm cold. My mouth is dry. I slowly come to, realizing by the overwhelming pile of sensations returning to me that I was probably in a medically induced coma. I know why doctors log you out and put you on blue-screen mode. I took premed before going to Juilliard. Whatever they did to me, I couldn't have endured it consciously.

I don't remember much. Actually...I don't remember anything at all. But my gut is telling me bad things have happened.

This wasn't a close brush with death. This was kissing its cold, blue lips, an inch from being swallowed by it.

I blink my eyes open, wondering how long I've been out for, and the first thing I see is my sister, napping on a recliner in front of me. Behind her is a blue, generic wall. My hoodie is draped over her chest, and it looks like she's been sniffing it for comfort.

My pupils turn to my right. Mom is sleeping in an upright position next to me. I avert my gaze to the left. It's stark black and crickets are chirping.

I try to swallow. Fail.

How long has it been?

What the hell did I do?

The memories of Thalia and the Juilliard letter tsunami back into my mind. I block them best I can. I'm not ready. Not yet.

Gingerly, I try to make a sound. Open my mouth and let out air. I can croak. I am grateful for this small miracle. For the simple pleasure of not losing my voice.

I close my eyes and take a greedy breath. This simple, involuntarily action fills me with hope.

I can breathe.

I can *still* breathe.

After everything I put my body through. Punishing it relentlessly. I am still here.

"Bails?" Daria croaks. My eyes are closed, so I'm guessing she knows I'm awake by the tears streaming steadily down my cheeks. My hospital gown is wet and I want to wipe my face, but I'm hooked to so many machines, it hurts to move my hands.

Daria stands up and pads on socked feet toward me. She joins me in bed, curling her long, agile limbs around mine and wiping my face gently. She kisses my cheek. She smells like our childhood— fluffy pillows and hot cocoa and sunshine. Her blond hair tangles in my own, and she hugs me like I'm a broken thing. Because I am.

Damaged goods are still goods, Bailey, Lev's voice reminds me in my head.

"I'm so happy you're here." Her voice sounds hoarse from crying. I cry harder, my body trembling with my sobs. This can't be good for my health. This flood of emotions that's drowning me whole.

"Shh." Daria strokes my head soothingly. "You'll wake Mom, and she'd been awake for over seventy hours. As you can *clearly* see on her skin."

"How long have I been out?" I whisper.

"Two days."

I breathe in sharply. Close my eyes. Oh Marx.

"I'm so sorry," I say.

"So am I."

Why should she be sorry? She didn't do anything. Unless… unless she isn't sorry for something anybody did. But for the situation. The realization must be painted on my face because Daria sucks in a breath.

"Bailey…" My sister hesitates. "Don't look down, but…"

I look down instinctively. Because that's what people do when you tell them *not* to look down. Plus, my leg is hurting really bad despite a monstrous amount of painkillers, I'm sure. My eyes widen when I see the huge bump poking from the thin hospital blanket. "What is it?"

"They had to put a rod in your tibia. You injured yourself pretty badly, practicing through the pain. The painkillers probably allowed you to push through, but you literally broke your bone clean."

My chin is trembling. Rather than being mad at myself, or at Juilliard, or at Thalia, or at the world, I am overwhelmed with gratitude. I've put myself through a lot and I'm still here. I can't believe it.

"Ballet…" Daria starts.

I shake my head violently. "I can't. Not right now."

"Okay." She sits upright, tucking me under her arm. "You're right."

"Are Mom and Dad angry with me?" I bite down on my bottom lip, feeling like a small child all of a sudden.

Daria rolls her tear-filled eyes, trying to look strong. "That's not even going to be their fiftieth emotion when they find out you're awake. But, Bailey…"

I know. They want me to go to rehab. To stay there. To be serious about getting better. Stupidly—and perhaps unbelievably too—I can't contemplate doing something like that right now. Being away from my family. I just want to bury myself in Mom and Dad's bed and never leave their sides.

"Can we not talk about this, either?"

This time Daria doesn't say anything. We stare at each other for a few beats before my sister asks, "Can I show you something?"

I nod slowly.

She pulls out her phone from her pocket. Her screensaver is Penn and Cressida making faces to the camera, with Sissi's fingers painted red. They were making Daria a card for Mother's Day. *Sissi.* If I had died, I wouldn't be able to hug her anymore.

Daria unlocks her phone and gets into her video gallery. She scrolls up for long moments, searching for something.

"I had some time to burn on the plane from San Francisco to Todos Santos, so I went through our old childhood videos. The ones Mom showed us last Christmas?"

"Yeah," I croak. "Yeah, I remember those videos."

Kind of. I was too busy ogling Lev and popping pills.

"Ah. There it is!" Daria jacks the volume all the way up and sticks her AirPods into my ears.

I don't recognize this video, but I know where it was taken. It's a video of me, when I was four or five, in a ballet class. I am tiny and wearing a bright neon-green tutu and leotard, against all the pale pinks and whites of the other girls around me.

"Stand in line, Bailey," I hear the teacher in the background—I can't even recall her name—but instead, the camera follows me as I hop on the ballet barre and hook the back of my knees against it, dangling upside down with my arms stretched, giggling.

Mom laughs behind the camera. A real laugh, a *rich* laugh, that dances in my own lungs as if it comes out of me. Something warm fills me.

"What are you doing, Bails?" Mom coos.

"Getting ready for my big number!" I flash my nonexistent guns at the camera, like I'm a superhero. My two upper teeth are missing, and I look ridiculous yet so confident and happy, carefree.

"Oh, I cannot wait to see what that looks like." I can hear the grin in Mom's voice. "Which song do you wanna dance to?"

"'Smooth Criminal'!"

"It's not a ballet song," Mom points out.

"Says who?" I challenge. "Everything is a ballet song if you're good at it."

"Bailey, are you coming?" the teacher reproaches in the background.

"Yes, Ms. McFadden!" I hop down to my feet and throw a sassy smile behind my shoulder. "Mom, check out my dance moves!"

And then…then I break into the Fox dance. I kid you not. With the groovy smile and ridiculous moves. Mom snort-laughs now, following me with the camera. The video goes on for a few more seconds. I stand in line with the rest of the girls—stand out with my outfit and uneven ponytails—and dance with all of them. I'm not the best in the class. I'm not even the third best in the class, to be honest. But the entire time I'm dancing, I look…thrilled. Filled with joy. The smile doesn't drop from my face, not for one second, even when Ms. McFadden corrects me over and over again.

The video ends, and immediately I want to watch it again and never watch it again at the same time. It is so bittersweet to see the way it all started—not with the pressure of Mom's projected dream. With the pure simplicity of a girl who simply loved to dance.

Untucking the AirPods from my ears, I deposit them in Daria's open palm.

"You always enjoyed the journey and didn't care so much about the endgame," Daria says quietly. "Remember when we went on vacations, to resorts, and there would be lame dance parties at night for the kids? You always danced in those. Everybody else thought they were too cool for it. Not you. You did the Macarena like nobody's business."

"I did," I croak out. "It's such a catchy song."

Both Daria and me burst into a laugh-cry sob.

"What happened?" Daria croaks.

My gaze flutters to where Mom is asleep. Only she isn't asleep anymore. She's been listening to this entire exchange, judging by the tears in her eyes. She is watching us, pressing a tissue to her nose.

"I happened." Mom leans forward on her elbows, grabbing my arm. "I did this to you. The same way I did it to Daria. Put so much pressure on you. Once I realized you were both so talented, I wanted you to have everything I hadn't been able to get. Daria was more assertive, though. She stood her ground when I tried steering her in the ballet direction. But you, Bailey…" Mom looks down, wrecked. "You always aimed to please. I should have been much more careful with you. I pushed and I pushed. And look what happened. You ended up with a broken leg too. Only in my case, it was an accident. In yours, you did it to yourself. They put a *rod* in your tibia, Bailey."

Wow. They're both really bad at pep talks. "Because of me. I—"

"Not because of you," I cut her off. "Because of *me*. I have to take accountability for what happened. Yes, you pushed me to succeed. To go to Juilliard. But I could've shut you down at any point. You wouldn't have put up much of a fight."

"Yes, and lived your adolescent years feeling like a complete failure," Mom says, not ready to let herself off the hook. "I've been a terrible mother to both of you."

Daria tips her head back and laughs. "Marx, Mom. *So* dramatic."

"One of my daughters ended up being abused by her principal, and the other became a drug addict," she reminds us.

"We're a family of winners." Daria pumps the air.

I have to smile a little too. Because if she finds it amusing, maybe I could one day too. I mean, Daria seems happy with her life, and back in the day, it seemed like hope was gone for her.

This is my moment of epiphany.

Apparently, motivation doesn't come from rock bottom. It comes from seeing all the things I'm going to lose if I don't turn my life around. My family. My passion—yes, dancing is still my passion, even if it didn't work out with Juilliard. *Lev.* I've been so horrible to him. To everyone around me.

I want to be that girl in the video again. To dangle upside down, break into silly dances, wear neon-colored tutu dresses. I want to be *happy*. Even if happy means not being the most successful girl in the room. Even if my happily-ever-after doesn't include big stages, a shelf full of trophies, and worldwide recognition.

The door opens, and Dad walks in. As I suspected, he is holding a coffee cup holder with fresh coffees for him, Mom, and Daria. At the sight of me awake and at all three of us crying, his eyebrows shoot up.

"She's awake." He drops the coffee on the floor. All three cups explode, brown liquid spilling everywhere. No one in the room even bats an eyelash.

Somehow, I find it in me to smile. "I'm back, Dad, and I'm never *ever* doing this to you again."

He rushes to me, dropping to his knees by my bed, kissing the back of my hand, even with all the needles inside it.

My dad is crying now. The big Jaime Followhill. The rulebreaker. The man who pissed all over tradition, and expectations, and married his high school teacher. The man who built an empire. The man who raised two firecrackers. Married one too.

Crying. Like a child.

You have too much to lose, Bailey. This is worth fighting for. This is worth living for.

We all gather into a group hug. When we disconnect, I clear my throat.

"Juilliard…" I start.

Mom jumps in. "I'm so sorry I opened your letter. I didn't mean to overstep. I was just so worri—"

"Mom, let me finish." I touch her wrist.

She makes a sign of zipping her mouth shut. She's shaking. So am I. I can't do this anymore. I can't ruin everyone's lives just because mine didn't work out the way I wanted it to.

"Juilliard wasn't a good fit for me. I wanted to succeed but didn't draw one ounce of satisfaction from it. I hated New York. Hated the cold. Hated the competitiveness. I was so good at excelling at things—school was always fun for me, dancing used to be a piece of cake—"

"All right, Miss Humblebrag, we get it," Daria mumbles. We all laugh.

I continue, "So when I started doing badly at something, I didn't admit defeat. I kept pushing and pushing through. And I ended up making friends with the wrong type of people." I think about Payden. "I'm ready to go to rehab. I need to do this right. I *have* to. I'll always be an addict. You can't turn the wheel back. But I want to be a sober one who is safe to be around. I don't just owe it to myself but to the people I love."

Hands enfold me from all angles. A flurry of tears and kisses ensues. And I know, in this moment, surrounded by the loved ones I'm probably not going to see for a long time, that somehow, I will be okay.

Because that's the thing about damaged goods.

They're still good. They just need a little fixing.

CHAPTER THIRTY-ONE
BAILEY

I stay in the hospital for ten days before they let me go.

Lev doesn't visit me once.

Actually, that's not true. He does arrive here daily, but he doesn't come in. I keep hearing him outside of my room, talking to Dad and Penn and Mom and Daria. Asking how I'm doing. I want to yell at him. Tell him I'm happy to email him my hospital chart first thing every morning and save him the time and traffic, since he isn't here to see me anyway. But I know I have no right to be a brat.

Why doesn't he come in? I think I know why, and the reason is frightening to me.

Good news is, I'm officially accepting visitors.

Knight and Luna arrive with Cayden and a stack of books Luna purchased especially for me.

Vaughn and Lenora arrive sans the twins and stay over for a DoorDash dinner and a two-hour conversation about art.

Daria and I watch movies every night and talk about the past—always the past, never the future. The future is too big, too vast, too threatening. We don't touch it.

I arrive back home in a wheelchair. My leg is in a cast and I can technically use crutches, but my parents are told I have to take it easy. It is an extremely humbling experience to sit in my backyard and crochet beanies for NICU babies without being able to jump to my feet and dance every time a song I like comes on the radio.

I'm not sure why I don't contact Lev. It's not pride—I've never been a prideful person. I guess a part of me understands why he put distance between us. Why he let go. I treated him horribly and put him through hell. Then to top all of it off, used again, despite his valid and healthy pleas. Mom always says love is an exercise in endurance, but I think she means general curveballs life throws at you. Not when one of you decides to become abusive and not themselves.

Still, I know we'll talk before he goes off to college, wherever that might be.

Before I enter rehab. Whenever *that* might be.

How's the sky looking, Dove? his voice asks inside my head.

The sky fell on me and crushed me whole. And still, I survived.

———

I end up choosing a rehab center in the same way I used to choose ice cream flavors when I was a kid. Squeeze my eyes shut real tight, run my finger along a curated list, and halt at a random place.

Mom, Dad, Daria, and Penn are sitting next to me. My built-in support group.

"No peeking!" Mom coos, trying to make the whole ordeal fun, rather than horrifying. I stifle a smile. I let my finger slide along the handwritten list and stop.

Silence. My heartbeats are drumming between my ears.

"Is it good? Is it bad?" I ask, eyes still closed. "Can you even tell? Daria's penmanship is awful."

"Hey!" Daria laughs.

"Aww! This one looks so good. We loved the pictures," Mom says finally. "Open your eyes now, Bailey. It's the beginning of the rest of your life."

The rehab center is in Pennsylvania. My decision to go out of state stemmed from my need to cut off the invisible cord running between me, my parents, and Lev. I wanted to focus on getting better, not on expecting weekend visits with my loved ones. Sometimes you have to live without people to remember how much they're worth keeping in your life.

Though, I guess Lev could be crossed off the list of hypothetical visitors. He doesn't even visit me from across the street.

Three days after I chose a rehab program, I'm sitting on the front porch of my house, surrounded by suitcases and duffel bags.

"You better come back clean, happy, and chill as fuck," Daria warns somewhere above my head, shoving my pink headphones and favorite glittery socks into my carry-on bag and struggling with the zipper. "This thing cost Mom and Dad sixty grand. Are they handing out bachelor degrees at the end of it?"

"Dude, guilt trip much?" I tilt my head up to glare at her. But I'm not mad, not really. She is right. Plus, she dropped everything to be with me for this entire duration since I OD'd.

"*Much.*" She tosses her Rapunzel hair to one shoulder. "You deserve to feel guilty—not ashamed. I had to take time off work. *And* stop a juice-cleansing stint."

"I'm sure you and Penn can still pay the bills." Her husband gets paid a gazillion dollars per season for the 49ers.

"It's not about money. It's about my responsibilities. Aspirations. My *passion.*"

"Are you talking about your job or the juice cleanse?" I frown.

"Both." She laughs. "My hot-girl-shit routine is perfected down to an art, and I miss my students sooo much."

Is she really that passionate about her role? I hadn't realized. Possibly because I've always secretly believed Daria took this job out of necessity, to do something with her life.

"Do you really like what you do?" I can only imagine the type of pep talks my sister gives the youth of America. There's tough love and then there's whatever Daria Scully is giving people. Which is more like...*BDSM affection.*

"Love it." A tender smile traces her lips, and her eyes soften. "You know, Bails, there's life after the glitz and glamour of professional ballet and cheer. It's really nice to do something quiet and rewarding. To work out because you want to, because it's fun, and not because it's your job." This, I can believe. "I make more of a difference as a counselor than I did as cheer captain. My positive footprint on this world is greater. Don't look at this as failure." She shakes her head. "We all fall. Those who get back up—they're the real winners. And once you've been down, you learn to appreciate the ups so much more."

Her eyes snap from mine to the mansion across the street. She arches an eyebrow and swivels toward the front door. "This is my cue to make myself scarce. Dad'll start the car in about ten minutes, so that's how much time you've got to say goodbye to lover boy."

Daria disappears into the house. I stare ahead and watch Lev crossing the cul-de-sac from his house to mine. He is wearing a black hoodie and low-hanging gray sweatpants. His sharp jaw tics when he sees me fenced by my suitcases and bags. He doesn't smile when his forest-greens meet my ocean-blues.

My heart is in my throat. I know this is goodbye, at least for right now. But what if it's goodbye for*ever*? What if too many things have happened for us to move on?

He jogs the few steps of the ivory marble leading to my door and stands in front of me.

"Is now a good time to talk?" Despite everything, his voice is sweet and familiar.

"No better time, since I'm leaving for rehab in..." I check my phone. "Nine minutes and twenty-three seconds."

I can't keep the bitterness out of my voice. I don't blame him for wanting me gone after everything I've put him through. But it still rips me to shreds. We both made so many mistakes ever since I came back, and I don't know how to move on from all the bad memories that muddied up all of our good ones.

Lev takes a seat next to me. I don't dare look at him. At his sharp, straight nose or delectably symmetrical lips.

There's a mountain of unspoken words wedged between us.

Lev closes his eyes, swallows, letting those words collapse like rubble.

"Since the moment you overdosed, all I've been doing is trying to find the right words to say to you when you woke up. It took me all these days to realize there are no right words in our case, so instead of saying what's right, I'm going to focus on saying what's *true*."

The truth is always a sucker punch. I hold my breath.

"I'd like to start by apologizing to you. This apology has been a long time coming. When my mom died, I looked for someone to replace her energy. You were the easiest choice. I put an unfair burden on you. Expectations no kid should be faced with. You were my everything—mother, sister, mentor, best friend, potential lover. You were the whore and the saint. The illness and the remedy. You made my favorite food, you slept in my bed, you prepared my backpack the night before school, and also starred in every fantasy I've ever had. There is something about you, Dove. You're very dependable. So people just throw shit at you, thinking you'll succeed."

I watch him in horror. I have a feeling I know where this is going.

He continues, "When you put the entire world on someone's shoulders, don't be surprised when they break their back. And when you sank, Bailey, my love for you began turning into hate. I don't want to hate you. I don't want to dread every moment with you. But I am. Around you, I'm acting like a fuckboy who won't keep himself in check. I break my own rules. I…" He rakes his fingers through his hair, which has grown. "I do shit with you I would never do with someone under the influence. There are no boundaries. There are no norms. I spent my entire life trying not to fall into the same life of thrill-seeking addiction my dad and brother struggled with. I don't want to lose myself, even if it means gaining you."

I know exactly what he means, even if I don't want to. Normal Lev would die before taking advantage of someone who is high or drunk. I made him loathe himself.

"We've done everything together ever since we were born. I think it's time we stand alone."

"I...I'm sorry for what I've put you through—"

"It's okay."

"It's not," I insist.

"It doesn't matter," he says flatly.

My gaze lingers on my sneakers. I can feel him slipping away from me. From *us*.

"What were in the boxes you gave me?" I blurt out. I've been meaning to ask, but it was never the right time. "I mean, nothing, obviously, so I guess I missed an important gesture there."

"A piece of the sky." His smile is like a lick of sunray over my skin. "I'd go up to the roof of my house and cut you a piece every day. I wanted you to remember you have limitless options. Endless possibilities. Doves are good at finding direction. Ballet isn't the beginning and the end of your life. And you're my dove, so I know you'll find your way. The sky is yours, Bailey." His voice is so sad, so full, I can't breathe. "Yours to find your way again. So just...just forget about Juilliard and ballet and competitions for a second and think about *you*."

Feelings clog my throat, and everything is beautiful and ugly at the same time.

"I need you to do me a favor while I'm in rehab," I hear myself say.

"Of course," he says. "Anything."

"Payden." I turn to look at him, gathering my knees in my hands.

Lev's face clouds. "I'm not doing Payden, no matter how fond I am of you."

Attempting a smile, I explain, "Payden was my dealer. My guess is he isn't dealing anymore, but...I can't be certain."

"Oh shit. He might be still doing that," Lev murmurs under his breath.

"For months, I've walked around with this hole in my chest that I'm letting him get away with what he did. My last thought before I go to bed every day is—has he killed anyone yet? So I did a thing." I lick my lips, reaching for the duffel bag next to me and pulling out a preprinted stack of papers. "I typed out my entire statement for you to give to the police, including my contact number in rehab. All his details are there too. I'm going to be available to them."

Lev grabs the papers, tucking them under his arm. "Consider it done."

"Thank you." I try to smile again. Fail—*again*. "I really appreciate it."

There's an awkward silence. This is brutal. I've never experienced awkward silence with Lev before. Maybe before we learned how to talk.

"I'm glad you're going to rehab," he says.

"So am I," I huff, adding bitterly, "It helps that my schedule is all cleared up, now that Juilliard kicked me out and my parents refuse to let me stay in their house unless I graduate rehab."

He doesn't crack a smile. "You need to go in there knowing you've lost everything. To fight for it back, you understand?"

"Not everything." I hang my gaze on his face anxiously. "I still have you, right?"

It is in that moment that I *do* lose everything. In the moment when Lev fingers his dove pendant, then slowly removes it from his wrist. We're both watching, mesmerized. It is like he is cutting off a limb or something. I don't think I've ever seen him without it since the time he gave me mine. I hurry to touch mine, then realize Thalia stole it. The doves are gone.

When we look up at each other, we both have tears in our eyes. His nose is red. He is *that* close to crying. And if he realized my bracelet is not with me anymore, he hasn't said anything. Maybe it's best. Maybe I don't want to know what he has to say about my losing it.

"I'm sorry, Dove. We'll always have the past, but your present needs to be yours, and you can't have my future."

"Lev…"

He stands up. I do the same. This time, I feel my tibia pain in all its glory—even through the cast—and even though fresh tears spring into my eyes, it's oddly satisfying to *feel* again. For the longest time, the pills made me so numb to reality.

"I love you, and for me to continue to love you, I have to let you go. You need to do the same."

"But Rosie made me promis—"

Lev cups my cheeks, bringing me close to his face. Our noses touch. His breath skates along my face, and I shiver with pleasure, like a junkie stealing a hit.

"I know what Mom asked. I'm asking you to disregard it. If there's one thing I've learned recently, it's that we need to try to rebuild our lives around the hole my mom left. I have to move on. Let. Me. Go."

My nails sink into his arms, and I do the opposite of letting him go as I sob into his chest. His breaths are labored and I can feel his heart jackhammering, threatening to pierce through his rib cage.

"I hate you," I croak out, balling my hands into fists and pushing him away from me. The garage door slides open. Dad is going to come out any minute now to start loading my stuff into the trunk. "I hate you so much."

But I don't hate him. I love him. I'm just angry that I lost him.

Lev wraps his arms around me, absorbing my punches. Even now, seconds before we say goodbye, I'm hurting him and he is taking it.

"I hate myself." I change my tune, finally saying the truth now. "I hate myself so much."

Lev angles my head down and presses a kiss to my scalp. "*I* love you."

"Thalia stole my dove bracelet," I hear myself sulk. Fuck, I'm such a big baby. "I would never have taken it off!"

He loosens his grip on me, stepping backward, toward his house. Before he turns around, he touches his lips again with his fingers. "Maybe you didn't need it anymore."

CHAPTER THIRTY-TWO
LEV

Miserable Fa… Nope. Not doing this anymore. Life is too short to be obsessed with death. It is time to live without feeling like it's somehow betraying Mom.

Dixie is waiting for me when I cross the street back to my house. I can see her through a screen of unshed tears, peering through the kitchen window, like it's amateur creeper hour or something. I've always liked her, but recently she's really been growing on me. What she did with the Air Force Academy application should win her a Bad Bitch award, even if I am now perpetually anxious I won't make the cut. Honestly, my chances aren't looking great. I could've fluffed my résumé a lot more. Sent out more references and letters of recommendation.

When I push the door open, I hear Dad telling her, "…can't believe you're screening my calls when you're right fucking *here* in my house. That's some next-level bullshit, Dix."

Eh. I see he is back to *Dicks*.

"I'm here for Lev, not for you. Besides, you never did call Jessica for that appointment," Dixie explains wryly, strolling from the window to the patio, following my lead.

"Well, you're here now, so—"

"Not for long. Knight is picking Lev and me up for dinner in ten minutes. Lev is having a day, you know. With Bailey going to rehab and everything."

"You're unbelievable." Dad shoots her a glare. "Of course, I know! He's my *son*! I should be the one taking them to dinner, not you."

"Dude, no offense." I down a Gatorade and smash the empty bottle in my fist. "You're not much company right now, and I need to lick my wounds."

Dixie turns to Dad with a serene smile. "You seem angry. Would you like me to return the keys to you?"

"No," he bites out acidly. "Keep them. It's only a matter of time until your rundown apartment needs something else fixed and you have to move in here again."

"I happen to like my 'rundown apartment' quite a lot." Dixie air quotes his miserable choice of words. "Every penny used to buy it was hard-earned and symbolizes my financial independence."

Dad blushes. Legit. Fucking. *Blushes.* "Poor choice of words. That's...that's not what I meant."

I wonder if he knows how miserable he looks and sounds, now that he doesn't have her complete and utter adoration. I can already see that if they *will* be together one day, they'd be nothing like he was with Mom. It would be less big, all-consuming love and more...two people keeping each other from falling into an abyss that will always be open and right in front of their feet. But that isn't a bad thing. Having a security blanket to clutch on to. I could use one right about now.

On the patio, Dixie hands me a cup of that bomb-ass bakery coffee. My usual order. I accept it and take a sip.

"I did it." I fish my dove bracelet from my sweatpants' pocket. "She says Thalia stole hers."

Fucking bitch. Thalia is high if she thinks I'm not getting it back.

Dixie gives me a sympathetic look. "I'm proud of you. I know it wasn't easy, but she needed to know she has to fight for everything she's ever taken for granted. The more you have at stake, the harder you fight."

I'm taking her word for it because she started from the bottom too. Sometimes it takes a fighter to make a fighter. Bailey needs to use her teeth and nails to claw her way out of this addiction. Breaking her heart was the hardest thing I had to do, and still, I did it because it means helping her mend her life.

Dad joins us on the patio, sulking. With his hands tucked inside his front pockets, he asks, "So how was saying goodbye to Bails?"

"Awesome. Thinking of making it a daily occurrence."

"Jaime told me she signed up for a ninety-day program." He toes his loafer over the dirt, refusing to look at Dixie, like a preschooler. "Seems like a reputable place. You should be happy."

Happy? Not in this lifetime. Hopeful, sad, exhausted, and relieved, however? Yeah. Honestly, my thoughts are a tangled mess. I won't be able to truly tell what's going on until we're on the other side of this and Bailey is out of rehab.

Pressing my lips into a hard line, I admit, "It fucking sucks being in love with a girl and not knowing if she is going to make it through the night."

"I know," Dad rasps. "I've been there. It's also the best to wake up and see that she is still there, breathing."

I can practically *hear* Dixie swallowing hard, glancing between us. "I'll leave you two to it." She disappears back into the house. I stare at Dad, and he stares back, and for a moment, I think he is going to go after her.

But he clears his throat instead. "The Air Force Academy? I hope you get in. I can't think of anyone more capable. Knight...I always knew what he needed from me. A father figure. A mentor. Not you. I always kind of felt like you could be more of a father figure to me than vice versa. And that scared me. So sometimes..." He heaves a sigh. "*Most* times, I just left you to your own devices, trusting you'd do the right thing. I'm sorry I wasn't more involved. More alert to your needs and wants."

Chewing on my upper lip, I say, "It wasn't just your fault. I saw an opportunity to make you happy, and I have this awful savior complex since I couldn't save Mom. And you *wanted* to be saved." I shrug. "I sometimes miss Mom's family gatherings on your bed. We'd sit there and talk for hours about our feelings. Doesn't work so well, though, with three six-foot-three dudes."

Dad laughs. "Not so well, no. I'll need two California kings to squeeze the three of us together. But you can still always talk to me."

"I know." I screw my mouth sideways. "I mean, now I do."

"And for my part, I promise not to hang all my hopes and dreams on you and Knight. I have a few ideas in mind, though."

My eyes travel to the glass door, and I raise an eyebrow. Dad shakes his head. "It's not what you think, but yeah. Guess Dixie is a part of that plan too. It'll just have to be…unconventional. Hug it out?" Dad suggests.

Mom always used to demand we hug shit out before we parted ways. She didn't like it when we left on bad terms with each other. Said it is a trait of people who took life for granted because you never really know if you'll see the other person again. You just *assume*. She even went as far as calling it a god complex when Knight and I would brawl about shit like who ate the last Nakd Bar (always Knight. Also, side note: I'd never felt so cheated as when I was fourteen and Knight teasingly offered me a Nakd Bar, and I thought he was taking me to my first titty place).

Now, Dad steps into my space, gathers me in his arms, and squeezes me so hard, my bones are grinding against one another.

I laugh into his shoulders. "Cut it out, psycho."

"What are you gonna do if…?" He leaves the rest of the question unfinished. If I don't get into the Air Force.

"Enlist. Prove myself while I serve. Then reapply."

His body goes rigid against mine, but he doesn't argue.

"I love you, Levy."

"Love you too, Dad."

"She'll be okay," he says, and I know exactly who he means.

I let my forehead drop on his neck and take a deep breath. "I know."

CHAPTER THIRTY-THREE
LEV

The day after Bailey goes off to rehab, I return to school.

I haven't been in over two weeks. Spent my entire time loitering outside her hospital room. Then after she was discharged, I was too much of a wreck to pretend to give half a crap about my grades. I'm not the only one. Pretty much everyone I know who has been accepted to a college or already sent their application has checked out mentally.

But I need to be here today. At school. I have unfinished business to take care of.

When Bailey was in a coma, and Mel and I were sitting outside her room, enjoying lukewarm hospital coffee and anxiety-inducing conversation, I remembered the moment before Jaime called us up when he found Bailey unresponsive. Mel had just said that Thalia had visited Bailey a few hours before she overdosed and pointed out that she and Jaime had conducted a thorough drug search of the house hours before. I put two and two together. Thalia was Bailey's *only* point of contact other than me for a good chunk of time. And I sure as fuck didn't give her drugs. Which leaves me with one candidate…

The person who actually *threatened* to give her drugs. Where there's smoke, there's usually fire. And Thalia right now is stinking of fumes.

I find her leaning against her locker, hugging her textbooks to her chest while Austin looms close, flirting with her. When she sees me heading in her direction, a teasing smile touches her lips. She thinks it's an incoming jealous scene. This girl is about as observant as a pair of dirty underwear.

Pushing Austin out of the way casually, making him stumble and fall down on his ass and drawing a few chuckles, I get all up in my ex-girl-something's face. "Have a little walk with me."

Thalia pouts, giving me her good profile. "I don't know, Cole. You're not making it awfully attractive to me right now with that tone of yours."

I flash a seductive smile, lowering my face to brush my lips over her ear. "If you don't take a walk with me right now, I'm going to report you to the police for soliciting and buying hard drugs, and then whatever options you still have to go to college will go down in flames, along with your reputation. How 'bout that, sweetheart?"

She jerks her head back and stares at me in horror. "Lead the way." Thalia turns around, shoves her textbooks into her locker, and slams it shut. I'm already on the other side of the hallway. She follows me hurriedly. I'm doing everything I can to remain calm, but it's hard when this idiot almost *killed* the person I love more than anything else in this life. I slip into the lab, and she does the same. I lock the door behind us, plastering a hand over her head. Her eyes widen in fear. Honestly? She should be scared right now.

"Whatever Bailey told you," Thalia starts, erecting her finger between us, "I wouldn't believe her. After all, she's a junk—"

I press a finger over her mouth, and the idiot immediately melts into my touch. "Let's get one thing out of the way—the next time you refer to Bailey as a junkie or any other questionable epithet, I'll send one of your nudes to the entire grade's WhatsApp group. I wouldn't put anything past me. Don't let the dimples and good grades fool you—we both know I'm an asshole when I want to be."

She swallows and licks her lips. I move my hand from her mouth. She nods, letting me know she got the message.

"Now, let's establish a few things." My hand curls around her neck. "I know you sold and/or led Bailey to drugs. I know you *gave* her drugs the day she overdosed too. And I know you did it because, despite my explaining to you in simple fucking English that you never were more than a warm hole, you thought you had a chance at us being something more. Correct me if I got anything wrong so far."

Tears fill her eyes, but she says nothing. I hate the words that come out of my mouth, but I hate her more for what she did. Plus, maybe if she hadn't reintroduced Bailey to drugs, Dove wouldn't have to go to rehab and could be right here with me. This is an unhealthy thought. It is *good* for Bailey to be in rehab. But my feelings for my best friend may forever skim the line between love and obsession. I don't need someone like Thalia maliciously sabotaging Bailey.

"Whatever, let's go with that." Thalia's voice is hoarse, like she's been internally screaming for months now. Maybe she has. I have no doubt I haven't heard her cries. I was too attuned to one girl and one girl only. "Yeah, that's pretty accurate. So what? You're gonna fuck up my life in retaliation?" she bites out. "Get your rocks off by ruining a poor girl's life?"

"Your financial situation has nothing to do with it. The fact you almost killed my best friend does." I bang my open palm just above her head and she jumps with a yelp. The sound echoes around the room. I need to control my temper before I lose it.

"Bailey could have said no." Thalia tries to push me away from her, desperate for an escape. "She didn't. She cared about drugs more than she did about you. You can point fingers at everyone and every-thing, but the truth of the matter is, Bailey wanted to be corrupted and I'm the only one who dared show you that."

"You're a waste of fucking space," I spit out, ripping myself off of her body. She disgusts me.

"Yeah, well," she huffs, dropping to one knee to rummage in her backpack for something. "What are you gonna do about it? Just tell me what my punishment is because I know you have something in store for me."

"How do you know?" I ask, surprised. Thalia doesn't strike me as a genius, to put it mildly.

She rolls her eyes, finding an elastic for her hair and wrapping it in a high bun. "If you wanted to hand me over to the police, you would have done so without this showdown. You've never had much interest in talking to me. It was more my pussy you were into."

"You're going to give me your drug dealer's deets so I can nail this motherfucker's coffin and put their ass in jail for a long time," I start.

Thalia nods. That's an easy sacrifice. "What else?"

"You're going to write Bailey a genuine, heartfelt, *sorrowful* letter of apology for what you did to her." I continue, "And you're going to then give it to me to hand over to her when she is out of rehab."

"She went to rehab?" Her eyes light up. "Actually, I'm glad to hear that. I was...I don't know, worried after hearing she ended up in the hospital," Thalia mumbles, shifting her gaze down. Astonishingly, I believe her. I don't think Thalia is a horrible person. I think she is misguided, with a side of fucked-up, but she lost herself too.

"And then you will remove yourself from our lives completely," I finish. "That means I don't want you to be anywhere in Bailey's vicinity, ever, for eternity."

"We live in the same area," Thalia protests.

"Go out to Carlsbad," I drawl out. "You gave her drugs that put her in a fucking *coma*, you moron. It's jail or staying the hell away. Todos Santos is off-limits to you in eighty-nine days, when Bailey gets out."

If she gets out. Maybe she decides to stay for longer. Maybe she relapses as soon as she leaves. Maybe she won't even complete the program. And what if she decides not to come back here? Needs to start fresh somewhere new? I need to stop thinking about it before my head explodes.

Thalia takes a deep breath. "And you won't tell anyone what happened if I do all those things?"

I shake my head slowly. "Oh, and one more thing."

She stares at me expectedly as I stretch my palm open before her. "Bailey's dove pendant. *Now*."

She screws up her nose, looking around us. With a huff, she shoves her hand into her pocket and hands it to me. I can't believe she is brazenly carrying it around like it was given to her, not stolen. For a keepsake. I put it in my pocket and immediately feel the relief of having something of Bailey's with me.

This is not the goodbye I had in mind from this girl, who was my first time.

Then again, a lot of shit went sideways in the past few months.

"You know," Thalia chokes out, "I knew you hated football. And I knew you were lukewarm toward me. But I always thought you'd cave." She sniffs. "That you would accept what life offered you. It was a pretty sweet deal."

I perch against the teacher's desk, crossing my ankles. "It was," I agree. "But I've never had a sweet tooth."

Three days pass, then four. I visit Jaime and Mel every day and ask about Bailey. They don't know much. They get updates through her counselor.

Bailey doesn't have phone privileges yet. Her counselor says she is making progress. That she is an excellent rule-follower, and that she enjoys helping others. If this isn't the most Bailey thing I've ever heard, I don't know what is.

In the absence of Bailey, and so close to graduation, I don't actually have much to do. I visit our doves. I find a recipe book Mom left behind and decide to memorize it by heart. Learn how to make all of her signature dishes. Stop depending on Bailey.

So I make Mom's rigatoni, chicken noodle soup, and cinnamon-silan waffles. Dad complains I'm bad for his six-pack and threatens to kick me out of the house. Knight and Luna conveniently drop Cayden off every afternoon so I can feed him dinner.

One person I'm not seeing much of is Dixie. I want to ask Dad where they stand, but I also don't want to come off as pushy. Wasn't that my whole unspoken beef with him in the first place? To each their own.

It's a random Friday night when Grim finally manages to drag me out. Only because there's a fair in town and I'm trash for blue cotton candy. Grim and I patched things up quickly after he became captain, but not before I did some groveling. Before I go out, I tell Dad I won't be home before midnight. Grim and I like to knock back a few beers after we go out, and I usually Uber it home. But this time, I come home at ten thirty. Grim's fault. Guy's got a talent for hooking up with people and ditching me halfway through the night.

I push the door to the house open and hear voices coming from upstairs.

Dad's bedroom.

Holy fucking shit. I'm so stunned and excited I straight up don't even *contemplate* not eavesdropping. Nope. I tiptoe like a cartoon robber to the stairway and strain my ears.

"...sure you want to do this?" Dad asks. I'm just happy I tuned in before he and Dixie started doing the nasty. I'm definitely bailing before it's showtime.

"Yeah," Dixie voice sounds certain yet a little wobbly. "I'm sure. Are you?"

Ew. They sound like fifteen-year-old virgins. Which is kind of adorable, knowing that Dad slept with, like, four digits of women before he and Mom got together.

"I want this," Dad admits, clearing his throat. "Actually...I *need* this. Lev's going off to the military and I'm going to need something to do with myself. And that something can't be butting into my grown-ass children's shit, you know?"

"You have a great way with words," Dixie compliments. Dad chuckles. So do I.

C'mon, Dad. Make a move.

But instead of listening to rustling of clothes and the sound of wet kisses and being scarred for life, I hear Dixie saying, "All right. Great. We'll do this. As friends."

"*Best* friends," he corrects. "Yeah."

"So I'll put down an offer right now. No point in waiting until Monday. The house is showing again on Sunday and I'm afraid someone will offer cash and snatch it."

Uhm, what?

They're talking about Dixie buying the house down the goddamn street? What a letdown. I thought they were gonna pork.

"What's the problem? You'll be paying cash," Dad says.

She laughs. "Whose cash?"

"Mine."

"Dean, I—"

"No, you listen to me. For this to work, you need to live close by." For what to work? What's happening? "I have the means. You have the will."

"I—I really don't feel comfortable with that," she stammers.

"That's great for practice, since you'll be feeling all kinds of uncomfortable when you have my baby inside you. Lev came out almost eight pounds. It was a hot mess. We Coles are really huge babies."

Ho. Ly. Shhh. His dirty talk is so rusty. Poor Dixie.

"Are you okay with...the process?" She clears her throat.

"You kidding me? Jerking off has become my specialty since Rosie died."

Yeah. Okay. Dude's a lost cause.

I hear the clack of Dixie's heels as she walks around the second floor, and before I can make myself scarce, she appears at the top of the stairway. Our eyes meet. I'm caught red-handed. But somehow, I'm more excited than embarrassed about everything I just heard. I give her a thumbs-up.

Dixie smiles, winking at me.

I wink back.

Thank you, she mouths. I nod.

I trust her with my dad's heart. And that's huge.

CHAPTER THIRTY-FOUR
LEV

I check our mailbox religiously, because Mel told me the rehab center Bailey is in encourages them to write letters to their loved ones.

I never get one, and it always surprises me, even though it shouldn't. I took off our goddamn friendship bracelet. Then told her we're done. Expecting a letter is some next-level bullshit. I should be happy she didn't set my house on fire.

A letter with the Californian government logo catches my attention. It is addressed to yours truly. I've no idea what I could have done to piss the entire state of California off. I'm one of the only citizens in this damn place who knows how to separate all the recycling into the colored bins correctly.

Maybe they want to celebrate me for that. A street after my name sounds like a good idea. Maybe jury duty?

I pluck the letter from the mailbox and walk inside. Leaning a hip against the dining table, I rip the envelope open. My mouth slacks and dries up when I see its contents.

It's a copy of a letter of recommendation from the mayor of Todos Santos, Graham Bermudez. My eyes skim over the words frantically.

"…as per your request, we have sent the original to the United States Air Force Academy. We wish you the best of luck. Please let us know if we can do anything else…"

Holy shit.

Along the years, Bailey had encouraged me to volunteer with the city to clean up trash from the beach and hand out leaflets during election months. I mainly did it so we could hang out because *she* did that, never because I thought a letter of recommendation could come out of it. But Bailey must've remembered. Because I sure as fuck didn't. This letter of recommendation is *huge*. But…how did Bailey know I applied to the USAFA? That makes no sense.

I dial up Dixie's number. She answers before the first ring.

"The answer is yes." She sighs. "I had to ask Bailey for help, Lev. I knew you needed all sorts of things you didn't include in the application and Bailey knows your life better than I do. What's more, did you know she keeps an entire folder with your résumé and potential places to get your recommendations from? There are, like, ten more letters like that coming."

I'm bracing the dining table with white knuckles, about to lose it. Bailey did this. Even while she was fighting her own demons, she went and collected letters of recommendation and whatnot to support my application. She helped me chase my dream while hers was dying in front of her very eyes.

And I, in return, told her she doesn't have me anymore. Dick move. Definitely a dick move. The road to hell is full of good intentions and all.

"How do you know I called about that?" I ask Dixie, stunned.

"I knew you should be getting an answer back any day, so I figured your nerves were shot."

"What did Bailey do exactly?"

"To my knowledge?" Dixie asks. "Got you ten letters of recommendation, including one from the mayor and another from the director of that airplane museum you volunteer at. She also did your extracurricular composite—I'm sure she padded it a little—and contacted your teachers for the teacher evaluation portion. Basically, she gathered all the things your application was missing."

"But she must've done it after the deadline."

There's silence on the other end of the line. My heart is pounding so hard, I'm surprised it hasn't jumped all the way to Pennsylvania.

Finally, Dixie answers. "She called to explain your...uh, *circumstances*. They gave her twenty-four hours to submit the additions to your application. Don't ask me how, but she made it happen. One thing's for sure—when this girl wants something, she gets it."

I close my eyes and breathe through my nose. I feel like I'm falling apart. Bailey did the undoable. She moved mountains for me. If she can only overcome her own struggles, the sky will be the limit for us.

Dixie must know what's going through my head. "You did the right thing, Lev. You gave her a shot at claiming her life back. It's not too late for you two."

"How do you know?"

"Because I've seen the way you look at each other," she answers, her voice steady and resolute.

"And?"

"And the fire you ignite together vanquishes every shadow around you."

CHAPTER THIRTY-FIVE
BAILEY

"Great work, Bailey. You're making excellent progress." My counselor stops by my table during dinner. I smile up from my granola-and-yogurt combo. There's a plate of fresh garden vegetables and a soy pudding next to it for dessert. I can't remember the last time I ate so well. Heck, I can't remember the last time I ate *period*. Appetite was not my friend these past few months.

"Thank you." I reach to take Ms. Hall's extended hand, smiling and actually feeling the smile on my face for a change. "My energy levels are up," I admit.

Not everything is dandy about my life. I can now see exactly why my parents and Lev insisted I commit to an inpatient rehab program. My schedule is grueling. The detox is no joke, and we are forced to undergo intense therapy and really dig into those issues that brought us to where we are. I've cried here more than I did my entire adolescent years combined.

I'm overwhelmed, lonely, and hungry for something no pudding or drug can satisfy. But I am feeling a full range of emotions right now, so I'll take that as a win.

"Are you coming to play pickleball in the evening?" Ms. Hall inquires.

I shake my head. "I really ought to take care of this leg of mine."

Ever since I became sober, I've been taking better care of my body, and it shows.

Ms. Hall grins, obviously satisfied as she slips her hand from mine. "That's what I wanted to hear. Enjoy your book tonight."

Ms. Hall thinks it's books I'm reading in my room every evening, based on the impressive stack of paperbacks by my nightstand. But the truth is, my reading material is different.

That diary Mom bought for me for Juilliard and I gutted and made my drug stash? She took it home with her sometime during my hospitalization in New York. She must've because I found it in one of my suitcases when I moved into rehab. Only now it's not full of drugs. The box is full of notes she wrote for me. Ninety-one notes, to be exact. *One for every day, and an extra one, just because I love you.* When I found it in my bag, I just about fell all over myself sobbing.

I finish my meal, tidy up, check on a few friends I made here, and walk over to my room. It is a *really* nice room, which makes me feel guilty for making Mom and Dad spend all this money. I fling myself over my queen-sized bed and sigh, staring at the diary Mom gave me that seems to be chasing me everywhere. I pull another note and open it. Mom's tidy handwriting, cursive and long, like a wedding invitation font, appears.

Day 28

Bailey,

I read somewhere that flamingos lose their pink when they raise their babies because raising your offspring is such an intense experience. They get their pink back when they're done with their parenting duties.

I remember thinking I wish it were true for humans too. I don't think we parents ever get our pink back. I think we will forever worry sick about you.

And the bigger the babies, the bigger the problems.

But I want you to know that being your mother is the greatest honor. You're smart, creative, good-hearted, and innovative. You are a rare gift. A celebration of the best that could come out of your father and me.

I wish you would cherish yourself half as much as we do you.

Love, Mom

I smile and wipe away my tears.

I look up, at my window. The last rays of light slither through the glass, painted yellow and pink. A dove lands from seemingly out of nowhere on my windowsill. It taps its feet impatiently, as if looking for a nest. It is holding something inside its beak. A twig...no, not a twig. A branch. An olive branch? Impossible. This is Pennsylvania. An olive tree would have to grow in a greenhouse in order to survive.

But it's here. Just like me. A sign sent to Noah's Ark when all hope seemed to be gone.

A symbol of dry land. Of hope. A ground to land on. *A safe haven.*

There's one valuable lesson I learned at Juilliard, and it wasn't taught to me by the professors: Your self-worth is a price too high to pay for success.

It is, in fact, your most treasured possession.

There's no currency for knowing your worth.

It is time to rebuild my life and start from scratch.

CHAPTER THIRTY-SIX
BAILEY

SEVEN MONTHS LATER

I ended up staying an extra four months in rehab. I didn't feel ready when it was time to say goodbye. Honestly, it felt right to give my injuries the rest they deserved. My body is repaying me in kind. I'm no longer weak, dizzy, nauseated, and frail.

I'm waiting for my parents to pick me up from the San Diego airport, encircled by my worldly possessions and a mild case of anxiety. I'm wearing a cropped, pink argyle sweater, a white tennis skirt, and knee-high socks along with my black Mary Janes. The persistent drizzle threatens to ruin my perfect bow-tied ponytail.

Lev and I haven't spoken to each other in seven months, and the way we parted ways suggested there was nothing to come back to.

The only update I've been given about him from Mom was that he got accepted to the Air Force Academy. Can't say I'm surprised, considering the effort Dixie and I went to, paired with his own unquestionable merit.

This means I'm not exactly sure if he is still in Todos Santos anymore, but there's a teeny, tiny part of me that hopes he'll come to the airport with my parents to pick me up.

Hence why I'm dressed like a blow-up doll ready to rock some lonely virgin's world.

A Porsche Panamera pulls curbside in front of me. Being kidnapped by a rich man with a midlife crisis isn't a lifelong dream of mine, but it still beats a Lev-less life.

The passenger door flings open and I step back instinctively, expecting a stranger, but come face-to-face with Mom. Dad slips out of the driver's seat. My heart tumbles down my chest to my stomach, then splits and rolls to both my feet.

"You got a new car!" I put on a fake smile (where is Lev?). "Congrats! It looks…" *Green. So green. Radioactively green.* "…cool."

"Oh, honey, you don't have to pretend." Mom is clutching me like she doesn't believe I exist, she hugs me so tightly. "We both know that car is entirely too green for its own good. It's your father's age."

"Better a neon Porsche than a twentysomething secretary with daddy issues."

Mom flashes him a tender smile, smoothing a hand over her cardigan. "Oh, but, honey, she would look so good next to your prenup-less divorce papers!"

"Wow. Two hundred hours of intensive therapy down the drain in two minutes. You guys are the best." I erect two thumbs-up. They grin at each other, then burst into laughter. It was their way to break the ice, apparently.

(WHERE IS LEV?)

"Bails! My goodness, how we've missed you." Mom gathers me into her chest again. Dad enfolds me from behind. I eventually untangle myself from their octopus arms.

WHERE. IS. LEV?

Dad hoists my bags to the trunk of the Porsche, while Mom is pushing me into the back seat like I'm about to make a run for it. I'm in a daze. He's really not here. Foolish as I was, a part of me was certain Lev would show up. That he'd had a change of heart while I was away all these months and realized he still wants me to be a part of his life, despite everything.

A gaping, ravenous hole tears open inside me. It feels like my emotions are devouring my inside organs. Which is…not fun. But I'm fresh out of rehab with a bevy of coping mechanism tricks and tools. So I just take ten calming breaths, redirect my thoughts, and… yup, life still sucks.

But my sobriety isn't at risk. I can be sad and *still* resist drugs.

"I'm starving," I announce as I buckle myself up. Dad slides into the front seat. He and Mom exchange more knowing grins.

I scowl. "Something funny?"

"Nope," Dad says at the same time Mom explains, "You hadn't been hungry for months before you went to rehab. I had to chase you down and shove energy bars down your throat. You look terrific, Bailey. You look like…well, *you*."

"I'm me, and I'm starving, definitely not for energy bars." I sniff. "Can we stop at Pizza My Heart on our way home?"

"Can an eighties baby sport a fanny pack without feeling embarrassed?" Captain Random, aka Dad, pumps the air with his fist. "I thought you'd never ask."

The car slides back into traffic, weaving out of the San Diego airport. We're ten minutes into a journey before I break down and blurt out, "Is Lev already in Colorado, or…?"

I feel pathetic asking, considering all signs show he has forgotten about me. So I hastily add, "I wrote him an apology letter as a part of our seven stages to recovery, but I haven't sent it yet. Should I slip it into his mailbox or…send it to his school?"

This is actually not a lie. My lying days are over, now that I'm sober.

"He's in Colorado," Dad says regretfully, and my entire soul slumps in disappointment. Dad tugs at his lower lip. "If it makes you feel any better, Dean says they're chewing him out like a squeaky toy. Fire-hosing info and ripping him several new ones every day. Apparently, being practically a pro athlete ain't enough there. He throws up every day just from the physical strain of it. Most of his peers are Sea Cadets, Young Marines, or previously enlisted, so they're used to a lot of the stuff he's now adapting to."

"That is…not comforting at all to me." I wince, thoroughly PTSD'd from Juilliard.

"It is to me." Dad taps the steering wheel. "Considering he makes my daughter sad."

Now's not a good time to confess his precious daughter made Lev literally *crawl* to her feet in front of his entire class so she wouldn't hook up with his enemy.

"I'll send the letter to the academy," I say decisively.

I want to ask if it looked like he missed me. If he asked about me at all. But the truth is a powerful weapon, and I don't particularly want it to blow up my fragile ego right now.

"Oh!" Mom snaps her fingers, mustering excitement again. "Daria said she is bringing her family down for a visit this weekend. Sissi learned how to spell Yves Saint Laurent."

"That's…"—I'm trying to come up with the right word—"frightening."

"And Luna got you tickets to see Ali Wong."

"That's amazing. Thanks for telling me, Mom."

"Sure thing!" Mom squeaks. "She also mentioned something about being swamped admin-wise. She is writing another book, you know. She asked if she could use your top-notch organizational skills and ability to turn everything into a bullet-point list. And pay handsomely for it, of course."

That is the nicest pity-job offer anyone has ever extended to a recovering addict, so of course, I feel complied to reply, "I won't charge her a penny. And I'm happy to. It'll keep me busy."

"Great!"

"Fun."

Ah, crap. Lev may have been relying on me, but I have been living with his attention. Now that it's gone, who am I anymore?

It's not just the three of us sitting in the car. There's also a million-dollar question nestled somewhere between my pile of duffel bags and me.

What are you going to do with the rest of your precious life, Bailey?

Competitive ballet is not on the table. Heck, it's not even in the same zip code as me. Even without Juilliard giving me the boot, every battle scar on my body reminds me I've survived once—best not to tempt my luck.

If I'm honest, I don't even think I *want* a second chance at becoming a ballerina. These past couple years, I've been miserable. Overworked, overstressed, and underappreciative of my good fortune.

I'm not one hundred percent sure what I want to do, but I know what I *don't* want to do: chase a dream that punishes you for hoping.

We stop by Pizza My Heart and I get three greasy slices with mushrooms and pineapple (don't come at me for it), along with a milkshake. I devour everything before the car slides into the garage, which is less than ten minutes. It does nothing to fill the hole inside of me.

When we get to the house, I don't unpack right away. I walk over to my bedroom window and watch Lev's house. It is amazing how inanimate it looks now that I know he doesn't live in it anymore. I now understand that before, when he was always a breath, one text message, one pebble thrown at a window away, his house felt like a person. Like a body. Like a friend.

Staring outside, I lift the hem of my sweater and finger the dove-shaped scar on my hip bone. Our doves are sitting on a branch in front of his window, waiting for him to come out. To feed them.

Doves always know their way back home.

I pull the edge of my sweater down and go in search of food to give them.

I'm home now. Back on shore.

I decide pretty quickly that I don't want to live with my parents. The house, which used to harbor my favorite childhood memories, is now soaked with flashbacks of broken glass, hidden drugs, and nasty arguments.

I rent a small studio apartment in La Jolla, about twenty minutes away from my parents' house. Close enough that they can get here in time if I need them—Marx forbid—but far enough that I don't feel like I'm strangled by their worried gazes.

My apartment is tiny, simple, and clean. It overlooks the beach, and I wake up to the seals yelling at tourists to leave them the heck alone. Every day is an opportunity. Each morning—a blessing. And I try to fill those days with things that will build me back up. Not to who I was before—that girl is never coming back. But to the girl Old Bailey and Addict Bailey made together. She's a stronger version of both. And yes, she still craves drugs, but when she does, she hops on the phone with her sister. Goes shopping with her mom. Or reads a really good book.

Mom and Dad paid for my rehab stint, and I'm determined to pay them back every single cent of it. Which is why, as soon as I take Luna's offer as her organizational guru and realize she really *is* in need of a full-time employee, I agree to take payment from her.

I go to her house every day for five or six hours, doing her filing, answering emails, processing book orders, and managing her social media.

"You're a godsend." Luna collapses her head on my shoulder every time she walks into the game room, which she converted into my makeshift office. She is pulling crazy hours trying to write her next motivational book, and Cayden only goes to daycare three times a week.

"Marx-send," I correct with a wink.

To supplement my income, I also tutor high schoolers in the afternoons. Finally, the one hundred thousand APs I took in high school come in handy. Precalculus is my love language, and statistics is my game of seduction. Daria says this place is my Geekdom Come. She *also* says ever since I got out of rehab, I'm "hotter than a tomato in a grilled cheese sandwich."

Which—let's admit it—is a legit compliment.

I attend biweekly support group meetings and actually have a sponsor I text every day. I no longer feel alienated and defensive during those meetings, like I don't belong in them. I one hundred percent do.

My sponsor, Will, tells me what I already know—that I have to send Lev the letter of apology. That it has nothing to do with my tangled feelings for him. It's about moving on and paying one's dues. About dismantling action from the human. I know he is right, but I can't help but feel like I'd be pestering Lev. He has obviously moved on and doesn't need this added complication when he is laser focused on succeeding at school. Not when it seems like things finally settled down for him now that I'm no longer in the picture.

One day, as I make my way from the support group back to my car, I stop by a storefront. *Pointe Made.* I've been to it a thousand times before. Mom is big on buying from small businesses, so we always got our supplies here and not online.

Behind the shiny glass is a six-layer platter tutu skirt. Neon green, with a thick satin wrap. It catches my eye immediately, and my heart starts thumping in an uneven tempo in my chest.

Just keep swimming, Bails. This life isn't for you.

But I can't move from my spot. Can't stop staring.

You know you want to feel me on your body, the green, hilarious tutu says. *You know how good I'd feel wrapped around you.*

File under: things both the tutu and Pedro Pascal can say and would still be true.

If there was only a way to reenter the world of ballet without competing…without putting my heart on the line…

Feeling dangerously close to the point of no return, I fish my phone out of my backpack and call Will. He answers before the first ring stops.

"Everything okay?" He sounds alarmed. I love that I have him.

"Yes! Not to worry. I just…I'm having a weird, impulsive reaction to do something I shouldn't."

"Talk me through everything that's happening." I hear him sitting down. "I'm here. I'm present. I'm with you."

Will was a star baseball player in a prestigious private school in NorCal. His cocaine addiction lost him not only an amazing spot at an Ivy League school but also his baseball career, his girlfriend, and eventually his parents, whom he had stolen from repeatedly. It took him six years to get where he is today. And still, not all of his relationships are mended. Plus, instead of being a pro baseballer, he is here sponsoring other recovering addicts and working a nine-to-five job selling solar solutions. Not that there's anything wrong with doing that. But it wasn't what he *wanted* to do.

Clearing my throat, I admit, "I'm just a girl, standing in front of a tutu at a storefront, asking herself not to walk in and buy it."

The cultural reference flies right over Will's head, because he isn't Lev and didn't watch *Notting Hill* with me while massaging my feet after I won a ballet competition in eighth grade. "Remind me why it's bad for you to wear a tutu dress?"

I huff out the obvious response: "Because dancing led me to use."

"No," Will replies solemnly. "*You* led yourself to use. Not ballet. Ballet was an innocent bystander. Ballet didn't force you to go pro. Ballet didn't force you to push yourself to the brink."

"But I did." My knees buckle and I hang my head down. "I did all those things, and now I will forever associate ballet with my downfall."

"Disentangle those two, then. Doing something you love is good, Bailey. I coach the little league baseball team for the elementary school near my house. And I don't even have a kid!" He laughs miserably. "Which is kind of creepy when you think about it. Sometimes your downfall isn't really your downfall. It was just something that happened in the background when you were in a very dark place."

I'm silent for a moment. I can't look away from that tutu.

"And hey!" Will says desperately. "Remember you told me when we first met that one of the reasons you loved rehab so much was because they let you teach a dance workshop to other patients one hour a day, five times a week? Your eyes were shining when you said that. Maybe it's time to rethink your passion, you know?"

They say those who can't, teach, and maybe that is true. But it is also true that some people can perform but find the experience of giving back more fulfilling. Not everyone wants to be the flower. Some blossom by being the gardener.

I'm that kind of person. A nurturer. A giver. Watching a thirty-five-year-old surviving alcoholic doing her first arabesque, to me, was more fulfilling than taking the stage when I competed in the nationals.

Teaching people the joy of dancing, the beauty in the body language, is no small feat. And if I can show one or two Baileys in this world that it is okay to love something without letting it kill you—then I'll have done my part.

"Teach," I mutter under my breath. "I should teach."

"There she is." I hear the smile on Will's face. "You're already teaching, aren't you? Tutoring. Helping. Assisting where you can. This is your calling, Bailey. Don't ghost it. *Answer* it."

Resolute, I step into the store, buy the tutu, and purchase a new pair of pointe shoes. Old man Gaston, the owner of the store, tells me he missed me. That he is happy I dropped out of Juilliard. That ballet is a passion, and passion can't be taught.

When I get back to my tiny apartment, I flatten my back against the door, slide down to the floor, and press the shoes against my nose, inhaling. The scent of glue, leather, and hope hits my nostrils and I hum with pleasure. The satin gleams, the shank untouched and full of promise.

For the first time in a long time, I know what to do.

I slide the shoes on. Wrap the tutu around my everyday clothes. I'm air. I'm fleeting. I'm everywhere. I'm invincible.

And start to move for the only person whose tune I dance to from now on.

Myself.

CHAPTER THIRTY-SEVEN
BAILEY

My Lev-less (*read: heartless*) existence is bearable. In the same way sugar-free, water-based oatmeal is bearable. I'm in a constant state of flavorlessness.

Three more weeks pass after I bought my new pointe shoes before I gather the courage to slip Lev's apology letter in the mailbox. I ran out of excuses and, frankly, damns to give. Yes, I've been horrible. Yes, I've done horrendous things. Yes, I'm willing to work hard to repent for them. But I can't turn back time. And we both need this closure, even if that means shutting the door to friendship—anything. I'm tired of being in the dark.

After getting the address from Dean, I send him the note and force myself to forget about it. Kind of like an audition.

Speaking of—I'm relieved not to have to face those anymore. Not to be constantly measured by a moment or two of excellence. Now I'm focusing on applying to colleges. I want to study education. And I want to study somewhere nice. Sunny. Beautiful. Somewhere that makes me flourish. Which is why I send applications to UCLA, Stanford, and FAU.

I don't know what I expect after I send Lev the letter. A phone call? A text? A handwritten reply?

I'm trying to keep my expectations down. Explain to myself that he is super busy with his workload. But it stings. The silence that drags day after day after day as though he was happier to forget about me. Yes, some terrible things happened between us.

But we were once best friends.

In fact, we were once best *everything*.

You don't throw that away when things get hard.

Unless…unless your best friend also made you feel the *worst*.

On the sixth day after I send the letter to Lev, I finally come to terms with the fact that he might never reply. That sometime down the line—a month or two from now—we'll meet at a mutual function between our families and exchange smiles, and pleasantries, and half-hearted apologies. We'll both pretend my letter didn't arrive so as not to embarrass the other. We'll be strangers. Cordial. Nice. Cold.

"Do you need anything else from me?" I ask Luna before I exit her house, my backpack slung over my shoulder. I'm already in a black leotard, a warm-silver knit top, and white leggings. I'm going to teach my first-ever volunteer dance class at a local retirement community. I imagine if word got out to Katia, my dormmate at Juilliard, I would become another Lauren anecdote. A sad story about a girl who didn't make it. Only I did make it—I made it out alive and with a dream of my own.

Luna looks up from a pile of pages making up her first draft, lost in thought. "What? Oh, no! All good here. Thanks so much, Bailey. You're a lifesaver."

I wink at her with a smile.

"Hey." Her voice halts my steps toward the door, but I don't turn around to face her. "He's busy, okay? Knight says he barely has time to talk to him on the phone. Only once a week." She's trying to make me feel better about Lev not making contact.

Nodding, I choke out, "I know." I don't know. So I cope. I take my deep breaths. I promise myself I'll call Daria when I leave here.

Slipping into my car, I make my way to the gated complex I've been invited to. Mom found me these gigs as soon as I told my parents I wanted to volunteer. When I get to the gym, which also moonlights as an auditorium, there are only a couple more cars in the entire parking lot. Mom said she'd be here to show support, so I guess she's running late.

I kill the engine, take a deep breath, remind myself that everything is okay, and get out. There's only a handful of elderly women in the studio. They're chatting to each other.

I draw a deep breath and introduce myself. "Hi. I'm Bailey and I'll be your dance teacher today." I give them a little wave, smiling—and noticing that for the first time in forever my smile isn't forced. The three of them turn to look at me. Their smiles are genuine too.

"Oh, we've been waiting for you. We're excited but also worried about breaking a hip!" one of them blurts out in a laugh.

I laugh too. "Don't worry. I'm not here to train you for the Olympics. I'm here to make you happy. To celebrate your bodies and have fun."

"I haven't been celebrating my body since I turned eighty, which was three years ago." Another one of them laughs. "It's all a string of disappointments at this point."

I grin. "I like a good challenge."

"Then you're going to *love* working with me."

They introduce themselves as Alma, Ruth, and Mariam.

I hook my phone up to the stereo and get started with a very light warm-up. I'm trying to shake off the fact that only three people came as I roll my shoulders back. I inhale positivity. Exhale negativity. Also—*where is Mom?*

This is supposed to be my come-to moment. The beacon of light I've been looking for. If only I had my dove bracelet, I'd be able to clutch it and get through this. But no one even *wants* this here. Other than these three ladies.

Who matter, I remind myself. *A lot.*

I pinch my shoulder blades together, and they repeat my action. The soft music fills the air-conditioned room. I'm too deep inside my own head to hear the door open, but at some point there's a figure standing by it. Mom finally came. Ten minutes late, but better than nothing.

"Now let's move to the barre and I'll show you some...um, simple moves. You don't have to be on your tiptoes, but good posture can strengthen your spine and...eh, its supporting muscles."

Marx, I need to pull myself together. My insecurity is showing. I'm really not great at this, which is crushing, because it was supposed to be my plan B.

Approaching each of the three ladies, I correct their posture, curling their fingers around the ballet barre. We go through all five positions. They're giggling like schoolgirls, but I'm still tense, stumbling over my words, slipping out of tempo with the music. I handed out leaflets beforehand and advertised it everywhere I could. This was supposed to be my redemption. I don't want it to turn into my failure.

They're having fun. Lighten up.

"Are you okay, little lady?" Mariam inquires.

"Don't be down about the poor attendance. People our age don't like trying new things," Alma adds.

"I don't! I mean, I'm not!" I chirp. "It's totally fine. Everything is great."

"Got a spot for another student?" I hear the figure at the door pushing off the wall and heading toward us. Only it doesn't sound like Mom at all.

I raise my head and see...*Lev.*

Achingly tan and handsome. Heartbreakingly kind. *Perfectly* Lev.

He is still in his uniform of blue dress pants and buttoned-up shirt. His hair is newly buzzed close to the scalp, and my breath hitches at how absolutely delicious he looks. His eyes glimmer playfully, and my heart liquifies inside my chest as he takes his position by the barre, looking at me seriously despite the hilarity of it all.

"You don't seem to fit into our age group, young man." Ruth is fawning over him. Really, though, they're all staring at him with open, unadulterated adoration.

He glances behind his shoulder to wink at her. "Trust me, if anything, I'll just slow you down."

So many questions run inside my head. What is he doing here? When did he come? Doesn't he have school? He can't just take off in the middle of the year. My mouth falls open, and I'm about to start firing questions at him, but he just whispers, "Dove, we're waiting."

Shaking my head to rid myself of the magic dust he sprinkled everywhere when he walked in here, I return to my position in front of them. Lev, astonishingly, completes the entire class, acting as my moral support. He groans as he slides from fourth position to fifth, raising both his arms in the air, looking ridiculous and adorable as he spins around. Every now and then, he winks and smiles at me, silently reassuring me that I'm doing a good job, and the ladies don't only look like they're having fun—they're also over the moon every time Lev so much as breathes.

"Girls." I clap my hands seriously at one point when he lowers himself to a demi plié and his round, muscular ass sticks out. "Your eyes should be on me, not on Mr. Cole."

"Oh, but you'll be here next week too. You can't promise the same about Mr. Cole!" Mariam giggles.

When the hour is over, the three thank us profusely—not just for the class but also for the entertainment. They trickle out of the room, and it's just Lev and me standing in front of one another. We're both panting from the class. His expression melts from humorous to serious all at once.

"Lev, I—" I start, not sure exactly what's going to leave my mouth but unable to take the silence anymore.

He cuts me off, fishing my letter from his front pocket and

unfolding it in front of me. "Here. I don't want your apology." He presses the paper to my chest.

My heart drops. This wasn't what I was expecting when I saw him here.

"You...you don't?"

"No." He shakes his head. "I want your forever."

It is extremely possible I'm about to have a heart attack. Twelve out of ten chance, actually.

"But you said—"

"We need to talk somewhere else." He leads me outside by the arm. I think I left my duffel bag behind and I don't even care. We walk past the door and toward my car. I guess he Ubered here.

"How did you know I was here?"

"I went to your parents' house as soon as I received the letter. A letter that—by the way—I've been waiting for, for weeks. A sign of life from you. Something to give me an excuse to seek you out again. Your mom said you were here. You're not mad I showed up instead of her, right?"

I barely manage to shake my head no. When we get to my car, he assumes position in the driver's seat and starts driving. It looks like he knows where he's going. Actually, I know where he's going too. The universe quickly restores itself, everything falling into place, erasing the last couple of years we grew apart.

We get to the woods not too long after. He kills the engine and we both hop out, me following his lead.

To our canvas. To our world. To our doves.

It is here, in our little snow globe, that he turns back to look at me with tears in his eyes. We're both standing in front of one another. As if on cue, Perseus descends the treetop, landing on Lev's shoulder.

Andromeda follows soon after, landing on mine. We both smile at each other. How could I ever question that we were meant to be? That we were endgame?

"I'm sorry I told you, you don't have me." Lev's voice breaks. "I didn't want you to rush through rehab. I didn't want you to focus on anything other than getting better. I had to truly let you go in order for you to find your way back to yourself. I had to."

He falls down to his knees in front of me, pressing his head against my midriff. I instinctively gather his head in my arms. The texture of his buzzed hair feels different. I can't resist running a hand over it again and again, until it becomes familiar.

"I know." Tears run down my cheeks. "I know you had to do that, and I want you to know that I appreciate it. I'm not angry. Just ashamed of everything I've put you through. Not just you. Everyone around me."

He looks up from my belly button, his green eyes glittering with tears. His arms are enfolded around my waist tightly. "Can I try this again?" he asks. "The love declaration? Same scenery. Same girl. Different year?"

I stroke his cheek lovingly. "I'm not the same girl," I croak. "I'll never be the same girl."

He presses his cheek to my palm, closing his eyes. "You're right. You're even more lovable than her. With the scars to prove you've been through a hard-won battle."

Drawing a deep breath, I nod. "Let's try again."

"Bailey Followhill, I'm in love with you. I don't remember a time *before* being in love with you. And I can't see my life without you. It was you before I was even born. It will be you long after I die. You are my beginning, my middle, and…well, the death of me, probably." We both laugh. "So please, *please.*" He puts his palms together. "Please help me write our happily-ever-after. Fuck knows you're so much better with words than I am."

Lev reaches for his back pocket. I know he won't pull out an engagement ring. There's a time and a place for everything, and we still need to experience so much more before we're ready. I want dates. Make-out sessions until our lips are swollen. I want days where we laugh together and days where we cry together and days where we're just *together*, curled one inside the other, making love.

What he produces from his pocket makes my heart stop beating. I gasp. "You fixed the bracelets. The strings are brand-new."

"But the doves are the same. A constant. Just like us."

"But Thalia..."

"Is gone from our lives. Forever."

Perseus and Andromeda fly off. It would be the last time we saw them, and somehow—don't ask me how—I felt it in my bones that it was their goodbye to us.

Rosie sent them to show us the way back to each other.

Now, they're no longer needed.

EPILOGUE
LEV

"You going home this early, bro?" Bryan, my bunkmate, raises his eyebrows at me, like it isn't eight thirty in the evening and I haven't been on my feet since five.

Frowning at my watch, I swing my bag over my shoulder. "Gotta make it in time for a flight to Florida."

First-year cadets get just about zero time off, and Bailey and I have been rocking the long-distance thing since we picked things up when she got back from rehab, so to say I'm in a hurry is putting it mildly. I'll only have a couple weeks with her, and I'll have to spend the first one pretending to like her college roommate, Sienna, who is just a little less boring than plain toast with a nice layer of unsalted butter smeared on top.

The second week we're spending in Jackson Hole with our families. And—thank fuck—sans prescription drugs.

Bryan rolls his eyes. "How do you have time for a girlfriend?"

The truth is, I don't. One thing that I learned in life is that you make room for things that are important to you. Sleep is for the weak.

"She's worth it. A'ight. See you here in two weeks." Bryan and I fist-bump and I dart like an arrow to freedom. To the civilian world. I get a cab to the airport, where Grim is waiting for me, looking rested and smug as all fuck. He goes to Boulder. Strong football team, and he shines there, despite being a total asshat when he wants to be.

"Wow, Lev. I'd say you look like shit, but I've met dumps fresher than you."

I believe him. There's a cadet saying that the Air Force Academy is a $150,000 education stuck up your ass a nickel at a time.

Clapping his back in a bro-hug, I release him and step back, laughing. "You look happy."

"I *am* happy," he admits seriously. "Thanks for getting your head outta your ass just in the nick of time."

"Can we stop with the shit metaphors?" I grumble.

He slaps a brown paper bag with a bagel inside it against my chest and hands me a coffee. "We can, but I'm not done just yet with busting your balls."

We both start making our way to our gate. I bump my shoulder into his. "Still feeding yourself the lie that this thing with the Miami Grand Prix race driver is casual?"

This is why he's headed to Florida right now instead of spending his vacation days with his family in Todos Santos. At least I'm going to see the love of my life. He met this dude literally five seconds ago and is already trying to find a way to transfer to Miami for him.

"It's casual," he maintains. "And for the millionth time, it's not the Miami Grand Prix. It's the Key Biscayne Motorpark. More prestigious than F1."

"All I heard was he has a jet lane in his backyard." I smirk.

The flight to Fort Lauderdale is painfully slow. I spend the entire duration texting Dove.

Lev: What are you wearing?
Bailey: A pair of black Lululemon leggings, your Moschino
  sweatshirt, and fluffy socks. Sienna puts the air-con on 70!
  So not environmental, and I'm always freezing.

Lev: Okay. I'll rephrase: what are you wearing for the sake of my warped fantasies?

Bailey: Nothing but a pair of Jimmy Choos and an edible thong.

Bailey: Bacon flavored, of course.

Lev: I LOVE YOU SO FUCKING MUCH I AM GOING TO MARRY THE SHIT OUT OF YOU.

Bailey: I love you so much I am going to have your babies. Like, literally five hundred of them. My stomach is going to look like cookie dough by the time I'm done.

Lev: I love cookie dough. How do you always get even more perfect?

Bailey: What are YOU wearing?

Lev: My heart on my fucking sleeve, ofc. You rob me of my cool.

Bailey: How long until you land?

Lev: Forty minutes, baby.

Bailey: K. Gonna go see if I can find an edible bacon-flavored thong by then.

The sun is almost up by the time we land.

Bailey waits for me at the airport, wearing a checkered pleated skirt, sneaks, and a white cable-knit Polo sweater. Her yellow hair is wrapped in a big, black satin bow, and she looks every inch of the girl I used to secretly glance at during dinners and high school functions and pinch myself that I was allowed to talk to her freely.

She hops on me, wrapping her legs around my waist as my fingers sink into the back of her thighs and I devour her mouth in a starving, wet, and sloppy kiss.

"There better be an edible bacon-flavored thong under these clothes, Dove," I growl into her mouth.

She giggles into mine. "Only one way to find out."

"Get a room," Grim moans behind me. "Actually, make it an entire bunker."

Bailey is still wrapped around me, kissing my face, oblivious to the looks we're getting as I give Grim my back and a middle finger and walk off toward where she parked her car. "See you in two weeks, fuck-face."

"Not if I can help it," Grim mumbles.

As soon as we get to Bailey's apartment, Sienna makes an executive decision not to be a total waste of oxygen and announces, "I'm going soap shopping! Be back later."

Yup. Soap shopping. As I said—blandest of the bland. Not that I'm complaining. It gives Bailey and me the opportunity to rip each other's clothes off right there in her living room. We have sex twice in a row before she offers me something to drink and three more times before we reluctantly DoorDash the first thing that pops on our phone screen. Cuban—thank God. A salad would have sucked. Then, finally, eight times later, when it's evening and Sienna is back with a bag of dessert-scented soaps and a lot of uninteresting anecdotal information about how her day has been, Bailey and I cuddle in her bed and talk. During the weekdays, all we do is talk. But it still feels different with her warm body draped over mine.

"How's school, Dove?" I stroke her daffodil hair, breathing in her warmth.

"I love it." She runs her nails over my chest, giving me shivers. "Yours?"

"Hate it. But they say the years get progressively less awful as you go along."

Bailey and I are going to do this long-distance thing for a long time. Until she graduates, at least. It will be hard, but it will be worth it. Our forever was hard-earned. Failure is not an option. Which is why I have to do to her what I'm *about* to do to her.

"Hey, Dove?"

"Hmm?"

"How would you feel about taking a trip to California before we go to Jackson Hole?"

"I would feel…" Her eyebrows are drawn into a confused frown. "Slightly jet-lagged, I guess. Why?"

I pull the two tickets I bought for us from my bag under her bed. Her eyes widen. "Lev, it says our flight leaves in four hours. From *Miami*."

I blink at her innocently. "You're a fast packer."

When we land in California, I don't even bother to visit home first. There'll be time for that later. As requested, Dad left me the Tesla parked at the airport, along with the key. Bailey spends the entire drive staring at me with a mixture of suspicion and excitement.

"This is not the way to our houses," she says when I pass both turns into the gated community of El Dorado.

"Very perceptive." I pat her thigh lightly, immediately getting a semi. Fuck military life. "You've always been incredibly smart."

"You're dodging." She narrows her eyes.

"See? Insightful *and* quick-witted."

"*Lev.*"

"That's my name."

"It's also going to be your most important organ, dumped on the car floor if you don't tell me where you're taking me."

We pass by downtown. More gated communities. The library.

"Do you really think the heart is the most important organ in the human body? I mean, it is, don't get me wrong, but you also can't function without your lungs or liver. Yet they don't get even half the glory—"

"Lev!" Bailey laugh-yells in frustration. "Where're we going?"

"It's a surprise."

"I hate those."

True story. Bailey thrives when in control. But she'll have to indulge me, just this time.

"Well, you love me, so suck it up, buttercup."

Ten minutes later, we're in our spot in the woods. Now, this part required some preparation. Dad and Knight had to pull some strings. Get some work done. They cleaned up the canvas, hung light strings from tree to tree, and brought a generator to make the place look like something out of a fairy tale. The combo between dusk and the lights really brings out the magic of our secret spot. Or maybe I'm just feeding myself some bull crap to convince myself she'll say yes.

I lead her by the hand and watch as her face lights up at the sight of our spot.

"Lev!" She turns to hug me. "This is wonderful."

"You're wonderful," I reply gruffly. *Sulkily.* I'm a little nervous, okay?

"Who did all this?" She looks around.

"Dad and Knight. They owed me."

"For what?" she asks with a smile, exploring our beautiful surroundings. What is she, the CIA?

"I dunno, existing." I glance around. "Hm, you're getting away from me. Come back here."

I'm really nailing this, aren't I? But I'm stressed. And hopeful. And *fuck*, my entire life is on the line here.

Bailey turns around, looking alarmed and a little amused. She ambles over to me, resting a hand over my shoulder with a smile. "I'm here."

"Good. Stay this way. No wandering off."

"Why are you sweating, baby?" She grins.

Because I might have my heart destroyed in about thirty seconds.

I gather her face in my hands like it's precious diamonds and glide the tip of my nose over hers. I'm not going down on one knee. She already knows I'd crawl for her. "Bailey. You're my one. You're my only. You're my *everything*. Life without you was something I've tasted for a short time, and it was by far the worst of my life. If there's one thing my mom taught me before she passed away, it is that time is too rare to spend away from the one you love. Our doves are gone—and not by accident. We don't need them anymore. There's something else to remind us we're in it for forever—*us*. So make me the luckiest motherfucker on planet earth and say yes."

Slipping Mom's engagement ring out of my pocket, I hold it between us, staring deep into Bailey's eyes. Dad initially refused to give away anything of Mom's—*especially* the ring he gave her—but I reminded him the kind of shit he put me through and added that at least with Bailey wearing it, he'd be able to have it in front of his eyeballs all the time and be reminded of her and the love they shared. I think it's the latter that convinced him.

But Bailey still hasn't said yes. She is looking at me now with an expression I've never seen before. Then she does something I wasn't expecting.

She punches me in the chest. "Lev!"

Oh shit. "What?"

"I thought you'd never ask!"

I blink, confused. "So…is that a yes?"

"It's a heck yes!" She *rips* the ring from between my fingers, putting it on. She doesn't even look at it. She doesn't even care about the diamond. God, I love this girl. "I love you!"

"I love you too. Now, Dove?"

"What?"

"Stay very still and give me a kiss."

BAILEY

"Oh my Marx, Bailey. This ring is obscene! So huge. So flashy. I love it." Daria clutches my hand in a death grip, drooling all over my engagement ring. We're having dinner after a long day of skiing. Last time I went to Jackson Hole, I was at the height of my addiction. I still find this place triggering, but not as much as Lev obviously suspects I do, since he keeps throwing me his golden retriever glances, making sure that I'm okay.

Lev, who is sitting next to me, clasps my free hand—the one not held hostage by the women under this roof—and drops a casual kiss to the tip of my shoulder.

"No joke." Lenora's eyes widen as she studies the ring. "I could sculpt a life-sized toddler with this thing."

"No more babies," Vaughn mumbles.

"It screams money," Luna agrees.

"It screams Rosie," Dean corrects from across the table, spearing a brussels sprout and popping it into his mouth. This is the part where he chides all of us and calls Rosie his wife—present tense—but when we all stare at him, all he does is shrug and get back to his food.

Without realizing it, the entire room breathes in relief.

Dixie puts a hand on Dean's shoulder, smiling at me. "You look wonderful, Bailey. Healthy and happy. And the ring suits you very well. How lovely that you and Rosie are the exact same size."

"Thank you, Dixie." I smile back. "You look radiant. I…" I catch myself, desperate to say the right thing. "You look right at home."

The rims of Dixie's eyes gleam emotionally. "Excuse me." She starts to stand to bring herself a tissue, but Dean produces a handkerchief from his suit and hands it over to her. She pats her eyes dry, laughing. "Sorry, I get so emotional these days. And seeing Lev and Bailey so happy…" She trails off.

"Yes," Uncle Vicious drawls, staring at the bottom of his wineglass, his arm slung over Aunt Emilia's shoulder. "I'm sure that's why you're emotional and not because you're seven months pregnant with the devil's spawn."

Dean gives him a scalding look. "Watch your mouth."

"Physically can't," Vicious quips tersely.

"So, are you guys ever gonna tell us how you two got pregnant? Turkey baster, or..." Knight points his fork between Dean and Dixie.

Dixie turns bright red and stands up. Her big bump is covered by a black evening dress, and she caresses it protectively. "This is my cue to declare heartburn and go hunt for Tums. Thanks for dinner, Millie."

Dean glances at her from behind his shoulder. "Be right there, Lady D."

Lady D is a better nickname than Dix. I'm sure she appreciates it. I know Lev does.

Dean turns to stare at Knight. His nostrils flare. "What is wrong with you?"

Knight sighs and sits back. "Oh God. There's a long list. Make yourself comfortable, Dad."

"Who asks something like that?" Mom interferes, unhappy with where this conversation is headed. "That is Dean and Dixie's business. Where are your manners?"

"I have the answer as for the whereabouts, but you're not gonna like it," Vaughn grumbles.

"But they're not even together," Knight whines.

"But Dad *did* buy her the house," Lev adds thoughtfully. "And not as a loan. He straight up paid in cash so she could live down the street from him, close enough that he can see her and the baby all the time." Lev pauses.

The truth Knight and Lev can't seem to accept is that Dean and Dixie absolutely did not conceive their unborn child in the biblical way. Dean isn't ready for that. This whole *moving on from Rosie* part. Perhaps one day he will be, but that day isn't coming in the next few years. He is ready to love again, though. Another child. Another member of his family.

Dean and Dixie have a very unique relationship. They're on the frayed veins between friends and lovers, and always will be. I trust they'll be amazing parents to their child, but the Rosie-shaped hole in Dean's heart will never mend. Which is fine. He looks content. Fulfilled. Excited for the new baby. "Do you know what it is yet?" I squeak, trying to change the subject. My fiancé throws me an I-see-what-you're-doing look in my periphery.

Dean grins, and for the first time in five years, he doesn't just look content—he looks *happy.* "It's a girl," he says, pink spreading to his cheeks. "And," he adds, "we are going to name her Rosie."

READ ON FOR A LOOK AT THE FIRST
BOOK IN THE ALL SAINTS SERIES

PRETTY
RECKLESS

PROLOGUE
DARIA/PENN

It started with a lemonade
And ended with my heart.

This, my pretty reckless rival, is how our
screwed-up story starts.

DARIA, AGE FOURTEEN

The tiles under my feet shake as a herd of ballerinas blazes past me, their feet pounding like artillery in the distance.

Brown hair. Black hair. Straight hair. Red hair. Curly hair. They blur into a rainbow of trims and scrunchies. My eyes are searching for the blond head I'd like to bash against the well-worn floor.

Feel free not to be here today, Queen Bitch.

I stand frozen on the threshold of my mother's ballet studio, my pale pink leotard sticking to my ribs. My white duffel bag dangles from my shoulder. My tight bun makes my scalp burn. Whenever I let my hair down, my golden locks fall off in chunks on the bathroom floor. I tell Mom it's from messing with my hair too much, but that's BS. And if she gave a damn—*really* gave one, not just pretended to—she'd know this too.

I wiggle my banged-up toes in my pointe shoes, swallowing the ball of anxiety in my throat. Via isn't here. *Thank you, Marx.*

Girls torpedo past me, bumping into my shoulders. I feel their giggles in my empty stomach. My duffel bag falls with a thud. My classmates are leaner, longer, and more flexible, with rod-straight backs like an exclamation mark. Me? I'm small and muscular like a question mark. Always unsure and on the verge of snapping. My face is not stoic and regal; it's traitorous and unpredictable. Some wear their hearts on their sleeves—I wear mine on my mouth. I smile with my teeth when I'm happy, and when my mom looks at me, I'm always happy.

"You should really take gymnastics or cheer, Lovebug. It suits you so much better than ballet."

But Mom sometimes says things that dig at my self-esteem. There's a rounded dent on its surface now, the shape of her words, and that's where I keep my anger.

Melody Green-Followhill is a former ballerina who broke her leg during her first week at Juilliard when she was eighteen. Ballet has been expected of me since the day I was born. And, just my luck, I happen to be exceptionally bad at it.

Enter Via Scully.

Also fourteen, Via is everything I strive to be. Taller, blonder, and skinnier. Worst of all, her natural talent makes my dancing look like an insult to leotards all over the world.

Three months ago, Via received a letter from the Royal Ballet Academy asking her to audition. Four weeks ago, she did. Her hotshot parents couldn't get the time off work, so my mom jumped at the chance to fly her on a weeklong trip to London. Now the entire class is waiting to hear if Via is going to study at the Royal Ballet Academy. Word around the studio is she has it in the bag. Even the Ukrainian danseur Alexei Petrov—a sixteen-year-old prodigy who is like the Justin Bieber of ballet—posted an IG story with her after the audition.

Looking forward to creating magic together.

It wouldn't surprise me to learn Via can do magic. She's always been a witch.

"Lovebug, stop fretting by the door. You're blocking everyone's way," my mother singsongs with her back to me. I can see her reflection through the floor-to-ceiling mirror. She's frowning at the attendance sheet and glancing at the door, hoping to see Via.

Sorry, Mom. Just your spawn over here.

Via is always late, and my mother, who never tolerates tardiness, lets her get away with it.

I bend down to pick up my duffel bag and pad into the studio. A shiny barre frames the room, and a floor-to-ceiling window displays downtown Todos Santos in all its photogenic, upper-crust glory. Peach-colored benches grace tree-lined streets, and crystal-blue towers sparkle like the thin line where the ocean kisses the sky.

I hear the door squeaking open and squeeze my eyes shut.

Please don't be here.

"Via! We've been waiting for you." Mom's chirp is like a BB gun shooting me in the back, and I tumble over my own feet from the shock wave. Snorts explode all over the room. I manage to grip the barre, pulling myself up a second before my knees hit the floor. Flushed, I grasp it in one hand and slide into a sloppy plié.

"Lovebug, be a darling and make some room for Via," Mom purrs.

Symbolically, Mother, I'd love for Via to make my ass some room too.

Of course, her precious prodigy isn't wearing her ballet gear today even though she owns Italian-imported leotards other girls can only dream of. Via clearly comes from money because even rich people don't like shelling out two hundred bucks for a basic leotard. Other than Mom—who probably figures I'll never be a true ballerina so the least she can do is dress me up like one.

Today, Via is wearing a cropped yellow Tweety Bird shirt and ripped leggings. Her eyes are red, and her hair is a mess. Does she even make an effort?

She throws me a patronizing smirk. "*Lovebug.*"

"*Puppy,*" I retort.

"Puppy?" She snorts.

"I'd call you a bitch, but let's admit it, your bite doesn't really have teeth."

I readjust my shoes, pretending that I'm over her. I'm *not* over her. She monopolizes my mother's time, and she's been on my case way before I started talking back. Via attends another school in San Diego. She claims it's because her parents think the kids in Todos Santos are too sheltered and spoiled. Her parents want her to grow up with *real* people.

Know what else is fake? Pretending to be something you're not. I own up to the fact I'm a prissy princess. Sue me. (Please do. I can afford really good legal defense.)

"Meet me after class, Vi," Mom says, then turns back around to the stereo. Vi *(Vi!)* uses the opportunity to stretch her leg, stomping on my toes in the process.

"Oops. Looks like you're not the only clumsy person around here, Daria."

"I would tell you to drop dead, but I'm afraid my mom would force me to go to your funeral, and you legit aren't worth my time."

"I would tell you to kiss my ass, but your mom already does that. If she only liked you half as much as she likes me. It's cool, though; at least you have money for therapy. And a nose job." She pats my back with a smirk, and I hate, *hate*, **hate** that she is prettier.

I can't concentrate for the rest of the hour. I'm not stupid. Even though I know my mother loves me more than Via, I also know it's because she's genetically programmed to do so.

Centuries tick by, but the class is finally dismissed. All the girls sashay to the elevator in pairs.

"Daria darling, do me a favor and get us drinks from Starbucks. I'm going to the little girls' room, then wrapping something up real quick with Vi." Mom pats my shoulder, then saunters out of the studio, leaving a trail of her perfume like fairy dust. My mom would donate all her organs to save one of her students' fingernails.

She smothers her ballerinas with love, leaving me saddled me with jealousy.

I grab Mom's bag and turn around before I have a chance to exchange what Daddy calls "unpleasantries" with Via.

"You should've seen her face when I auditioned." Via stretches in front of the mirror behind me. She's as agile as a contortionist. Sometimes I think she could wrap herself around my neck and choke me to death.

"We had a blast. She told me that by the looks of it, not only am I in, but I'm also going to be their star student. It felt kind of…" She snaps her fingers, looking for the word. I see her in the reflection of the mirror but don't turn around. Tears are hanging on my lower lashes for their dear lives. "A redemption or something. Like you can't be a ballerina because you're so, you know, *you*. But then there's *me*. So at least she'll get to see someone she loves make it."

Daddy says a green Hulk lives inside me, and he gets bigger and bigger when I get jealous, and sometimes, the Hulk blasts through my skin and does things the Daria he knows and loves would never do. He says jealousy is the tribute mediocrity pays to genius, and I'm no mediocre girl.

Let's just say I disagree.

I've always been popular, and I've always fought hard for a place in the food chain where I can enjoy the view. But I think I'm ordinary. Via is extraordinary and glows so bright, she burns everything in her vicinity. I'm the dust beneath her feet, and I'm crushed and bitter and *Hulky*.

Nobody *wants* to be a bad person. But some people—like me—just can't help themselves. A tear rolls down my cheek, and I'm thankful we're alone. I turn around to face her.

"What the hell is your problem?"

"What isn't?" She sighs. "You are a spoiled princess, a shallow idiot, and a terrible dancer. How can someone so untalented be born to *the* Melody Green-Followhill?"

I don't know! I want to scream. *No one wants to be born to a genius. Marx, bless Sean Lennon for surviving his own existence.*

I eye her pricey pointe shoes and arch a mocking eyebrow. "Don't pretend I'm the only princess here."

"You're an airhead, Daria." She shakes her head.

"At least I'm not a spaz." I pretend to be blasé, but my whole body is shaking.

"You can't even get into a decent first position." She throws her hands in the air. She isn't wrong, and that enrages me.

"Again—why. Do. You. Care!" I roar.

"Because you're a waste of fucking space, that's why! While I'm busting my ass, you get a place in this class just because your mother is the teacher."

This is my chance to tell her the truth.

That I'm busting mine even harder precisely because I wasn't born a ballerina. Instead, my heart shatters like glass. I spin on my heel and dart down the fire escape, taking the stairs two at a time. I pour myself out into the blazing California heat. Any other girl would take a left and disappear inside Liberty Park, but I take a right and enter Starbucks because I can't—*won't*—disappoint my mom more than I already have. I look left and right to make sure the coast is clear, then release the sob that has weighed on my chest for the past hour. I get into line, tugging open Mom's purse from her bag as I wipe my tears away with my sleeve. Something falls to the floor, so I pick it up.

It's a crisp letter with my home address on it, but the name gives me pause.

Sylvia Scully.

Sniffing, I rip the letter open. I don't stop to think that it isn't mine to open. Seeing Via's mere name above my address makes me want to scream until the walls in this place fall. The first thing that registers is the symbol at the top.

The Royal Ballet Academy.

My eyes are like a wonky mixed tape. They keep rewinding to the same words.

Acceptance Letter.

Acceptance Letter.

Acceptance Letter.

Via got accepted. I should be thrilled she'll be out of my hair in a few months, but instead, the acidic taste of envy bursts inside my mouth.

She has everything.

The parents. The money. The fame. The talent. Most of all—my mother's undivided attention.

She has everything, and I have nothing, and the Hulk inside me grows larger. His body so huge it presses against my diaphragm.

A whole new life in one envelope. *Via's* life hanging by a paper. A paper that's in my hand.

"Sweetie? Honey?" The barista snaps me out of my trance with a tone that suggests I'm not a sweetie nor a honey. "What would you like?"

For Via to die.

I place my order and shuffle to the corner of the room so I can read the letter for the thousandth time. As if the words will change by some miracle.

Five minutes later, I take both drinks and exit onto the sidewalk. I dart to the nearest trash can to dispose of my iced tea lemonade so I can hold the letter without dampening it. Mom probably wanted to open it with Via, and I just took away their little moment.

Sorry to interrupt your bonding sesh.

"Put the drink down, and nobody gets hurt," booms a voice behind me, like liquid honey, as my hand hovers over the trash can. It's male, but he's young. I spin in place, not sure I heard him right. His chin dipped low, I can't see his face clearly because of a Raiders ball cap that's been worn to death. He's tall and scrawny—almost scarily so—but he glides toward me like a Bengal tiger. As if he's found a way to walk on air and can't be bothered with mundane things like muscle tone.

"Are we throwing this away?" He points at the lemonade.

We? Bitch, at this point, there's not even a you to me.

I motion to him with the drink. He can have the stupid iced tea lemonade. Gosh. He is interrupting my meltdown for a lemonade.

"Nothing's free in this world, Skull Eyes."

I blink, willing him to evaporate from my vision. Did this jackass really just call me Skull Eyes? At least I don't look like a skeleton. My mind is upstairs with Via. Why does Mom receive letters on her behalf? Why couldn't they send it directly to Via's house? Is Mom adopting her ass now?

I think about my sister, Bailey. At only nine, she already shows promise as a gifted dancer. Via moving to London might encourage Mom to put Bailey in the Royal Ballet Academy too. Mom had talked about me applying there before it became clear that I could be a Panera bagel before I'd become a professional ballerina. I begin to glue the pieces of my screwed-up reality together.

What if I had to migrate to London to watch both girls make it big while I swam in my pool of mediocrity?

Bailey and Via would become BFFs.

I'd have to live somewhere rainy and gray.

We'd leave Vaughn and Knight and even Luna behind. All my childhood friends.

Via would officially take my place in Mom's heart.

Hmm, no thanks.

Not today, Satan.

When I don't answer, the boy takes a step toward me. I'm not scared, although…maybe I should be? He's wearing dirty jeans—I'm talking mud and dust, not, like, purposely haphazard—and a worn blue shirt that looks two sizes too big with a hole the size of a small fist where his heart is. Someone wrote around it in a black Sharpie and girlie handwriting *Is it a sign?—Adriana, xoxo* and I want to know if Adriana is prettier than me.

"Why are you calling me Skull Eyes?" I clench the letter in my fist.

"Because." He slopes his head so low all I can see are his lips, and they look petal-soft and pink. Feminine, almost. His voice is smooth to a point it hurts a little in my chest. I don't know why. Guys my age are revolting to me. They smell like pizza that has sat in the sun for days. "You have skulls in your eyes, Silly Billy. Know what you need?"

For Mom to stop telling me that I suck?

For Via to disappear?

Take your pick, dude.

I shove my free hand into my mom's wallet and pluck out a ten-dollar bill. He looks as if he could use a meal. I pray he'll take it before Mom comes down and starts asking questions. I'm not supposed to talk to strangers, much less strangers who look like they are dumpster diving for their next meal.

"Sea glass." He thrusts his hand in my direction, ignoring the money and the drink.

"Like the stuff you get on Etsy?" I huff.

Great. You're a weirdo too.

"Huh? Nah, that shit's trash. Orange sea glass. The real stuff. Found it on the beach last week and Googled it. It's the rarest thing in the world, you know?"

"Why would you give a total stranger something so precious?" I roll my eyes.

"Why not?"

"Um, hello, attention span much? Weren't you the one who just said nothing in this world is free?"

"Who said it's free? Did you get all your annual periods today at once or something?"

"Don't talk about my period!"

"Fine. No period talk. But you need a real friend right now, and I'm officially applying for the position. I even dressed the part. Look." He motions to his hobo clothes with an apologetic smile.

And just like that, heat pours into my chest like hot wax. Anger, I find, has the tendency to be crisp. I really want to throat punch him. He pities me? *Pities.* The guy with the hole in his shirt.

"You want to be my friend?" I bark out a laugh. "Pathetic much? Like, who even says that?"

"Me. I say that. And I never claimed not to be pathetic." He tugs at his ripped shirt and raises his head slowly, unveiling more of his face. A nose my mom would call Roman and a jaw that's too square for someone my age. He's all sharp angles, and maybe one day he will be handsome, but right now, he looks like an anime cartoon character. Mighty Max.

"Look, do you want the lemonade and money or not? My mom should be here any minute."

"And?"

"And she can't see us together."

"Because of how I look?"

Duh.

"No, because you're a boy." I don't want to be mean to him even though, usually, I am. Especially to boys. Especially to boys with beautiful faces and honey voices.

Boys can smell heartbreak from across a continent. Even at fourteen. Even in the middle of an innocent summer afternoon. We girls have an invisible string behind our belly button, and only certain guys can tug at it.

This boy…he will snap it if I let him.

"Take the sea glass. Owe me something." He motions to me with an open palm. I stare at the ugly little rock. My fist clenches around the letter. The paper hisses.

The boy lifts his head completely, and our eyes meet. He studies me with quiet interest as though I'm a painting, not a person. My heart is rioting all over, and the dumbest thought crosses my mind. Ever notice how the heart is *literally* caged by the ribs? That's insane. As if our body knows it can break so easily, it needs to be protected. White dots fill my vision, and he's swimming somewhere behind them, against the stream.

"What's in the letter?" he asks.

"My worst nightmare."

"Give it to me," he orders, so I do. I don't know why. Most likely because I want to get rid of it. Because I want Via to hurt as much as I do. Because I want Mom to be upset. *Marx, what's wrong with me?* I'm a horrible person.

His eyes are still on mine as he tears the letter to shreds and lets the pieces float like confetti into the trash can between us. His eyes are dark green and bottomless like a thickly fogged forest. I want to step inside and run until I'm in the depth of the woods. Something occurs to me just then.

"You're not from here," I say. He is too pure. Too good. Too real.

He shakes his head slowly. "Mississippi. Well, my dad's family. Anyway. Owe me something," he repeats, almost begging.

Why does he want me to owe him something?

So he can ask for something back.

I don't relent, frozen to my spot. Instead, I hand him the lemonade. He takes it, closes the distance between us, pops the lid open, and pours the contents all over the ruined letter. His body brushes against mine. We're stomach to stomach. Legs to legs. Heart to heart.

"Close your eyes."

His voice is gruff and thick and different. This time, I surrender. I know what's about to happen, and I'm letting it happen anyway. My first kiss.

I always thought it would happen with a football player or a pop star or a European exchange student. Someone outside of the small borders of my sheltered, Instagram-filtered world. Not with a kid who has a hole in his shirt. But I need this. Need to feel desired and pretty and wanted.

His lips flutter over mine, and it tickles, so I snort. I can feel his warm breath skating across my lips, his baseball cap grazing my forehead and the way his mouth slides against mine, lips locking with uncertainty. I forget to breathe for a second, my hands on his shoulders, but then something inside me begs me to dart my tongue out and really taste him. We're sucking air from each other's mouths. We're doing it all wrong. My lips open for him. His open too. My heart is pounding so hard I can feel the blood whooshing in my veins when he says, "Not yet. I'll take that too, but not yet."

A groan escapes my lips.

"What would you have asked of me if I took the sea glass?"

"To save me all your firsts," he whispers somewhere between my ear and mouth as his body brushes away from mine.

I don't want to open my eyes and let the moment end. But he makes the choice for both of us. The warmth of his body leaves mine as he takes a step back.

I still don't have the guts to open my mouth and ask for his name.

Ten, fifteen, twenty seconds pass.

My eyelids flutter open on their own accord as my body begins to sway.

He's gone.

Disoriented, I lean against the trash can, fiddling with the strap of my mother's bag. Five seconds pass before Mom loops her arm around mine out of nowhere and leads me to the Range Rover. My legs fly across the pavement. My head twists back.

Blue shirt? Ball cap? Petal lips? Did I imagine the whole thing?

"There you are. Thanks for the coffee. What, no iced tea lemonade today?"

After I fail to answer, we climb into her vehicle and buckle up. Mom sifts through her Prada bag resting on the center console.

"Huh. I swear I took four letters from the mailbox today, not three."

And that's when it hits me—*she doesn't know*. Via got in, and she has no idea the letter came today. Then this guy tore it apart because it upset me...

Kismet. Kiss-met. Fate.

Dad decided two years ago that he was tired of hearing all three girls in the household moaning "oh my God," so now we have to replace the word *God* with the word *Marx*, after Karl Marx, a dude who was apparently into atheism or whatever. I feel like God or Marx—*someone*—sent this boy to help me. If he were even real. Maybe I made him up in my head to come to terms with what I did.

I open a compact mirror and apply some lip gloss, my heart racing.

"You're always distracted, Mom. If you dropped a letter, you'd have seen it."

Mom pouts, then nods. In the minute it takes her to start the engine, I realize two things:

One—she was expecting this letter like her next breath.

Two—she is devastated.

"Before I forget, Lovebug, I bought you the diary you wanted." Mom produces a thick black-cased leather notebook from her Prada bag and hands it to me. I noticed it before, but I never assume things are for me anymore. She's always distracted, buying Via all types of gifts.

As we ride in silence, I have an epiphany.

This is where I'll write my sins.

This is where I'll bury my tragedies.

I snap the mirror shut and tuck my hands into the pockets of my white hoodie, where I find something small and hard. I take it out and stare at it, amazed.

The orange sea glass.

He gave me the sea glass even though I never accepted it.

Save me all your firsts.

I close my eyes and let a fat tear roll down my cheek.

He was real.

ACKNOWLEDGMENTS

I had always maintained that Lev and Bailey would only get their story if a great idea came up to me. With the way All Saints had ended, Lev and Bailey appeared to be a low-conflict couple. They were both nauseatingly perfect. I loved them, but I wasn't invested in their story. Perfection is boring. It is the flaws that make people worth fighting for.

Bailey's substance abuse came to me through a real-life, terrible journey a friend of mine had been going through. Her husband—the perfect, overachieving, romantic man she married—became an addict. And she loved him. But she loved her children and their future more.

This had me thinking about how all of us are vulnerable. Addiction finds us at our weakest points. We should always be on guard for it. This friend is the first person I'd like to thank, for sharing her story, her trauma, her tears, and her hopes with me. Your input was priceless for this story. Thank you.

Special thanks to my amazing designer, Letitia Hasser, who always brings it, as well as Stacey Ryan Blake, my interior designer.

Huge thanks to my beta readers, Tijuana Turner and Vanessa Villegas, and to my beta/alpha editors and proofreaders—Sarah Plocher, Leslee Vessels, and Cate Hogan.

All the gratitude in the world to my agent, Kimberly Brower, and Bloom Publishing for picking up this series. Thank you, Dom, Christa, Letty, Pamela, Madison, Gretchen, and Kylie.

I would also like to thank LJ's Influencers, the Sassy Sparrows Facebook group, and anyone who has supported this series currently or in the past—Instagrammers, bloggers, or BookToker.

If you need help overcoming an addiction, please consider calling this free and confidential Substance Abuse and Mental Health Services Administration line: 1-800-662-HELP (4357).

Thank you so much for reading,

L.J. xo

ABOUT THE AUTHOR

L.J. Shen is a *USA Today, WSJ, Washington Post,* and #1 Amazon Kindle Store bestselling author of contemporary romance books. She writes angsty books, unredeemable anti-heroes who are in Elon Musk's tax bracket, and sassy heroines who bring them to their knees (for more reasons than one). HEAs and groveling are guaranteed. She lives in Florida with her husband, three sons, and a disturbingly active imagination.

Website: authorljshen.com
Facebook: authorljshen
Instagram: @authorljshen
TikTok: @authorljshen
Pinterest: @authorljshen